Lost Creek Books presents

Wesley Murphey's books—

Fiction

A Homeless Man's Burden: She was only nine

Based on the actual still-unsolved 1960 bean-field murder of little *Alice Lee* near Pleasant Hill and Dexter, Oregon. Wesley Murphey picked in that very field for many years and, as a teen, worked for Alice's father. Murphey's father was Alice's school bus driver and the mail carrier in the area for 25 years. This somewhat autobiographical story begins on the McKenzie River in 2010 with a dying homeless man's confession. (306 pages)

Girl Too Popular

Being the most popular girl in town is not all it's cracked up to be—Carly Cantwell finds out why when she is kidnapped to a remote location in the forest. Is her abductor connected to her ex-stepfather who she rejected? Or is someone or something greater at work here? (176 pages)

To Kill a Mother in Law

Dan Thurmond got more than he bargained for when he married Brenda—a lot more. He got Maureen Muldano, the mother in law from hell. With his marriage on the rocks, and shut out by his wife's restraining order, Dan has taken all he can take. Now his hypocritical, pseudo-spiritual, controlling mother-in-law and the other wolves in her family are going to reap what they sowed. (306 pages)

Trouble at Puma Creek: A Vietnam vet, a deadly hunt

While hunting deer in Oregon's Fall Creek Forest in 1980, Vietnam veteran Roger Bruington is murdered by an Oregon State Police officer after discovering a suspicious shack. Did finding the shack get him killed? Or was this a government hit because Bruington was finally going to reveal the U.S. Government's cover up of the evidence he turned over in 1974 proving American POWs were still being held captive in southeast Asia a year after all POWs were supposedly released? (338 pages)

Nonfiction:

Blacktail Deer Hunting Adventures (172 pages)

A classic. The only true adventure account ever written on hunting the Pacific Coast's blacktail deer. "Anyone who has ever hunted blacktail deer can relate to this book and can gain some good hunting lore from reading this book." -- Boyd Iverson author Blacktail Trophy Tactics

Conibear Beaver Trapping in Open Water (110 pages)

Recognized as one of the best beaver trapping books in America.

Coming in 2013:

Fish, Hunt & Trap with the Murpheys (3 volumes approx 172 pges each)
   True Tales and Tactics by Wesley Murphey and his father, Don Murphey
   Includes many articles previously published in national and regional
   publications—and many great never-before-published articles.

Trapping with Wesley Murphey: Beaver, Otter, Raccoon, Nutria and other animals (approx 172 pages)
   Wesley Murphey's many published trapping articles and possibly some
   other stories.

To Kill A
Mother in Law

Wesley Murphey

Lost Creek Books
La Pine, Oregon

To Kill a Mother in Law

Published by Lost Creek Books, La Pine, Oregon
http:lostcreekbooks.com

Cover Design: Wesley Murphey

ISBN 978-0-9641320-6-1
Library of Congress LCCN 2012900542

Printed in the United States of America by Sheridan Books

Fiction: Suspense-Thriller

Part One

1

The Wong Place

In The Wong Place, he leaned toward the table where his estranged wife sat with her mother and step-father, and said to the parents, who were facing him, "I forgive you guys for what you have done to our lives and to our marriage."

His mother-in-law, Maureen, immediately pointed at him and laughed, mocking him like a kid would do to hurt another kid's feelings. Her mocking brought back some deep hurt from his childhood. His wife said, "Dan!" as a warning that he was violating her two-month-old restraining order against him. Immediately, he withdrew from their table, once again crushed by the fact that his marriage was on the rocks with little hope for reconciliation in sight. His mother-in-law had been a controlling, devastating influence in their lives, family and marriage for the past seven years: his wife had allowed it and, in fact, needed her mother's abuse.

Dan's broken heart ached as he walked back to the table on the other side of the room, where his nineteen-year-old son was sitting. He sat down to wait for their number to be called knowing they had to get out of there as soon as they got their Chinese food; he didn't know how long he could control the anger welling up inside him. Soon their number came up, he picked up their order and they made a hasty exit.

As he drove the four miles home, Dan grew more and more angry. He talked of going back to the restaurant with his shotgun to make those hypocrites pay. How much was a man supposed to put up with? His son, John—who knew how bad these people had treated his dad—tried to talk him down from his anger.

At home, when John went into the house, Dan headed into his shop to grab his twelve gauge shotgun, and some ammunition. The shotgun was the only firearm he had kept on the property after being served with the restraining order. As he stepped out the door to get to his vehicle with the gun, John—a handsome, dark-haired, powerfully-built, young man of 180 pounds—jumped in front of Dan's six-foot, 200 pound frame, and said, "Dad, you can't do this!"

"You darn right I'm going to do it!"

John grabbed the gun with one hand on the barrel and one on the stock and said, "There's no way I'm going to let you ruin your life; and what about Megan and me? We need you. If you kill them, or even go into the parlor with the shotgun you'll be locked up forever. I know how bad you've been hurt Dad, but these people aren't worth it. Please stop!"

They struggled momentarily with the gun, each trying to take control of it from the other. Finally, Dan eased his grip, "You're right son. You and Megan do need me, and those people aren't worth it." John took the gun.

Dan's anger was under control for now. But in the weeks and months ahead, his mind would run wild with the plans he contemplated for how he was going to put an end to that bitch of a mother-in-law, as well as others of his wife's family and even a couple people in his church. These people who had helped destroy his marriage, and put him through more pain than any man should have to take, were going to pay dearly for it.

2

Taste of Things Ahead

In the spring of 1998, Brenda, an attractive, forty-five-year-old, slim, five-foot eight-inch, blue-eyed red-head, and Dan, a stout, brown-headed, handsome, six-foot, forty-two year-old, were married in a very nice church wedding service that was well attended. They were a blended family. She had two daughters—five-year-old Jackie, and seventeen-year-old Annie (her only adopted child)—while he had a thirteen-year-old son, John, and ten-year-old daughter, Megan. Brenda also had three grown sons in their mid-to-late twenties. Her children were each by different fathers; she never married two of the men. This was her fourth marriage and Dan's second.

Dan should have seen the handwriting on the wall when Brenda spelled out the problems her mother had caused in each of her four siblings' marriages, and in her own previous marriages, the most recent having ended seven years earlier. She told him that each of the other four couples had been forced to move out of the area where the mother lived in order to save their marriages. Yet Brenda still lived in the same area as her mother, and always had.

Ironically, Maureen was the one who introduced Dan to Brenda. Dan had met Maureen years earlier when he went to high school with Brenda's younger siblings. At one point, when he was in his early twenties, he attended the same church Maureen did. Even back then, her Christianity never added up for him, because she tried to impress others with how "spiritual" she was.

In early November 1997, Dan ran into Maureen in the gym at the conclusion of the local grade school evening assembly. They hugged, and he asked, "What are you doing here?"

"My oldest daughter, Brenda, got in the flesh several years back and had a baby girl out of wedlock. I came to watch my grand-daughter tonight. She sang that song with her kindergarten class."

He was taken back that she spoke that way of her own daughter, as though she had to separate herself from her daughter's sinfulness. A few minutes later Brenda came by, and Maureen introduced her to Dan. Dan learned later from Brenda that it was not uncommon for her mother to introduce her to others as, "This is Brenda, my second oldest child. She was always the smartest of my children, but she never did anything with it." Fortunately, she wasn't introduced to him that way. It would have been quite awkward for both of them.

A couple weeks after their meeting at the grade school, Dan spotted Brenda at the local high school where her daughter Annie was playing in a volleyball game. He took the initiative and asked her out for some hot chocolate at one of the diners nearby. She accepted, they hit it off immediately, and within two weeks they were seeing each other practically every day. They became best friends, and within three months he asked her to marry him. She was thrilled, and they were married two months later in April.

A week before their wedding, Maureen arrived home from spend-ing the long winter in Arizona at a sister's place, while leaving her husband to winter alone at their home outside Monroe, Washington. Since Maureen had left the Everett-Monroe area just as Brenda and Dan began dating, he never got the chance to see any interaction between Maureen, Brenda and Brenda's daughters, particularly Jackie.

Trouble began one week after their wedding when Maureen disregarded Brenda's request for her to bring Jackie and Megan to the church for their evening dress rehearsal after she took them shopping with her. They finally arrived an hour late, missing much of the rehearsal. Maureen acted like it was Brenda's fault, and then she refused to come watch the girls in their Easter play at church the next morning. That was the first indication Dan had of how Maureen's overpowering personality and complete disregard for others would chip away at their marriage and blended family.

While they were dating—and during the first year of their marriage—Dan hated to be away from Brenda. He loved the way she always burst out laughing in the middle of her punch line when telling a joke. She seemed happy so much of the time. After they got married, whether they were walking the beach hunting seashells, hiking in the forest, swimming at the lake, camping in the mountains, looking for mushrooms, fishing, cuddling up at night, or just walking around the neighborhood holding hands, they enjoyed just being together. Over time, Maureen managed to take all that away from them, directly and through her negative influence on other family members.

A couple months after the wedding, one of Brenda's female cousins clued Dan in on a couple family circumstances in which Maureen had demonstrated her spiritual hypocrisy.

The cousin said that two years earlier, when Maureen's youngest sister's seventeen-year-old grandson got his sixteen-year-old girlfriend pregnant, Maureen—the self-professed, staunch anti-abortionist—encouraged the young couple to get an abortion. That had surprised, *yet* at the same time *didn't surprise*, the sister and a number of other family members.

Fortunately, the sister's grandson and the girl friend chose to keep the baby. When the grandson turned eighteen, six months after the baby girl was born, they moved in together; they were married a year later. Today, they are happily married with three kids— including *the one Maureen would have aborted.*

The cousin also told Dan that throughout Brenda's pregnancy with Jackie, Maureen had ragged on her non-stop for getting "knocked-up" out-of-wedlock *again.*

Ironically, after Jackie was born, Maureen took a strong liking to her, to say the least. She had retired from her career as a secretary a year earlier, so she filled her retirement hours with her newborn granddaughter.

In no time at all Maureen had established the ground rules for her visits with little Jackie. She could drop by Brenda's place and take her at any time, with no prior conversation, or permission, and Brenda had no say in the matter. That is, she had no say unless she wanted verbal hell from her controlling, boundary-breaking pseudo-Christian mother. Having been beaten down by her mother for over twenty-five years, Brenda rarely tried to stand up to her. Consequently, Maureen always got her way in regard to Jackie.

When Dan came into the picture, he saw immediately how Maureen consistently put Brenda in a no-win situation.

A favorite tactic that Maureen used was to drop by their house with no warning and catch Jackie playing outside. Maureen would tell Jackie that she was going shopping, or to MacDonald's, or somewhere else, "with Grandma." Then she would help Jackie climb into her big pickup. Maureen would then go into the house and tell Brenda, "I'm taking Jackie with me to…*wherever.*"

The few times that Brenda even started to object, not only would Maureen jump all over her, but as the argument moved outside near Maureen's pickup, Jackie would break into tears over the possibility of not getting to "go with Grandma." So Grandma would get her way.

One day, a year and a half into their marriage, Maureen told Brenda that she was taking Jackie overnight with her. Brenda told her that Jackie wouldn't be able to do that, because Dan, Brenda and all the kids were going camping as a family for the weekend. Maureen said, "Why does Jackie have to go?" *Excuse me?* What did Maureen not get about, "going camping *as a family*"? What she didn't get—and refused to acknowledge—was that *they were indeed* a family and she should keep her hands off.

Dan and Brenda's pastor preached a sermon one Sunday, less than four months after their wedding, about the proper relationship between a husband, wife and their families and friends. He had said, "The Bible says a man and woman are *to leave* their mother and father, and *cleave to*, or become attached to, their marriage mate, and the two shall *become one flesh*. This relationship is to be above all others. When family members—or anyone else for that matter— is allowed to have a negative influence and impact on a marriage, one of the mates has not left their mother, father, or someone else behind in order to put his or her spouse first."

Dan saw the application to their situation immediately. Brenda had never "left" her mother or a couple other family members when she married Dan. When those family members (most notably her mother, sister and oldest son) began interfering in her and Dan's family's business, he told Brenda that her relatives were not respecting their boundaries as a couple, or as a new blended-family, and that was having a negative effect in their home. That comment fell on deaf ears, as did so many others in the years ahead.

Little did Dan know then that Brenda was actually feeding the fire against him by talking to those family members about anything that she disagreed with him on, especially in his role as little Jackie's new step-father. It didn't take long for the in-laws to begin their behind-the-back and frontal assaults against Dan. Then Brenda was put in the middle of the very thing *she helped fuel*. Since she dared not stand up to her mom, sister or her oldest son—and back

Dan—his respect for her slowly evaporated.

Over time they began to relate to each other more like just roommates, then eventually enemies, instead of the most special person in each other's life. Because of the disrespect that Brenda allowed her family and especially her daughter, Jackie, to show toward him, Dan gradually withdrew his affection and romance from her. Eventually he grew to despise her. She was starving for his time and affection, yet she refused to listen when he told her what was killing their relationship. What began as a beautiful love affair crumbled a little at a time until reaching the breaking point in late 2004.

3

Maureen Muldano

There was a time when Maureen was a much different person—or at least much more self-controlled. *Supposedly*, up until her first husband, Gerald Gregory, died in a car accident that also claimed one of his brothers, Maureen actually tried her best to live her professed Christian beliefs. After his death, her stubborn, cold-hearted, self-willed nature took root, and she became one of Christendom's biggest hypocrites. She had always showed signs of these seedy qualities, but was loved so much by her husband that she was much more relaxed and secure, and genuinely desired to please both her husband and God. Gerald's death crushed her and caused bitterness to grow inside her like a cancer.

Gerald had been highly respected in his community. He was a hard-working sawmill worker who, somehow, found or made the time to teach and participate almost daily with *all five* of his very athletic children—three boys and two girls.

His oldest son, Doug, was the most gifted. He not only starred as a third baseman at the University of Southern California, but

9

went on to play eleven years of professional ball, predominantly at the triple-A level. He made several forays into the major leagues with various teams, but could not stick permanently. He was a good fielder and had good power, but his batting average in the majors hovered around .200. In triple-A ball he was a solid .270 hitter and typically batted a slot or two down from cleanup. Wherever he played he was a leader because he mirrored his deceased dad's strong Christian character.

Sadly Gerald died during Doug's senior year of high school, never getting to see the full extent of what his genes, encouragement, and investment of time had accomplished in his oldest son's adult life and sport's career. Ironically, neither did he get to see the person his wife turned in to, and the terrible damage she did in her adult children's lives—at least those who allowed it. God rest his soul.

Brenda told Dan on several occasions that her dad, Gerald, had always loved her deeply, but that she always had problems relating to her strong-willed mother, who she said was too different from her. That struck Dan as odd, because, as their marriage deteriorated, he saw many similarities between mother and daughter. The most notable traits, and those that caused the greatest negative effect on their marriage, were Brenda's dishonesty (especially regarding money, debt and her behind-Dan's-back derogatory conversations she had with her mom and others of her family), her argumentativeness, and her stubborn, strong-willed nature.

Maureen, for her part, was dishonest whenever it suited her needs, she never allowed her husband, Horacio Muldano—they call him Horay—to lead. She never consulted him on purchases (like when she bought a new pickup, or a rental property that turned out to be a huge repair project for him, one on which they lost thousands of dollars), and she ruled the house. Dan felt sorry for Horay from the start, because Maureen was so overbearing and disrespectful to him.

When Horay married her, the red-headed Maureen was five-foot-three, athletically built and weighed 140 pounds. At thirty-nine, she was quite attractive for a woman who had birthed five babies. Within four years she had ballooned to 250 pounds and eventually made the 300 pound mark, looking fittingly like a powerful, but squatty, Sherman Tank. Not only was she known to shoot the verbal cannon rounds out there like nobody's business, she physically bowled people over if it suited her. One time while she was in her fifties, she was even charged with misdemeanor assault for shoving a woman who had offended her.

Instead of the beautiful red hair she once wore, Maureen traded that in years ago for jet black hair that she keeps full, but cut short, halfway between her jaw and ear lobes, giving her the added feel and look of power that is so important to her.

The advertisement says, "You can tell a lot about a man by the truck he drives." That's not true of just men. It describes Maureen, except that it should say, "...by the truck she drives *and how* she drives it."

Maureen has a big, powerful, black, three-quarter ton, Ford diesel-powered pickup that she loves to run right up the rear of all smaller vehicles in front of her. She makes sure they know she owns the road. Of course, when you drive like that, you better pay attention to the front at all times, and have good brakes and good tread on the tires. Unfortunately for Maureen, sometimes she gets too involved in gossiping with her passenger, or someone on her cell phone. She has rear-ended other vehicles twice in the past three years alone.

4

FM: The Priest

On the second Monday in July, two weeks after the Chinese restaurant incident, Dan decided to visit the priest at Aberdeen's St. David's Catholic Church. His own Protestant pastor had proven to be worthless as a pastor to him during his marital struggles and then during the long separation period. Since Dan was raised in the Catholic Church up until his parents divorced, he thought, who knows, maybe a Catholic priest would be of some help to him. He hadn't been to a Catholic Church service in over twenty-five years, let alone talked to a priest. He really didn't know what to expect. Dan just knew he wanted some kind of spiritual help with what he was going through.

Sitting behind a desk in the Catholic Church office was a very attractive, dark-haired woman, who Dan guessed to be in her early forties.

She noticed him at once. "Can I help you?" she asked, as her eyes twinkled. He thought: *if you only knew*. I've been celibate for months and could really use the company of a beautiful woman like you about now.

"I was hoping to maybe speak to the priest," he said. "I'm going through a difficult time."

"I'm sorry to hear that," she said. "Are you a Catholic?" Dan thought, do I have to be a Catholic to speak to the priest? What does that matter?

"No, I'm not a Catholic. But I was a Catholic when I was a kid," he said, hoping that would qualify him. Then he thought, why bother? If I have to qualify to get a hearing from the priest, I don't want one. "Does my being a Catholic or not, make a difference?"

"Not at all," she said, "I was just curious. I didn't mean any offense." Dan was relieved. She seemed even prettier now. She picked up the handset on her phone and punched a button on the base. "Father Michael, there is a gentlemen here that would like to see you."

Dan just knew he would ask, "*Is he a Catholic?*"

Dan's childhood experience in the Catholic Church wasn't exactly exhilarating. After his parents divorced—and he and two brothers went to live with their dad—Dan was thrilled that his dad didn't make them attend church anymore, even though they moved directly across the road from the Catholic Church they had attended all their lives.

After the move, Dan had actually organized many neighborhood baseball games in the church parking lot. The kids broke a couple of stained-glass windows on the east side of the sanctuary with a regular baseball, so they switched to using rubber balls. Dan's jack-of-all-trades dad repaired the broken windows. The kids also played basketball under the covered, exterior entryway to the sanctuary; they used a twelve-inch plastic ball and shot at one of the panes of glass ten feet up the wall.

During the week there was rarely anyone at the church. The priest was only there two days a week: Sunday mornings for mass, and on Wednesday nights for catechism classes. So, along with playing basketball and baseball, Dan, along with his younger brother, and some neighbor kids, pretty much did whatever they wanted on the church property. They often rode their bikes all around the sidewalks, played a lot of army, and hunted birds on church property with their BB guns. Their favorite thing to do with their bikes was to ride off the two-foot concrete ledge at the west end of the sanctuary entryway.

When it got cold enough during the winter, the kids ran water from one of the church's side faucets into a bucket, then dumped it on the walkway so it would freeze. They would then run and slide there in their hard-soled shoes. It didn't take too many women falling on their backs or faces on the Sundays that followed to put a stop to that practice. The church staff turned off the water supply to the faucets.

"Bring him on back," said the priest. Surprisingly, he didn't ask if Dan was a Catholic.

The pretty receptionist led Dan down a short hall and through an open door on the left. The room was large, the floor covered with plush, light-brown carpet. Arranged in a semi-circle on the left side were three dark-brown upholstered chairs and a couch. A desk, swivel office-chair, filing cabinets and book cases were on the other side of the room. Dan noticed several Civil War and World War II books among the other books on the shelves of one of the book cases. The white walls were adorned with several large paintings, one of an American aircraft carrier stirring up an impressive wake as it cruised in the deep blue Pacific Ocean.

Immediately, a smiling, distinguished looking, tall, medium-built, salt and pepper-haired man in his mid-sixties, wearing glasses, blue jeans and a blue, long-sleeved, plaid shirt, stepped out from behind the desk and said, "I'm Father Michael." He reached out his hand to shake Dan's. He wasn't the formal guy Dan always remembered a priest being when he was a kid.

"Father Michael, this is…," she hesitated, realizing her blunder.

"I'm sorry; I forgot to get your name."

"Dan. Dan Thurmond," he said, as he shook Father Michael's hand.

"Nice to meet you, Dan; come sit down." He gestured toward his comfortable-looking furniture. The receptionist, whose name Dan didn't get, slipped out of the room and back down the hall.

Dan felt at ease immediately, as he sat on one of the cushioned chairs. Father Michael sat down in the chair across from him. "I like that picture of the aircraft carrier," Dan said. "We called those 'bird farms' when I was in the Navy. I served as a torpedoman on submarines during the mid-to-late seventies."

"I'm retired from the Navy myself," said Father Michael, totally surprising Dan. He thought all priests went directly to seminary after high school, didn't pass go or collect 200 dollars, and lived a dull life throughout their entire adulthood.

"I served extended duty as a psychologist on a couple different aircraft carriers and at several shore stations. In the early part of my career, in sixty-eight to seventy-two, I served in-country in Vietnam and also off the Vietnam coast aboard the aircraft carrier USS Constellation. That's her in that photo. I helped many U.S. servicemen who were struggling with the emotional trauma of their combat duty." Dan knew he never got to talk to his older brother, Victor, a combat marine.

A psychologist, Dan thought, I don't know about this. I don't want a shrink messing with my head. But on the other hand, maybe Father Michael's psychological background could actually help me.

"How did you end up in the priesthood?" Dan asked.

"I was raised a Catholic, and had actually considered going into the Navy as a chaplain, but opted for the psychology field instead. I wanted to help servicemen and women with their emotional issues, but I didn't want the limitations I felt would be placed on me as a Catholic chaplain. After I retired with twenty years active duty served, I went directly to seminary, and earned my ordination." Then looking to establish rapport, Father Michael said, "So, Dan, tell me a little bit about your submarine training and duty."

"Right after high school, a friend and I joined the Navy together on the buddy program," said Dan. "We were kept together in the same company for the nine weeks of boot training in San Diego. From there, we went our separate ways to class-A schools. My Torpedoman A School was in Orlando, Florida. After that I went to Groton, Connecticut for submarine school. After sub school I ended up on the USS Queenfish SSN 651, where I spent over 3 years as a torpedoman. I got out after my four year hitch was up."

"Thanks for your service, Dan. I'm not sure I could have handled being on a sub myself." Switching gears, Father Michael said, "Tell me why you came here to talk to a priest today."

"Well, like you, I was raised in a Catholic church, at least until my parents divorced when I was eleven. Even made altar boy my last year or so. I can't say that I ever really liked going to mass, but I liked the friends I had at the church, and I always liked the coffee and refreshment hour after mass."

"Yeah, the food was always good at my church when I was a kid, too. Have you been a member of the Church since you became an adult?"

"No, I've attended several different Protestant denominations, but had no interest in the formality of the Catholic Church. I don't mean any offense by that. Right now I go to a non-denominational church here in Aberdeen, but I have a lot of hard feelings toward the pastor. My wife left, and took my step-daughter with her, this past winter, the day after Christmas. Great timing."

"I'm very sorry to hear that, Dan."

"Three weeks after she left, she told me that she definitely wanted to reconcile with me, 'even if it takes a miracle from God.' At that time I *was not* interested in reconciliation, but a couple weeks later I came completely around. Unfortunately, the longer she was away from me, the further she grew from me. The influence of her family, which had been a terrible influence in our home and marriage for over six years, pulled her completely away from me after we separated.

"I think one of the things that hurts the most is the way my wife, just out of the blue, cut off all communication with me. We were talking normally by phone the night before Easter; ended the conversation with each of us telling the other, 'I love you.' Then two days later she wouldn't answer her phone to talk to me, and hasn't talked to me since. A week and a half later she slapped a restraining order on me like a muzzle. I never did anything to deserve it. The only thing she has said to me in the last two and a half months was at a Chinese restaurant a couple weeks ago when she said my name as a warning that I was too close to her table. Her shutting me out like that hurts deeply and makes me very angry."

"I can certainly understand that, Dan. You mentioned that you were angry with your pastor. Tell me about that."

"I need to change churches. My pastor has proven to be one of the most arrogant, uncompassionate people I've ever met. He takes lots of time to put together his power-point presentations for his Sunday morning sermons each week, but has never had any time for me or my marital issues. He's one of those eight to five pastors. You know what I mean by that, don't you?"

"I think I do. They are never available after hours, and they really don't want to do any counseling or anything else that would take a commitment from them, even during their regular hours. The Catholic Church, historically, has had plenty of those kinds of priests. I call that type of priest or pastor, the 'professional minister.' They seem to be in the ministry to prepare their sermons and do their masses each week, do their confessions, marry and bury and collect their pay checks. I almost didn't go into the priesthood after I got out of the Navy for that reason. I didn't want to be a professional minister. But I decided that I didn't have to be like the others, I could do the ministry in the way I believed God wanted me to. Not the way the Church has been doing it for hundreds of years."

"I'm glad to hear you say that," said Dan. "I've had my fill of professional ministers. Believe me I've met some good Protestant ministers that would have given you their arm and leg. But this guy at the Church Of The Uncompassionate in Aberdeen is worthless as a pastor. He preaches good, professional sermons, but there's no humanness in him. He can't relate to hurting people at all."

"So how did he fail you?"

"I don't want to get into all the details, but I'll tell you a few things that happened, enough for you to see where I'm coming from with my feelings towards him."

"That sounds good."

"When each of my parents died within the last two years, he never once called to express his sorrow or to ask if there was anything he could do. Then when my wife got the restraining order against me, he blamed me, saying that I hadn't given her the space she wanted. The guy was clueless as to what was going on with her. He's a joke.

"The thing he did, though, that really made me mad, happened when I called him up one day last week. The restraining order had already been in effect for over two months. Even at that, it had a provision that allowed for my wife and me to meet together with the pastor or a deacon. Yet in all that time, not one effort was made by the pastor to bring us together, nor had there been in the four previous months of our separation. This was the same guy who came to my house two and a half weeks into the separation spouting that he believed in a God of reconciliation, that he knew that God wanted my wife and I to be reconciled.

"So one day I called him up and asked, 'what are we waiting for to get my wife and me together?'

"'That's a fair question,' he answered. 'Actually, we're waiting on you.' Instantly, I was fuming inside. That arrogant idiot was laying all the blame on me.

"'What do you mean you're waiting on me?' I asked.

"'We haven't seen enough spiritual growth in you.'

"I was furious. I went off on him. I said, 'What do you do, stick a spiritual thermometer up a person's butt to determine if he's spiritual enough to get back together with his wife?' I mean it wasn't like I was a drunk, druggie, adulterer, or a wife beater. I never laid a hand on her, nor ever threatened her the whole time we were together. I told him, 'That's a bunch of crap. I'll never be spiritual enough for you then. You want some super-spiritual Christian. Who are you to determine when I'm spiritual enough, and what about my wife's spirituality? This whole thing has been so one-sided. You're just a huge hypocrite. I don't have to listen to your crap.' Then I hung up."

Dan didn't tell Father Michael that it was that conversation with the pastor that convinced him that he had to deal with the man. He didn't know when or how, but he knew he had to.

Shaking his head in disbelief, Father Michael said, "I can really appreciate your frustration and anger at the pastor and the whole situation. Just from the little bit you've told me—and I'm guessing there's a lot more—I would agree with you that your pastor *is no pastor*. And I don't say that lightly. It's not my intent to run another minister down, but just from what you've shared, I can't understand at all where that guy is coming from."

Dan knew he had an ally here. But how was that going to help him and his situation?

"I've often asked myself," Dan said, "why did he even bother to come to my house that first month talking about reconciliation if he was going to sit on his lazy, unaccountable butt and do nothing toward that end?"

"I sure can't answer that one," said Father Michael. "So how can I help you?"

"I'm not sure, honestly. I just know I'm not getting any spiritual support from that pastor. I'm struggling with angry thoughts much of the time. I guess I need a spiritual friend, and someone to pray for me and this situation."

"I would be glad to be those things for you, Dan. Let me give you my cell phone number. Feel free to call me anytime." He gave Dan his number.

"Well, I'm not the kind of guy that would become a nuisance to you, so you don't have to worry about that. I may not call at all; I don't know. But just knowing that I can means a lot to me, Father. Thanks."

"Can I pray with you right now, Dan?"

"I would appreciate that," said Dan.

The father prayed what sounded like a genuine heart-felt prayer, unlike the formal, spiritually-dead prayers Dan's pastor prayed. At his words, Dan felt a connection to his childhood, but didn't know why. A spiritual conscience and yearning had been planted in him during those early years as a Catholic. Maybe that's what he felt, that spiritual consciousness. He already really liked Father Michael. He was a pastor and psychologist all in one. But it was his pastor's heart that came through loud and clear to Dan.

After the prayer, he asked Dan if he could do anything else for him today, or if there was anything else Dan wanted to tell him. There *were* other things Dan thought he might talk to him about later, such as his childhood for one, his first wife, and his older brother, but he had said enough for now. Dan considered asking Father Michael if maybe he could try to contact Brenda in Aberdeen to talk to her about reconciliation, but what would be the point? There was little hope for that now. Plus, she might turn him in for trying to contact her through a third party—forbidden by the Restraining Order—since Father Michael wasn't his pastor or a deacon in Dan's church. His pastor and church had failed him, and there was nothing he could do about it. Nothing he could do *to fix it*, that is. There was plenty Dan contemplated doing about it. But, for now, he would wait.

On his way out of the church, Dan visited briefly with the attractive receptionist. He mentioned to her that he was in the middle of a long separation that looked hopeless. She said she would pray for him. Her name was Julie. She was a widow with three teenage children. And *she was* a life-long Catholic.

5

Brenda Moves

In early August 2005, two months after the incident at The Wong Place, Brenda and Jackie moved in with her mother near Monroe, Washington, about three hours away from Dan, and only twenty minutes southeast of Everett, where they came from several years earlier. During the last two months Dan had only seen Brenda twice, but had no direct contact. As far as he could see, her move ended all hope for reconciliation, despite her having supposedly told the gullible pastor two weeks earlier that she still loved him and intended to reconcile with him. She sure had a funny way of showing her love. But self-deception and hypocrisy come easy in that family.

The idiot pastor still hadn't made any effort to bring Dan and Brenda together. By now Dan knew he could never reach the required level of spirituality that would justify the pastor making any effort to bring him and Brenda together. Dan wanted to hurt him and hurt him bad. But that would be like hurting God since he considered himself to be God's right-hand man. *The arrogant bastard!*

Hope of reconciliation was one of a few things that had kept Dan from actually doing many of the things he had been plotting since the restraining order was placed on him. Besides God, other considerations were that he could end up incarcerated or dead, and his kids would lose their father. In the best case scenarios Dan felt confident he could escape without getting caught, but might never be able to live a normal life or see his kids again.

Brenda knew the day she got the restraining order that Dan wasn't a threat to her, at least not up to that day he wasn't. She obtained the Order for one purpose—to shut him out of her life, a sort of *legal muzzle and shackles*.

Brenda was kidding herself if she really believed the restraining order would keep her or her family members safe when Dan decided to physically harm any of them. He still had his firearms, or at least ready access to them. Besides that, Dan thought killing up close with a knife, club, rope or his fists would be plenty simple and much more satisfying. Heck, he could even burn them up. There was hardly a limit to the various ways he could handle them. Any day of the year he could go to any of their houses or where they work or shop, hide behind a bush or a car, wherever, and catch them in the dark and kidnap or kill them. He had the power of life or death over every one of them.

Before Brenda moved out of the Aberdeen area and back to her mother, Dan thought about putting up a big sign on the main road that she had to travel into town on, that read,

Restraining Orders Can Not Stop Bullets, Knives, Ropes, Clubs, Fists, or Fires.
But They Can Sure Make Someone Mad Enough To Use Them!!

Brenda, you have no idea what you have started, thought Dan. I was a good guy, but your deception and the silent treatment you gave me with that damn restraining order, and the way your family treated me, has brought some old, deep hurts up out of my past. Now you're all going to pay, especially your bitch mother. She should be very concerned at how easy it would be for me to kill her, especially since she and Horay live in a rural house that has plenty of bushes around it and access from several directions. Maureen should remind herself of her own words, spoken less than two years into our marriage, "Dan is a sick man. He needs to see a psychiatrist!" I'm sicker now than I was then, Maureen, and now I have the motivation to kill you.

6

FM: Second Meeting

A few days after Brenda and Jackie moved away, Dan called St. David's Catholic Church hoping Julie would answer. He knew now that his marriage was mostly over, so what would be the harm in chatting with a beautiful widow like her.

"St. David's Catholic Church; how can I help you?" It was Julie; her tender voice was music to his ears.

"Hi Julie, this is Dan Thurmond. Do you remember me?"

"Sure I remember you. We haven't heard from you, so I really didn't know if we would, you not being a Catholic and all." Of course, Father Michael probably wouldn't have told her anyway, if he had talked to Dan on his cell phone during that time.

"I know, you don't mean any offense by that, do you?" said Dan. He liked her already.

"Of course not," she answered. "How have you been?"

"About the same. My wife moved back to the Monroe area a few days ago. I'm sure it's over now."

"I'm sorry, Dan. I know that has to be very rough for you. Did you want to talk to Father Michael?" She was a good Catholic and, as a single woman, was not about to string out her conversation with a man in a failed marriage. But Dan hoped she might have wondered about the possibilities. If his wife was ditching him and leaving her marriage vows, how wrong could it be for him to be attracted to, or think about, another single woman? He knew it probably wasn't right by the Bible's standards, but right now he felt anything but spiritual. Thinking of being with other women *couldn't be any worse* than thinking of, and plotting, murder.

"Yes. Well, actually, I was hoping to get in to see him, if he's available."

She looked at his schedule. "He doesn't have any appointments for this afternoon. Let me tell him you're on the line and would like to meet with him."

She put Dan on hold and punched the father's line. Father Michael told her to have Dan meet him at the church at 12:30. He would buy Dan lunch at The Fish House. That sounded good to Dan.

They met for lunch, enjoyed a great meal of fish and chips, and small talked about some of their naval experiences, as well as how many outdoor recreation opportunities there were in the Aberdeen area. Dan was surprised to learn that Father Michael was an avid hunter and fisherman. Somehow, because of his childhood experience, Dan assumed that all priests lived unexciting lives with no wives or women, no kids, no recreation and no hobbies or interests outside the Church. Father Michael didn't fit his model of a priest at all. Dan liked him more all the time.

After lunch Father Michael drove them back to the church, where they went into his office and sat on his comfortable furniture. He had been sensitive enough to know that Dan didn't want to talk about any of his problems in a restaurant.

"How are things going for you with the separation?" asked Father Michael.

"My wife moved back to the Everett area three days ago—supposedly because she was struggling financially. But I know it was because she wanted to be close to her mother, step-father and other family members. She told the pastor a couple of weeks ago that she still intended to reconcile with me. She had to be kidding. If her mother and other family members worked so hard to tear us apart while she was living with me, you can be sure they have multiplied their efforts since she's been away. And now that she has moved in with her mother, you can be sure it's over.

"Only an idiot like my pastor could be so naïve to believe there is any chance for reconciliation. I mean, first she leaves me, moves in with an older spiritual woman in the church and makes it clear that she wants to reconcile with me, even if it takes a miracle from God. Two and a half months later, she tells me I just need to be patient with her. A couple weeks later she gets a bunch of her stuff and furniture from the house and moves into her own apartment. Two weeks later, Easter evening, she cuts off all communication with me. A week and a half after that, she gets a restraining order against me. Two weeks later, she brings with her *to our church* the very same family members who worked hard to tear our marriage apart. I mean if that wasn't heartless, I don't know what is. Then now she moves to her mother's, three hours away. Does she take me for a jackass, telling the pastor that she still loves me and intends to reconcile with me? She didn't fool me. Satan runs that family, and he has controlled my wife for years, through her mother."

"I can sure sense your anger over this, and I can understand it," said Father Michael. "Just from what you have described, it's hard for me to see much chance for reconciliation, unless God somehow intervenes and gets through to your wife's heart. And even then, if she isn't willing to drop the restraining order, to move away from her troublesome family members, and to cut off her communication with all those who have had such a negative impact on your marriage, and open the lines of communication with you, I see little-to no-hope for reconciliation. I'm just being realistic. And I think you see it the same way."

"Yes I do. So where do I go from here?"

"I wouldn't advise you to take any legal action, other than to protect whatever assets you can. You should speak to an attorney about that. I would move ahead with your life as if your wife is never coming back, and I would try to draw close to God."

"It's hard to get close to God when I know the many ways I failed as a husband, and with all the hostile thoughts I have toward my wife and her family, not to mention the pastor and a couple other people in my church."

"I understand that, but consider that God knows all about your situation, your failures, your hostile thoughts, your pain and your anger. All of it. Yet, He loves you. His son, Jesus, died and was resurrected, not only to pay the penalty for your sins, but to give you a new abundant life. I know it doesn't seem like that now. But God does still love you and He forgives you. You need to trust him." If the father knew of the murder plans that Dan contemplated, maybe he wouldn't be so generous with God's forgiveness toward him.

"It's very hard for me to trust God for anything in my life, with all that has happened," said Dan. "I trust His Son as my savior, and I always will. But as far as I can see, God doesn't involve himself in the daily lives of people today."

"I understand how you feel about that," said Father Michael. "I've had those same thoughts plenty of times. When I was in the Navy during the Vietnam War, I saw many coffins filled with the bodies of young men from good American families. I also dealt with soldiers fresh off the battle field, who were emotional wrecks, mere shadows of the strong, energetic young men they left boot camp as, some of America's finest. It's hard to see that without wondering how a good God could allow it to happen."

"Why does He allow it?"

"Heck, I can't explain something that I don't understand myself," he answered. "I just know that, somehow, we have to trust Him. Where are we with all this pain and suffering, if we don't?"

"I don't know, Father." Dan took a deep breath, and let it out slowly.

Father Michael saw that, and sensed Dan was about to open another chamber of his hurting heart. His tender eyes looked at Dan's, as if to say, "It's okay; I'm here for whatever it is you need to tell me."

Dan remembered his dad looking at him that way sometimes. He often wished his dad could have shown his love for him more easily. His rare hugs and words of affection were almost always a bit awkward for both of them. It was the way much of his dad's generation was raised, "The Greatest Generation;" the heroes of World War II. Why did it have to be so hard for a father to show his son physical affection? Dan struggled with that toward his own son.

"My oldest brother, Victor, was killed in Vietnam in 1970," said Dan. "He was a marine."

"I'm so sorry, Dan. Man you've had a lot to deal with in your life." His empathy and compassion came through clearly, such a contrast to Pastor Bill.

"He graduated from Monroe High School in 1969. He and his life-long friend joined the marines a month later. They were going to go help America win the war. I was only twelve when Victor left for boot camp in San Diego. After boot camp, he took a fourteen day leave at home. It was the last time I saw him. One of the last things I did with him was go fishing on the small creek not far from our house. We'd fished there together many times. I knew he was going off to war, but I couldn't picture him ever getting killed.

"He was a star quarterback on the high school football team—a natural leader. He made first team all-league his senior year. His buddy, the fellow marine, was his fullback. The team tied for second in the league, so they didn't go to state, but they won six of their nine games. Victor was also a good baseball player. He mostly played catcher and outfield. He made second-team all league at catcher his senior year.

"When Victor was killed, it was a blow to the whole community.

He had been popular mainly because of his quarterbacking. They held a memorial service for him in the high school gym, and over 300 people turned out. The varsity head football coach gave a short talk in which he spoke of Victor's athletic ability, leadership, and work ethic. He also mentioned his faith. Victor was a Catholic, an altar boy for many years, but he didn't attend church his senior year. I know he died a believer, and I will see him again some day."

"I know you will," said the father. He paused, then said, "I'm sure enjoying getting to know you Dan. I hope I'm being of some help."

"You really are, Father. Getting some of this stuff off my chest is a big relief. You're nothing like my pastor. I know you really do care about me."

"Well, I do care about you, Dan. I can sense that you have some good values and that you are a genuine person. I'm sorry for all you've been through and what you're still going through. I just encourage you to reach out to God and open your heart to let His love fill you. I'm not going to tell you that you have to forgive those who have wronged you. You'll do that when you're ready. Just know that God loves you, and He's always there. You can talk to Him anytime, just like you have talked with me."

"It's just not the same, Father," said Dan. "He never responds to me. He's just silent. I need a real person."

"Read the Bible," said Father. "He can speak to you through it, and He can speak to you in a still small voice, inside your head. But I'm with you on the person part of it too. We do need other people. God uses people like me and many others to listen to His people, to pray with them, and to encourage them. Like I said before, feel free to call me anytime." He paused. "Can I pray with you?"

After his prayer, they stood up. Both knew they had accomplished what was needed for the day. Father hugged Dan, then walked him to his door. Dan hoped he wouldn't walk him to the front office, because he wanted to flirt a little with Julie. "Have a good day, Dan. Call me." They shook hands and Dan left.

Julie was all smiles. "How'd it go today, Dan?" she asked.

"It went very well. I really like Father Michael." Man she's beautiful, Dan thought.

"I really do to. I like him better than any priest I've ever had. When my husband died in a small plane crash two years ago, Father Michael was so compassionate, and he made sure that church members checked up on me regularly and brought meals. He came by my house several times himself. He even took my son, Aaron, who was thirteen at the time, to several Aberdeen baseball games. He's become like an uncle to me."

"I'm very sorry about your husband. I wondered what happened to him."

"Thanks," she said.

"I agree with the uncle part," said Dan. "I was thinking the same thing about him myself."

Part of Dan wanted to ask her if maybe they could get together for coffee or lunch some time, but he thought better of it. Why potentially ruin a good thing? There would be other opportunities. Besides, he was still married, and part of him still wanted to reconcile with Brenda, no matter how bleak that prospect looked, or how bad a marriage it had been.

They small talked for a few more minutes, then he left.

7

Conner Willingham

Conner Willingham, Brenda's oldest son, a six-foot-two, 400 pound half-white, half-black, ex-con, pumps septic tanks for a living. He's been working for "PUMP IT BABY SEPTIC COMPANY—Your Sewer Sucking Specialists," for six years. When they hired him they told him, "We'll pay you eight dollars an hour and all you can eat." It sounded too good to Conner to pass up. He was a bit slow on the take, ended up with just the eight dollars an hour. He makes ten now. Unfortunately for him, the two assault charges he rung up for fighting in a bar, and at a Washington Husky football game since starting the sewer sucking have prevented him from getting a better job. He had to do up to two weeks jail time, and pay restitution for both misdemeanors. Maybe someday he'll learn, though only a fool would put money on that.

Conner spent four years in the Washington State Felons Center in his early twenties for his part in the gang-rape of a nineteen-year-old woman. The rape occurred near Bellingham, Washington in August

1991 when Conner and five of his buddies were spending a week-end get-together at a rented, secluded cottage near the beach.

They had been driving the Bellingham city streets around 9:30 pm when they spotted the shapely, long blonde-haired, inebriated woman staggering along on the sidewalk, wearing crotch-length shorts and a skimpy tank top. The sight of her got the young men's testosterone boiling. There was some joking about picking her up, then suddenly lust overcame a couple of them. They jumped out beside her, pulled her into the Chevy Blazer, and then took her to their cottage. Once they had the woman inside, Conner and one of the other young men held her down. Three of their friends stripped her clothes off and then took her, one after the other, while she struggled and screamed. When they were done, four of them loaded her back into the rig, took her to the other side of town and dropped her off.

Unfortunately, for the young men, the woman was a local loose woman known by the Bellingham Police Department. When a police officer spotted her stumbling and crying along a sidewalk fifteen minutes later, she poured out her heart to him about the rapes.

Twenty-five minutes after that, two Bellingham police squad cars and two Whatcom County sheriff rigs pulled up and parked on the road, a hundred yards from the cottage. The disheveled, crying woman pointed to the cottage and said, "That's it. That's where they raped me!"

The police officer in the car with the woman asked, "Did you see if they had any firearms or other weapons?" In her drunken condition, he didn't figure she saw too much, but he wanted to glean any helpful information that he could.

"No, I didn't notice any weapons." She was trembling, as she looked at the cottage.

The five lawmen all drew their service issue .38s, spread out and cautiously approached the front of the building. The window shades were closed. But they could see lights on inside, and hear what sounded like a typical drinking party inside—young men laughing and being vulgar and loud. Three of the officers walked to the front door that was lighted by a porch light. The other two circled to the back of the house in case an attempt was made to flee out a back door.

One of the officers in front spoke quietly on his radio to an officer in the back to make sure they were all in position. When he received the OK, one of the officers at the front knocked on the door. One of the young men inside opened the door and, upon seeing the uniforms and drawn guns, knew his evening was going sour in a hurry.

"Bellingham Police! I need you to step out here on the porch with your hands on your head."

"What's going on here?" the man slobbered.

"Just step out now!" ordered the officer.

The drunk took three clumsy steps out into the open and was immediately grabbed, and cuffed by the other two officers. The first officer asked him, "How many more of you are there inside?" as he stayed up against the building and watched the doorway, pointing his gun there.

"There are five more. What do you want? We didn't do anything wrong." The two officers pulled the man away from the house and forced him to lie face down on the grass. The officer at the front door, yelled inside where things had gotten quiet, "The rest of you come out here one at a time, with your hands on top of your heads. Count to thirty, then the next man step out. You are all under arrest for raping a young woman here earlier this evening."

Conner was the fourth one out. As they cuffed him, he knew that his life was not turning out anything like his Uncle Doug's (the professional ball player) or his Grandpa Gerald Gregory, who died when he was a newborn. He also knew his mom, Brenda, was about to get the second saddest news of her life. Only the death of her father when she was seventeen was worse.

The sixth and last man out was Rob, who had refused to assist in anything to do with the rape and, in fact, had pleaded with the others not to do it when they had first grabbed the girl. After Rob came out, the two officers who had come around from the back entered the building with guns drawn and did a search.

"Clear, nobody left inside," they reported as they came out to assist with the six prisoners.

"You men, if we can call you that, are all under arrest for the rape of the young lady we have in the squad car over there," said one of the officers. "You have the right to remain silent, if you give up that right, anything you say, can, and will, be used against you in a court of law." He finished quoting them their Miranda Rights.

Rob spoke up immediately, "I didn't help with any of it. I told the others from the start not to do it, but they wouldn't listen to me." He was actually sober, having only drunk a couple of beers. The others, by contrast, were obviously drunk. After the rape, they had come back and tried to soothe some of their guilt. They had no thought that they would get caught. The only one who had worried about that was Rob.

The six men were all cuffed, frisked and then led away to three of the squad cars. The woman was taken in the other one. They were driven to the Whatcomb County Jail and booked. Ironically, with a little finesse, all of the men probably could have had their way with the woman without having to rape her.

Rob, the young man who had refused to assist in the rape, later gave his eye-witness testimony in exchange for a misdemeanor charge and two years probation. Conner and the other man who helped hold the woman down, but didn't actually rape her, got four years. Their three friends, who did the raping, got seven years each. The three rapists also *got gonorrhea* for their efforts.

Now that Brenda was away from Dan and back with her family in the Everett area, she was able to spend lots of time playing with the two grandsons that Conner had allowed her to see very little of since the big Christmas blowup at Maureen's house in 1999.

That was the day Maureen got in Dan's face and verbally tore him to pieces in front of the whole family, saying cruel things about him as a husband, him as a father, him as a person, and him as a Christian. One of the coldest things she said to him, in reference to her granddaughter, Dan's step-daughter, Jackie, was, "My blood runs through her. Yours never will!"

The only thing Dan had said to her in rebuttal of all the terrible things she had said was, "At least I'm not a gossip!" alluding to her regularly getting on the phone to this relative or the other with the "latest" about Dan's failings as a husband, failings as step-father, or something else that wasn't done that Maureen thought should be.

After Maureen finished ripping Dan apart at the Christmas party Brenda and Horay managed to get her out of the house. That's when Conner said to Dan, "The last time someone mouthed off, I knocked him cold," referring to Jackie's father.

Dan replied, "You lay a hand on me and you're going back!" meaning, *to prison.*

At that, Conner totally lost control of his anger, and immediately moved toward Dan, grunting. Brenda, right at the door, along with her youngest son, Leroy, a 200 pounder, jumped on Conner and knocked him off his feet. Someone else, Dan couldn't remember who, also helped hold him down. Dan told his son, John, to call 911, but Brenda said, "Don't you dare call 911." So no call was made. In a few minutes, Brenda and Leroy got Conner to go outside and leave. That was the second time Conner had wanted to fight Dan. The other time occurred seven months earlier in Dan and Brendas' own house, barely a year into their marriage.

They say that blood is thicker than water: that blood relatives will stick together. One thing Dan found true the day of the Christmas blowup, and increasingly so, was that for him to say even one thing to Brenda or any of her relatives about their interfering in his and Brenda's family, was asking for a fight. He knew that if he ever got into a fight with one of her sons, Brenda would never forgive him, no matter what the outcome. On the other hand, since he was just her husband and not blood to her, if one of her boys started a fight with him, she could easily forgive the son. That was a deck loaded against Dan.

8

Sister in Law

Dan was quite depressed the week following Brenda's move back to Monroe, even after his second meeting with Father Michael. His mind raced with various plots. He finally settled on the one that would make a huge impact and in which he felt he could definitely get away with.

Brenda's little sister, Jan Walden, who was as strong-willed and bitchy as her mom, had taken sides against Dan as soon as her mother had gossiped to her by telephone about the argument she started at Dan's house in February 1999. Looking back, Dan was sure Maureen said plenty of negative about him to Jan even before that first argument.

Maureen, never able to mind her own business and keep her mouth shut, had not only instigated Brenda's and Dan's first argument that February, she had proceeded to jump in and berate him verbally in front of his kids in his own home. With Dan sitting across the room, twelve feet away, Maureen said things like, "This situation is worse than I thought. We really need to pray for him."

Finally, he had said to her, "Maureen, you don't have to put yourself up on a spiritual pedestal with me. I've seen the way you treat Horay." Brenda had managed to get Maureen out the door soon after that, but Dan caught hell from her afterwards. He learned that day where he fit on her priority list—definitely not at the top. Over time, he realized he was way down the list. Not quite what he imagined the day they said their, I do's.

Ironically, several months after that February incident, Dan had gone to Maureen to try to patch things up. When he apologized to her, Maureen had hugged him and said, "It's okay, Dan. You just don't know how things work in our family." She said a mouthful with that comment.

Jan and Mike Walden lived in a secluded forest not far from Chehalis, Washington. She worked in the main office at a local lumber mill, while he was a police officer with the Centralia Police Department. Dan knew Jan from high school, when she was a little pre-Madonna, very athletic, very attractive with her long brown hair and shapely five-foot three-inch figure. She was a little flirt in those days, and every boy Dan knew would have liked to have been her boyfriend. He learned, too late, that being her brother-in-law was a whole different proposition.

Jan's husband, Mike—a friendly guy with a slender, but strong build, six foot tall, perhaps 175 pounds—always liked Dan. At a family get together at Maureen's, the second summer Brenda and Dan were married, Mike told Dan that he could see Dan was getting the same treatment from Maureen that Mike had received early in his marriage to Jan.

Mike said, "You've probably noticed that I stay out on the periphery of whatever is going on, and I don't join in any of their games. By not participating, Maureen can't put me down or try to stir up family members against me. When I first quit joining in, she and Jan pressured me to participate by laying guilt trips on me. I figured that wasn't as bad as what Maureen dished me when I did get involved. They both finally quit harassing me for not playing, and now I pretty much stay out of trouble. You might have to do the same thing."

Fortunately for Mike, he and Jan lived over two and a half hours away from Maureen, and they didn't have any children. Dan often thought that if Brenda didn't have Jackie, they could have had a good marriage. But Jackie was constantly used in different ways to tear at their marriage and parenting by all of the meddling family members.

As much as Dan liked Mike, and wished he could handle things differently, Mike was going to get caught because he was married to Jan. Dan was going to have to kill both of them in order to make it look like a robbery. If he killed only Jan, the police would immediately start looking at who would have a motive to kill her. He would certainly come up on their list because of her past harassment of him and the influence she had in turning his step-daughter against him. Dan's intention was to crush Brenda and Maureen with Jan's death, especially by murder.

Dan remembered how torn up Maureen was one holiday the first year of his and Brenda's marriage upon getting a phone call saying that an older brother had just died. She bawled inconsolably. Back then he felt sympathy and compassion for her. Now he would enjoy seeing her experience that kind of pain. He had cried dozens of times in the last several months. He was haunted by her devilish glare at him in his own church two weeks after the restraining order was placed on him, and then the mocking in The Wong Place Chinese restaurant two months later. The woman was mean and cruel and *satanic*. She needed to feel some of the pain she had made others feel, then Dan needed to kill her. He could kill her anytime he wanted, but he would rather drag her pain out for a while before putting her out of her misery.

Jan and Mike's house was a large, two-story place, about ten years old. It sat in the middle of their thirty acres of mostly one-hundred-foot-high, second-growth Douglas fir trees. Their place was surrounded by BLM land on two sides, and an undeveloped large private forest on the north side, which butted up against the Lewis and Clark State Park. The eastern boundary of their property ran along Boone Road which joined Tucker Road. There were no neighbors within a mile of their place. The driveway to their house was about two hundred yards long. On the back side of the house, there was a large manicured lawn, as well as a large, uncovered deck that butted up against the house. The front of their house had no lawn and only about a thirty foot space between the house and the younger firs.

Brenda, Dan and the kids visited Jan and Mike there the first summer they were married. Dan remembered thinking how quiet and peaceful the evenings and nights were and how lucky the Waldens were to have such a secluded home. Now he was going to use that seclusion to his advantage. Jan and Mike owned a German shepherd dog in the past but fortunately he died two years ago. Last Dan heard he hadn't been replaced. A dog would throw a definite wrench in his plans, because he would somehow have to shut the dog up before he could approach the house.

On September 12th, Dan set up his mushroom picking camp, in an off-the-beaten-path location, inland from the northern Oregon coast south of Astoria. Megan was going to spend the following weekend with a friend, and she knew that he would be spending a fair number of nights away from home picking mushrooms. He gave her permission to spend the nights he was gone at one of her friend's house, or have a friend stay at her house with her. She had no idea that the following weekend, instead of going mushroom picking, Dan was headed to Portland to rent a vehicle to drive to his secluded parking spot in the forest within a mile of the Walden's place.

Back in early July, he had made a day trip to the Chehalis area to do his reconnaissance in preparation for a possible murder mission to the Walden's later on. He had received word before that weekend, through his daughter's continued contact with her step-sister, Jackie, that all of the family was gathering at Monroe for their annual re-union. Therefore, he knew there was no danger of the Walden's seeing him in their area then. That trip had given him all the information he needed.

After getting his canvas tent and various other things set up in his mushroom camp, Dan drove back to Aberdeen to spend two days waiting for Thursday.

In the previous couple of months Megan had heard Dan say some angry things about her step-mother, Brenda, and Brenda's family and knew of his anger the night of the Chinese restaurant incident. She also knew he was taking some medications that were supposed to help him, but she still worried a lot about him. She knew how bad he was hurting, and actually hoped that his doing the mushroom picking would be a step back toward normality.

On Thursday morning, he gave Megan a ride to school and kissed her goodbye. She would have died if she knew what he was about to do.

After dropping Megan off, Dan drove his brown 1992 Jeep Cherokee to the northwest outskirts of Portland and parked in a huge shopping center parking lot that had several twenty-four hour stores, including a WINCO Grocery Store. He then carried his big duffle bag filled with clothes and walked seven blocks to a used-car rental shop, where he rented a brown 1990 Toyota Camry. He paid cash to avoid a credit card trail.

He told the rental attendant that his car developed a mechanical problem earlier in the day and was now in the shop. He said he was driving to the Eugene area for a family get-together, and had come by way of Portland for some business. He might be gone as much as three days, depending on whether his buxom, drop-dead beautiful, blonde-headed cousin Windy—who looked like she should be a movie star—was there or not. The attendant chuckled at that.

From the time they were little kids, Dan and Windy, a year younger than him, were attracted to each other. She lived an hour away in Bellingham, so they didn't see each other that much except over the holidays, or when she stayed with Dan's family for a week most summers.

They didn't know if their parents ever figured out how many good kissing sessions they had out in the barn or the neighbors' retired chicken barns, but the parents probably knew much more than Dan and Windy realized. They never went beyond kissing, even though they wanted to, because of the cousin connection. Dan knew other cousins had crossed that line, even in his extended family. But he and Windy just never did, maybe because he didn't want to have to confess that to the priest. Dan's family get-together was actually the next weekend. By then he would have blood on his hands and almost hoped Windy wouldn't be there. He was sure he would feel dirty in a way he never had.

After he left the car rental, Dan drove back to his vehicle at WINCO and carefully transferred the suitcase, containing his broken-down Remington twelve gauge shotgun and Smith and Wesson .357 magnum pistol, into the trunk of the Camry. He had purchased both guns two weeks earlier from a private party in McCleary, with no names or information exchanged.

With the restraining order in effect, Dan could not legally possess any firearms. Therefore, any gunshot residue found on him would be incriminating. What to do? He picked up a used forest green colored diving suit, full head mask, and gloves at a recent yard sale in Westport.

He put his sleeping bag and foam pad in the trunk over the gun case. If he had to spend a night in the woods, he wanted to be comfortable.

9

Childhood Death

An hour after leaving WINCO's parking lot, Dan was cruising Interstate Five north, in Washington about thirty miles north of the Columbia River. For some reason he couldn't quit thinking of his beautiful cousin Windy. Paying minimal attention to the road ahead, his mind drifted back to her summer stay in 1967, when Dan was ten. As he thought of her, he remembered the tragedy.

All of them—Dan, four of his siblings, his mom, several neighbor kids and Windy—were playing baseball in their largest horse pasture, located next to Highway 530 northeast of Monroe, having a grand time. Finally, it was time to quit, so everyone except Dan left the field and went to the house, or to the back yard. As always, he was the one left scrounging for a lost ball in the high grass near the fence line adjoining the highway. He was a stickler for finding lost balls, and never understood why no one else saw the importance of that.

Soon, he heard two older boys talking and laughing as they rode their bikes nonchalantly on an old road running along the opposite side of the highway. He didn't know their plan was to cross the highway near the Thurmonds' front yard.

A minute or two later there was a terrible crash and crunching of metal from that area. Instinctively, he looked toward the sound, just in time to see one of the boys catapulted out of the dirt cloud and land dead on the pavement of the old road. "Larry!" Edwin yelled pathetically, after the boy landed on the pavement. Sadly, Larry had waited before trying to cross the highway, while Edwin had ridden his bike directly into the path of an oncoming car. That car swerved to miss Edwin, went part way into the right ditch only to come back out, cross the centerline, and hit a car going the opposite direction. That car rolled into Larry.

At that moment Dan felt more alone than he had ever felt in his life. He ran to the house. Everyone was running to the front yard to see what had happened. No one else had witnessed the accident, so he alone was left to be haunted by the memory.

Dan kept on driving north, mechanically. Death from his past continued to mull through his mind. Why now?

Now it was June a year after the kid was killed on the bike. Dan's mom and dad were in the middle of their breakup. He was eleven. Two sets of his favorite neighbor kids had moved away in the past month. His world was falling apart.

In late March, about ten weeks before Dan's dad and older brother, Victor, moved out, his dad had bought a dozen week-old mallard ducklings, and put them in a pen in the cottage house. The Thurmond kids loved the ducklings, played with them every day and watched them grow.

Two weeks before Dan's dad moved out he said the ducklings were too big to remain in the cottage; so the kids turned them loose outside.

At that time the Thurmonds owned a black Labrador retriever named "Boots," and a Norwegian Elk Hound that they called "Prince." On this particular afternoon, another black Lab was also hanging around. Anticipating the worst, Dan and his younger brother Randy, along with their new friend, Mike, stood ready with their BB guns to shoot the dogs if they made any move toward the ducklings. Immediately the dogs went for the clueless ducks. The boys held them at bay for at least an hour by stinging them with a BB every time they approached the ducks. It didn't take too many hits before the dogs got the message.

Then it was time for everyone to go to bed. The ducklings (two-thirds grown) huddled in together next to the step that led to the back porch. The boys felt they had gotten the point across to the dogs. Not a chance! The dogs' instincts kicked in some time during that night after sleep had overtaken the Thurmonds.

Dan was the first one up in the morning; what he saw through the windows devastated him. The ducks were massacred all over the place. One hung from a limb several feet up the Holly tree outside the kitchen window. Dan cried out and, immediately, his mom and brothers and sisters were there. They all cried as they looked out at their dead ducklings. Suddenly, Dan noticed that one duck in the front yard was flopping around trying to get to its feet. He raced outside, wearing only his underwear, and rescued the survivor. On careful examination, one other duck was saved. The Thurmonds nursed both ducks back to health over the next week, only to have them die about six weeks later.

Dan's mind persisted in playing that summer's tape—a tape that had been comfortably in storage for many years.

About a month after the duck massacre, the Thurmond kids were playing in the front yard next to that deadly highway that had claimed the older boy a year earlier. They watched helplessly as their dog, Prince, ran out into the highway on his way to the neighbor's bitch that was in heat on the other side. He didn't have a prayer. The big truck hit him as if he were a decoy that no one cared for or would miss. When the truck had passed, there was Prince lying motionless on the opposite shoulder. The Thurmond kids all cried, while looking desperately for any signs of life. There was only silence and a slight breeze. It never would have happened except for the neighbor's bitch!

In less than a minute, the merciless highway came back to life paying no attention to what had just transpired. One car after another sped past in either direction. Some of their drivers surely saw the dead dog. But it's doubtful they made any connection between it and several kids crying while holding on to the fence on the other side of the highway.

The dog was just one more casualty to go the way of Dan's mom and dads' marriage. One more pet they had lost on that same stretch of road. Dogs, cats, they even had a pony killed there several years earlier. Tough stuff for any kid to experience.

For the rest of that summer and many months after, Dan often dreamed about both the ducks and Prince coming back to life. In his dreams, Prince would suddenly get up and run back across the highway to the kids. Then Dan would awaken, and the sad reality would hit him once again. No more ducks, no more dogs, no more cats, no more pony. And worst of all (now that his parents had split up and his mom had moved her half of the family to Texas), no more sisters, no more youngest brothers, and no more mom. Kids shouldn't have to deal with so much pain.

10

At the Waldens'

Flashing lights up ahead brought Dan back to the present, as he approached a Washington State Patrol car that had a green, late-model Pontiac pulled over. The flashing lights caused anxiety to stir inside Dan. He was beginning to wonder if he could really get away with the planned killings. He sucked in some air and told himself that he was just worked up because of the flashbacks to the deaths of his child hood. He'd be alright.

Dan finally reached exit 63 at highway 505 which would take him west to the Jackson Highway, which he would then take north to his destination point half a mile south of the Lewis and Clark State Park. The Waldens' place was over a mile east of there. The sky, that was dark and threatening to rain over Portland when he left there seventy minutes earlier, was clear here. His luck was running favorably. He knew the Waldens' nightly routine was to sit out on their back deck, reading and relaxing, until well after dark during these warm summer nights. If things didn't work out for him the first night, he could stay another. Any more than that and his chances of getting caught escalated. He didn't even relish the idea of staying in the area for a second night.

At the last rest stop Dan had pulled on his wig of shoulder-length brown hair, and his thick brown beard. He had dyed his eye brows and mustache the same color brown, with a washout dye, before leaving Portland. He didn't want anyone to be able to remember his real physical appearance should they see him. If by some chance he passed the Walden's on the highway now, they would never recognize him. He would remove the wig and beard before putting on the dive suit later.

Once he reached his spot south of the State Park land on the Jackson Highway, Dan parked his vehicle back in on an old logging road in the second growth fir forest a mile west of the Walden's. He had passed a number of cars going the opposite direction on Jackson Highway.

At five o' clock Dan put on his backpack, strapped on his holstered pistol, grabbed his shotgun and headed up the old, moss-covered logging skid-road that would take him to within 250 yards of the Walden's forest. He had twenty rounds of three inch 00 buckshot shotgun shells and a box of fifty hollow-point rounds for his .357 magnum revolver; twelve hollow point rounds were already accounted for, six in the gun's cylinder, and six in the cylinder quick-loader. He wore rubber gloves when he handled the ammu-nition to avoid leaving any fingerprints. In the worst case scenario, he would get into a shoot out with the police.

He took his time walking the skid road so as not to work up a sweat. When he got to the end of the grown-over road, he got into some thick brush and took off his clothes, along with the wig and beard, and then put on the diving suit. He had kept the suit in a sealed bag with Douglas-fir and incense-cedar fragrance for a week with the intention of covering his scent.

At 6 pm he moved through the Walden's timber—no way he would get away with that if their shepherd was still alive. When he got to the back of their house and could see the deck, he moved in closer, quietly positioning himself behind some thick salal bushes that were about five feet tall. Sword fern lined the edge of the driveway just outside the salal. He was shaded well by the great canopy of fir trees overhead. He took his pack off and sat down to wait silently for the Walden's to come out for their nightly routine. He laid the shotgun down beside him and took a drink from his quart canteen.

By 6:45 he grew concerned that maybe they wouldn't come out tonight. He had learned by way of the grapevine that Mike had recently been undergoing some tests for possible lung cancer. He smoked all of his adult life. Maybe he was in too bad a condition to come out. Dan thought that better not be the case or it would have been a wasted trip.

Just then Mike came out onto the deck through the sliding glass door. He was carrying a plate with what looked like some thick steaks. He set them down on the table to his left and proceeded to light up his gas barbeque. He looked healthy to Dan.

In a couple of minutes, he placed the steaks on the grill, closed the lid, and then sat down to read a book. Dan couldn't tell what Mike was reading, but Dan knew he liked murder mysteries. Smoke drifted out of the cooker within a few minutes as that juicy fat was doing its job. Dan could hear the sizzling even from where he was.

There was nothing Dan loved more than a fat-laden, juicy, barbequed beef steak. The wind, which was out of the north, carried that wonderful odor, in its mysterious way, right to his nose—a sort of punishment for what he was about to do. He hadn't eaten barbequed steak in several weeks. He lived a lonely life now that his mother-in-law had stolen his wife from him. Part of him wanted to walk out of the woods, take off the diving suit, and come up the Walden's driveway to join in for the steaks.

He longed for the way things were the first year of his and Brenda's marriage. Then he was still liked and accepted by pretty much the whole family, though negative rumors about him had already made the rounds, most of them started by Maureen.

Dan knew Mike still liked him after these seven years, and believed that he had been wronged, because they had conversed at the annual Gregory family reunion the summer before last. Mike's wife, Jan, on the other hand, had no use for Dan. In one of her harassing phone calls four years earlier, Dan asked her what he had ever done to her. She said, "It's what you have done to my mom."

Dan had answered, "Your mom is the biggest hypocrite on the face of the earth." Jan hadn't spoken to him since. Up until Brenda left Dan, Jan hadn't spoken to her either during that time. Amazing considering they had always been close.

Dan wished he had videos of all the interactions he had with Maureen and Conner to show the family. No court or jury in the country would side with those two. But that is the kind of pull Maureen had with certain members of her family. No one held her accountable. "That's just the way Grandma (or Mom) is, accept it." None of those who said that ever had to be her son-in-law and step-father to the grand daughter that was so much like her.

The sun had disappeared behind the trees and the west side of the house nearly two hours earlier, but it was still light and the air was warm. Mike turned over the steaks which were on the top rack, and brushed sauce on them. Dan could almost taste them. Mike called for Jan and said the steaks would be ready in about five minutes.

Three minutes later, Jan came out carrying a tray which contained a bowl of salad, some French bread, a couple of glasses filled with milk, some plates and utensils. Dan could see the salt and pepper were already on the table. Knowing Jan, she had her cell phone with her too. She wasn't one to miss any gossip. The cell phone was his biggest concern, because in a flash 911 could be punched in and his goose would be cooked. He had to be certain she wasn't holding the phone when he started shooting.

He grabbed the shotgun and slowly stood up. He had removed the plug right after he got it. With the plug in, which was required for hunting, the scatter gun would hold only three rounds, with one of those in the chamber. Now it held seven rounds. He eased the safety off knowing the time had come. Mike picked the steaks off the grill and set them on the table. Mike and Jan now both stood at the table facing him, offering Dan a front-on shot at their torsos. Mike was not a praying man. But Jan, no longer a church-go-er, though still a spiritual hypocrite following in her mom's shoes, started to say grace. It wouldn't get any better than this.

Dan aimed at Mike's chest. Because of his police training, Dan had to get him first, and quickly follow up with Jan before she could get to her phone which Dan could see laying on her chair's armrest five feet away. There was a chance that a couple of the balls from the first shot would hit her in the torso, too, at that range. He would jump out of the brush after his first two shots, careful not to eject the second spent shell until he was clear of the brush, and run up to make sure they were dead. Then he would take Mike's wallet, dump Jan's purse and get her wallet, go inside and run upstairs to their bedroom which was where he knew he would find her jewelry— there and in her bathroom. He would leave the empty jewelry containers sprawled on the floor. He would quickly pull out other drawers and empty their contents. He had to make this look like a quick cash/jewelry robbery.

After leaving the house, he would grab his stuff and the single spent casing from the brush, pick up the other spent casings nearer the house, then throw down an equal number of wiped down empty casings in the driveway and closer to the bodies. He wanted to make the shots look like they came from the corner of the house and up closer. Of course a ballistics expert would probably figure out that distance was too close for the shot pattern of the buckshot in the bodies. To muddle the shot-grouping pattern, he would take several shots at the corpses from up closer. He knew he could easily do that to Jan, but didn't know about Mike; he had to though to confuse the evidence. After gathering up his stuff from the brush and scattering the empties, he would hustle back through the woods to the old skid road he had hiked in on, get to his rig and head home.

He wasn't worried at all about any distant neighbors, or someone driving by, hearing the gunshots. The timber in that entire county was popular for target shooting and its many hunting opportunities. People there took the sound of gunfire in stride year-round.

With his bead in the middle of Mike's chest, Dan put some tension on the trigger, but his finger wouldn't complete the squeeze. I have to do it. I can't do Jan without doing him too. Mike never did anything to me. He doesn't deserve this. I'm not a killer. Dad, don't do it! I need you. My baby girl. John needs you. I have to make Jan and Brenda and Maureen pay. It's not Mike's fault.

"Amen," Jan said, and they both began filling their plates.

He took another breath and held it. Now! I've got to do it now. I love you Dad. Don't do it. But the pain they have caused me. I haven't deserved it. What did Mike ever do to me? *I can't.* **I'm not a killer**.

He couldn't do it; at least not tonight. I'll come back tomorrow night. I'll do it then. No harm in waiting. She can't get away with what she has done to me.

Dan got back to his rental car at dark, pulled out his pad and sleeping bag and got comfortable for the night. His vehicle was hidden back off the skid road in a densely brushed area with thick, tall salal bushes surrounding it. After he had arrived there earlier in the day, he had closed off the opening with some small dead trees and brush. He knew he would be fine there. Just in case, he hid his firearms and ammo in a hollow fir log fifty yards back in the brush. Even if a law enforcement officer, by some fluke, came back there and found him, it wouldn't matter. He was just camping. No laws against that.

Sleep did not come easy. On one hand he felt relieved that he hadn't killed anyone. On the other, he wrestled with having to do it the next night.

He thought of Megan and John. When they were very young, he

used to take them cat fishing. One night when Megan was four, she tripped in the dark and fell face first into the hot lantern, scalding the skin on her chin. Dan immediately grabbed the worm and fish slime towel and soaked it in the cool lake water and placed it on her face. The coolness helped ease the pain, but she still cried. He held her and comforted her. John snuggled in close to them. Dan wanted to keep fishing, but soon he knew they needed to get home to clean up the wound, put medicine on it, and give Megan something to ease the pain. He reeled in the two fishing lines, removed the worms, and secured the hooks to a guide.

It was a quarter mile hike uphill through the woods to the pickup. Dan strapped on his fanny pack and put John on that with his arms around Dan's sides. He picked Megan up in his right arm and the fishing poles, lantern and the bucket with his left hand. He carried both kids and the gear out of the woods. How tired he had been by the time he reached the truck. As he thought about that night, he grew more and more groggy. Sleep finally overtook him.

11

Second Evening

The next day, Friday, Dan lay on his sleeping bag, reading John Grisham's "A Time to Kill," while he snacked on crackers and summer sausage. Of all Grisham's novels, he found his first to be the best. He also read the Friday edition of the Portland "Oregonian."

Everything was right for Dan the second day. The weather was perfect, about seventy-five degrees. He knew this time he had to go through with it.

As evening drew near, he thought, killing indirectly by poisoning someone, where you don't have to see them die, would be much easier on the conscience than actually taking that step where you see the person alive one minute, and the next he is lying life-less, at your hands. Then there's the blood and the gore, the visual image that would be stamped in your mind forever. How does one live with that?

No matter, he can do it.

Again Dan hiked up the skid road with the same equipment as

last night. When he got near the house he spotted a big, black Ford diesel-pickup parked in the driveway. It can't be! Maureen is there. That bitch always has a way of showing up at just the wrong time. What now?

He set up in the bushes, same as last night. He could hear Maureen talking inside, so the glass doors had to be open. He loathed that voice. In a moment, out she came with Jan right on her heals. They sat down in a couple of wooden deck chairs and began gossiping in earnest. After about three minutes, he heard his name mentioned.

"Brenda finally got away from that psychopath Dan for good," said Maureen.

"I thought he was a loser clear back in high school," said Jan. "I never did understand what Brenda saw in him."

"I can't believe I encouraged her to marry him, and that I sang at their wedding," said Maureen.

You hypocrite, Dan thought. You sang at that wedding for one reason and one reason only: to be at the front and center of attention. Brenda told me that herself. We already had our whole wedding planned, already had two solos. But you forced your way in—no way would you miss that chance. Then the song you sang had that line in it, "Your family will be there to support you, no matter what the cost." You bitch. You should have sung, "Your mother in law will be there to destroy you at every chance she gets."

"How long is she going to live at your place Mom?"

"She can live there as long as she wants. I love having Jackie there. She needs my positive input, especially after living with the devil himself."

One time Brenda had told Dan she had lived with her mom for short periods of time in the past, and it never worked out because Maureen had always tried to run her life.

"You seem so much happier now, Mom."

"My heart has been broken since Brenda and Jackie moved down to Aberdeen. He wanted to get them off to himself and keep me from being able to see Jackie."

You don't have a clue do you? Dan thought. Two years into our marriage, Brenda begged me to move our whole family away from Everett in order to get away from you. You have no idea how much she hated your control. Yet, she could never cut the psychological umbilical cord to you. Sadly, part of her desperately needs your abuse. Even after we moved, she kept the door open for your further mistreatment of her, Jackie and our family.

"He's a very controlling guy," said Jan. "He came between our whole family and Brenda and Jackie. It was pretty bad that he, Brenda and the kids didn't come to any family gatherings for those last five years."

I'm controlling? Take a look at yourself and your mom. And neither of you take an ounce of responsibility for our family not being at your family get-togethers, do you? After the verbal assaults on me by you guys and Conner, and never any thought of needing to apologize, there is no way I was coming to any of your get-togethers. Only a fool would. Brenda was hurt deeply by your excluding her from family times, and the fact that her husband was ostracized, and criticized mercilessly. What kind of people are you? Not a single member of my family ever interfered in my marriage or criticized Brenda.

"Well that's all behind us now," said Maureen. "We have Brenda and Jackie back home where they belong. It's just too bad that John and Megan have a father like that and they won't be a part of our family anymore," said Maureen.

"Yeah, I loved those kids," said Jan, as she stood up. "I better go get the hamburgers ready for cooking."

Mike came out and fired up the grill.

Here goes again, Dan thought. What do I do? I could kill all three of them tonight and be rid of two of my biggest enemies. But if I kill Maureen, I will be the prime murder suspect. I've said way too many angry things about her. Darn it. I can't do it. I feel like the sniper in one of the World War II movies who has Hitler in his sights but can't take the shot. If a sniper had been able to take out Hitler early on, hundreds of thousands, even millions of lives would have been spared. If I could just take out Maureen now… But I can't. I would go to prison or get the death penalty. No point in sticking around any longer. I'll just get pushed closer to my limit and end up killing anyway.

Just then he heard a car coming up the Walden's driveway. Oh no: a Lewis County Sheriff's squad car. He ducked as low as he could in the brush and quickly pulled his stuff together. What are they doing here? Have they found my rental car? I'm about to be in serious trouble.

The car stopped directly between Dan and the Waldens' deck. The deputy looked in his direction. Dan knew he couldn't possibly see him in the shade of the thick brush and overhead canopy, not at this hour, surely. He wanted to slink deeper into the trees and run away, but he didn't dare move. The deputy couldn't know that he was hiding right there, could he?

The driver's door opened and a big, young deputy got out and quickly looked around at the woods surrounding the large back lawn. Dan could see the barrel of his riot gun, standing vertical, strapped in its holder between the front seats.

At once, Mike said, "What's up, Bruiser?"

"We got a call twenty minutes ago that a guy was popping off shots at some deer on up the way here on Highway 12. We have a good ID on the suspect vehicle. It's a candy-apple red, mid-eighties vintage Camaro. It was seen heading south, but we don't know if it came down Tucker or not. I tried to reach you on your cell phone, but could only leave a message. I figured since I was coming by, I would swing in here for a minute to let you know."

"Thanks, Bruiser," said Mike, as he walked up to the squad car. "I have my phone off right now. Sorry about that. Is there anything I can do?"

"No. It smells like you're getting ready to have a barbeque. You're off-duty, and besides the vehicle is way out of your jurisdiction. I only called ahead thinking maybe you could have hustled out to Tucker to head him off if he came that way. Don't worry about it; we county boys will get him." Mike chuckled at the young deputy's pride and confidence. He obviously really liked the guy.

"My mother-in-law is here for a couple of days," Mike said. Then lowering his voice to a level Dan could barely hear, he added, "I've got to be on my best behavior. I'm getting my ears full, as usual. But as long as I keep my mouth shut, I may get out of this visit without a scuffle."

"Ha! Been there, done that," said Bruiser. "My mother-in-law is hell on wheels. When she comes around I make sure to put my flak jacket on." They both burst into laughter.

"What's going on over there?" Maureen demanded, scowling.

"Just a good joke," Mike assured her.

Speaking louder again, Bruiser said, "I better get on my way. If you see a candy-apple Camaro, give us a holler."

"Can you believe that," said Mike, "someone would be stupid enough to use a candy-apple-colored car for his escape?"

"No one ever said being a criminal took any brains," said Bruiser, as he got in the cruiser. They laughed some more.

Just then a report came over Bruiser's radio that the suspect's speeding vehicle had been pulled over by a Washington State Trooper on Interstate 5, near milepost 48.

"Well," said Mike, chuckling, "I guess you county boys aren't as good as the state troopers, are you?"

"You got me on that one, at least this time. But we'll get the next one. I gotta run."

"Catch you later, Bruiser."

"I'm looking forward to it," said the big deputy through his open window, as he backed his car around, and then headed down the driveway.

With his heart restarted, Dan headed through the brush and trees back toward the rental car. He knew after Mike told them of the poacher, Maureen and Jan would have something else to talk about now. At least they wouldn't be burning his ears.

As he approached his rental car, Dan circled to see if anyone had come up the old road. No problem. No one had been there. He stripped the dive suit, threw it, his pack and weapons in the trunk, put his clothes on, and hit the road. He knew he couldn't return the vehicle until morning, so he slept in the woods east of Kalama.

The next morning he returned the car and was back to Aberdeen by mid afternoon. Megan was glad to see him. She mentioned that his cousin Windy had called to see if he was going to the get-together. Knowing she would be there for sure set his mind to wondering.

The following morning, Sunday, he left early to get to his mush-room picking area. Since he wasn't working anywhere, he had to make as much picking mushrooms as he could. Megan would stay at her best friend's house.

12

Windy has Stormy Eyes

Dan thought about his beautiful cousin Windy off and on while he hunted mushrooms. Unfortunately, he also ruminated over the wrongs done him by his wife and in-laws. Walking miles a day was great exercise and good for his mind when he steered it to good thoughts. He wondered if Windy might be single now. She and her husband were separated last year when he saw her. He and Brenda were still together then, though both were quite miserable.

The following Friday afternoon, Dan picked Megan up early from school and they headed down to his cousin Sam's place in Veneta, Oregon, a small community fifteen miles west of Eugene. This would be the first mini-reunion that his son, John, missed.

When they pulled into Sam's driveway, Windy came rushing out of the house.

"Dan, Megan, I'm so glad to see you. Where's John?" asked Windy. "Kristin has been looking forward to seeing him."

"He's in Arkansas working with a friend. He may be back for the

Christmas season. He's kind of playing it by ear," said Dan.

"She's going to be disappointed. She, Amy and Sam's kids went out to Fern Ridge for a couple hours. They should be back pretty soon. I'm so sorry, Dan, about all that has happened with you since last year. I'm sorry that Brenda left you. I didn't think she was capable of the legal stuff she has pulled." Someone in the family had obviously filled her in.

"I didn't think so either. So, how are you doing, Windy?"

She hugged Dan tightly, then stepped back while keeping a grip on his triceps. He gazed into her gorgeous blue eyes. He could always get lost in those eyes, mesmerized as if a storm had swallowed him.

"Steve and I are through. The divorce will be final next month. The kids are broken hearted over it, but even they know it's been coming for some time. Steve's drinking controls his life now and has for over three years. He's not the man I married, or the one you knew. I don't know what made him change so much. I just couldn't take all the uncertainty anymore. I worried constantly about him getting in an accident all those nights he drove drunk. He became very verbally abusive to me when he was drunk. He said I drove him to drink and to the other women because I bitched at him all the time. I didn't think I bitched at him at all. I just cared about him, and wanted him to give up the drinking and be interested in me and the girls again."

"I really doubt that you did bitch at him, Windy, unless you were a completely different person at home than the one I have always known and loved. I'm very sorry for you and the kids."

"Oh, you've always been so sweet to me, Dan. Brenda and her family didn't know what a gift she had been given when you came into her life. And you've always done so well with your kids. I never could understand how they could find so much fault with your parenting of Jackie. I saw you try to show her a lot of love. From what I could see, she was quite disrespectful to you, and Brenda rarely dealt with that. If Jackie was that way around other people, I can imagine what it was like around home."

She hooked her arm through his and said, "You guys come on in," as she led him to the door. He could feel those old vibes awakening within him. Things were looking up.

Dan and Megan had a wonderful three-day weekend with their extended Thurmond family. They all went to the lake one day, played volleyball and horseshoes, and ate a lot of good barbequed food and all the fixings. Dan and Windy hit it off like they hadn't had a chance to since he went into the Navy. They talked a lot about the good old times they'd had. As Windy was leaving, she and Dan vowed to keep in touch. He didn't know what that meant, but he knew she would be often on his mind, if nothing else.

13

Harriet Allison

After Dan and Brenda moved to Aberdeen in 2001 and started attending the interdenominational Church Of The Uncompassionate on Spring Drive, Brenda had become good friends with Harriet Allison, a woman about her age who was head of the women's marriage-wrecking ministries. Harriet and her husband, Dave, had been members in the church for many years.

Harriet served as a kind of mentor to Brenda on spiritual matters and issues within her home and marriage. Dan knew that because Brenda occasionally told him about some advice Harriet had given her on how to handle a specific situation in her marriage or as a parent. There were times when Harriet had also reportedly told Brenda that Dan was wrong about how he handled some situation.

At first Dan thought Harriet's influence on Brenda was probably helpful. But as time wore on, he began to see her as his wife's bitching board, and he didn't like their dirty laundry being aired to Harriet. One man in the church told Dan that Harriet was a busy body. Apparently she had gossiped to the man's wife about other people in the church and in the community. Dan suspected she included his and Brendas' marriage and family problems as part of her fare.

Harriet had made it clear through things she said to Dan—and about him to a couple of other people who confided it to him, that she didn't like him one bit. Yet, she continued to be the one person involved in working with Brenda during the separation. In his few efforts to speak to Harriet, before and after the restraining order had been placed on him, she made it clear she didn't want to talk to him. If this was the attitude of the person who was the only one-to-one spiritual influence on his wife after she moved into her own apartment in late-March, what chance did they have for reconciliation?

A few things Harriet had said to, or about, him were:

"You never listened to her." "Dan is not a good guy." "I've never been able to talk to him."

Dan thought it was interesting that a person who never wanted to listen to anything he had to say concerning his home, marriage and family, could possibly know who never listened to whom. Was she in their house twenty-four seven? And for her to tell others that she has never been able to talk to him. She never even tried. Besides that, after listening to Brenda bitch about him for over three years, how could she even begin to view him objectively and fairly? He's not a good guy? What right did she have, not even knowing him, other than through his wife's bitching about him, to say that he was not a good guy? Another spiritual hypocrite—Dan's life was full of them.

Because of Harriet's involvement with Brenda during the separation, particularly since the restraining order was placed on him, Dan developed a lot of anger toward her. Now that Brenda had moved back to Monroe, and the marriage was obviously over, he had mulled over many different ways of making both Harriet and Pastor Bill pay for their contribution to the failed reconciliation. He wanted to kill both of them. Getting away with it was the hang-up.

While there was still a chance for reconciliation, Dan had to kiss Harriet and the pastors' butts because of their connections to Brenda; he didn't want to make them anymore his enemies than they already were. But he didn't have to kiss their butts now. He couldn't wait to be the one in control of their lives, when they would *beg him for mercy*. How do you think I have felt all these months while one of you talked ill of me and influenced my wife negatively toward me, while the other arrogant, uncompassionate bastard sat on his unspiritual, hypocritical butt and did nothing?

If either Harriet or the pastor came up missing, Dan would undoubtedly eventually come up as a possible suspect in their disappearance. But if no body was found, they couldn't prove there was a homicide. He might even be arrested, but they would have no solid evidence on which to hold him. They couldn't make him take a lie-detector test. And according to the law, he was innocent until proven guilty. There were many missing persons cases in which prime suspects could not be prosecuted because the body was not found and the only other evidence was circumstantial and speculative. Murder cases must be proven beyond a reasonable doubt, and the jury *must be unanimous* in finding the defendant guilty.

Dan had thought through several different plans. He would wait several months from the time he took Harriet to when he dealt with the pastor. He was sure Pastor Bill would have strong suspicions about his involvement in Harriet's abduction, because Dan had expressed some strong feelings of anger about her to him. If Harriet's disappearance had the effect that Dan hoped it did on Pastor Bill, he would realize that he was at the top of Dan's list, too. Maybe he would even find some humility out of his fear for his own life. That was doubtful. Someone that arrogant could only find humility staring down the barrel of a shotgun or .357 Magnum.

Dan hated that man so much. He always acted like he had everything together, and he had a condescending spirit about him that gave anyone who had to meet with him the feeling that he considered himself smarter, better, or more spiritual than they were. Dan had seen and heard about some of the pastor's little meetings where he instituted some form of church discipline. Now Dan *must discipline him.*

Dan felt the best plan was to catch Harriet at her car, in the dark, on a Wednesday night after church. She was one of the leaders in the kids' program. She and her husband always drove separate vehicles because of her need to be there earlier, and he left to go home before she did. Dan had noted that she was often the last person to leave the parking lot. There were no houses in sight of the Church Of The Uncompassionate, which was on the outskirts of Aberdeen, on the way out toward the Olympic National Forest. Coastal pine trees surrounded the church, making it nicely secluded—a beautiful setting for a church. The close proximity of the trees and salal brush made a great place to hide close to the parking lot.

A week before he kidnapped Harriet, Dan would drive his brown, 1970, half-ton Chevy pickup up into the Olympic National Forest to within a mile of where he would ultimately dispose of her vehicle. After ditching his truck back in some heavy brush, he would ride his mountain bike out of the area to Coast Highway 101 and then back to Aberdeen from there. He had ridden his bike all over that area. Bikers were very common, so no one would ever make a connection between him and a vehicle found at the bottom of a mountain canyon weeks or months later.

The pickup was Dan's second vehicle, and he rarely drove it, other than for bringing in firewood. Megan knew that he sometimes left it parked for days back in the woods behind their place when he was in the middle of a load. If she asked about it, which was doubtful, he would tell her it was parked there.

He would have his SUV hidden in the back woods, on the Wednesday—or Wednesdays—if for some reason he couldn't successfully snatch Harriet the first week, so no one would see it and then figure out that he was not picking mushrooms. He lived a mile and a half from the church, so he would walk there the evening he made the snatch.

When he captured Harriet, he would be wearing the dive suit and mask again and be armed with his .357 magnum pistol. This time the suit would be to keep any of his DNA from being left behind in her vehicle. He would hide at the opposite side of her car from the church. When she came out to get into her car, he would step around and grab her mouth, while sticking the gun barrel in her neck. He had played the scene over in his mind a dozen times.

"Keep your mouth shut or I'll shoot you." He presses the pistol barrel hard against her neck. "Give me your purse."

She hands him the purse, and he tosses it in the back seat. Her cell phone flops out. That's what he wanted to see.

She thinks maybe this is just a robbery, but something about his voice sounds familiar. She can't place it.

"Get in the car, bitch."

She has never heard his angry voice, so she doesn't recognize it as his. She gets in behind the steering wheel, as he gets in the back seat directly behind her.

"How does it feel to not be in control? Start the car, and take us north on Highway 101. You and I have a lot to talk about."

"Dan?"

"Hey, you're not so dumb after all."

"What are you doing?"

"Isn't that obvious? Uh, I have a gun aimed at the back of your head and if you don't do exactly as I say, I have every intention of spreading your brains and skull all over the inside of the windshield and on the hood of your nicely polished car. How does that sound bitch?"

"Why are you doing this?"

"Where have you been? You've been against me since the first time Brenda ran to you with our problems. You're as arrogant and uncompassionate as Pastor Bill. The both of you think that you are more spiritual than the rest of us. You should have had babies together. *They would have been angels.*"

"What do you want from me?"

"If you do what I say, I might spare your life." He lies. "If you so much as blink your head lights, or do anything to alert another driver that you need help, your obituary will be posted in the Aberdeen News in the next few days. When we go through Humptulips, I'll be crouched low behind you, but—so help me—I will kill you in a heartbeat if you do anything stupid. Your only chance is to co-operate with me."

"Are you planning to rape me?"

"Give me a break. I'm not a rapist. All I ever wanted was to be a good husband and a good father, and to be loved by my wife and kids. Was that asking too much? But then Brenda's mother caused hell in our marriage and home right from the start. Finally we moved down here to Aberdeen and started going to your church. When we went to the pastor for help with our marriage, he said he wasn't qualified to help us—so things continued to get worse. You didn't help the situation one bit, so don't try to tell me otherwise. Then after Brenda left me, you showed no compassion to me, you blamed me, and you took her side completely. You formed your nasty opinions of me based solely on Brenda's griping sessions. Did you ever bother to consider that I'm not as bad a guy as she makes me out to be? At least I wasn't until she got the restraining order. That pushed me over the edge. Or did you ever try to see the problems that her family was causing in our home and marriage? No.

"You specifically told me after Brenda left me that the Bible says to 'Honor your mother and father.' Since both of my parents are dead, I knew you meant that we had not been honoring Brenda's parents, at least not the way you, *the eternally wise woman*, thought we should. I know you encouraged her to keep a relationship going with her parents and other family members, *at all cost.* It didn't even matter to you that her mother stole from her own grand-daughter twice. The one time she stole over $500 from her, money that was donated by church members and community members for her trip to Washington DC.

"People like that are sick. You are so naïve. They were destroying our marriage and undermining me as Jackie's father in every way they could think of. But you told Brenda she needed a relationship with them. Now you're going to pay for that and all the other ways you helped end our marriage."

"Please Dan, I never meant to harm you or your marriage. My husband and I have prayed every day for God to reconcile your marriage."

"Then why is it that my wife grew further and further away from me during all those months when you were involved mentoring her? I know that you encouraged, or agreed with, her getting the restraining order on me. How do you think it feels to have your own wife use the law to keep you from talking to her, or seeing her? Not once in our marriage did I ever harm her physically or ever threaten to harm her. I bet she didn't tell you about her hitting me or throwing glass cups at me. I'm sure you never considered how difficult it must have been for me to endure the constant criticism of her family.

"The pastor and brother George came to my house to get me to consider reconciliation, which I didn't want any part of. Then when I finally came around, not one of you, other than George, worked toward that end. It's bull crap. I've died inside every day for months. Many days I've considered killing myself. But I couldn't do that to the kids. Besides, that would please Brenda, because she would get the house. You probably would have been pleased with that. Then the two of you could sit at our dining table, with your coffee, talking about how all of this was caused by Dan's mental illness. You self-righteous, little bitch."

"You have it all wrong Dan. Yes, I did tell her that she needed to honor her mother and father and maintain her relationships with her family. But I wasn't against you."

"That's really funny Harriet. I tried to talk to you several times, and you said that you were Brenda's friend and weren't going to talk to me about our problems. The last time I tried to talk to you, you told me that your husband told you not to talk to me anymore. Now there's a piece of work. Next to you and the pastor, Dave is another, uncompassionate, arrogant idiot. I hate him too, but I figure that I can hurt him most by what I'm going to do to you."

"What are you going to do to me, Dan? Please, I sensed a long time ago that there was good in you."

"That's hilarious. The good just wasn't good enough, right? You're just trying to save yourself. I don't blame you. I would be too. Now just shut up and drive."

Four miles past Humptulips he said, "Take this road to the right."

"Why are you going there?"

"I told you to shut up, and I meant it! I'm the one in control now. You and Brenda have been in control of me and my pain for all this time. It's my turn."

Through the rearview mirror, Dan can see her lips moving. He's sure she's praying for God's protection and mercy. He doubts she's praying for God's forgiveness. People like her don't think they ever sin. She should ask Him if this is His wrath for all the ways she helped end his and Brenda's marriage.

Soon they hit gravel, and at each intersection where the road branches off he tells Harriet which way to go. They climb into the thick Douglas firs of the southern end of the Olympic National Forest. He loves these woods.

In the four years he has lived in Aberdeen, Dan has become well acquainted with these roads, both with his vehicle and his mountain bike. He's killed a couple deer and numerous upland birds in this forest. *Harriet will be his first human.*

Twenty minutes after leaving the pavement, he notices she is trembling badly. They haven't passed or come upon a single vehicle since leaving the Coast Highway. He thinks she has fully grasped the helplessness of her situation.

"Is something wrong, Harriet?" he asks.

"Dan, I know how bad you are hurting, but you can't handle it like this."

"I can handle it anyway I want to, damn it! And you're the last person who is going to tell me how to handle anything. I hate your guts for the pain you have caused me. Did you think that this guy who deserved to have a restraining order on him could just stand back and take the pain day after day? What is it with you bitches? You think you can stop violence from happening with a stupid little piece of paper?

"To set your mind at ease, I'll tell you how I'm actually going to handle it, Harriet. I'm going to walk you back in to a certain area in the woods and tie you up with duct tape and rope so there is no way you can escape. I will leave you some water in a couple containers hanging from the tree you will be tied to. You'll have just enough of a hole in the duct tape over your mouth to get a drink from the containers. I'll hike out and then make a phone call to Dave, asking for ransom money to be dropped at a specific place. I'm paying someone five thousand dollars to make the pickup there, and then deliver the money to another place for me. I will give the authorities the coordinates to your position only after I am safely out of this country. I plan to start a new life. You see, I'm not a killer. What I want to do to you, isn't kill you. What I want to do is torture you. Whether I do or not, partially depends on you."

Harriet feels some relief learning that he doesn't intend to kill her, and that if she cooperates, he may not even hurt her. She thinks maybe God is working in the situation, and says, "Dan, could I pray with you?"

"Absolutely not! I don't pray with pseudo-spiritual, arrogant, hypocrites. Unless you want to be tortured, you damn well better shut up. Get it?"

"Yes." It feels great to be in complete control of her, to cause her such emotional distress.

She drives for another ten minutes, and then he orders her to turn left onto a logging road that takes them into a remote canyon. They finally arrive at the end of the brush-choked road. He makes her get out of the vehicle and walk ahead of him, in his flashlight beam, on the overgrown, moss-covered spur road.

A hundred yards up the road, he makes her lay face-down on the dew-dampened ground. Then he grabs his stashed backpack from the brush nearby. He's sweating. He takes off the mask and puts it and his pistol into the pack beside the rope, tape and other miscellaneous supplies. He tells Harriet to get up, and they continue walking. They have to go around blackberry patches and scotch broom, and duck under low-hanging limbs. She trips and falls to the ground several times; serves her right. He wonders how righteous she feels now about all the things she said and did to help end his marriage. They walk the old road for half a mile, then reach the place where they dive off into the canyon. She's shivering; her brown suede jacket and blue jeans are soaked from rubbing against the dew-laden brush.

From here their path is marked with orange surveyor-ribbon tied to brush at twenty-to thirty-foot intervals. He will remove the markers on his way back out. He leads the way now. Harriet follows behind, holding part of a sheet that he wraps around his waist. She stumbles and falls into the brush below them a few times. She cries. Maybe she should have treated him fairly. He pulls her back to her feet each time. They hike side hill on the steep hill for three hundred yards and reach a little bench in the thick, young firs.

Immediately ahead of them is the eight foot deep grave he has dug, dirt piled up on its sides, a shovel lies on top of the dirt. He dug it extra deep because this area receives over two hundred inches of rain in the average year, and he doesn't want her body to ever be washed out. Harriet steps up beside him, just as he shines the light on the open grave.

"No! Please, Dan, no! Please, Dan! I'm sorry for everything.

Forgive me."

"You don't need my forgiveness. You need God's. Don't worry Harriet, that hole is only to impress your rescuers when they come for you. I'm not that bad a guy; just ask Brenda. Oh, that's right. You already did."

He doesn't want her fighting him; he can't have any scratch marks or bruises on him. He tapes her arms alongside her body, leaving her forearms free. He then tapes her upper legs tightly together, and finally tapes over her mouth while wrapping the tape around her head three times. He walks her to the edge of the hole to let her see inside. She is shaking badly. Does she really think he would move out of the country and leave his kids behind? Not a chance.

He knows that when he pushes her into the hole, she won't be able to get out. The hole is too deep. Once she's in the bottom, he'll pull out his pistol, point it at her head, and order her to sit down.

He will throw in a couple shovelfuls of dirt at a time. He wants to drag it out. He's leaving her forearms and lower legs free so she can struggle harder. But the end result will be the same. She needs to feel the fear, the helplessness, the anger of knowing "it is over and I can't do a thing about it," just as he has felt it for endless months.

Self-righteous people like Harriet stood by and did nothing to help him. In fact, they stood by and judged him. You deserve the best eight-foot-deep hole in the forest, and by George, you're going to get it.

After he buries her body, he will scatter the excess dirt into the nearby brush, cover the grave with moss-covered soil and then brush-over the top of that. He will then hike out to her car, drive it to the logging road that skirts a deep canyon a half hour from there, and run it over the 150 foot rocky embankment, where it will likely burst into flames upon hitting the rocky bottom. He will then hike the mile through the forest over a ridge to his pickup which is parked on a completely different drainage and forest road system.

It will probably be a long time before anyone discovers the car. When the authorities do find it and they can't locate her body, more questions will be raised. They may speculate that she staged the whole scenario in order to run off with another man. If all goes well, they will never put a serious finger on Dan.

14

FM: Dan's Sick Neighbor

On October 8th Dan called Father Michael on his cell phone and arranged to meet him in his office the next afternoon. The next day, Dan had a nice exchange with Julie in the church office. But after spending a lot of time with Windy at the recent Thurmond family gathering, his flame for Julie was on pilot. No woman would ever be able to light his fire the way Windy did. And now that Windy's marriage was over and she was going to be available, he knew he didn't want to get something started in a different direction. A man couldn't ask for a better woman than her.

"It's great to see you again, Dan," said Father Michael, as he shook Dan's hand and led him into his comfortable office once again.

"Thanks, Father. Good to see you, too."

"How did your family gathering go?"

"It went real well," said Dan. He wasn't going to tell him about Windy yet, and he certainly couldn't say anything about his trip to the Waldens' in Centralia the week before the Thurmond family gathering, or his imminent plans to kill Harriet.

"Was there a good turnout?"

"Not bad. My three brothers and several cousins were there with their families. We had a great time."

"What did you want to talk about today, Dan?" said Father Michael, getting to the point rather quickly, which was fine with Dan. Maybe he knew more about Dan than he realized. When Dan was a kid, he often wondered if priests had a direct line to God, and knew when you weren't telling everything in confessional. That's probably why he could never look a priest in the eyes.

"Something that happened in my childhood has bothered me for years. I've only told a couple of people about it, and never any clergymen. But I wanted to get it off my chest. I suppose I could do it in a confessional, but I'd rather do it right here, with you, right now."

"We don't hold so rigidly to confessionals nowadays Dan. At least I don't. I believe, and I teach, that a person can actually confess his sins directly to God. He doesn't have to go through a priest to confess them. Don't get me wrong, I think it's good to confess one's sins to another believer, particularly a clergyman. The Bible even admonishes us to do so. But the Old Testament require-ment of a person needing a human priest to be a go-between them and God just isn't necessary. The Catholic Church has been locked into that Old Testament teaching since its beginnings. Somehow, the Catholic hierarchy missed the point that Jesus was the final sacrifice and that he is the one true priest, the ultimate go-between sinful man and God."

"Your theology sounds like what I've heard for years in Protest-ant churches, and what I believe through my own study, Father," said Dan. "Are you really a Catholic priest?"

"Oh, I'm definitely a Catholic priest, but you can think of me as an enlightened priest." They both laughed. "Now what is it that you want to get off your chest?" said Father Michael.

"When I was in sixth grade and all the way through eighth grade,

I had some neighbors that were quite dysfunctional," said Dan. "There were four kids, two boys and two girls, who lived with their dad and his parents, their grandparents. In a lot of ways the grandparents were the parents to these kids. My brother Randy, the one a year younger than me, and I became good friends with the boys right away. The oldest brother, Paul, who was in my grade, had some issues. If there was trouble to be found, he found it. Unfortunately, the grandmother died of a ruptured blood vessel in her brain during the summer after Paul's and my sixth grade year. It devastated the kids, as well as the dad and grandpa." He looked at Father Michael's face, but avoided eye contact as he told the story.

"Something inside Paul really went south after he lost his grandma, because he started gathering up stray cats from around the neighborhood and torturing them—nothing real serious at first. And he only maybe did it to one cat every few weeks or so. He'd place a cat in one of the small sheds at the back of their property and throw rocks at the building, beat on the outside of the walls, that sort of thing. The cat would freak out, climb the walls, and try to escape through the windows. I watched this with curiosity at first, and I let him know that I didn't like what he was doing.

"After a few months, he started getting inside the shed with whatever cat he was *working* on, and he would strike at it with a stick. He got some sort of sadistic satisfaction out of being in control of the cat and scaring it, making it panic. I thought about telling my dad, but didn't want to get Paul in trouble. My brother Randy and Paul's little brother saw some of this go on, too. But we all had a boyish curiosity about the whole thing, so none of us told anyone else. His youngest sister caught him at it, but he warned her to stay away and keep her mouth shut or she would deeply regret it. When you see a person acting like that, you take his threats seriously, which she did. She never said a word.

"It was about that time that my brother Victor was killed in Vietnam. I was devastated." Dan looked down at the brown carpet as he continued speaking. "I had had so much pain in my life by that point, that losing Victor seemed to break my conscience. The next time Paul captured a cat and brought it to his shed, I joined in with what he did to it. I can't explain it, but when I made that cat afraid of me and it ran around climbing the walls, it felt good to be in control of something, to have that power. I hadn't been in control of anything in my life for a long time."

He took a chance and looked into Father Michael's eyes, not sure what he was looking for. Father looked back into Dan's and didn't speak right away. Dan knew he wasn't judging him. Dan thought maybe he wasn't quite sure what to say, or perhaps he wasn't sure if Dan had said all he was going to say.

Finally, Father said, "I can appreciate the pain you must have been going through back then Dan. And the pain your friend Paul had too. Losing a loved one and feeling like you're totally out of control of everything in your life is very tough, especially when you're young like that." He paused for several seconds, then said, "Was there any more you wanted to tell me about what you guys did to the cats, or was that it? Did you ever actually hit the cats with sticks? I don't want you to say anymore than you're comfortable telling me. But at the same time, I guess the priest in me would like to see you get the whole thing off your chest now since you took the step of saying anything about it in the first place. Does that make sense?"

"Yes, it makes sense to tell all of it," said Dan. "I wanted to anyway. I wish I could say I only messed with the one cat, but it was several over a few month period. And we did resort to actually striking the cats. I never hit them with the same enthusiasm as Paul. I don't think I ever actually injured one. Paul broke some bones. It was pathetic—the painful cries the cats made, and all.

"Then one day I went back there and looked in the shed window while Paul was in there with a cat. An orange and white, long-haired tabby was hanging from the rafter with a rope around its neck. It was struggling, while Paul's small dog kept jumping up nipping at its feet. I shouted at him, through the window, that he had gone too far. He wouldn't listen to me, so I left. I didn't tell anyone, nor did I sleep much that night.

"The next day I went out to the shed to see if the rope had been taken down yet. The cat was hanging there, dead, with coagulated blood dripped off both back paws that the dog had been nipping at. There were puddles of blood on the floor under the cat, and the cat's mouth had blood all around it; the chin fur was soaked, as well. I got sick to my stomach. I wondered what kind of a maniac I lived next to. I wondered how my best friend could do such a thing. Then I realized that I was just as much to blame. I didn't stop him, and I had even joined in several times. I knew that I could have done something to save the cat's life—that I should have done something. I realized that Paul was a monster. A *sick* monster. *But I was too.* I ran home and vowed never to be involved in anything like that again."

"Did you ever tell anyone what your friend had done?"

"I never told anyone about him killing the cat. I could relate so much to the pain that caused him to do it, and I didn't want anybody to think of him as a psychopath. Nor did I want anyone to know I stood by and let the cat be killed. We both needed all the friends we could get."

"Did you ever ask God to forgive you for doing those things?"

"Yes, I did, Father, a long time ago. In fact, I've asked his forgiveness for it many times. Every time it comes to my mind, I ask him to forgive me."

"So you have to accept His forgiveness by faith as the Bible says, and not let it keep eating at you. You were a badly hurting kid back then. You are a different person today, right?"

"Mostly, I guess I'm different," said Dan. I've graduated from killing cats to killing humans. He has no idea.

"What happened to your friend Paul after that?"

"I never saw him torture another animal. I guessed that the reality of the depth to which he had stooped with that last cat had shocked him. We never talked about the cats again after that."

"In high school, he got heavy into drugs and alcohol. We drifted completely apart. I heard that later he became a drug dealer. When he was twenty-five, he was found dead on a country road not far from where we grew up—a self-inflicted gunshot to the head, they said."

"I'm sorry Dan," said Father Michael. "That's a sad ending. He seemed to have a lot of cards stacked against him from early on."

"He sure did, and I didn't help things by not telling someone who might have been able to help him.'

"You were just a kid. Don't be so hard on yourself."

"Dan, you have alluded to a lot of pain in your childhood, even before your brother was killed," he said. "Can you tell me a little about that? I'm interested to see the connection between your taking your aggressions out on the cats and what in your childhood could have been a factor. The psychologist in me would like to sort this out a bit, if you don't mind."

"I don't want to get into a lot of detail, Father, but I'll give you enough of it to hopefully help you figure me out."

"That's fine," said Father Michael.

"My mom was overwhelmed with taking care of eight kids, so she ended up abusing us. She choked us, dragged us around, gave us the silent treatment, locked me outside at night some times; even hit me with a baseball bat. Then, to add to the trauma, we watched several of our animals get killed on the highway by our house. One time I saw a boy get hit by a car, and killed, while riding his bike on that highway. Kids made fun of me a lot; I had broken front teeth, a flattened nose, and was basically your run-of-the-mill-ugly kid. That's pretty much it in a nutshell. Just a good Catholic family that played church on Sunday mornings and Wednesday Catechism nights."

"That doesn't sound like too a good Catholic family to me."

"Honestly, Father, I had no idea what a good Catholic family was, or even what normal was back then. In fact, my whole life, I've never known what normal is. I don't even have a clue."

"To tell you the truth, Dan, I'm not sure there is such a thing as normal. Everyone, and every family, has problems, some worse than others. Some people are just better than others at hiding their problems. It's all part of our human condition." He paused for several seconds, then said, "Dan, I've been curious about what happened in your relationship with your first wife. Would you like to tell me anything about that?"

"She was the girl of my dreams, her name was Katie. We met in college, and it was love at first sight. She was gorgeous, five foot five with long brown hair and green eyes, a committed Christian, full of love and laughter."

"So what happened to that marriage?"

"Seven years after our wedding, she suddenly came down with cerebral meningitis. It came on hard and quickly. She died within a few weeks. Nothing has crushed me like losing her. It was like I died that day. But I had to somehow pull through for our two kids, John and Megan, who were six and three. The ladies in the church we were attending really pitched in and helped with the domestic chores and taking care of the kids during the weeks immediately following Katie's death."

"I'm terribly sorry, Dan. You really have been given some tough circumstances to deal with. I can see why you struggle with your faith. I want you to know that I'm here anytime you want to talk."

"Well thanks, Father. You have a way of helping me to not be so hard on myself, and to know that God is there to help me through my hard times, if I will let Him."

"I'm glad I'm of help to you, Dan. Are you ready to pray?"

"Yes, go ahead," answered Dan. Father prayed, they said their 'good byes', and Dan stopped to visit with Julie for a couple minutes on his way out of the church.

15

Waiting

Dan was having second thoughts about following through with killing Harriet, the pastor too, for that matter. Maybe Father Michael was getting through to him, at least a little. They both deserved to pay the ultimate price for their deeds, but he would wait until spring before he did anything to either of them.

November rolled around and Dan was doing better emotionally. It had been ten months since Brenda and Jackie left him. He was still taking anti-depressants, still had bad dreams almost every night involving Brenda's rejection, and he woke up severely depressed every morning, but he was improving. He still hurt deeply inside, and struggled with tremendous anger. But he was functioning better on a day to day basis. And he didn't think of suicide most days now.

His bi-weekly phone conversations with Windy had been a big encouragement to him. She and the girls were planning to come to his place for the Christmas holidays. He was thinking they could have a future together, but that was premature.

With Thanksgiving coming up, and knowing that much of Brenda's family, including all those who had wronged him, would be gathered at Grandmother Muldano's place, Dan was considering a major massacre. It would be the ultimate justice for Brenda's family, but it would be a big blow to his. He would end up dead in a police shoot-out, or arrested and then sentenced to die. Was revenge to those who had wronged him important enough for him to bring devastating pain on his kids, along with his brothers and sisters? He didn't know. If someone told him that they would inflict that kind of pain on his kids, there was no way he would let them do so. Yet, he was considering that himself. Maybe he was sick.

Dan's son John arrived home on November 20th. He and Megan would be going to their maternal grandmother's place in Olympia for four days over Thanksgiving, November 23-26. That would give Dan an excellent window of opportunity for going up to Monroe to ambush his in-laws at Maureen's and Horay's house on Thanksgiving. They always ate dinner at 1 pm. The first two years of his and Brenda's marriage, he looked forward to that dinner with all its fixings. One thing he couldn't deny was that Maureen and her daughters were excellent cooks.

Why did all this crap have to happen? Why couldn't he and Brenda have been left alone to make their own family? They were bucking tough odds as it was just bringing a blended family together. The last thing they needed was interference from outside. Those damn relatives of hers. Now he was going to be spending Thanksgiving alone, while Brenda was with four of her five kids, her sister and brothers, their kids, and her mother and step-father. All that good food and family time, while he sat alone. Those bastards needed to pay for this.

Recently Dan learned that there was some friction in the Muldano-Gregory family. Actually, there always was. You couldn't have a matriarch that was so self-righteous, judgmental, and outspoken without hard feelings being stirred up from time to time.

Most the time the family managed to fake a form of harmony, as most of them had learned to keep the topic of conversation around Maureen on an impersonal, surface level.

The big source of friction currently revolves around Brenda's second-oldest brother, Kevin's, twenty-one-year-old son, Edward. A year ago he got his girlfriend of two years pregnant. She was a senior in high school at the time. Several months before Sylvia got pregnant the two of them began talking about getting married in a couple years. Everyone in the family liked Sylvia, so all the feedback on the impending engagement from the family was positive. Then last March the news broke that she was four months pregnant, and that the couple had decided they would give the baby away in an open adoption.

Crap hit the fan. Not only did Edward's older brother and older sister get on him about his plans to give the baby away, but, predictably, his cousin Conner (Brenda's oldest son), and Grandma Maureen Muldano got on his case non-stop, too, so it seemed. He stayed away from all of them, and rarely answered their phone calls.

Of course, Maureen wasn't about to let him off the hook that easy. Sometimes he'd look out the window of the house he rented to see her bossy black Ford pickup pull up. Then he knew he better put on his flak jacket and clamp his tongue. He didn't want to get any deeper in the crapper with her. He should've just told her to go to hell, and to stay away from him. But no, like everybody else in the family, he had to try to get along with her, at any cost.

16

Edward Gregory

Edward Gregory, Kevin's son, spent many days during his early childhood at Grandma Maureen Muldano's house, back when she was only working three days a week. Edward's father, Kevin, and his mom, found it convenient to let grandma watch little Edward, rather than pay for childcare. Sadly, they ended up paying a much steeper price than any paid sitter or care provider would have cost them. Grandma Muldano got her controlling hooks into him and into Kevin's home. It was actually similar to what happened later with Brenda's daughter Jackie, because of Brenda's reliance on her mom for childcare.

The big difference was that Edward's father, Kevin, saw what was happening. After four years, when Edward was seven years old, Kevin moved his family about two hours away to Centralia. After that, he vowed to never let his mom be in a position to negatively affect his family again. Unfortunately it didn't work out that way. Edward already had a strong attachment for Grandma.

To her credit, Maureen really did love Edward, as she did and does all of her blood relatives. But her kind of love can be stifling at best and devastating at worst.

At sixteen, Edward was a stunning-looking, young-version of Tom Selleck; he already stood six foot three inches tall and was a stout 210 pounds. Like his older siblings, he was a gifted athlete. His sophomore year, Edward, a right handed thrower and hitter, started varsity and made second-team all-league playing third base, the same position his uncle Doug Gregory, the professional, had played. That was quite an accomplishment in a league with a history of turning out college players. The future looked bright for a possible professional baseball career.

After Edward's sophomore year of high school, in the summer of 2000, he moved back to Monroe to live at his Grandma and Grandpa Muldanos' house. His dad and mom both objected, but, ultimately, they let him make his own decision.

Unfortunately, at the beginning of his junior year at his new school, Monroe High, Edward sustained a severely torn anterior cruciate ligament in his right leg (his plant leg for throwing and hitting in baseball), when he was tackled scoring the winning touchdown in the fifth league game. The injury required surgery. Not only could Edward not play anymore football that fall, but he was unable to come back to play basketball or baseball that year.

His senior year, he tried to play football, but couldn't take a tackle on that right leg without significant pain. Grandma Maureen Muldano—who had raised five super athletes, including two who played college ball: Kevin (Edward's father) and Doug—began to get on his case consistently with comments like,

"If you worked harder, your leg would get stronger."

"Your dad never took the easy way out; he worked his rear off to come back from his injuries."

"I love you Edward, but I can't stand by and let you be a sissy. If you wanted to play bad enough, you would make it happen."

"You have all that potential to play college ball, or even professional ball, but you just want to feel sorry for yourself."

Grandpa Horay Muldano, for his part, didn't think Edward's injury should be as limiting as it seemed to be, but he figured Maureen did enough criticizing for the both of them. It hurt Grandpa Muldano to not see the Edward he remembered. He had so much enjoyed the leadership and flashiness Edward had demonstrated in his sports from middle school through his sophomore year at Centralia.

During the winter, Edward limped noticeably while playing basketball and didn't make the starting team. In fact, he was played sparingly. If the varsity coach hadn't been a Monroe High School team-mate of Edward's Uncle Denny, back in the mid-nineteen seventies, he would have been cut.

In the spring baseball season Edward was relegated to playing first base, where his limited mobility wasn't as much of a factor. He had a good season at the plate, where he batted .343, stroked 7 homeruns out of the park, and led the team in runs batted in with 24. His average would have been close to .400 if he could have run like his old self, and he would have had several more extra-base hits, as well. Still Edward made first team all-league.

Unfortunately, with the leg problem, there would likely be no college ball or professional career in his future, though he hadn't completely given up on those dreams, even if other people had. He thought that more surgery could possibly correct the leg problem.

Late in Edward's senior year, 2002, he had a conversation with his dad, Kevin, on one of his weekend visits up from Centralia to watch Edward play baseball, concerning how Grandma Muldano had treated him since his injury.

Kevin told him, "You've always given Grandma the benefit of the doubt and stuck up for her, even when she has said something very hurtful to someone at one of our family gatherings. Many family members, especially the older grandkids, make excuses for her, 'that's just the way Grandma is.' The only way to be at peace with her is to limit your visits to a few days, or to stay completely away from her. I'm very sorry for the way your life with your grandparents has turned out. If I could, I would turn the clock back, so you could re-do your last two years, you could live at home with us."

17

Muldano Thanksgiving 2005

John and Megan drove to their maternal grandmother's house, in Olympia, on the morning of November 23rd, the day before Thanksgiving. This gave Dan plenty of time to pull things together and get up to Monroe by Thursday morning. He decided to go to the Muldanos' place prepared to wreak devastation. He didn't have to decide for sure that it was a go until he was set up and everyone was there.

Still he wrestled with, does he dare do that to John and Megan? And now he had to consider, was there a possible future with Windy? He knew this opportunity would not present itself again until possibly Christmas—most years the families got together at the Muldanos', but every few years they had it at one of Brenda's siblings' homes. Dan didn't know if it would be in Monroe this year or not. Christmas wouldn't work anyway, because Windy and her girls would be at his place then. That is, they'd be there if he didn't do any killing tomorrow.

Dan went to bed early and got up at two. He had to be in the

Muldanos' hedge before daylight.

The drive took him three hours, because he had to go the long way around through the forested hills south of the Muldanos' place. The late archery season was open in that county, so his vehicle wouldn't draw any special attention, if anyone even saw it. He hiked the three-fourths mile through the young-growth timber, mostly by way of a skid road, went through the Muldanos' neighbors' overgrown grape vineyard, and from there was able to get inside the Muldanos' hedge. He hung back in the hedge forty yards away from where he wanted to be later. It was 7:15. He was very tired. Soon he drifted off.

He awakened and checked his watch. It said 11:10. He waited until noon, then moved up closer to the garage door, in the dark shade of the hedge brush, and sat there. Waiting was the hard part. When he waited, he thought. Thinking was not good.

He may get caught before he kills anyone. What if they storm him instead of doing what he tells them? He could only get a couple shots off before he is overwhelmed and probably beaten to death. He's sure his buckshot would kill at least two if he's rushed. Would they risk that, or hold back and try to talk him out of killing anyone. Two of Brenda's brothers were millionaires—one was actually worth over five million. Maybe they'd try to buy their lives? Dan had his doubts about that.

Brenda was dirt poor when he married her, even more than he knew. She had almost $9,000 in credit card debt, and revealed none of it to him when he asked. Obviously, her brothers hadn't shared any of their wealth with her. Maybe they figured out what she was all about years ago. Her son Conner's past financial actions and attitude toward them may have been a factor. A year and a half into their marriage, Brenda forged Dan's signature on a Discover Card application, then transferred half her debt into his new account. He discovered his credit card account about a year and a half later when he inadvertently found a Discover Card bill statement in his name.

Now his one regret was that he hadn't gone through with filing a case against her. She would have done prison time for forgery and credit card fraud. But at the time he held out hope that they could somehow still make the marriage work, in spite of Brenda's dishonesty.

What if Brenda doesn't show up? This will be her first Thanksgiving with her family in over five years, thanks to Maureen who was unwilling to acknowledge her wrongs and apologize to Dan. Brenda has to be here so she can see what her restraining order has caused, rather than prevented like she hoped.

What if Jackie isn't here? Dan wants her to witness this killing, to see what a little respect toward him could have prevented. He tried and tried to be the father she so desperately needed, but several family members undermined him on every turn. They not only cheated him out of having Jackie treat him like a father, they cheated her out of having a father. Her own father, who she never lived with and who was never married to Brenda, was on death row for raping and brutally murdering two college girls that he picked up one night while he was high on speed. He'd been in prison since Jackie was four. His criminal record was so long it burned up a printer. Yet Maureen had compared Dan unfavorably to him.

What if Conner doesn't come? What if he and his wife are at *her* family's dinner? He, as much as anyone, has to be here. He will be. They always come to the Muldanos' first and then have a six o clock dinner at his wife's parents' place. That's why he's so fat? He never misses a meal; he'll be here, right on time. In fact, he'll be here early to fill his gut on appetizers. Dan had never seen a man that could out eat Conner. He must have two separate three gallon stomachs, one for snacks, drinks and desserts and one for the main meal.

One thing Dan did know: Maureen would definitely be here; it's her house.

As he continued to wait, leaning up against the trunk of the arborvitae in its darkness, forty-five minutes passed. He felt himself getting sleepy again. He hated it—a form of torture, fighting to stay awake. Sometimes he was fine. Then other times, this happened. Driving a car made him sleepy within twenty or thirty minutes, almost guaranteed. He thought his sleepiness was because he rarely got a good night's sleep, and his mind needed stimulation because of his creative intelligence. When he didn't get the necessary sleep or mental stimulation, his brain wanted to go into standby. Years ago, a friend helped him more than the friend would ever know when he suggested that Dan eat sunflower seeds if he got sleepy while driving. Dan tried that, and found it really helped. Now he always kept some sunflower seeds in the car for that very purpose.

Unfortunately, he didn't have any seeds with him now, and he was getting sleepier by the minute.

Finally it was one o clock. He slipped inside the house, careful not to be seen or heard. This was the scariest part for him. He breathed heavily. Quickly, he ducked into the small bedroom on the right with his loaded firearms and extra ammunition in his belt. The belt also held a long, fix-bladed hunting knife, not that it would do him any good in this situation anyway. He listened for the Thanksgiving prayer. He knew the routine.

As soon as Grandpa Muldano finished praying, they went quickly around the tables giving each person the chance to give thanks for something in his or her life. Dan always liked this part. In fact, he always did things that way in his own home on Thanksgiving when not at a relative's place.

It was time. He moved slowly up the hallway. He could see them. Three huge tables, surrounded by family, loaded with turkey and all the trimmings. It was so unfair. He was the outcast. He couldn't be part of this anymore. That damn restraining order. His damn wife. That damn mother-in-law. Where is she?

He stepped out into the open. His movement was noticed instantly by a few family members who gasped.

"Every cell phone on the floor now or I start shooting." Cell phones hit the floor immediately from all around the tables.

What a shame that so many people nowadays are tied, like Siamese twins, to their cell phones. Darned if he'd ever be one of them; he didn't even own one.

"If even one person keeps a phone and makes a call, the blood in this room will run out those double glass doors," he said. A couple more phones hit the floor. Jan was holding one of them. He was tempted to execute her right then.

"Any more?" he asked. "If I find that any of you kept a cell phone, I will blow your damn head all over your fellow family members. Is that clear? This is your last chance, if you have a phone, get it on the floor right now." Maureen's phone hit the floor.

"How sad that even in your own house you have to be a slave to that damn phone," he said. "I take that back. I know you aren't a slave to the phone; it's a slave to you. I guess you don't want to be even a second late on catching the latest gossip, or in sending yours on the way, do you Maureen?"

No answer.

"I said, do you?"

"I guess not," she answered. Dan decided not to push things with her yet.

"I locked the door to the garage on my way in, so no police officers can come through there," he said. "Jackie, I want you to close all the shades, and lock the front door and the double sliding doors. Then stand right by that divider, and stay there. I want you to have a front row view. You deserve that after all the years of showing me so little respect."

Jackie was shaking badly, but got the shades shut.

"Did you lock the doors?"

"Yes."

"So now, when I have someone go check that the doors are actually locked, they will find them so?"

"Yes."

"If either door is not locked, the person checking is dead. Are you okay with that Jackie?"

"No!"

"You mean the doors aren't locked?"

"No, the doors are locked. I mean I'm not okay with you killing anyone," she said, stifling tears.

"Now, Jackie, get a paper sack from your bitch grandmother and pick up every cell phone. I hate to tell you guys this but if the police show up, I will empty my guns into all of you, no questions asked. I sure hope no one has already tried to be a hero by hanging on to their cell phone and punching in a rescue code."

Jackie got the sack and gathered up the cell phones.

"With the exception of Brenda, Conner, Jan, Maureen and Jackie, I want every one of you to lie on the floor, belly down. Stack chairs however you need to make room. Jackie, you get your back against that dividing wall. She quickly did what he ordered. One false move and Jackie won't have a heart." He trained his shotgun on Jackie's chest.

Chairs were shuffled and finally everyone was on the floor, except the five.

"Now, you other four each space yourselves out and stand in the middle of a group of your family who are on the floor. Since you four are the chosen few and so worthy of special treatment for how well you treated me, you get to stand so that I can easily blow you all over your family members with this 00 buckshot. By the way, for those of you who know firearms and want to consider your odds based on the number of rounds in this gun, I'll let you know that I pulled the plug. Instead of three rounds, this shotgun is loaded with seven, and it's a pump action; I can get shots off rapidly.

"What I am really happy about right now is that no one has tried to be a hero by attempting to negotiate with me. I will call all the shots here. I don't particularly want to kill a bunch of you, but I will if I'm pushed. It should be of some concern to Maureen that she has known for years that I am crazy and *need to see a psychiatrist*. She said so on my answering machine."

Then, projecting his voice directly at Maureen, he said, "You know that if I'm crazy, you may not be able to reason with me, right Maureen?" She was terrified. First time he'd ever seen her speechless.

"I said, 'is that right Maureen?'"

"Yes."

"Is that yes, I'm crazy. Or yes you may not be able to reason with me?"

She hesitated, she was so afraid of giving a fatal answer. She knew good and well how badly she had treated Dan.

"I mean, yes I said what you said I said." She was obviously not thinking clearly with that answer.

"What do you think about me now, Maureen?"

"I don't know what to think."

"You better come up with something fast."

"Mom, just tell him that you're sorry. That we're all sorry," said Jan.

"I *am* sorry Dan," said Maureen. "I'm terribly sorry."

"You told Jackie four years ago that you needed to apologize to me. Do you really think your apology now is going to make up for those four years that you continued to mistreat me, my marriage and my family? And now look at my family. You finally broke it apart."

"I can't change any of that," said Maureen. "I can only tell you now, that I am sorry. And that I will—we all will—welcome you back into our family right now."

"What do you take me for, Maureen, a fool? Your death-bed apology means nothing to me."

"Dan, we can work all this out," said Brenda.

"I don't even want to hear your voice Brenda. You haven't wanted to hear mine in months. You used that damn restraining order to put a muzzle on me. That restraining order was to shut me up, so that I couldn't influence you back toward the marriage.

"Within the first three weeks of when you left, you told me that you were believing for the reconciliation of our marriage, even if it took a miracle from God. I guess God wasn't up to the task, *was He?* A month and a half later you told me that I just needed to be patient with you. A month after that you were intimate with me for the last time. Two weeks later, the night before Easter, we had our last civil conversation on the telephone. We talked for two hours. We ended the conversation with both of us saying, 'I love you.' I called the next night to talk to you, on Easter, and you were mean to me; you cut me off. No resurrecting our marriage, huh? A week and a half later a sheriff's deputy showed up at my door with a restraining order. You haven't talked to me since, other than giving me that warning in The Wong Place. That was the Christian way to handle things wasn't it?"

No answer.

"I said, wasn't it?"

"I don't know," she said.

"Of course you know, damn it! But you never cared about what the Christian way to handle anything was in our marriage and family. You're just like your bitch mother." Brenda wanted to object, but somehow managed to keep her mouth shut—a rarity.

"During all the months of our separation you opened wide the door for your satanic mother, and these other wolves here that wanted our marriage to end, to give all their negative input about me and our marriage. You're not your own person, you never have been, and you never will be. You're just a pawn to be pushed around, controlled and manipulated by whichever one of your evil family members wants to. You're just a little girl in a woman's body. How do you think it feels to have a restraining order put on you by the very person who should be the closest person to you in the world? You know I never once abused you or even threatened to."

"You never abused me physically, but you abused me psychologically."

Instantly, Dan's anger exploded inside; he swung the shotgun barrel directly toward her.

"No Dad!" screamed Jackie, in unison with Brenda and several other family members who yelled, "No," believing that Brenda was about to die, and wishing she would have the sense to keep her mouth shut.

He heard crying from a couple of the kids. No one thought they were going to get out of this alive. The way things were going, they might not.

"*Dad?*" Dan said to Jackie. "You're kidding me. After all this time you're going to call me *Dad?*"

The only time she ever used that title with him, or addressed him at all, was when she wanted to manipulate him into doing some favor for her. The rest of the time he was the nameless "it." She once suggested to Brenda, Dan and his two kids, "Maybe I'll just call him 'It'."

Dan couldn't believe a nine-year-old could be so disrespectful and heartless, especially toward someone who had spent countless hours hitting her softballs, pitching to her, and playing catch with her—someone who genuinely tried to show her love.

"How can you be doing this Dad?" said Jackie, apparently figuring calling him Dad now might still get her her way. He swung the shotgun barrel back to her, training it on her chest. Part of him wanted to shoot her right then for once again trying to manipulate him. But part didn't. She'd hurt him so bad with her rejection. He just wanted to love her, and have her love him. But she got some sort of sadistic pleasure in manipulating his emotions with her disrespect and rejection. Surely she had the same spirit of anti-Christ that her mom, Aunt Jan, and grandma had.

"Don't start that with me. You never wanted to call me Dad before, or anything else, but 'it'. You even called the dogs by name when you wanted their attention. Me, I got nothing. That problem should have been solved the first year we were married. You were only five when Brenda and I got married, for crying out loud. But your bitch mom didn't care about your lack of respect for me. Nor did she care that some of her family members showed no respect for me. In fact, she fed their fires against me. How do you think all of that felt for me for all those years? The best thing you can do right now is keep your mouth shut—for once. I know that comes as a shock for you, the strong-willed, stubborn, arrogant granddaughter of the biggest satanic hypocrite I've ever met. For once you are not in control.

"Now I want you all to relax and listen to a little story. I know that not one of you could possibly relate to the person in this story, because if you could, you could never treat a person the way you've treated me since I married into your *loving* family. Nor could you have allowed others to treat me that way. What amazes me even more is how a family of tremendous athletic stars, who worked so hard and overcame so many odds, out performed so many opponents, could sit by and do nothing when you saw your mom, grandmother, sister, son, or nephew attack, criticize, or steal from me and my family."

Dan paused for several seconds to let his words sink in. As angry and hurt as he was something inside him hoped that, somehow, maybe his words would get through to these people and they might still find a place in their hearts and in their family for him.

"There was a little boy who was the black sheep of his family. His mother abused all of her kids, but she saved the worst kinds of abuse for little Dennis. Like his brothers, Dennis was dragged around the house by his biceps, his mom's long fingernails digging into his flesh, making his arms bleed. His sisters were dragged by their long hair. Whenever he cried too much, Dennis's mom choked him by putting her hand over his mouth, which also blocked off the air to his nose. He would panic, desperate for air, and begin flailing his arms and legs. His mom held tighter. Finally, Dennis would grow weak from lack of oxygen and quit struggling. Then his mom would release her hold. Dennis's brothers and sisters all endured this same abuse, but since they behaved better than Dennis, they were abused less often.

"Once in a while, in the evenings when Dennis misbehaved, his mom locked him outside in the dark on the large, open, back porch. Dennis's family lived out in the country, so Dennis was terrified that a wild animal might get him, or maybe the "wild man," that the neighborhood kids and his own siblings talked about, would. When Dennis was a preschooler, a seven-year-old girl had been murdered one summer while she and her family worked in a local bean field not far from Dennis' house. The girl's body was found eighteen days later. They never found the killer. Dennis worried that the killer would come for him some night while he was alone on the porch.

"One day when Dennis was eleven, he did something that must have been pretty bad, though he doesn't remember what it could have been. His mom dragged him out onto the big porch, with his siblings following, and she proceeded to hit him on the legs with a baseball bat. He knew he must be an awfully bad kid to deserve being beaten with a baseball bat.

"Dennis's parents soon divorced, and he didn't have to endure his mom's abuse any more. His father became an alcoholic and neglected him. Eventually his father remarried and the decision was made to move to the step-mother's house in a new school district.

"When school started in the fall, Dennis got a new name before the bus had even reached the new school that he and his younger brother were to attend. One of the girls on the bus that first morning thought that with Dennis's crew-cut brown hair, flattened nose, short chin, and broken front teeth, he fit the description of a vampire."

"'He looks like a vampire,' she said, pointing her witch's finger at Dennis. 'Let's call him *Vamp.*'"

"So, because of one cruel kid, Dennis's name was now officially 'Vamp.' With the exception of a couple friends that Dennis made, and a few girls, all the kids called him "Vamp." That crushed his spirit even lower than all the other things that had happened to him throughout his young life. Dennis and his brother both hated that school with a passion. Dennis had stuffed down so much pain already in his life that he was very quickly running out of room for more.

"Over the next two months, things fell apart in Dennis's relationship with his new mom. She finally kicked him out of her house and made him live in a camper; his dad was forced to split up with her and moved him and his brother back to their old neighborhood and school. Things were much better back at his old school, where he was now a freshman in high school. But he could never get a girl friend, and he was often the butt of jokes. Still, at least the kids used his real name instead of calling him Vamp."

Dan looked around the room at his in-laws on the floor and saw many teary eyes. He heard sniffles too. He then looked at the wolves that were standing. Brenda was crying. Jackie was crying. Even Maureen was crying.

"Jackie, who do you think Dennis is?" he asked.

"*It's you, Dad*! It's you."

18

Real Meal Deal

A car horn sounded, startling Dan from his sleep. It was *just a dream*. Fixing the breakup had always been just a dream. Who was he kidding to think it could ever have been anything else? He looked at his watch. It was 12:30. He had only slept for about five minutes, but it seemed much longer. He wept silently, as he looked out of the hedge, through blurry eyes, to see Brenda and Jackie standing next to his and Brenda's Toyota pickup. Jan had pulled in behind them with her SUV, and honked her horn.

This was the first time Dan had seen Brenda and Jackie in over four months. The last time he saw them was from a distance at a 4th of July Festival at the Aberdeen City Park, before they moved back to Everett. Part of him ached for them, to be with them. Part of him was so angry that he wanted to rush out of the bushes and shoot both of them and Jan right then, while he had the chance. He stayed put. He would go into the house during the meal. *He had to go in.* He couldn't continue to live this way. But what about Megan and John; what about Windy?

Finally, it was one o'clock. No one else had arrived in the last ten minutes. There were fourteen cars parked in the driveway and parking area. It was time.

Dan slipped into the house through the garage door. He was sweating badly, breathing hard. Everyone was out of sight around the corner at the end of the hallway—so far, so good. He moved quickly past the utility room on the right, to the small bedroom, also on the right, opened the door and stepped inside. The door had been open a few inches, but he determined no one had been in there. No jackets were lying on the bed, and the computer screen was off. He heard Horay praying over the Thanksgiving meal. He needed to move into position for the standoff just as the prayer was completed. He double checked his ammo belt and his holstered pistol. He held the 12 gauge, short-barreled shotgun by the neck in his right hand and eased the hammer back silently as he squeezed the trigger gently and then released it.

He started to step out of the small room, but he couldn't lift his left leg for that first step. He tried again. It didn't work. His hands and forehead were soaked. He struggled for a breath. He had to go now. But he couldn't. Neither of his legs would budge. Was this God—or just nerves?

He still thought of God often, but rarely prayed anymore. He went to church most weeks, and even read his Bible sometimes. But *God had let him down.* God had let him down? Yes, God *had* let him down. God had let many people down, the many people in Dan's church and community who had prayed for his and Brenda's reconciliation. Yes, God let him down. If He couldn't fix their marriage, why should Dan trust Him for anything?

Since Dan couldn't seem to move out into the hall, he decided to stay in the small room and listen to the family's conversation while they ate. If he was going to confront the family, he would have to do it before the kids finished eating and began leaving the table to go play. If he wasn't going through with it, he had to escape before then.

After the prayer they went around each of the three huge tables and gave each family member an opportunity to briefly share about a blessing they had to be thankful for. It amazed him how Brenda could say her piece as if she wasn't separated from her husband, as if she didn't have her husband restrained, as if her life was going just the way she wanted it to. That hurt.

When the giving thanks part was over, Dan could hear the hospitable conversation as everyone dug into the fixing's; silverware clanged against serving plates and bowls. He could smell the turkey, dressing, gravy and sweet potatoes. Suddenly, he felt very hungry. If he walked in to join them, could this family, who had just prayed to God and thanked Him, extend His love and forgiveness to Dan? He thought some of them could and would. The hypocrites wouldn't, and there were several of those here. He was violating Brenda's restraining order just being here; even if he hid the guns and took a chance on being accepted, the hypocrites would call 911. He would be arrested.

As the relatives ate, various topics were discussed around the tables. But it didn't take long for Maureen to spoil a good time.

"Edward, aren't you and Sylvia about due for your first visit with your baby?" she said, opening up a can of worms.

The festive mood vanished; a chill came over the room instantly. That never bothered Maureen. She never considered how awkward or damaging her words could be to others.

"Uh, yeah. We go to see her on December tenth," answered Edward. He hoped that would be the end of it, but knew better.

"Have you been getting any pictures of her since she was born?"

"Actually, they sent us some three weeks ago that were all taken during her first month," said Sylvia. "We know they're going to give us more when we go see her, and we're going to take some then ourselves."

"Did you bring the pictures?"

"Yes, I'll get them out of my purse," said Sylvia, beating

Maureen to the next step. She dug out the package with the photos and handed them to Maureen. Why couldn't they all just enjoy the good meal now without having to be passing pictures around? Sylvia thought.

With the exception of the kids, who couldn't care less about anything the adults were talking about, *all conversation* in the room had come to a standstill. Everyone had been here plenty of times before—fortunately not so much on holidays—and knew that sparks could fly at any moment. Maureen never seemed to notice the suffocating effect her words had in a room, and she sure as heck didn't know when to shut up. Nor did she care to know.

Listening from the bedroom, Dan sensed all hell was about to break loose; and he wasn't even the cause of it. Part of him was relieved to not be part of this anymore.

"Your baby's darling," said Maureen, as she looked at a couple of photos. "Well, I guess she's really not your baby now since you gave her away. How could you do that anyway, with your own flesh and blood?"

"Grandma, we've been over all this ground before, and we don't want to get into it again, especially on a holiday and with the whole family here," said Edward, answering for Sylvia. "We have enough of our own feelings to deal with regarding all of this. Can you give us a break?"

Kevin, Brenda's second-oldest brother, felt very proud of his son at that moment for having the courage to stand up for himself and his fiancée. He wouldn't have dared stand up to Maureen at that age. In fact, he still couldn't stand up to her. Unfortunately, Grandma Maureen Muldano wasn't letting anyone dictate to her when a topic could or should be discussed and to what extent.

"I think now is a perfect time to bring it up, Edward," said Maureen. "We're all family here, and if you can't talk about anything and everything amongst family, it isn't much of a family, is it?"

"Please Grandma!" said Sylvia, "this is not an easy topic for us.

We've had our own regrets and remorse over our decision. We just don't want to deal with it right now, certainly not here with the whole family together."

"Sylvia, I hate to say it, but *you aren't* family yet. No female in our family has ever given her baby away." (Though at least one would have been aborted if Maureen had had her way.) "There are many of us in our family that consider you to be a selfish, immature, spoiled brat who gave your baby away—so that you could pursue your career goals—instead of taking responsibility for screwing around without protection and then reaping the consequences."

Everyone was aghast at this frontal assault on Sylvia, who all the other family members liked all along, regardless of their feelings about her giving up her baby.

"Grandma, I am not going to sit here and let you talk to Sylvia that way!" said Edward. "All of us know that the person in this room who is selfish is you. Nobody ever wants to say that to you, or stand up to you about anything. But *it's* true. This family is made up of a bunch of weaklings that let one person—YOU—run over all of us as if our ideas, opinions, and feelings mean nothing. I'm done doing it."

"You're not going to talk to my grandma like that," said Conner, Brenda's oldest son. "She's right about both you and Sylvia, so buck up and take it like a man."

"You're just the person I would expect to jump in and defend Grandma. And by the way, she is my grandma, too, as much as I sometimes hate to admit it when she acts like this," said Edward. "You've been defending her for years. I first realized that four years ago when she was getting on my case over my injuries. Grandma can do no wrong in your eyes. I used to look at her the same way, but I grew out of it."

"You grew out of it," said Conner, slamming a fist on the table, knocking over a salt shaker. "What are you implying with that comment?"

"Boys, this conversation isn't going anywhere good." said

Grandpa Horay Muldano.

"Poppa," Kevin jumped in, "you sat there, like you always do, and let mom tromp all over my kids and said nothing. I agree that this conversation needs to stop. But for crying out loud, Poppa, have the balls to stand up to Mom for a change and put her in her place."

"You know I can't do that."

"Why can't you do that?"

"When have you ever done it, Kevin?" said Horay.

"I never have, but maybe it's time to start. My son showed the fortitude to do it, and I'm proud of him for it."

"Uncle Kevin, your son doesn't respect authority, and he certainly isn't respecting Grandma," said Conner, again acting like her little side-kick. Little? Not.

It was ironic that Conner would call anyone else on the carpet regarding their respect for authority. He only had a father figure in the home for a total of seven years of his childhood, including two step fathers and one of his mom's live-in lovers. Consequently, he despises all authority figures.

Controversy can go full-circle quickly with this family, and Dan discerned it was headed there now, as he continued to listen from the bedroom. Even the kids were paying attention now.

"What is your idea of respecting Grandma, Conner?" said Edward. "Letting her verbally rip me or other family members to shreds, saying any darn thing she pleases to us. I can imagine some of the things she said about you in the past." He was careful not to mention Conner's criminal record. "I consider myself too much of a man to let her rip me or Sylvia to shreds."

"You think you're quite a man, do you Edward?" said Conner. "Why don't you and I step outside, and I'll show you who the man is."

"You never change, do you," said Edward. "Every time there's a conflict, you want to settle it with your fists. When are you going to grow up and handle things like an adult?"

Edward just bit off more than he could chew with those words.

Conner was a replica of his grandma. A bull in a china shop who knew how to do one thing: run people over with his physical size and overbearing personality.

"Let's go outside you punk kid!" said Conner, shoving his chair back and getting up.

"You people never learn do you," said Edward. "This whole situation sounds so familiar, only I was a naïve teenager then. Conner, Grandma and Aunt Jan, you all teamed up on Dan. It was the last Christmas that he and Brenda and their kids spent with us. In fact it was the last time they spent any holidays with the family. If it wasn't for the Gregory family reunions, none of us would have ever gotten to see them in all these years since then.

"Thank God the Gregory family is a loving family, which would rather get along with each other than find fault," Edward went on. "They act like the Christians that many of them are. That's a far cry from the hypocrisy modeled by you Grandma and Grandpa. You don't even get along with each other. You talk and treat each other with disdain. When I was a kid I didn't pay attention to it, but the last few years it's bothered me whenever I've been around you. Personally, I think you should both *live* what you *read* in the Bible and *preach* to others. I will say that I have at least seen you Grandpa trying to get along with Grandma sometimes. Grandma, I've rarely seen you try to get along with Grandpa or anyone else."

"Son, you need to put a lid on it," said Kevin. "It's not your place to point out, or correct, your grandma and grandpa's faults."

Kevin's words came just in time. Grandma Muldano had leaned forward in her chair in order to get up, and started to speak, but bit her lip to hold back her words. She would let her middle son defend her. She mis-figured that one.

"Dad, I'm twenty years old now, and I've sat through holiday after holiday, family get-together after family get-together and said nothing, while the same family members—Conner, Aunt Jan, and Grandma—have said and done whatever they wanted to anybody and everybody. And not one person ever holds them accountable.

Frankly, I've lost much of my respect for Uncle Doug (Brenda's oldest brother), Uncle Denny (Brenda's youngest brother), Uncle Mike (Jan's husband), Grandpa, and even you, Dad (Kevin, Brenda's middle brother)."

"The men in this family have never stood up like men within this family system. At least I haven't seen it. From everything I've heard and everything I've read in your scrapbooks and yearbooks, all three of you brothers were great running backs and defensive players on the football field and wouldn't back down from anyone. Why are you all so intimidated by your own mother? Did she abuse you, and you never said anything about it before?"

"Son, you just crossed the line with that comment, so back off!" said Kevin. "Some things are just the way they are, and that's *just the way it is*. You learn to keep the peace by not rocking the boat."

"I don't like what I'm hearing Dad. You're not even answering my questions. I feel like I'm in the middle of an interview with a politician that doesn't want to make any waves."

"Edward is right," said Doug, the one son Maureen had never berated. The one son she would at least listen to on the rare occasion when he spoke up about anything. As her first-born, she looked at him in much the way she had looked at his father. He actually strongly resembles his deceased father, not only in his physical appearance, but in his personality. A big difference was that Gerald never would have stood by impotently, as Doug had always done, while Maureen verbally battered those around her.

"I don't mean any disrespect to you, Mom, but it's time I spoke up. As the oldest son of our deceased father, I should have stepped forward years ago and taken a leadership role. God knows I had no problem doing that in high school or college sports, or on the professional baseball teams I played on."

Speaking to the rest of the family now, he said, "Back when Mom married Horay, I saw how she had changed from when Dad was alive. Even when Dad was alive, she struggled at times having to bite her tongue and submit to Dad's leadership. Dad loved her so much, and he corrected her in such a gentle, but manly way. He knew the formula with her. There was never any doubt about who the leader was in our family then. I don't think mom has ever gotten over Dad." Maureen and the other women in the family were wiping their eyes. "She has taken her pain of losing him out on all of us at one time or another—some of us a lot more than others. Probably on Horay more than anyone."

"I haven't deserved any of the way she has treated me," said Horay, whose timing has never been good.

"You have never loved me like Gerald did," said Maureen, through her tears.

"You're not an easy person to love, picking at everything the way you do," said Horay.

"You're not half the—"

"That's enough, Mom," Doug cut her off. He had listened to her humiliate Horay before. He wasn't standing for it now.

"Why do you guys have to get right back after each other?" he continued. "Can you just cool it?" No one dared say a word now. All eyes were glued on Doug. Aside from his wife and kids, none of the relatives had ever seen or heard him take such a strong stand before. They were impressed. It seemed like he was back in high school, taking the handoff from the quarterback and breaking through the off-tackle hole on the line to go for one of his big runs. Maureen saw her deceased husband, Gerald, in him now. But she didn't like his next topic one bit.

"Edward brought up a very sore subject in this family when he brought up Dan's name earlier. We need to talk a little about that now," said Doug. What I mean when I say sore subject, I'm sure, is different from how others in the family may think of the soreness. Personally, I liked Dan from the first time I met him. I thought he was a good kid back in high school when I came to a few of Kevin's spring baseball games; Dan played in the outfield on that team. Then years later when Brenda got hooked up with him, I knew he was a genuine, honest man. I still believe he is, no matter how

Brenda and anyone else involved in getting the restraining order tried to make him look. It's time to call a spade a spade. Dan is not the spade. Brenda, Mom and the other wolves in this family are the spades.

"Mom, it's a shame the way you have done your dead-level best to bring him down to nothing in the eyes of various family members with your regular gossiping about him. And you've been successful with several of them. Unfortunately, one of those people is Brenda, the one who counts most. And Brenda has done a bang-up job of playing the victim role. Honestly, I couldn't blame Dan for being extremely angry over all of this."

"You don't know what you're talking about, Doug," said Maureen. "From the moment he got into this family he caused problems. He did his best to keep my grand daughter away from me."

"That's not how I saw it at all, Mom," said Doug. "I saw a man who, obviously, came from a family that knew what respecting family boundaries meant. Brenda never made any boundaries her entire adult life, and she knew if she tried to, you would disregard them. She was lucky to marry a man like Dan who knew the way things should be, and then had the strength of character to attempt to make it that way. Unfortunately for him, the wolves in this family were far more than he could have imagined. They're more than any man could deal with. No man could survive the—"

"Why don't you ask the rest of the family what they think?" Maureen interrupted.

"Frankly, I don't care what they think. There's right and there's wrong, and that doesn't change no matter how many people are convinced otherwise. This is wrong. I do know that Edward, Kevin and Denny all agree with me. But even that doesn't matter. We could line the whole family up, draw a line on the carpet with chalk and separate ourselves. It wouldn't mean a thing. *What does God think*? That should be the only thing that matters. Certainly in a family that calls themselves Christians. Not one of you wolves, or you Brenda, can justify Biblically the action you've taken against Dan. And I'm sorry to admit that I've sat here for years and minded my own business, instead of speaking up.

"It amazes me, how one person—you Mom—have so much control over a family," Doug went on. "You turned several family members against Dan, and then some of them turned against Brenda as well. Conner and Jan cut themselves off from having anything to do with her. Conner even went so far as to pull his kids away from her because she was married to Dan. Talk about really hitting a person where it hurts. I don't know how any of you can say that you love Brenda and Jackie when you pull that kind of manipulative crap."

"I don't understand why you're standing up for that loser," said Conner, who wouldn't acknowledge he was holding a losing hand even if a royal flush was laid down across the table from him. "He caused problems in this family right from the start. And Brenda didn't like the way he took over in the home trying to parent Jackie. There were a couple of other things she told me about Dan, too, during those first few months."

"What the heck was she doing talking to you, her son, about anything that was going on in that home?" said Doug. "You were the wrong person."

"Why was I the wrong person?" said Conner, jumping on the defensive again as he does so naturally. His involvement in the rape and the ensuing prison term years ago, caused Conner to think that everyone had their eye on him; that they looked at him as though he was in no position to judge others or give his opinion. The funny thing was, other than his grandmother, no one gave his opinion more freely than him.

The family as a whole was leery of Conner for more than one reason. First, he used his size to intimidate the men whenever he disagreed with them; he'd always had a short fuse. Second, his character was suspect at best; he was known for his situational ethics. If Conner could benefit by adjusting the right and wrong of a situation, then he had no problem doing so. Shortly after he got out of prison he swindled two of his uncles, Kevin and Denny (Brenda's youngest brothers), out of thousands of dollars. Like his grandmother, he would never admit his wrong doings or ever try to make them right. It was in his blood.

Maureen once said to Dan in front of the family when she was ripping him a new one in regard to his step-daughter Jackie, "My blood runs through her; yours never will." At the time she spoke it, those words struck him as coming directly from the bottom of an outhouse. After watching Conner, Jan and Brenda over the years, Dan was actually very thankful Maureen's blood didn't run through him.

"No woman should run to her adult kids to talk about her marital problems or disagreements she has with her husband concerning the parenting of kids still at home," said Doug. "Those things are none of the grown kids' business. In most cases nothing but more problems will come from that kind of exchange."

"I don't know why any of the stuff with Dan should matter to you anyway, Uncle Doug," said Conner, refusing to even try to see where he himself was at fault.

"It matters because Brenda is my sister, and I've stood by for years and watched her go through one man after another; marrying some of them and not others." Doug was too diplomatic to say that she shacked up with the ones she didn't marry, or just had sexual relations with them. Nor did he mention the fact that three of her five kids were either conceived or born out of wedlock.

"Dan is far and away the best man she ever had," Doug went on. "Yet, you, your grandma and grandpa, Jan and Jackie all did nothing but focus on Dan's faults. From the start, he wasn't allowed to be Jackie's father. Years ago, I heard talk in the family of how Mom, Brenda and others had prayed for God to bring a Christian man into Brenda's life that could be Jackie's much needed father, since her birth father was in prison for life for his heinous crimes.

"When Dan and Brenda first got married, everyone was overjoyed with God's answer to prayer. But as soon as Dan stood up as a man to be the leader, including setting family boundaries, all of a sudden, he was Satan incarnate. There were the big blow ups with Mom and Conner; then Dan became the black sheep in our family. What really amazed me was how Mom was able to suck all of the rest of you in to pack up like wolves against Dan. From the get-go, the man didn't stand a chance of making the situation work."

As Dan listened from the bedroom, he wanted to run out there and hug Doug for his insight and the fortitude to finally speak up on Dan's behalf. He wanted to hug Edward too. Maybe there still was hope for reconciliation after all.

Dan decided to get out of there before he was discovered. This mission was well worth it, even though he didn't carry through with his plans of devastation. Thank God he didn't go through with those plans. How could he have even considered such a thing? Hurt, rejection and anger can do that to a man. There were still a lot of people in that family that cared for him and were in his corner. Thank God for Doug and Edward, and even Kevin.

Dan quickly slipped out the bedroom door and escaped out the door to the garage. His legs worked perfectly. In fact, he felt a spring to them he hadn't felt in months. Maybe his marriage wasn't over.

As He hiked back up the hill through the woods to his rig, Dan considered all that he had heard. Then he thought of the things that were not spoken, or rather, of the people who had not spoken up. Two who had not said anything while he was there, other than to say what they were thankful for after the family prayer, were Annie and Jackie, his two step-daughters.

Jackie, now twelve, was turned against him by the wolves' influence during the first year they were married. Fortunately, Annie, who was now twenty-four, never did take sides against him—but she also never stood up for him either. Her being adopted and not Maureen's blood granddaughter probably had a lot to with her having a gentle, kind nature about her rather than the rebellious, obnoxious, controlling nature that Brenda, Jan and Jackie all inherited.

Dan was sure the discussion about him and the state of his and Brenda's marriage would continue that day and in the days to come. He bet Brenda would enlighten Doug, Kevin and Edward—and perhaps others who may not be in the wolves' circle of gossip—as to all the crap that she had to put up with from him. How he didn't show her any affection, how he didn't let her be herself, how he was controlling, and any other of his faults she could think of to justify her leaving him. He would also bet that she wouldn't be candid with them about how she sabotaged their family financially, how she lied to him, how she dishonored him, how she refused to make Jackie respect him, how she argued with him about everything, and how she verbally berated John and picked at him endlessly.

Dan had openly acknowledged that both he and Brenda had many faults. But the worst problems in their marriage revolved around the interference by Maureen and the manipulative tactics used by her, Jan and Conner.

Dan arrived back in the Aberdeen area at 7 pm and decided to have turkey dinner at North's Chuck Wagon. At least there he didn't have to eat alone.

19

Christmas Break 2005

Christmas break was here for Megan.

Dan hadn't heard anymore from or about Brenda. He was told way back when she got the restraining order, eight months earlier, that she only intended to keep it in force until she saw that he was under control. Boy he got angry when he heard that. And he got angry at his naïve pastor who relayed the message from her to him. The pastor had no idea what Brenda, her mom and other family members were really up to with that restraining order.

Who was she to put a legal muzzle and shackles on him until "she sees that you are under control"? What did he need to be under control from? And what made her think it was her place to control him? He still got angry just thinking about that. Why would he want to reconcile with her anyway? Maybe because she was still his wife; his God-given wife. At least he thought so when they got married.

At just after one in the afternoon on December twenty-third, Megan shouted, "They're here, Dad!" as she looked out the front window.

John rushed down the stairs. He was dying to see his cousin Kristin. The house was in tip-top shape. Dan wanted to make a good impression on Windy. Not that anything he could ever do could dampen her opinion of him.

"Hi everyone," said Windy, with that gorgeous perfect smile of hers. She and Dan hugged and held each other tighter and longer than they had in years. She'd kept her figure so nice all along, actually filled out some, which made her even more attractive to him.

"How was the trip?" Dan asked.

"It was beautiful!" she said. "We took I-5 to Salem then drove to the coast and traveled the coast highway all the way here. I just love the view of the ocean that you get in a lot of places. I've always loved the ocean."

"Me too, that's one of the main reasons we moved here."

The kids had no problem settling in. Megan and Amy were the same age and had always hit it off perfectly. And, of course, John and Kristin had the similar affinity for each other that Dan and Windy always had. Dan had a talk with John the day before reminding him to use good judgment and not let physical things go where they shouldn't.

Dan, Windy and the kids all had a great Christmas, exchanged gifts, and ate an excellent meal, compliments of Dan's stormy-eyed cousin.

On December 28th, Thursday, at 10 a.m., Dan, Windy and the kids had just finished eating a late breakfast when a sheriff's deputy pulled his rig up outside. *What are they going to get me for now?* Dan wondered. The knock came on the door. He opened it. "Good morning," he lied to the officer.

"Are you Daniel Thurmond?" the officer asked, as he held what appeared to be some kind of legal document. Windy stood right behind Dan, with a hand on his hip. Dan and the deputy had seen each other around the Aberdeen community before, though they had never spoken.

"Yes, I am."

"These are dissolution of marriage papers from your estranged wife, Brenda Thurmond. I just need you to sign here for receipt of service, and I'll be on my way." Dan signed and took the divorce papers.

"Sorry to be the one to serve you, especially over the holidays. It's one of the unpleasant parts of my job. Best of luck to you, sir." He got in his car and drove out the long driveway.

And that was that. The marriage was actually over. Done deal, no reconciliation. Months of holding on to some kind of hope, no matter how slim. Even Doug and Edwards' words at Thanksgiving meant nothing. Maureen, the bitch, *the anti-christ*, had won. She had completed her mission. Well, now Dan was going to complete his mission too. She would get what she had coming.

"Dan, are you alright?" asked Windy. "Why don't you close the door and let's all go sit in the living room." She nudged him away from the door in her ever gentle way, pulled him around and looked tenderly into his eyes with her loving, still youthful, sparkling, encouraging, stormy, blue eyes which seemed to say, "It will be okay. We will be okay." He probably read the "We will be okay" into them. But maybe he didn't.

All six of them—John, Kristin, Megan, Amy, Windy, and Dan— took seats in the living room. Dan and Windy sat together on the light-blue love seat, and Windy took his right hand in her left hand.

"Dad, did I hear the officer right?" said John. "Are those the divorce papers from Brenda?"

"Yes, son, they are. I guess it's finally over. There's no going back now."

"Do the papers say anything about what she's trying to get out of you in the divorce?" he said.

Dan took a minute to skim through the papers, then said, "Yes, she wants the speed boat, camp trailer, alimony, and she wants half of the equity in the house, plus half of my inheritance from my parents. It's unbelievable to me that coming into the marriage with absolutely nothing, except over $9,000 of hidden credit-card debt, she thinks she is entitled to all that. It shows you what she was really all about."

"Can she get alimony and half the equity in the house and half your inheritance, Dad?" John asked, obviously very concerned.

"There's no way I see her getting alimony and I don't think she can possibly get half the equity, or any of my inheritance. But I'm afraid she will get plenty more than she deserves, considering she brought nothing but all that hidden credit-card debt into the marriage," said Dan.

"Do we stand any chance of losing our place?" said Megan. Windy and her girls were letting Dan and his kids interact without giving any of their input. He was impressed with that.

"I won't let that happen, Sweetie." He was actually scared to death it would happen, that he wouldn't be able to stop it from happening. "I'll have to get a good lawyer. In these months of separation, I've talked to a number of different people about what my potential of losing big in a divorce would be. Mostly I have been told that I have a tough battle ahead of me. Let's hope those people are wrong, and that the couple who said the laws have changed, and property isn't routinely divided in half anymore are right. Supposedly, each person's contribution to the marital assets are considered and distribution made accordingly. I can only hope that my attorney will keep me from losing an arm and a leg."

Then changing the subject, Dan said, "Well, it's Christmas season still. So let's forget about all this and get up in the forest and go sledding. That's what we were planning to do, and by golly that's still what we're going to do." The kids—glad to end the brief, tense discussion—jumped up and ran to get their heavy clothes, mitts, boots, hats, and the tubes and sleds loaded into the rig.

Windy put her arm around Dan, then did what she hadn't done in years, she pulled his face to hers and kissed him on the lips. It felt so good. She always had such big, soft, succulent lips that could kiss so tenderly. A short thirty seconds passed with their lips gently rubbing each other. She tasted so good to him.

Then she gently drew back, looked him square in the eyes, and said, "Dan, you just got some closure. You can look at this as good news, if you will. You have the freedom to make a new start now. Brenda will get what she has coming to her, and I'm not talking about money or material assets. I'm talking about the life she deserves. She's right back where she has always been—before you—with her mother to control her life and make it miserable in the process. I'm not saying that we should wish that on her. Just that that is what will happen. I think even you know that."

"You're right. And I'm so glad you were here when I was served. It's almost like it was meant to be. Now let's go have some fun." Now, he knew things were going to be okay, no matter if he lost everything he owned.

They got up, grabbed their warm clothes, the hot chocolate-filled thermoses, the sandwiches and chips, and joined the kids in loading the rig. They then drove up into the higher elevations of the Olympic National Forest where a wet, cold spell, in the past several days, had dumped over two feet of snow. They went sledding one other day during the Christmas break, played lots of board games and watched a bunch of good movies. It was fun to feel like part of a family again.

On New Year's Day they had a fantastic meal with ham and all the trimmings. Windy had always been an excellent cook. She and the girls left on January 2nd to return to Sutherlin, Oregon, where Windy worked as a hair dresser. Amy was a junior at Sutherlin High School, and Kristin was in her second year at Umpqua Community College. She was working toward a nursing degree.

20

Her Time

After receiving the divorce papers Dan made up his mind that Maureen had to pay the ultimate price for what she caused. But he knew he didn't want to jeopardize the future he now knew he would have with Windy. So how would he handle Maureen without getting caught?

He knew Horay, now 82, had suffered some dementia in the last two years—brief periods of not making sense, problems remembering things, and minor outbursts of anger and profanity. Dan thought highly of him the first two years of the marriage, but he allied up with Maureen and the other wolves after the big Christmas blowup. It was hard to admire a guy who took an active role against you, which he had done. Unfortunately for Horay, that would make it much easier on Dan's conscience when he carried out his plan for Maureen and Horay.

John and Megan were spending the weekend of February 17-19 at their grandmother's place. John drove them over there right after Megan got out of school. They would be back late Sunday night. This was the perfect opportunity.

At 3:30 on Friday afternoon, Dan left Aberdeen and drove to the woods south of the Muldanos' place, five miles east of Monroe, arriving there at 7:10 pm. He parked near the same place he parked on Thanksgiving in the young-growth Douglas fir forest about three-quarters of a mile from their place. He didn't need to worry about anyone finding him there, especially after brushing in the scotch-broom-laden road he parked on.

He leaned his seat back in the SUV and relaxed, as much as he could for about an hour before descending down the same hill he hiked on Thanksgiving. He got to the Muldanos' house by nine. They never locked their outside doors until just before they went to bed at about eleven, after the evening movie, or the ten o clock news. He was traveling light this time. Once again he wore the diving suit and mask, as he entered the house through the garage again, wearing his holster belt loaded with ammo and the .357 pistol. He deliberately left his shotgun in his rig, and wasn't planning to use the pistol. After getting inside the house, he slipped his mag-light into the fanny pack that also contained a roll of duct tape and a few other odds and ends.

He knew Horay had a very nice gun collection—or at least did have—containing over two dozen firearms, half of them pistols. He and Dan had looked through it a couple times when Dan was over in the past. He was quite proud of it. Dan thought he used other people as an excuse to look at the collection himself. Unlike most gun owners, Horay kept his weapons and ammunition locked up in a gun safe. None of his guns were kept loaded either.

As he entered through the garage, Dan was careful to listen to the program on the television. He made sure it was not on a commercial, then slipped into the house and went into the little bedroom. Horay and Maureens' bedroom was at the other end of the house beyond the twenty by twenty-foot family room. He would wait in the closet of the little room until twelve to ensure they were asleep. From there it would be a piece of cake.

At just after eleven, he heard one of them come past the little bedroom and then heard the locking mechanism on the door to the garage being handled. He then heard the outside, double-garage door close electronically. He was locked in. No problem, he'd go out the front door on his way out. He heard Maureen say something from the far end of the house.

"I'll get to it. Do you ever let up?" Horay muttered, just loud enough to gain some satisfaction, but not loud enough for her to understand him. Dan felt sorry for the man. He made the bed years ago when he didn't put her in her place and keep her there. The only thing that surprised Dan was that Horay wasn't an alcoholic after all those years.

Dan's dad once told him, "A lot of women drive a man to drink." Dan guessed that was a good excuse for him. The Lord knew he drank his share.

Dan only had two years to get to know Horay before all hell broke loose in the family toward him. But it was enough time to hear him tell a lot of stories, which Dan thoroughly enjoyed. In his younger days he was one bad logger. He could get down in the canyon, set a choker, and get back out of the way faster than any man alive—at least by his own account. All the various certificates, for winning logging skills contests at the old-time logging conferences, plastered on the wall of his study did add credibility to his claims, however.

When he got a little older, in his late twenties, he became a top-notch timber faller. Standing six-foot-two, and going 220, he had no problem packing one of the old heavy McCulloch chain saws around all day on a steep hill side. He was one big Mexican, though he was born in La Jolla, California. His parents, with his four oldest siblings, had migrated up there around 1915 from northern Mexico. There were nine kids in all. Only Horay, an older brother and two younger sisters were still alive. Dan was going to shorten that list tonight.

It was midnight. Dan reached behind him to put his pocket watch back into his fanny pack. He wouldn't need it anymore tonight. He snuck out of the bedroom with his loaded pistol in hand. The thick shag carpet was soft and quiet under his feet. Several dim wall lights illuminated his path to the Muldanos' bedroom. The door was open, and he stepped in, silently. He stood at the foot of their queen bed, looking at them snuggled up together, mostly covered by a light-brown comforter. They were both snoring lightly.

Horay had flannel pajamas on, while Maureen was wearing a flannel nightgown. His belly was up against her back, his right arm around her. How cute. They could bicker all day long, then cuddle up so cozily like newlyweds do just after they've been intimate. Frankly, anyone that had heard them bicker wouldn't think they'd sleep in the same bed, let alone cuddle up together. Dan was surprised Horay didn't wear ear plugs to bed. When Maureen wakes up she probably bitches at him for having his arm over her. That won't be a problem for him after tonight.

This was probably the closest either of them ever got to being their true self. The self that admitted it needed to be touched, to be understood, to have intimacy, companionship, to be loved. What a shame they couldn't let the love of God be real in their lives. Dan thought *it takes so much less effort to feel and express positive emotions than it does to express the bad ones, the hateful ones*. Was he preaching to himself?

In a few minutes he would wake them. But for now he just watched.

He will point his pistol at their faces. They won't recognize him in the dim light with the dive suit and mask on. They will think they are being burglarized by a stranger. He'll say, "How are you lovebirds doing tonight?" Looking down on them, he felt such a sense of confidence, of power.

They will say, "Dan? Is that you?"

"Why would I be here?" he will say.

"What do you want?"

"What have I ever wanted? When did either of you ever care about that anyway?"

"We do care about you Dan." Horay will say.

"Aren't you a little late with that line, Horay? I liked you the first couple years of Brenda's and my marriage. I even felt sorry for you. I couldn't imagine what hell it must be for you to be married to a bitch like Maureen." Horay couldn't deny the truth in that statement. Nor will he confirm it, even on his death bed. Dan continued to consider the verbal exchange soon to take place.

Maureen won't say anything; she'll wet her pull-ups. She knows there is enough evidence to convict her and earn her ten death sentences for all the harm she has done to the people in her life over the years. Well, on second thought, maybe she doesn't know.

As Dan continued to watch them, Horay rolled over onto his back for a few seconds, then to his other side, his right side. As if rehearsed, Maureen rolled over and then snuggled up against Horay, putting her left arm over him. Neither awakened; no sense of guilt emanated from them either. Neither of them knew they were being watched by their killer.

Dan didn't know how Maureen could sleep at night with the things she did during her waking hours. She had to buy a new cell phone every four months. A phone could only take so much gossip. He thought the limit was somewhere around six hours a day. How did she do it? She must have a good supply of shovels to dig up all the crap she comes up with. Bitch! I hate you so much.

He was in no hurry. No one was coming there at this hour of the night. He'd waited months—no, years—to be the one in control of the bitch. He was going to savor it a bit longer.

"I am God's tool of wrath," he will tell them. "You will do exactly as I say."

"Do what?" Horay will ask.

"Do what I say."

"What is that?"

"*Whatever* I say," Dan will sound like a politician—speaking, yet saying nothing. They hadn't said a nice thing to or about him in over five years. Why should he say *anything* to them?

"Get out of bed. Both of you get out on Maureen's side." He will back away from the bed, out into the room to give them space to pass him. The gun collection was in the second bedroom that was serving as a study. It was a big room, 15 by 18 feet, with the cabinet in a corner.

"Now take me to your gun cabinet and unlock it. Horay lead the way." Even though Horay's weight had dropped to 180 pounds in his old age, Dan knew he couldn't make a mistake. One of Horay's elbows in his chops could do some serious damage. He would keep Maureen between Horay and himself and keep the gun barrel in her neck, just below the skull. She will whimper, but will be smart enough to keep her mouth shut. She knows Dan has nothing but contempt for her, and that her only chance is to let Horay advocate for both of them. She doesn't realize that she has no chance. No way Dan would be talked out of completing his mission.

He will have Horay hand his Colt .45 revolver to Maureen and let her hand it to Dan; then the ammo. He will load both, while they stand in the opposite corner of the room from him. Dan's sure she will bawl buckets, but it won't change a thing. He's cried buckets and nothing changed.

He will make both of them get back into the bed, each on their proper side. He will move up Horay's side of the bed, pointing the .45 at him. He will tell Horay to look at the wall above his head board, and at the moment he looks there he will place the barrel under his chin and blow his brains out. Maureen will be a nut case, so Dan will quickly reach over and shoot her in the right side of her head, close to her ear. Since Horay is right handed, Dan will then put the pistol in his dead right hand and use his right index finger to pull the trigger for the second point blank shot into Maureen's head.

No more Bitch. No more bitching…or tearing marriages apart.

It will look like a murder-suicide. He shot his wife twice in the head and then shot himself. Since he's had some dementia recently, it will be accepted. She bitched at him their entire marriage, and hundreds of people witnessed it. They argued all the time. *He had* motive. *He had* mental issues. *He had* all he could take. *He finally* shot the bitch. But he couldn't live with that, so he shot himself, too. End of story.

Some may say, "Why would he shoot her twice, the first shot got the job done?"

"He held all that anger inside for all those years—a big man like that, having to submit to his wife and listen to her bitch at him for that long. Would you shoot her once or twice if you had the chance?"

Suddenly, Maureen turned onto her back. Dan thought she might wake up. He watched. No. She still slept. He was having doubts. Why did he have to have a conscience? Just be done with them. Horay is a good man, he's just a wimp. It's not his fault. Where has he heard that before? You know you're not going to do it. You're not man enough. It has nothing to do with being man enough. I have a woman who loves me now, kids who need me. I don't want to kill him. I want to kill her. Who are you going to listen to, God or Satan? I am *not* a killer. What do I do? Get out of here before they wake up and I'm forced to kill both of them.

He hurried out of the bedroom, across the family room, down the hall. But the doors were locked. He could unlock the house door, but if he tried to open that garage door now, they would hear it and come. What was he thinking? He already knew he wasn't going back out that way. Hurry! Back up the hall he went to the front door. The front door was only used by strangers; everyone else used the entry through the garage or the sliding glass doors in back. He undid the dead bolt and then the door lock, and slipped out. He relocked the door lock on his way out, but couldn't do anything about the deadbolt. If Horay found the deadbolt unlocked, he would think maybe he forgot it. If Maureen found it, she would gripe at Horay for forgetting it. Poor fella: can't win for losing. At least he was still alive.

Dan made a hasty retreat along the Muldanos' hedge, out through the neighbors' grape vineyard and up through the woods. He changed out of the dive suit in his vehicle, then headed home. He was in Aberdeen well before dawn. He *was not* a killer. He stopped at his special spot to stash the .357 magnum pistol and the shotgun. No way did he keep those around home. Brenda was mean enough that she might get a wild hair and tell the cops that she heard he had his firearms at home. He had a camouflage-colored cooler hidden in a thicket back off a side road several miles from his place, where no one would ever find it. It kept the guns and ammo dry.

21

Something's Missing

Dan got home, took a shower, then hit the sack for several hours of sleep. It was a long night. He still had his whole life ahead of him—a future wife... a future with his kids and future grandkids. Everything was okay. He hadn't minimized his options. He was not a killer. What a great feeling. Maybe he was not such a bad guy. Maybe he was not sick—just angry. There were better ways to deal with his anger. Father Michael was right. He needed to listen to his conscience. He needed to listen to God.

At noon he got up to eat and do some chores. He was going to the boys JV and varsity basketball games at the high school at 5:30. He put his clothes on, then grabbed the fanny pack to get his watch. His watch wasn't there. He dug around inside the pack. Not there. He dumped the contents of the pack. No watch. It can't be. Where is the watch? He went to the rig and looked around the back where he changed. No watch. He grabbed everything from the back and went through it. Nothing. He looked over every square inch inside the vehicle. No watch. *No!*

What if the watch is in the Muldanos' closet? He started to panic. Where else could it be? What if it fell out somewhere else in their house? It has to be the closet. That was the last place he handled it. He must not have gotten it all the way in the pack. Those gloves made it hard to feel.

What if they find it? They're going to immediately wonder who it belongs to and how it got in their house. If they show it to Brenda, she'll know it's his. No one else has a watch like that, with one half of the band removed. She knew that Dan used a regular small men's wrist watch, but made it into a pocket watch by removing one side of the band. He doesn't know of anyone else that does that. It's his signature.

If they find it and decide it's his, what will they do? There's no way his watch could, or should, be in their house. Especially since the morning before the big fight, the day Brenda left him for good, he had asked her to bring him that watch from his night stand. Would she remember that? If she did, she would know that this watch was lost in the Muldanos' house after she left him. She knows that he hasn't been in their house since the Christmas blowup over five years ago. How would they think it got there? They would know there is only one way it got there: if he had been in that house. They would call the cops. No doubt about it.

What does he do? It may be too late already. If it fell out any-where other than in that closet, he's screwed. Actually, he's not. What does his watch being there prove? No crime was committed. Nothing was stolen. Dan doesn't know if the police would even question him. Maybe they wouldn't even come out to the Muldanos' to take a report. It's just a watch. So what? But what if they thought that he had entered the house with the intent to commit a crime, or that he entered it while Brenda was there. If he did it while she was there, that would be a violation of the restraining order. They're not going to start an investigation of someone who lives two and a half hours away over a simple alleged violation of a restraining order. They don't have the man power for such things. At least Dan hopes they don't.

If the watch fell out in the closet, chances are good that it wouldn't be found for some time. The Muldanos don't use that closet for anything other than hanging the clothes that don't fit them anymore. Maureen's wanna-be thin clothes, and Horays broad shouldered, barrel-chested suits of old. The shelf above the hanger is a graveyard for Maureen's old shoes and hats. All that stuff should have been hauled off to Goodwill years ago. The only other reason they would ever get into that closet is because one of the two inside-the-house under-floor crawl-space access-openings is in there. At their ages, and in their health, Dan doubts seriously they would be going under the house.

He was going to let it ride for now. He definitely was not going back up there this weekend, and next weekend was out. Windy and the girls were coming up. He couldn't do it during the week, because he couldn't come up with a good reason to be gone overnight. Besides that, Megan had wanted a lot of his help on her U.S. history class work. That was quite a switch. She had never involved him in her homework the way she always dreamed a daughter would. He learned a long time ago, there was no point in forcing those issues. She seemed to want more one on one time with Dan lately than she had for several years. Maybe she realized her time with old Dad was beginning to run out—*maybe quicker than she imagined.*

He couldn't believe how fast the years had gone with both his kids. He had so many good memories with them. Megan was great for making humorous statements when she was dead serious about something.

When she was five and John was eight, Dan was lying on the bed with them one evening, something he often did with the kids, one on each arm. The kids had spent the previous night with Dan's widower father who lived a few miles away. They loved going to his house and spent many nights there; that gave Dan a break as a single father at the time. During the sharing time as they lay there,

John said, "You know Dad, Grandpa's not a bad cook." Before Dan had a chance to ask how he came to that conclusion, Megan piped up, "Yeah, he makes good toast." John and Dan both died laughing, and of course their little runt joined right in with the fun, clue-less that it was her statement that got them going.

Another time when they were about that same age, John and Dan were talking about something that the two of them were going to do. Megan wanted to be included, but John commented that only he and Dad were big enough to do it. Little Megan stretched herself out as tall as she could, stood on her toes, put her hands on her hips, and said, "See how big I am." She wasn't about to let them exclude her based on her size.

22

Candid With Windy

Windy and her girls came up to Dan's the following weekend. The weather was unseasonably warm, so they all went out to the beach. Dan and Windy showed each other plenty of affection, but limited the kissing to short interludes when they were alone. This had to happen gradually. On Saturday afternoon, while they were in the living room by themselves and the girls were outside, Dan brought up some tough stuff to talk to Windy about.

"Windy, do you remember that summer when that boy was killed on his bike on the highway in front of our place?

"Yes, every once in a while something on the news or on a TV program will remind me of that. It was terrible, the worst thing that ever happened around me when I was growing up."

"I talked to you after my folks split up, when we were teens, about all of our animals that were killed on that highway and the duck massacre the summer after the boy was killed. But I never told you certain things that went on in our household when you weren't around. You always saw our family at its best. We always had a lot of fun when you were around."

"What do you mean by that?" she said.

"Well, you didn't see the abuse."

"What abuse?"

"My mom was very abusive. She couldn't handle the pressures and stress of taking care of so many kids day after day. None of our friends ever saw what she sometimes did to us. She was careful to control herself when we had company. Actually, not too many kids came over to our house, at least not in it. We mostly went to their houses to play. When friends were at our place, we usually played in the yard, in the horse pasture, the walnut orchard, or out in the barn. Or we had a private place where we might take that special someone to mess around a little," Dan said, smiling.

"Oh yeah? I bet I know where that place was," she flirted.

"I bet you do too." They giggled like the two school kids they once were.

He let the spontaneous moment linger for a bit, then said, "I feel like you and I are headed for a possible future together. Am I right on that?"

"Yes, you are. I do want a future with you, Dan. From the time we were little kids, I loved you. When we were older teenagers, I often tried to figure out how it would be possible for us to get married some day. I even talked to my mom about it. She told me that cousins can't get married, because any kids they have could end up with serious birth defects. I wanted kids real bad, so I finally convinced myself that there was no way I could marry you—that I needed to quit entertaining the idea. So eventually I did."

"That's so sweet of you to tell me Windy. I loved you too when we were kids, even throughout our adult lives. I love you now. You were always the one that I really wanted to be with. Do you remember the movie 'Forrest Gump'?"

"Yes, I know what you're going to say," she said. "I always thought of you and I whenever I saw Forrest and his girlfriend, the one that cared so much about him. That is a very romantic story of true, unconditional love, don't you think?"

"Yes it is, honey," he said. "But at least I'm a lot smarter than Forrest."

"Yeah, but you aren't nearly as rich."

"Well I didn't have a black friend in the army that was a shrimp expert. And I didn't know a Lieutenant Dan. Does it matter to you that I'm not rich?"

"I want to be rich in love with you, Dan. Being rich materially means little to me."

"I'm glad you think that way, Windy. I do hope to be very wealthy someday. But even if I end up living on the street, if I have you with me, I will have all I need or want."

"You sure know the right things to say to a girl, don't you, Dan?"

"At least with you I do, I guess."

"If we are going to have a future," Dan said. "I feel like I need to tell you a few things that happened to me, and a few things I did. Those are not who I am today, but they lie dormant inside of me, my past. I'm not proud of any of it, and there is plenty of pain there. I'm not going to tell you everything, because I don't need to. Just enough for you to understand some things about me that you never knew of."

"Dan, no matter what happened to you or what you did, I've always known the real you, I believe, far better than anyone else. No one's perfect and we all have skeletons behind us, but what matters is who we are today, and where we go from here."

"I knew you would say that," he said.

He paused, then said, "You remember going to the Catholic Church with us several times, when we were kids, don't you?"

"Yes, I remember that," she answered. "I remember I couldn't wait until mass was over, so we could go dig into the goodies in the coffee room afterwards."

"Yeah, that was the only thing I liked about it. I could never wait to get home to play," said Dan. "Mass was so boring. I never could understand why the Priest had that section each week when he talked in Latin. What good did that do for all of us who couldn't understand it? Even the music during mass was like something out of the dark ages."

"You have that right," she said. "The Christian church my family went to was much better. I actually had fun there," she said.

"Well, after Brenda left me, and I started having so much anger, I realized soon enough that I couldn't get any help or satisfaction from my own pastor. Even the time we went to him to try to get marriage counseling just after we moved to Aberdeen, he was worthless. Said he wasn't qualified to help us, that our situation was too complicated. After the separation began, he proved to be uncompassionate and arrogant. Anyway, that caused me to consider other options for help. I thought back to my childhood, before Mom and Dad divorced, my Catholic background, and decided to go talk to a Catholic Priest in Aberdeen."

"That's interesting. Did he help you?"

"I was very surprised, actually. When I was a kid the priest seemed so formal, a super-spiritual person, the next closest thing to God Himself. He always wore his black robe. He liked kids, but he also knew just how bad they really were, since they told him about all their various sins at confessional.

"I hated going to confessional," he went on. "That long line of people waiting against the wall with the stained glass windows, waiting for their turn to spill their guts, to clear their consciences, to cleanse their souls, so they could go out and sin all over again the next week, or month, or however long it was before they couldn't carry the guilt any longer. Then when it would finally be my turn, I'd step inside behind the heavy purple curtain hanging over the doorway to the booth. I'd get in there and kneel down on a cushioned knee-bench facing this dark screen that separated the priest's room from mine. It was dark in both rooms. There was just enough light to see the form of the father's head. If I didn't already know who it was, I never could have recognized him. We both talked softly. *I did it* so no one outside could possibly hear how bad a sinner I was. Of course, there were a few things I couldn't even admit to the priest. I hate to think where I would have ended up if I died in that condition—probably Purgatory.

"I would say, 'Bless me Father, for I have sinned.' Honestly, I don't remember whether he said something before that or what he said at all. It's just those words that I had to say each time, that stuck in my head all these years. I would then go on to unload my guilt on the father. I never knew how he could even get up off his little seat, or whatever he was on—nobody could possibly kneel that long, even on a cushioned bench, listening to the sins of dozens of people—bearing the weight of all his parishioners' sins.

"I haven't been to confessional since that summer after fifth grade. Dad never made us go to church after we moved in with him. Before Mom divorced him, he only went to church on Easter each year, and that was just to please Mom.

"This priest in Aberdeen who I've been seeing is Father Michael," Dan said. "He didn't get into the priesthood until his late thirties or early forties. I think that's why he's so helpful. He's become a good friend. He's sixty-six. I actually look up to him like an uncle or something."

"That's great Dan. So you've been able to talk to him about everything."

"Well, not exactly. But many things. There are just some things I've seen or done that I can't share with any human. I have to save those for God."

"I understand," she said.

"I'm not going to tell you all the things I've told Father Michael, just enough so you can understand my pain, especially with the way Brenda has handled this whole separation and divorce situation. I hope you don't mind if I call her a bitch."

"It's okay, Dan. From everything I've seen and heard about the situation, I don't think you could put a better label on her."

"I know that's very un-Christian," he said. "But, this separation, restraining order and divorce proceedings have made me feel like anything but a Christian."

"I'm with you there," she agreed. "Since I was the one that filed for my divorce, I don't know if God will ever forgive me."

"Give yourself a break, Windy. You gave Steve many chances to get sober. You spent well over two years worrying yourself sick about his safety. He removed himself from any kind of involvement in yours and the girls' lives or activities a long time ago. He cheated on you. Alcohol became his God. You were fair in your divorce settlement demands. He made the bed that he has to sleep in now. So don't blame yourself."

"Thanks for saying that, Dan. I really needed to hear that, especially from you."

"That's what I want to be here for, at least one of the things."

"And I want to be an encouragement to you, too, Dan. I want to be the person who you can talk to about anything, and know that I will still love you, no matter what."

"That means so much to me, Windy. So now you get your first chance to listen. Are you ready?"

"I'm all ears. I think I would be lying if I said I wasn't a little curious."

"From the time I was old enough to remember, Mom used to take time each day for herself," he said. "She wouldn't pay attention to anything any of us kids said or did, unless we were fighting, or hurt. She shut us out completely; gave us the silent treatment. Acted like we were invisible and that she couldn't hear a word we said. It didn't matter what we wanted. This lasted an hour or two each day during the afternoon, often while she watched her soap operas. She sometimes picked other times of day to do it, too, whenever she felt like disappearing. It was a terribly rude and insensitive way to treat us."

"That's hard to believe a mother would do that," said Windy. "During our teen years, I sometimes saw a couple of my girl friends do something similar to a boy that was pursuing them, and occasionally to a boy friend. Just shut them out and ignore them, not answer their phone calls, that sort of thing. I thought it was childish. In a way it is saying, 'you're not on my level, so I'm not going to waste my time talking or listening to you.'"

"I wish that was the worst of it. And believe me that was plenty painful," he said. "Mom often choked us kids. I got it the most. She couldn't stand crying, so sometimes it pushed her over the edge. She would grab the crier and cover their mouth with her hand, which also blocked the nose. We couldn't breathe. It was terrible. Gasping for air, struggling with our arms and legs flailing—"

"You gotta be kidding me, Dan."

"I'm not kidding one bit."

"What did you do?"

"What *could we do*? She was much bigger and stronger."

"Did you see each other being choked?"

"Yes. It was horrible. But we had all learned at an early age not to get involved unless we wanted the same treatment."

"So what did you do?"

"We cried as quietly as we could, and hoped she would stop before our sibling was dead. When you're a kid, you don't understand the mechanics of death-by suffocation: that a person will always pass out from lack of oxygen at least a few minutes before they would die. Mom always seemed to quit when the kid finally stopped struggling. They were too weak from not getting any air. I don't know that any of us ever actually passed out. We weren't in any danger of dying. But we didn't know that then."

"Dan, that is so sad," she said with tears on her cheeks. His eyes filled too. "How could she do that?"

"You're asking the wrong person," he answered. "You know what is funny?"

"Nothing could be funny about that."

"No, I mean what's ironic," said Dan. "The last year before Mom died, when she had Alzheimer's, she often asked me, 'What kind of a parent was I? Was I a good parent?'

"What was I supposed to say? 'No, you abused the hell out of us.' Instead, I said, 'Mom, you loved all of your kids. You did the best you could, like every other mom.' Maybe that was the truth. I don't know. Was she a good parent? I'll let you judge that one."

"I'm so sorry, Dan. I had no idea. Your mom was always so sweet to me when I was around."

"She was good at hiding her real self for short periods of time. Even when you were there, she sometimes snarled at us, while giving us the evil eye, when she knew you or any other kids weren't nearby. She was very controlling. Her snarls and look communicated to us: 'You damned-well better mind me, even with your friends here, or else.' We did our best to behave when company was around because, even though she had never choked any of us when friends were there, who wanted to take a chance of having your friend see that?"

"I can't imagine what that was like for you guys. I guess I can understand why you didn't bring friends over to your house much."

"Yeah, but boy I loved the neighbor's chicken house," he said, laughing to lighten the mood. She laughed. She hugged him, held him tight. It felt so good. All he ever wanted was a female's unconditional love and acceptance. He thinks he has finally found it.

Dan was going to tell Windy more, tell her about being locked out in the dark, being beaten with a baseball bat, torturing the neighbors' animals, and being renamed "Vamp," but somehow, he didn't think he needed to. At least not then.

"Windy, with you holding me, I don't feel the need to talk about the painful stuff from my childhood anymore. Maybe I will another time. Do you mind?"

"I'm fine with not knowing. If you need to tell me later some time, for you, then I will gladly listen. I know what kind of a man you are, just the kind of man I want."

23

At the Muldanos'

Dan couldn't take the worrying anymore. He had to get his watch, or at least try to get it. Since he hadn't been questioned by the cops about it, he assumed that it either hadn't been found, or, so far, the law hadn't decided it was worth pursuing. If he could find it first, no more worries.

He was not looking forward to another trip to the Monroe-Everett area. It was too sad for him to go back to his old stomping grounds—too many painful memories. Knowing Brenda was there and didn't love him anymore, none of his siblings lived there anymore and both of his parents were dead. It was a lot to face. But he had to. He had to find that watch.

If he could get in the Muldanos' house, find his watch, and get out, he could rest at ease knowing none of that family could ever accuse him of a crime again. In several weeks, when the twelve months was up on Brenda's restraining order, she would have no grounds to get another. She wouldn't have any more control over him. Neither would Maureen.

Dan thought: Maureen is one lucky woman. I could have killed her at the Waldens'. I could have killed her on Thanksgiving. I could have killed her three weeks ago. There is still part of me that would like to put her in a begging position now. But I don't need to kill her anymore. I have a good life to look forward to. She still has to live with her misery. Only a very miserable person could treat other people the way she does. I'm not like her. I don't have to let my anger, the pain of my past, or the pain of rejection, control me anymore. Thank God I didn't go through with any of the violence. I am a good man. I don't care what you think about me anymore, Maureen.

The second Friday afternoon in March, on the 10th, two weeks after Windy and the girls were at Dan's and three weeks after he went to the Muldanos' house to kill them, he drove up to the hills southeast of Monroe and went through the same routine as he did twice before. They say third time's a charm. He hoped so. That would mean, he found his watch, got out with no problems and lives the rest of his life free of that family and the hell it caused him.

He waited until well after dark in the woods above the Muldanos' neighbors. At 8:50, he crossed through the grape vineyard. When he was a kid, he and his siblings, along with the neighbor kids, loved to hit all the local grape vineyards and other various fruit and nut trees, as well as the berry patches to eat whatever was in season from early summer through early-fall.

At 9:04, Dan snuck into the garage by his usual route. Maureen's truck was the only vehicle there. He wondered if Horay was gone, or perhaps his truck was in the shop. Dan knew that for years, if the two of them went anywhere together, they took her pickup. She— with the impeccable driving record, *NOT*—didn't trust Horay's driving, plus she liked to be in control of that too.

Dan got to the door to the house and found it unlocked. He eased in quietly, went into the small bedroom, shut the door most the way, and went directly to the closet. Hallelujah! There it was, his watch, laying in a well-shaded back-corner, where only a person specifically looking for it would have seen it. His worries were over. He heard no activity in the house as he moved back toward the door. Even the television wasn't on. That was odd. They have that TV on every night.

Just as he grabbed the door handle to open it, he saw red and blue lights flashing around on the wall inside the little room's window. What's going on? He panicked. He stuck his head out into the hallway, and still heard nothing. No one was moving, or talking. Then there was a loud rap on the front door, followed immediately by, "Snohomish County Sheriff." The lights were still flashing on the wall of the little bedroom. Was this a trap? Had they been watching him all along, waiting for him to make a false move, so they could nail him? What was he going to do?

Another hard knock on the front door, "Snohomish County Sheriff, will you open up?" He heard voices around back, it sounded like they were near the double glass sliding doors. From the sound of things there had to be at least two cops out back. He heard tapping on the glass doors that sounded like a flashlight hitting the glass. The cop out front was working the door knob, trying to get in. No one seemed to be trying to come through the garage door, the one that was unlocked.

I've got to hide, he thought, but where? I'm sure they will search the whole house. *The access hatch... under the house...* my only chance.

He lunged for the closet, struggled to get a grip under the edge of the lid, finally got it up where he could get through, and quickly dropped down under the house. It was cool and dark under there. At once, he pulled the hatch back over the top, into place... and he listened. Immediately, he heard cops coming in through the garage door. They moved in deliberately, checking each room as they advanced up the hall, guns drawn.

Are they looking for me? Dan wondered. He pulled his Mag-Lite out of his jacket pocket and shined it around to orient himself, to determine where he could hide if he had to.

"There's a woman in here," an officer said. "She's down. She's bleeding real bad."

He strained to hear what was said. He stayed near the hatch, but was ready to make a quick lunge away from it into the dark behind supporting posts if the cops came near.

"No pulse. She's dead. She hasn't been dead long." Whose dead, he wanted to yell? Is it Brenda? He still had love for her somewhere behind all that pain. Is it Maureen? Who is it?

"The house is clear," a cop said. They talked freely now. It sounded like several cops were there.

"We've got a deceased white female, short, black hair, age approximately seventy-five, extremely obese, with a severe gash to the back of the head, it appears her neck may be broken. No other visible injuries."

It sounded like the officer was reporting to a dispatcher. Dan breathed a sigh of relief. It's not Brenda. It must be Maureen. As much as he wanted to kill Brenda himself, he realized now that he really didn't want her to be dead. He has no sorrow over Maureen being dead. How did she die, he wondered?

"See if you can find some identification," one deputy said to another. "Dispatch says the 911 call was made by what sounded like a male, someone who was obviously disguising his voice. It came from a pay phone on Brigham Street. The caller said someone was seriously hurt at this address. They didn't give any other details. When the dispatcher asked for the person to stay on the line to give more information, he hung up."

"I found a purse," reported another deputy. "There's ID, a driver's license. Maureen Adel Muldano." He walked over to the woman lying lifeless on her back with a large pool of blood soaking into the tan-colored shag carpet, and looked at her.

"That's her," he said.

Dan wished his hearing was better. He lifted the hatch on the backside to listen. He continued to strain to hear the officers' words.

The bitch is dead, he thought, and I didn't even do it. Someone called this in? Why didn't they call it in from the house here? Was it Horay? Maybe that's why his truck is gone. Thoughts raced through Dan's mind. Maybe he and Maureen had a fight and it got out of hand. If it *was* Horay, where could he have gone? If it wasn't Horay, who was it? If it was a stranger, maybe a burglar, he wouldn't have called it in would he? Maybe he would have, if he just wanted money, and ended up in over his head. If the guy has a conscience, maybe he could have called it in.

"Dispatch says she is married to a Horacio Mateo Muldano, age eighty-two, six foot two, 190 pounds, gray hair, brown eyes, wears glasses. He drives a blue 2001 Chevy half-ton pickup, Washington license plate BLV 457. That vehicle is not here now."

"Does she have any other family living in the area?"

"Dispatch is looking that up right now. The CSI unit will be here in twenty minutes."

A couple of passersby pulled their cars up to the edge of the driveway. A sheriff's deputy strung yellow crime scene ribbon across the driveway, and then stood guard to keep curiosity seekers out and to raise and lower the tape as necessary to let law enforcement vehicles pass. The neighbors, who had walked over to the Muldanos' driveway, asked what happened. They were told "a woman is dead," but no other details were revealed. The cops questioned the neighbors to get information about the Muldanos.

"She was a very friendly woman," one lady said, "until you offended her."

"That didn't take much," said the man with the woman.

"Are you husband and wife?" asked the deputy.

"Yes, we live right there." He pointed to an older house, lighted by a couple of flood lights, a hundred yards down the road—the one with the grape vineyards adjoining the Muldanos' property.

"I take it you offended her," said the deputy, seeing potential motive.

"Yes. Some of her grand kids were over running around in our grapes like there was a war going on several years back," said the woman. "We simply asked her if she could have the kids chill out a little and quit all the yelling and screaming, making all the gun sounds. We didn't even mind that they played out there, or helped themselves to all the grapes they wanted. She thought we were way too sensitive. Said kids will be kids; one of those women whose grandkids can do no wrong. I'm sure you know the type."

"What is her husband like?" said the deputy.

"He can be a bit edgy, too, but generally he doesn't say much," said the man, "especially in recent years. I think he had some problems with dementia."

"How long have you known the Muldanos?

"We moved here in 1980, they were here then. So, what's that, twenty-five years or so."

"They have a few family get-togethers here a year, a huge family," she said.

"Do any of the family live local, in Snohomish County?" asked the deputy.

"Yes, I know her oldest daughter lives in Everett. She's going through *another* divorce right now. She moved back within the last six months or so. She was living near Aberdeen. Actually, she and her daughter lived here at her mom's for a couple months, but it didn't work out. One son also lives in Hamilton.

"Do you know the daughter and son's names?"

"The son is Denny, and the daughter is Brenda. I can't tell you the last names. I know that Horay is the step-dad, so the son's name is not Muldano," said the woman. "I know that Horay has a real son who lives somewhere in the area, but I don't know his name or where he lives. I've never talked to him, and his parents have only mentioned him a few times. I think they have a strained relationship. I don't know any more than that."

As they were speaking, the CSI (Crime Scene Investigating) Team arrived to process the scene. They went in and questioned the deputies in the house regarding the basics, name, age, etc. Then they began taking photos, dusting for prints, and looking for all possible evidence.

24

Brenda Arrives at Scene

Dan waited below knowing it would be a long night, and then some, before he had a prayer of escaping. Not a good way to cover his alibi situation. And he had no water or food. At least he had his heavy jacket on.

"Dispatch has contacted both of Mrs. Muldano's children who live in the area. They are on the way," said the deputy who was talking with dispatch.

That means Brenda will be here in twenty minutes or so, Dan thought. This will be rough on her. What do I care? She deserves any pain she has to suffer. With all she's done to me, and not one show of regret or remorse. Yeah, she deserves this pain. Maybe she'll know where Horay is.

One CSI guy, Spike, said, "She was moved from where she initially landed. See that blood smattering on the end table there." He pointed to the table, four-feet away from her body. "There's a five-inch pool next to the table leg, and a light blood trail on the carpet going from there to the blood surrounding her head."

"Why would they move the body?" the other CSI guy, Tom, asked.

"It doesn't make sense to me," said CSI Spike. "Whoever moved her, was strong, and moved her in one smooth pull. But why?"

"With the way she hit that table and landed, her neck was broken. The worst thing the guy could have done was move her," said CSI Tom. "Maybe he panicked."

"That's my guess. That would suggest it was someone who knew her. Would her husband be strong enough to move her? Dispatch reported that his driver's license describes him as six-two and 190 pounds, but he's also eighty-two, and she is a very heavy woman," said Spike.

"A little adrenalin rush can add a lot of strength," said Tom. "If it was someone who knew her, there was probably a lot more than a little adrenalin flowing."

"What does dispatch know about the 911 caller?" Spike asked the lead sheriff's deputy, Sergeant Allen.

"Said it sounded like a male who was disguising his voice," said Allen.

"Well, there's no doubt the body was moved by a strong male. That's undoubtedly your 911 caller," said Spike. "If it was an accident, where she just tripped, fell backwards and hit her head, the guy wouldn't have left would he?"

"It's doubtful, unless there's something about him that he was afraid would raise suspicions about it being an accident in the first place," said Sergeant Allen.

"Still, it's hard to see a friend or relative leaving their family member here alone in critical condition," CSI Tom said.

"That doesn't add up to an accident, does it?" Spike said.

Brenda arrived with her third oldest son, Leroy. Her face was soaked and red from all her tears. She walked unsteadily up the walkway to the front door, leaning against Leroy. He was never very close to his grandmother, though he connected well with Horay.

Brenda was unable to reach her other local area son, Conner. His wife said he went to lift weights at the gym, and after that was getting together with his buddies for their monthly card game. He wasn't answering his cell phone. The wife said that wasn't unusual. When Conner played cards he didn't want to be bothered. He figured that once-a-month guy-time was his exclusive time. Conner's wife takes advantage of that night herself by getting together with a few girl friends for movies and goodies. With her beautiful figure, she could afford the goodies, even if Conner couldn't.

Brenda didn't dare bring Jackie, who was spending the night at a friend's anyway. Brenda didn't know how she would break the news to her; she will be crushed no matter how she's told.

As Brenda entered the house, she saw her mom lying on the floor fifteen feet ahead of her, just off to the right of the entryway that joins the family room to the dining area. She fell to the floor sobbing, "Mom! Mom!" Leroy knelt down beside her, and put his arm around her back. He hurt deeply for his mom; his eyes filled with tears.

Sergeant Allen helped Leroy get Brenda onto a couch in the living room, out of sight of her mom's corpse. Then he left them alone to grieve. It was obvious they had correctly identified Maureen. The dispatcher told Brenda over the phone that Horay wasn't at the house. Brenda didn't know his whereabouts. He could arrive at any minute unless, of course, he was involved in the accident, or whatever it was. Then he might not show up at all.

The dispatcher put out an All-Points-Bulletin (APB) for one Horacio Mateo Muldano, driving a blue 2001 half-ton Chevy pickup, license plate BLV457. For now Horay made sense as the number one suspect. Husbands often are, especially when they are unaccounted for at the time immediately following the murder. This may not be a murder at all, but they were sure as heck treating it like one. That 911 call had murder, or at least non-accident, written all over it.

One problem the detectives would be up against if a friend or relative was involved was that fingerprints and DNA at the scene would mean little-to-nothing. If they were able to find either on the victim or the victim's clothing, however, that could be strong evidence.

Sergeant Allen allowed Brenda several minutes to cry and regain some composure before taking a seat in the chair beside her. After he explained the importance of gaining the information immediately, he began questioning her. He encouraged Leroy to jump in any time he wanted, but Leroy had never been one for conversation—definitely not with strangers. Both CSI specialists and one other deputy listened in as they continued searching for evidence.

Since there were no signs of a struggle in the house, Horay's pickup was missing, and the 911 call was made, the deputies were almost certain that Horay had *not* been abducted. "Do you have any idea where your father is?" Allen asked her.

"I don't know," said Brenda. "He's my step-father. He's always here with Mom at this time of night."

"So your mom didn't say anything to you about him going anywhere tonight?"

"No, she didn't. I haven't talked to her in a few days."

"Have they had any problems lately?"

"What do you mean?"

"Any problems getting along, any fights?"

"Why are you asking me that? Do you consider him a suspect?"

"I'm sorry; we have to consider all the possibilities. Someone called 911 at 8:58 tonight and reported a seriously injured person at this address. We got here and found your mom. The dispatcher reported that the person making the call was disguising his voice. Said it definitely sounded like a male. Your step-father is gone. No one knows where he's at, apparently. We have to consider him a possible suspect."

"I understand," Brenda said.

"Now, can you tell me if they've had any recent arguments?"

"Honestly, they have never gotten along very well. But he would never hurt her."

"A neighbor out front told one of our deputies that he has had some problems with dementia the last few years. Is that true?" said Sergeant Allen.

"Just in the last two years. It hasn't amounted to much. He would still never hurt her. He loves her."

"When you say it hasn't amounted to much, what do you mean?"

"He's had some problems, at times, getting confused and not remembering things.

"Has there been any violence?"

"No," she hesitated, "well, he shoved her once, I guess. At least that's what Mom said." She started crying again. Sergeant Allen waited a minute, while she wiped her eyes and cheek with a white tissue.

When she had pulled herself together, Allen asked, "Has any of the family observed him during one of his demented phases?"

"Yes, a few times. The thing that disturbed us was his free use of swear words. He's never been a curser. He's always been a religious man, for as long as I've known him, anyway. The person you should be looking at is my soon-to-be ex-husband."

Now she's done it, Dan said to himself. I can't believe this. After all she's done to hurt me. Now she's implicating me in her mother's death. I'd like to get my hands on her. Well, I guess it hasn't been any secret how I felt about Maureen. I'm sure some of the threatening things I've said have even gotten back to Brenda. Still, to hear with my own ears, my once lovely wife, point her finger at me as the probable killer of her mother. *I'm down here.* Obviously I didn't do it. Maybe I should climb out of here and tell them that myself. That's a smart idea. Crap, I'm down here, and she's going to have cops at my door before the night is over. When they can't find me… crap.

Surely they won't suspect that I hiked down here from the

woods, and send squad cars up in the hills around here looking for my vehicle. No, that's why I parked there. No one would think of that. I hope not.

"Why do you think your husband would be responsible?"

"He couldn't get along with my mom from the day we were married."

That's nice Brenda. Make it sound like it was my fault we couldn't get along. Your mom is dead, *now you have to cut* that umbilical cord. Quit defending her, and for once try to see things for the way they were. Didn't you listen to anything your brothers and nephew said on Thanksgiving?

"What is your husband's name?" asked Sergeant Allen.

"Dan Thurmond. Daniel Paul Thurmond, but everyone knows him as Dan. He lives in Aberdeen."

"Do you have an address and telephone number for him?" Allen asked.

"He lives at 32655 River Tree Road. The phone is 360-563-0852."

"Did your husband make threats against your mom?"

"Not to me, but I heard by the grapevine that he told some people he was going to make her pay."

"Pay for what?"

"For interfering in our family and breaking up our marriage."

"Did she do that?" he said, trying to get his hands on a solid motive.

"Well, she has always involved herself in her kids' lives more than she should." She's side-stepping his question. For crying out loud, Brenda, your mom can't do anything to you anymore. Be a big girl and tell it like it was.

"Dan didn't like the way she thought she could do or say whatever she wanted to anybody in our family. He and I often ended up at odds over things my mom said and did. Many times I actually agreed with him. But most the time, I couldn't take sides against my own Mom."

"Did your husband and your mom have any recent arguments or contact that you know of?"

"She hasn't spoken to him in over six years." (You mean she hasn't said anything nice to me, Dan said under his breath.) "They had a big blowup at her Christmas Dinner here at Mom's in 1999. The relatives were here. It got ugly. She jumped down his throat about a bunch of things. He stood there and took it. She was right in his face. It was terrible. At the time I was in deep turmoil inside. How could my mom be ripping my beloved husband to shreds, and to do it in front of the whole family, the kids? I was actually proud of Dan for keeping his mouth shut." That's funny you never told me that, Dan thought. Instead, after we left, you gave me a royal butt chewing.

"Finally, Dan spoke up and said to Mom, 'At least I'm not a gossip.' I hated him for it, but he was right. He wasn't a gossip, and she was the Queen of gossip. She finally went outside, but then problems escalated between my oldest son and Dan. It started to get physical."

"What do you mean by that?"

"I don't want to get into that now. My mom's lying over there on the floor. I don't want to talk anymore." She broke down and wept. Leroy held her hands in his on her lap. Her tears dripped onto both of their hands.

Sergeant Allen figured he had bothered her enough and that he had the information he needed for now. He got up from the chair and then asked one of the other deputies and the CSI guys to follow him. As they walked into the small bedroom above Dan, he eased the hatch down and lunged in behind the posts, back where a flashlight beam from the access opening wouldn't illuminate him.

"What do you guys think, does it look like definite foul play to you?" asked Allen.

"There's no doubt about it, as far as we're concerned," said Spike, speaking for both CSI guys.

"I agree with them Sergeant, the physical evidence of her being moved and the 911 call don't fit an accident scenario," said the other deputy.

"We all agree then that it wasn't just an accident. Now, as I see it, from talking to the daughter and the neighbors, I think we have two strong suspect possibilities, right off the bat. The dead woman's husband, Horacio Muldano, and the daughter's estranged husband, Dan Thurmond. We don't want to limit our focus to those two, of course, but they both have motive. We need to get someone over to Brigham Street, where the call was made from, right away to try to locate anybody that might have seen the 911 caller," said Sergeant Allen.

"I'll make a call right now, sir," said Deputy Rhinehart. "We're outside Monroe city limits here, but the call was made inside the limits. We can get some help on Brigham Street from the Monroe Police."

"Be sure and tell them to secure the area around the phone booth so we can get CSI over there right away to dust for prints," said Allen.

"Yes sir, Sergeant." He went in the other room to make the call.

The CSI guys left the room and continued their crime scene investigation. Sergeant Allen went out to talk to Brenda's youngest brother, Denny, who had just arrived from Hamilton. Denny didn't provide anymore information than the sergeant had already gleaned from Brenda.

Dan moved back under the hatch, so he could hear what he could.

The coroner arrived and removed Maureen's body after the deputies and CSI guys had completed gathering evidence from the area immediately around the corpse. Brenda wept as her mom's body was lifted onto the gurney and taken outside. Brenda wanted desperately for Horay to show up. She loved him, despite the problems he had getting along with her mom. She wanted to know he wasn't involved. And she needed him here to comfort her. He was the only father she had known for the past thirty years.

With Horay gone, it looks like he might be guilty, thought Dan. I wanted to kill Maureen and make it look like he did it. Now I think he actually did do it. But here I am not at home, and I have no alibi. Boy did I pick the wrong night to not be at home. I'm sure the Grays Harbor County Sheriff's Office already received the call to get officers out to my place to see if I'm home. They're probably there right now. Not finding me there, they'll probably hide out in the bushes nearby to wait for me to come home, then ambush me. If they had found me home, I couldn't have been involved.

Judging by the condition of the blood, and Maureen's body temperature, the CSI guys determined that the mishap occurred around 8:40 pm.

It was now 10:30. Both of Dan's watches said so. Thank God I found my watch, he thought. I couldn't have arrived more than fifteen minutes after the killer left. Now I just have to wait it out and get out of here when I know the coast is clear. I only hope that no one finds my rig up in the hills above here. If the cops find it, they will stake it out and do a relentless search throughout the hills, here on the Muldanos' property, on Ben-Howard Road, and maybe even under the house. They won't give up until they find me. But will they even look in the hills? Since I came by way of the hedge again, I know I didn't leave any footprints anywhere near the house.

It was beginning to rain hard outside. Even with the vents closed off for the winter, Dan could hear it coming down. If they didn't find his rig, he would still have to drive the roads over the hills to the Carnation-Duvall Highway then out to I-5, go south to Chehalis and then over to the coast highway so he comes into Aberdeen from the south. That route would take him a couple hours out of his way, but he didn't want any local cops to see him coming from the east. He could only hope that the Washington State Troopers wouldn't be looking for him. Horay had to be the prime suspect, since he hadn't shown up.

Dan knew he was in for a tough go, trying to convince the law that he wasn't involved. If they could just find Horay and get a confession from him, Dan's worries would be over. Poor old guy, he just couldn't get anything right with her. Maybe he had a final break from reality and won't even know who he is let alone who any of his family is. That would be nice for him, they could put him in an old folks' institution and let him live out his demented days. But where would that leave Dan?

Brenda, Leroy and Denny finally left the house around 11 pm. A couple of officers were still milling around looking for clues. Earlier, they were in the little bedroom for a few minutes. Dan got sick to his stomach considering what would have happened if he hadn't gotten there when he did and retrieved his watch. That would have been damning evidence of his presence in the house. He doubted the fingerprints would have been of any value, too many, all smudged together. But Brenda would have been able to identify the watch, and the thing would have been loaded with his skin cells for getting DNA samples.

Dan heard the cops in the bedroom across the hall, the one used as a study, talking about the locked gun safe. Brenda told them she didn't know where Horay kept the key. Apparently they plan to leave a deputy on the site for a couple of days, or until Horay comes home, whichever occurs first. Dan hoped the old man got back soon. Either way, Dan was going to be very dehydrated before he got out.

If he had to be there too long, he would have to get creative with one of the water pipes. He had his hunting knife with the saw back on it. Trouble was, he couldn't make any noise that would be heard above the floor. He would have to saw slowly. Just long enough to get a tiny leak going.

He took the insulation covering off of several cold water pipes to allow them to gather condensation. He would lick them for the time being. Dan wondered if there could possibly be a faucet valve down there somewhere. Very unlikely.

In the next twenty-four hours, the Monroe police were unable to locate a single person who remembered seeing someone making a call from the phone where the 911 call was made. None of the residents on Ben-Howard Road were paying any attention to vehicles that traveled that road last night, so no vehicle descriptions were obtained. The fact that it was dark didn't help. The APB on Horacio Muldano's truck produced nothing. Nor has anyone heard hide, nor hair from him.

The family was very worried. Many of them feared Horay was guilty of pushing Maureen down and causing her death. They suspected that he was either hiding somewhere, or was having more serious problems with his dementia. Some family members wondered why they couldn't see this coming.

The police didn't know what to think. Both of their initial suspects were still missing, with no explanation. No one in the family believed Dan and Horay could be in on the homicide together. But it sure was a coincidence that neither of them could be found. Megan and John were still at their grandma's, oblivious to Maureen's death and their dad's predicament, so they were no help. The police didn't know the grandmother lived in Olympia, or even who she was.

Dan had been sucking on cold pipes, getting enough moisture to avoid total dehydration, but was concerned that if he was stuck under the house much longer, he would have to break into a pipe. The problem with that was sooner or later someone would figure out there was a leak under the house, come down, find his work, get suspicious, and maybe call the cops, that is, if the whole thing wasn't settled by then. The cops would come out, gather up DNA and fingerprints, which Dan was leaving plenty of, and they would have him. Plenty of innocent people were on death row for crimes they didn't commit. He didn't want to be one of them.

25

Back To Aberdeen

On Sunday, the second day after Maureen's Friday night death, the cops decided Horay wasn't about to come home. They pulled the deputy from the property at about 5 pm. The coroner's exam and autopsy revealed that Maureen's neck was, in fact, broken and that she had multiple fingertip-sized bruises on her chest, just above her breasts. No other clues turned up. Surprisingly, *no tumors* were found *in her brain*, eliminating that as the possible cause of all her bitching and gossiping. The chest bruises confirmed the CSI specialists' theory that she was pushed. There was no doubt there was some kind of foul play, but the detectives could only speculate about the circumstances. They were convinced it was someone that knew her, argued with her, pushed her, moved her after she was down and probably unconscious, and then left immediately when they couldn't get her to respond. From there the person drove to Monroe, where they made the 911 call. Horay looked like the best candidate because he had never been missing before.

The Snohomish County Sheriff's CSI team came up with some

finger prints from the phone on Brigham Street, but so far the prints didn't match any in the police computer files. Of course, whoever made the call could have worn gloves, or covered the receiver handle with something to avoid direct contact.

All the relatives had been questioned. Other than Horay and Dan, the only other family member mentioned as someone having a distinctly rough history with Maureen was Edward. They finally reached him at home at 6:30 Sunday evening. He had no solid alibi for the night of the crime. He said he spent Friday and Saturday nights camped alone on a ridge near Troublesome Creek on the north fork of the Skykomish River east of Goldbar. He arrived home with his camping gear at four Sunday afternoon. He said he saw no one else on the trail and that he parked his car in an out-of-the-way location so no one would find it—too much chance for a break in.

Dan managed to escape to his vehicle through the grape vineyard and woods just after dark on Sunday evening, shortly after six. No cops were around the property by then. He was hurting for fresh air by the time he pushed the access cover out of the way. It reminded him of when they opened the hatches to the submarine after a long stint at sea. Those first gulps of fresh air were like heaven. The air on the submarine was much better, though, than what he just breathed for two days.

He pulled into his Aberdeen driveway at 12:45 am. Immediately, bright lights shined in his eyes from both sides of the drive. A flashlight banged on his window. He couldn't see anything. He rolled down his window. "Are you Daniel Paul Thurmond?" said the form outside the window?

"Yes, I am."

"Get out of the car. Keep your hands out where we can see them, then place them on the top of the car." Dan half expected this. He had nothing to hide. He did what he was told. Three Grays Harbor County Sheriff's deputies surrounded him. One frisked him.

He didn't know they had stopped his kids in the same manner, four hours earlier upon their return from the grandmother's house in Olympia. The kids were asked where their dad was, but weren't given any details. They had no idea where he was. But they worried themselves sick about him as they waited at the house after being stopped in the driveway.

"What's going on?" Dan asked.

"You are a suspect in the death of Maureen Muldano," said Sergeant Lang.

"That's my mother-in-law. She's dead?"

"Don't play dumb with us Thurmond. Where have you been?" Dan thought a man was innocent until proven guilty. They seemed to already have him headed to the electric chair. But he had plenty of time to plan for them.

"I was staying out in the woods near Rainbow Falls on the Willapa River."

They saw his sleeping bags, rolled up pad, and a blanket in the back of the vehicle, which supported his claim of being camped. From late fall through early spring he routinely kept those supplies, along with plenty of food and water, in the rig in case he ever got stranded.

"What happened to my mother-in-law?"

"We think you know exactly what happened?" said the oldest deputy.

"Why would I know?"

"Your wife believes you are guilty."

"She's divorcing me; that does not make me guilty of anything, other than being *her fourth discard.*"

"Maybe not, but you had motive and opportunity."

"Am I being arrested?"

"Right now we're just going to question you. So pull your vehicle up to the house and park it. The deputies will do a thorough search of the vehicle; we have a warrant to do so. You'll walk to the house with us. After you greet your kids, we'd like them to go into another room while we talk to you." One of the deputies got in the passenger side of his vehicle and rode the short distance to the house.

They didn't have a warrant to search the house. Deputies had originally arrived there before Dan would have had time to get back from Monroe, if in fact he was there and had committed the crime. He couldn't have hidden any evidence in the house, or anywhere else on the place. Two deputies had already come into the house, with the kids' naïve permission, and looked through his bedroom and office. Nothing they could have found would incriminate him, anyway. He had never written down any of his plans of violence for the Muldano clan or anyone else. Fortunately, the deputies that did the superficial search didn't make a big mess like they always seemed to do on TV cop shows.

The deputies who searched Dan's vehicle, took all his clothes, footwear, sleeping bags, pad, and his *Pig Boats* book, anything they might be able to get a clue from—such as carpet fibers, clothing fibers from the clothes Maureen was wearing when she died, or any other materials that would have come from the Muldanos' house. In the house, they had him strip and they took everything he was wearing. They also took his hunting knife and Mag light, which he had thoroughly cleaned off.

When he had gotten back to his vehicle, he changed his clothes and footwear, then bagged them up. He then stopped at a landing in the woods ten miles away, on his way out to the Carnation-Duvall Road, and buried the bag underground back in the brush. He didn't mind losing the clothes, but burying that jacket was painful. It was a nice wool/cotton lined cold-weather special that he bought the first winter after they moved to the coast. It had cost him $95. Maybe when all of the drama played out, he would go back and get it.

After talking to Dan for forty minutes, mostly about his background as it related to the Muldanos, Brenda, and the relational problems they'd had, his account of his whereabouts and what he did over the weekend, the deputies left. He was honest with them about all the family and marital friction, confrontations, and his frustration regarding the restraining order against him. They could verify those details with many people anyway. However, he wasn't about to tell them anything that indicated how strong his motivation had actually been to carry out violence against certain family members, or two people from his old church. Nor was he going to ever admit to being in the Muldanos' house twice, with the intent to kill, since November first of last year. He discerned that they sensed they weren't getting everything that was there, but what could they do about it? They said he would be asked to come down to the station for further questioning in a day or two, and they advised him to consider getting a lawyer.

After the cops left, Dan called Windy, waking her from a deep sleep, to tell her what had happened with the police. She was shocked. She asked if he and the kids were okay and if there was anything she could do. He told her she could pray. He let her know that the sheriff's investigative team would be talking to him in a couple of days, because he was considered a prime suspect. He assured her that he had nothing to do with it, that they were interested in him because of the restraining order and all of the problems he had getting along with Maureen.

Of course, he didn't tell Windy that he was in the house when Maureen's body was discovered. He needed her support now more than ever. She told him she would stand by him no matter what. She also said she and the girls would come up the following weekend.

26

Man in the Woods

On Tuesday, March 14th, at 4:07 pm, four days after Maureen Muldano's death, the Washington State Police (WSP) received a phone call from a couple of older teen-age boys about an old man they spotted a half hour earlier along Clear Creek Road, southeast of Darrington, which is approximately thirty-five miles northeast of Monroe, as the crow flies, but many more than that by road.

The boys had been down one of the side roads off Clear Creek Road plunking cans with their twenty-twos, and were on their way out when they ran across the big man walking along the road. When they didn't see any vehicle, they decided to stop and see if the old guy was okay. He told them he was fine, that he was just out in the woods enjoying himself; he used to be a logger. He seemed fine to them, just an old, foul-mouthed, ex-logger—could have been either of their grandpa's. They wouldn't have called it in at all, except that when they mentioned the old man to a friend upon their return to Darrington, the friend told them he had heard on the news that an old Monroe man was missing.

Horay, with his logging-woodsman background, knew his way around in the wilds. If he had any of his senses about him, he could survive indefinitely on what he could get from nature—*if* he had his senses about him. But did he? Why was he out there, if it was him, and why hadn't he contacted anyone in his family in four days?

At 4:45 pm two Washington State Troopers in their four-wheel-drive pickups pulled onto Clear Creek Road. It would be dark in a little over an hour; they hoped to locate the old man before that. The Snohomish County area Muldano-Gregory families had been notified about the possible sighting minutes after the WSP had gotten the call from the boys. They were asked if anyone knew why Horay would be in that area. Was it a family hunting spot, or anything like that? Were any family members familiar with the area? If it was Horay, would they know where up there he was most likely to be? None of the contacted family members knew anything about the area. They wouldn't be of any help. Brenda and Manuel both volunteered to go out there, but were told not to, at least not unless they were instructed to do so later.

If the law did locate the old man and it turned out to be Horay, there was no telling what would transpire. If he had shoved his wife and knew she was dying when he left her, would he give up peacefully, or would he start shooting at them? Did he even have firearms with him? The last thing the WSP wanted was a family member getting in the line of fire. However, they also knew that if things came to a face off, a family member or two might be able to reason with him, though it would have to be from a safe vantage point, and only at their direction.

A Snohomish County Sheriff's deputy that had come from Van Horn, arrived in the area just after the other two. He was instructed to wait at the lower end of Clear Creek Road, near the two mile marker, to hopefully, ensure that Muldano didn't drive out of the area from behind the troopers. All of the lawmen had topographic maps of the area as well as the description and license number of Muldano's pickup. However, they couldn't rule out the possibility of him being in a different vehicle either. They were concerned that he might have driven out of the area before they arrived. Since the teen boys had spotted him on the first road to the right past the eight mile-marker, both troopers decided to search there first. Two Snohomish County Sheriff's deputies, riding together in one cruiser, were on their way up from Everett.

The State troopers reached the eight mile post, then turned right down the gravel road that dropped off into a creek canyon. Cruising slowly down the road, they wondered what the possibility was that the boys had not actually seen anyone. It wouldn't be the first time the WSP or other local law enforcement officers had been sent on a wild-goose chase into the woods of Snohomish County. This was different, though. The police knew that an old man was four days missing. They knew the old man's wife had been pushed to her death four days ago, whether deliberately or by accident. And they knew the dead woman's family had said her husband had suffered some dementia in the last year or so. He was there all right. They just had to find him.

A mile and a half down the road, they came around a corner and immediately spotted the blue Chevy pickup pulled off on a wide spot on the right. There was a creek seventy-five yards farther down the road. At once, the troopers pulled their rigs at an angle to the right edge of the road, the second vehicle six feet behind the first one. It would provide protection on their backsides if needed. They had no intention of being ambushed. If the man was running from a homicide, shooting police officers would be a genuine option.

After radioing dispatch that they believed they had located Horacio Muldano's pickup—they didn't have a clear view of the license plate to confirm it—both officers got out of their trucks wearing their .38s. Trooper Miller, in the front Dodge, had his M-16 and a megaphone. He left the driver's door open and walked to the back of his truck. Trooper Smith was armed with a twelve gauge shotgun, loaded with the standard 00 buckshot. He moved up beside Trooper Miller. They both kept a watch to their back and sides.

On the megaphone, Trooper Miller announced, "This is the Washington State Police. If you can hear us, please step into the center of the road, and keep your arms straight out to the side where we can see them." No movement. Trooper Miller waited thirty seconds and repeated the order. Nothing.

Twenty seconds later, a big, old man, wearing brown coveralls, leather boots and an old ball cap, climbed up the bank of the road below the truck and walked toward them. With each step, water splashed out of the silver, two-gallon, metal bucket he was carrying. He appeared to be unarmed. He seemed oblivious to the orders that had been given. Maybe he hadn't heard them over the noise of the creek's running water.

"This is the Washington State Police. Stop where you are," said Trooper Miller. The man stopped immediately.

"Put the bucket down, and put your arms straight out to your sides." The old man complied.

Trooper Miller put the megaphone in the bed of his truck. The officers spread out and advanced down the gravel road to within twenty feet of the man. It was definitely Muldano. He matched the image of the man on their trucks' computer screens. They glanced at the license plate on the blue Chevy. It was his.

Trooper Smith radioed dispatch that they had a positive identification. "The old man is Horacio Muldano." They had found him with his truck. He appeared to be unarmed, in good physical health, and they were establishing communication with him now. Trooper Smith radioed the deputy waiting at the two-mile marker to come on in. The Snohomish County Sheriff's deputies coming from Everett were only a few miles from Darrington, and would come on in to Muldano's location as well.

"Are you Horacio Muldano?" asked Trooper Miller.

"No," said the old man. They looked at each other, with squinted eyes. They knew it was him. Was he lying to them, or did he actually believe he was not Muldano?

"Sir, you match the photos and the description we have for

Horacio Muldano. Is this your pickup?"

"Yes, that's my pickup."

"This pickup belongs to Horacio Muldano. You match the photos and the description for a Horacio Mateo Muldano." said Miller.

"My name is Mateo Muldadano," he said, with sincerity, showing no concern. The troopers were puzzled. Was this guy for real? He seemed to be normal, but he honestly didn't seem to make the connection between himself and Horay Muldano. Miller explained the discrepancy to dispatch and asked for a double check on the name. Dispatch confirmed Horacio Mateo Muldano was the correct name. No doubt about it, he was their missing man.

Troopers Miller and Smith small talked with Muldano for several minutes about the woods, his logging background, what he was doing out there by himself, and anything else they could think of, while they waited for the sheriff's deputies to arrive. The first deputy arrived six minutes later.

Miller and Smith determined that Muldano needed to be taken to the sheriff's office in Everett by the deputies for further questioning. There they could have family members come in to visit with him. Maybe they could get to the bottom of what was going on, and what had happened.

The troopers realized that in Muldano's present apparent state of mind, it would be best not to mention his wife's death.

After the other deputies arrived, they talked with the troopers a bit, and to Muldano, then led him to the back seat of their patrol car for the ride to town. He smelled sour, like he hadn't changed or bathed in several days. Before having him get into the back, one of the deputies frisked him and found a four-inch folding pocket knife, his wallet, car keys, a handkerchief and a comb. They didn't handcuff him, because he wasn't under arrest. They were merely giving him a ride to the station for questioning, and to meet with family members. All the officers agreed that something wasn't right with his thinking, and since he was the prime suspect in his wife's death, they weren't about to let him drive his own truck in.

The two troopers and the first deputy completed searching Muldano's truck and the immediate area around it, but found nothing they could consider evidence in a crime. Muldano had no extra clothes with him except for a heavy jacket. No bedding and no food. He must have had the bucket in the truck bed, where there was also a shovel and a couple of milk jugs filled with water. He probably slept in his cab the four nights he was missing, but he didn't seem any worse for the wear.

Who knows what he had eaten during that time, if anything. Spring was not like mid-to-late summer in that area when various wild berries were available in great numbers. There were some active beaver dams and ponds in some of the small streams in the area, and there was a fair population of cutthroat trout. But the troopers saw nothing to indicate Muldano had cooked anything, or even had a fire, at least not in the area where his truck was currently parked.

One of the sheriff's deputies drove Muldano's truck and followed the other officers to the sheriff's office. They were about fifteen minutes behind the deputy that had Muldano with him. Brenda Thurmond, Denny Gregory and Horay's son, Manuel Muldano, were informed by phone that the old man was, in fact, their dad and he was okay. They were asked to go to the county sheriff's office in Everett where the law officers were taking Horay.

27

At the Sheriff's Office

Brenda and her oldest son, Conner, were waiting at the sheriff's station when the deputy and Muldano arrived at 7:25 pm. Manuel Muldano arrived a few minutes later. After the deputies settled Muldano into a comfortable room with several cushioned seats and a few wooden chairs, got him some coffee and a couple of ham and cheese sandwiches, they went in to talk to the family members in another room furnished with a long table and wooden chairs.

The deputies discussed Muldano's condition and asked where he might have come up with the name he was using. Muldano's birth son, Manuel (a half-breed Mexican) explained that Horay's dad's actual name was Alberto Mateo Muldadano. Manuel's Grandpa Muldadano brought his wife and children (Horay's oldest siblings; Horay wasn't born yet) with him when he migrated to La Jolla, California in 1915. Manuel recounted that around 1962, Horay took his family, including Horay's mother, his white American-born wife and three kids (Manuel being the youngest kid), down to Manzanillo, Mexico to visit Horay's Grandma Muldadano—who was over ninety—and other relatives who still lived there. In time, many of the Muldadano kids and grandkids ended up in California. All of them eventually adopted English as their primary language, but they all also spoke excellent Spanish.

Horay got his middle name, Mateo, from his father (Manuel's Grandpa Muldadano). The interesting point was that Horay had actually gone by the name Mateo Muldadano until he was twelve. It was at that time, in 1936, that Horay's dad decided to shorten the last name to Muldano. He did it because so many people in America stumbled over the spelling and pronunciation of the original name. Though he was proud of his Mexican heritage, he was in "the land of opportunity" to stay. Eventually, all of the younger American born and raised generation on the Muldadano side of the family made the switch to the shorter name, as well.

The first part of the riddle was solved. But why did Horay go to that name now?

After ten minutes, Denny Gregory arrived and all the family members were taken into the room to see Horay. They had decided that when the time was right, Brenda would be the one to broach the subject of Maureen's death, since she had always been closest to him, even closer to him than Manuel.

Brenda broke down and cried when she saw Horay. He was surprised and pleased to see his family.

"Poppa," Brenda said, using the title the Gregory kids had adopted for him, their step-dad, in the early years following his marriage to their mother, Maureen.

"Brenda, Manuel," Horay said. He recognized them. The deputies looked at each other with relief.

The four family members crowded around him, and each gave a hug of affection and relief, which he readily returned. He had always been a demonstratively affectionate person, a trait he carried from his Spanish upbringing. He was glad to see them, but seemed to have no idea what all the fuss was about. All of these family members' alibis for Friday night had checked out, so none of them were considered suspects in the crime. Denny was at home in Hamilton with his wife and two daughters. Brenda and a friend, Patty, were together at Brenda's apartment. Manuel was with his wife and daughter at his middle son's city league basketball game; then they went out for pizza. Conner was playing cards with his four buddies at a house on Woods Creek Road.

The law enforcement officers inside and outside the room closely observed the interaction between Horay and his family. The deputies noticed that Conner seemed a bit stand-offish, but they attributed that to his probable suspicion of Horay's involvement in his grandma's death. They knew of other situations when a family member was involved somehow, through an accident (even a car crash) or homicide, in the death of a loved one, where other family members felt awkward around them and didn't know what to feel, how to act, or whether to blame the surviving family member in some way for the death of the loved one.

"Where have you been, Poppa?" Brenda asked. "We've all been worried sick about you."

"I was up in the woods when the troopers contacted me," he said. "I don't honestly remember what I went up there for in the first place, but I was really enjoying myself. You know how much I've always loved the woods. When the troopers arrived, I was getting ready to gather up some bracken fern, toss it in my water pail, put together a fire, and make myself some tea."

"Dad," said Manuel, "you've been gone four days. You didn't tell anyone where you went, or when you were coming back."

"I've been gone that long? Where's Mom?" the name he called Maureen since the first year they were married. Maureen's youngest son and daughter were fifteen and sixteen, still at home, when he married her.

All three of Horay's kids were dreading that moment. They glanced at the deputies in the room, not knowing quite what to say, or how to say it. Should they just come out with the truth now? Brenda would be the one. Why did they pick her? She could never address the tough issues before. That is with anyone besides her husband, who she seemed to contend with on every household or parenting point. Conner was the only one in the room who stood up to people, but it was always for the wrong reasons. Manuel and Denny were a couple more followers who let others handle their conflicts for them.

Horay sensed that the pause in answering his question was too long. "How come Maureen didn't come down here with you guys?"

Brenda took the dive. "Poppa, Mom died," she said, her eyes instantly filled with water.

"No she didn't!" he cried in disbelief.

"Yes, Poppa; she's gone."

"She can't be." He burst into tears, sobbing uncontrollably; his whole body shook as he let out a mournful moan that would tear the heart out of all but the hardest hearted person. All of the family, including Conner, joined Horay in his grief with their own tears. Brenda hugged him tight from his left side. The battle-hardened deputies and state troopers, who had all seen plenty of grieving, were moved by the genuine pain displayed by this family.

Watching through the one-way glass, Trooper Miller said to the other officers, "There's no way he's faking that. No way. They're all being real."

No one spoke again in the room or outside of it for a couple minutes. Then Trooper Smith said to Trooper Miller, "If Muldano shoved his wife, he either wasn't himself when he did it, or he broke from reality sometime after he made the 911 call. Maybe the accident pushed him over the edge. Either way, he isn't completely himself now, I'm sure of that. His mind is dealing with this death now as if it is the first time he became aware of it."

"If he did it and he was in his normal mind," said Miller, "when and if his mind gets back to normal, he may remember what happened. If he did it when he was in this current state of mind, he may never remember it. We can only hope."

After several minutes of bawling his eyes out, Horay managed to regain control of his emotions. The tough, old logger was coming to the surface. He asked, "What happened, how did she die?" The deputies paid close attention to him. They hoped something he said or how he reacted would give them some clues.

"She fell and hit her head on an end table in the family room," said Brenda, barely holding back another outburst of emotion.

"When did it happen?"

"Last Friday evening, sometime between eight thirty and nine."

"And I wasn't home? Dammit, something's not right here. I'm always home with her at that hour."

"There's a lot we don't know about it right now, Poppa."

"How did you find out about it, Sis?"

"Someone called 911."

"Where is she now?" He didn't seem to have any curiosity about the 911 call. That seemed odd to everyone. Did he, somewhere in his sub-conscience, know he had made the call? Or was this just another symptom of his current state of mind?

"She's at Burbank's Funeral Home. We've been waiting to hear from you before we decided what to do with her," said Brenda.

"I'd like to go see her."

Sergeant Allen cut in, "It's almost nine o'clock. I think we're going to call it a night. We'll let Horay go with one of you if you will sign for his care and custody. I want whoever takes him to bring him back in here tomorrow so we can continue where we left off tonight. I don't mind if a few family members are present when we talk with him tomorrow. In fact, I think it would be quite helpful."

"I don't need anyone to sign for me. I'm perfectly capable of taking care of myself."

"Poppa, you know how we've had the little talks about you having periods where you seem to get confused and can't remember things?" said Brenda. "Well, you are confused about a bunch of things right now. Will you just trust me, as your daughter, on this? You can come home with me and Conner. I'll be dropping Conner off on the way home. I can take the day off tomorrow."

"Manuel, what do you think?" said Horay, hoping his birth son would disagree with Brenda.

"Brenda's right, Dad. You need to go home with her. I'll meet you guys back in here tomorrow. We'll get all of this figured out. I would be happy to meet you at the funeral home. I know that's going to be rough on you."

"Okay," Horay conceded. "I know all of you just want to help me. I'll trust your judgment."

The deputies in the room stood up, and the Muldanos' and Gregorys' followed suit. A deputy from outside the room brought in the release form, Brenda signed it, and Horacio was released to her care.

"Can we see you back in here tomorrow at one in the afternoon, Ms. Thurmond?" said Sergeant Allen. "That should give you plenty of time to make your visit to the funeral home, get some lunch, and get over here."

"Okay," said Brenda. "We'll see you at one tomorrow." She was as anxious as the law officers to get this riddle solved.

28

Prime Suspect

Jackie spent the night with Conner's wife and kids at their house. Brenda had dropped her off there when she picked Conner up to go to the sheriff's office last night. Jackie got to see Grandpa Muldano when Brenda dropped Conner off. It was a very emotional time.

Brenda was making coffee at 8:30 Wednesday morning when Horay came into the small two-bedroom apartment's kitchen-dining room. Her stomach was in knots, worrying whether she would have to explain her mom's being dead to him all over again.

"Morning Poppa. Did you get enough rest last night?"

"I feel pretty rested, but what am I doing here?" he answered. She cringed.

"Can we talk about that after some breakfast? Why don't you sit here at the table? I have to make a couple of phone calls, then I'll make you some Cream of Wheat cereal, and get you a cup of coffee."

As he sat down, she left the room and discreetly grabbed the Everett Daily News morning paper off the TV stand in the small living room and took it into her bedroom. No way she wanted Horay to see today's issue. There was a photo of him at the top of the front page next to the headline, "Missing Husband of Dead Monroe Woman Found Safe in Woods."

Brenda immediately punched in some numbers on her cell phone.

"Conner, I need you to come right over. Poppa doesn't know why he's here. I doubt he remembers anything from last night. I'm scared."

"I'm on my way," said Conner, who had already arranged to take the day off from breathing septic fumes. He wasn't about to miss the talk at the sheriff's office.

As soon as Brenda got off the phone with him, she put some water in a large, glass, cereal bowl, and stuck it in the microwave for two minutes. While the water was heating, she poured Horay a cup of coffee from the freshly brewed pot, then got the instant cereal, sugar and milk out. When the water was ready, she mixed in the cereal and set everything on the table in front of him. She then hurried off to the bathroom to kill time until Conner arrived.

Soon after Conner got to her apartment, Brenda was forced to break the same news to Horay that she shared last night. His reaction was the same, but now it was just Brenda and Conner to comfort him. The tears flowed freely.

They went to the funeral home at ten, then to lunch at McGrath's Fish House. Horay ate very little, while Brenda managed to force down most of her meal. Conner, true to himself, ate all of his fish and chips, then polished off what Horay and Brenda couldn't eat. He couldn't stand to see good food go to waste, even when others at the table were filled with grief.

At the sheriff's office, Brenda took Sergeant Allen aside and explained that Horay was back to his normal self, and that she had filled him in on the same details about her mom's death as were discussed last night. She said he had grieved at the news just like he did last night, as if it was a new revelation to him.

They all went to the same room as the night before. Sheriff's detective Gonzales joined them in the room again. The same people from last night watched from outside the room.

"I'm Sergeant Allen, Snohomish County Sheriff's Detective. I'm very sorry for your loss, sir. I understand your daughter has filled you in a bit on our conversation here last night. I'm aware that you have had some problems in the recent past remembering things. How do you feel right now?"

"I just learned my wife is dead. How do you think I feel?"

"I'm sorry. What I meant was do you feel like you can talk to us now about what has happened?"

"You ask the questions, I'll see what I can answer."

"Do you remember being in the woods on Clear Creek Road last night before coming to the sheriff's office?"

"No, I don't remember any of that. I don't remember being here either. Where is Clear Creek?"

"Do you remember any of your activities in the last four days?"

"No."

"Miss Thurmond, has your dad ever had any times where he was confused for four days?"

"No, the longest time I remember, or that Mom ever mentioned, lasted only a few hours. Even that worried her a lot."

"Mr. Muldano, do you know where you were last Friday night?" asked Allen. "Today is Wednesday."

"I remember that my wife and I went out to eat at Home Town Buffet, one of our favorite places. I've always liked Friday nights, because it's fish night."

"What time did you get home?"

"We got home about seven."

Conner was a bit restless today, fidgeting in his chair and sometimes tapping his fingers on the table. The family knew that he was always nervous around the law because of his criminal record. He hadn't spoken a single word last night when they were in the sheriff's office, even when his mom and uncles spoke consoling words to Grandpa Muldano. He had just hugged his grandpa and cried. None of the family could blame him. Four years in prison can do that to a man.

"What happened after you got home?" said Sergeant Allen. "I need you to recall every detail."

"There's not much to say. I went into the bathroom in our bedroom and sat down and did my job. Afterwards, I changed into a pair of coveralls and went into the family room to watch some TV."

"A few minutes later my wife went into the bathroom, then came out complaining to me because I hadn't turned the fan on. She said the bathroom stunk like an outhouse. It wasn't anything new. I should have remembered to turn on the fan, and burn a match. I apologized, but that wasn't good enough. It rarely was. She started reaming me out over how inconsiderate I was. She came right over in front of my chair and continued her griping. I've taken that for years. Friday night I wasn't in the mood for it. After all, I had just taken her out to a nice dinner, listened to her latest gossip about the family members. She had gone on and on about Brenda's divorce proceedings, and what a scoundrel her husband was. I'd heard it all plenty of times before."

"I finally got her off that subject about mid-way through our meal and on to talking about some positive things that were happening at our new church. We changed churches again a month ago. Seemed like we were always changing churches, at least every year or two. Maureen would get into some conflicts with the church's leadership over some trivial issues. I was forever playing peacemaker. Over the years we wound up back at some of the churches we had left years earlier; there are only so many Pentecostal churches in the area."

"So your dinner didn't go so good?" said Allen.

"It went great after I got the subject changed."

"Okay, so let's get back to your argument at home after dinner."

"It wasn't much of an argument. You don't argue with Maureen, you get bull-dozed by her. She was never wrong." Brenda, Manuel and Denny looked knowingly at each other. Yet they also knew that Horay, himself, was a very opinionated, strong-willed person. He just didn't have what it took to stand up to Maureen. That and he learned early in their marriage that the price to do so was too great.

"What happened when she was standing in front of your chair?" The curiosity was killing everyone inside and outside the room.

"I finally said, 'I treat you to a good dinner, then we come home and you start chewing on me for something that I admitted I forgot to do, and I even apologized for it. I've got to get some air. I'm going for a drive.' I got up from my chair, grabbed my heavy jacket, and put on my boots. I figured I would get away for a couple of hours. I thought about doing that many times before, but never had. Friday night I just couldn't take any more of her jumping down my throat. So I got in my truck and left. She even followed me through the house, and down the hall into the garage, calling me names; her favorite one has always been, 'Wimp.' She was on quite a rampage. And for what, a little stink in the bathroom?"

"What time was it when you left?" said Allen.

"It was about seven thirty."

"You're sure of that?"

"Definitely, I looked at my watch when I was sitting on the pot. It was seven ten. I came out, sat down, listened to her harp for five or ten minutes or so, then left. No way was it any later than seven forty."

"Where did you go after you left?"

"I was driving out toward Lake Chaplain to get some air, and look at the stars."

"Did you get there?"

"I honestly don't remember. The next thing I remembered was waking up on my granddaughter's bed at my daughter's apartment this morning. That's a scary feeling, not knowing how you got somewhere. Or why you're there."

The officers looked at each other and wondered. What did this mean? Was he making all of this up to cover his rear, knowing that, according to his family, he had had some memory loss and confusion in the recent past? Was it possible that he remained confused for all four days? Maybe he was in and out of reality during that time. Was he acting the confused part when the boys and troopers found him? There would have been no reason for him to put on an act for the boys. And there was no denying the authenticity of the grief he displayed last night.

"What is your name, sir?" said Sergeant Allen.

"Why are you asking me that? You know that already."

"Would you tell us your name, please?"

Horay was puzzled at such a ridiculous question. He looked at each of his family members. What is going on here? He has to be kidding?

"My name is Horacio Muldano."

"Your full name."

"Horacio Mateo Muldano."

"Was your name ever Muldadano?"

"What difference does that make?" he said, obviously frustrated.

"Could you please just answer the question?"

"Yes, my birth name was Muldadano. My dad shortened our last name when I was twelve, a few years after my Grandpa Muldadano died. I hated him for it. He was willing to change our name to please the public, or at least to make it easier for them. That was the way I saw it. In a Spanish home in those days, a twelve year old did what he was told. So I had to go along with it."

Slipping into his story-telling mode with no prompting, Horay went on.

"Every time I heard the name *Muldano*, for the first couple years after the switch, I told myself that when I was eighteen I was going to change my name back to Muldadano. Eventually I got used to Muldano, and gradually my resentment over the change diminished. By the time I was eighteen, I had chicks crawling all over me. I was always very strong and handsome. And the fact that I was a dark-skinned Mexican seemed to make me more appealing to all the white girls. I loved the way they flirted with me, using the name Muldano. I realized there was no point in changing it. I actually grew to like it. And it was much easier for other people to say."

"Last night you told us that your name was not Muldano, but that it was Muldadano. Why would you say that?"

"If I was confused, how would I know that I said that, or why?" He was getting irritated. "Why are you asking me these questions? Is there something you're not telling me?"

Brenda and Conner had only told him that Maureen had tripped, fallen backwards, broke her neck on the end table and split her head open. That she had died quickly.

"Okay, I'll get right to the point," said Sergeant Allen. "Your wife was pushed. She fell backwards, hit her head on the coffee table, broke her neck, split her head wide open, and then was moved four feet to the side from where she initially landed. Someone disguising his voice made a 911 call at 8:58 Friday night from a phone booth on Brigham Street in Monroe. He said there was a seriously injured woman at your address. When deputies arrived, no one but your wife was there. She was dead. Do you see our problem?"

"My Lord. It definitely wasn't an accident?" he asked, in disbelief.

"What do you think?" said Sergeant Allen.

"Maybe it was an accident," said Horay, "at least the part about her falling backwards. Maybe the person who pushed her didn't intend for her to fall, and certainly not to hit the end table."

"Is that what you think? You seem to have the person's thinking figured out pretty well."

"What are you implying?" Horay's face turned red; his hands were trembling. He was getting angrier by the second.

"Try to see it from our position, sir. We know someone pushed her, and she ended up dead. I'm only doing my job here."

"Yeah, but you seem to be locked in on me as the guilty person.

The fact that I can't recall anything from soon after I left the house doesn't mean I'm guilty of anything. I've told you the truth about everything leading up to whenever it was in my drive that I got confused."

"Yeah, but it's quite a coincidence that during your entire marriage, by your own admission, you had never left the house for a drive during the middle of an argument with your wife."

"I told you it wasn't an argument. It was just her chewing me out. I did the right thing by leaving, before I got more angry and did something I regretted. I mean before I said something I regretted. Well I guess I didn't do the right thing, or she wouldn't be dead." Horay paused, then getting choked up from the weight of guilt, said, "Oh, dear God, why did I choose that night to leave?"

"You said that you had to leave before you *did something you would regret*. What did you mean by that?" said Allen.

"I meant, before I said something I regretted. Don't you understand how difficult this is for me to talk about? And you want to focus on a slip-up in what I said."

"That's our job in these investigations, to look for inconsistencies in what people say—to look for clues that give away certain important details."

"Have you guys considered or looked for anyone else? Are you doing that part of your job? It sounds to me that you're already convinced it was me."

"Dad," Manuel said, "I know this is rough; I know they seem to be totally focused on you as the guilty party. It even makes me mad that they're talking to you like this, but I also understand what they're trying to do. If you didn't do it, then their questions can help determine that too. Do you see what I'm saying?"

"Son, nothing they have asked me indicates that they are even considering the possibility that I didn't do it; that someone else did."

"Dad, even you, if you look at the circumstances of your disappearance, would have to admit, things look very suspicious. At least give them that."

"Son, you never could see things the same way I did. That's part of the reason we were never as close as I wanted us to be. At least believe me now, and try to give me the benefit of the doubt."

"I wasn't taking sides against you, Dad. I was just trying to talk to you as your son who wants more than anything to get to the bottom of this. To find out that you definitely were not somehow involved in Maureen's death."

"You know I always loved her, and would never hurt her. You know I've never gotten physical in any way with her, even when many men would have. You think that didn't take a lot of will power? There were times when she seemed relentless in her efforts to push me to violence toward her. You guys never saw those times. You saw plenty, but you never saw how mean she could get with me sometimes when we were by ourselves. I sometimes wondered if she had some kind of mental illness."

"Poppa," Brenda interrupted, "Mom told us a few months ago that you pushed her during one of your confused states. Do you remember that?"

"No, I don't remember that. Why would she say that? Why would you say that now?"

Sergeant Allen let the verbal exchange between family members go on without interrupting. He and the other officers were picking up some good insight by listening.

"Dad, the officers have already questioned all of the family about yours and Maureen's relationship," said Manuel. "They already had it on file that you supposedly shoved Maureen one time, at least according to what she told some family members. You know they're just doing their job. Your being missing the night of the crime, and for these days right after that, has raised a lot of questions, and doubts, even among our family."

"You can't mean that. How could my own family believe I could have killed Mom? If I had ever shoved her and she hit her head and was seriously hurt, there's no way I would have left her in that condition to die. She was my wife, for crying out loud. I loved her.

Think about it. Think about what you're saying."

"We didn't know what to believe, or think, Poppa," said Brenda. "You've never taken off like that before. You didn't tell anyone where you were going."

"I told your mom I was going for a drive. I needed to get some space to cool off from her harsh words."

"Yeah, but Mom wasn't here to tell us that, Poppa," said Brenda.

"Then you have to believe me!" he said, slapping his hand down on the table. "Who else is on the suspect list?"

"Right now we're looking at your son-in-law, Dan Thurmond, with a lot of interest, as well," said Sergeant Allen.

"You mean I'm on the same list as that idiot?" Horay was brainwashed by Maureen soon after the big Christmas blowup. After the separation Brenda only made all that worse with her false accusations.

"We're also looking at your grandson Edward Gregory," said Deputy Gonzalez.

"Edward loved his grandma. Have you guys lost your marbles? He would never hurt her. The boy lived with us his last two years of high school. He's always been a wonderful kid." He looked at Brenda for a hint that the deputy was not serious. "Why would they think Edward could have done it, Sis?"

"They haven't questioned him beyond just asking him about his alibi for last Friday night. He was camping by himself. He packed into the woods near Troublesome Creek, but no one can verify that he was there. They found out through various relatives how strained his and Mom's relationship has been the last few years."

"That doesn't make him guilty," said Horay. "He's never even hinted at violence toward Mom or any other family member."

"Poppa, the argument that Edward had with you, Mom, and Conner on Thanksgiving was mentioned by several family members when the cops questioned them," said Brenda.

But no one in the family had given the cops any details about the argument, particularly the challenges that Conner had made to

Edward. None of them wanted to feed the suspicion fires. With Conner's criminal record, they certainly didn't want the law digging into that. Besides they had all learned that Conner had a great alibi for the whole evening. He had gone from home to the gym, then straight to his once-a-month card game with his buddies.

"I never argued with Edward on Thanksgiving," said Horay.

"Well, I guess it wasn't really an argument with you," she said. "But you guys did go back and forth a little. And you have to admit that Mom opened up a terrible can of worms when she brought up the adoption issue with Edward and Sylvia. It made the whole family uncomfortable. Edward spoke out very freely about Mom's criticism and the control she had over the whole family. Even you have to admit that."

"That part is true. But he would never have laid a hand on his grandma. He loved her dearly."

Sergeant Allen thought about jumping in to question Horay about Conner's part in the Thanksgiving argument, but decided against it. No one the police had talked to said anything about Conner having any problems getting along with his Grandma Muldano. They told the police that Conner had stuck up for his grandma, as usual, on Thanksgiving, when Edward was speaking ill of her words and actions within the family. Since he had a rock-solid alibi for Friday night Conner wasn't considered a suspect. His four card-playing buddies had all vouched for his having arrived at the card game at just before 8:30, and Cindy Nickson, the front desk person at Gold's Gym, confirmed that Conner left Gold's at 7:45, no where near enough time for him to have driven to Monroe and back to the card game on Woods Creek Road, southeast of Dubuque Road. For whatever reason, the detectives didn't check to see if he had a police record.

"We all agree with you on that Poppa," said Brenda. "I'm not sure why the police aren't focusing more of their attention on Dan. He hated Mom, and she hated him."

"Yeah, well she was justified in that. He moved you guys down to Aberdeen to keep Jackie away from us," said Horay.

"That's not why we moved."

"Then why did you move?"

"I don't want to get into that, Poppa. It doesn't matter now anyway. We're back up with you guys where we belong. And he can't hurt our family anymore. Well, I thought that, but now I think maybe he did hurt us."

"If your husband did push her, why would he call 911?" said Deputy Gonzalez. "We know he had plenty of motive. We also know that you have a restraining order on him. But it doesn't add up that he would push your mom, then call 911. Does that make sense to you Ms Thurmond?"

"You don't understand how that man thinks," said Brenda.

Brother Denny thought, here we go again. He had listened to Brenda run her ex-husbands and ex-live-in boyfriends down for years with this same line of reasoning. He wished his oldest brother, Doug, was here about now, to jump in. Yet, he had his own suspicions about Dan's possible involvement, even though he always liked Dan, just like Doug did. The way his grandma treated Dan, Denny could understand why he hated her.

"Ma'am," said Allen, addressing her more formally. He had come to his own conclusions about Brenda's stand against her husband and the validity of the restraining order. "We are doing everything we can to get to the bottom of your mom's death. That includes questioning your husband. As a matter of fact, Deputy Gonzales and I are going to Aberdeen tomorrow to talk with him. He has already been questioned and his house was searched by Grays Harbor County Sheriff's deputies. So far we have no evidence to link him to your parents' home at the time of your mom's death. We do know that he has no alibi for Friday night. He said he was camping. That is the same thing your nephew Edward said he was doing. Is one of them lying?"

Allen continued, "Here it is, only mid-March, not exactly a popular time of year for camping. Yet, three members of your family all say they were camping, or in your step-dad's case, he said he went out to look at stars and he ends up camping for four days and doesn't remember any of it. All of this happens on the same weekend your mom dies; you're either a family of Grizzly Adams, someone is lying, or it is a very peculiar coincidence. Now do you understand why we have to consider Edward a suspect—especially given his recent history with your mom?"

"Dan is no longer part of my family, so I would appreciate it if you don't refer to him that way," said Brenda. All of the officers were seeing some of Maureen's traits in her, though they didn't know that.

"I know Edward didn't do it," said Horay.

"How can you know that?" said Allen, thinking maybe Muldano was on the verge of confessing in order to protect his grandson. All eyes were on Horay.

"He never would have hurt my wife; he never would have pushed her. You have no idea how she harped on him his last two years of high school, after his serious football injury. She was relentless. I felt so sorry for him. The few times I tried to stick up for him with her, she leveled me with her put downs." He looked at his kids. "None of you has any idea what that boy put up with. And not once did he say a disrespectful word back to her, or even come close to doing anything physical to her. With his size, he didn't have to be afraid of her. He practically could have thrown her across the room. Kevin and Sherry did an excellent job of teaching that boy respect. I only wish I had been a better surrogate father to him those two years. But it doesn't matter, this last Thanksgiving he showed me, that in a lot of ways he is a bigger man than every other male in our family."

At that statement, Conner started fuming inside. He had actually liked Edward when he was a kid. But ever since finding out about Edward and Sylvias' plans to give their illegitimate baby away in an open adoption, and actually going through with those plans—not to mention Edward's stand on Thanksgiving, when he had the nerve to speak of him and Grandma Muldano as he had—Conner had grown to hate Edward. He knew someday he was going to beat the tar out of him. The *boy* needed to be put in his place, and he was just the man to do it.

It was ironic that a guy, who fifteen years earlier, held a woman down while three of his buddies raped her, could be so judgmental of anyone, let alone his own family. The truth was, Conner was still an insecure little boy inside who hated himself—just as his grandmother had always been an insecure little girl who hated herself. Somehow, he always tried to elevate himself in his own eyes by putting other people down, by trying to overpower them, by intimidating them. No one could say that his Grandma Muldano's blood didn't run through him. Obviously it did. So even though she was dead, yet she still lived. Of course she still lived in that same awful way through her two daughters, Brenda and Jan, and her granddaughter, Jackie.

Sergeant Allen and Deputy Gonzales continued questioning Horay for another half hour, but gained nothing of value in their attempts to figure out what had happened to his wife Friday night. His account of that evening did not place him at the scene of the crime at the right time. They felt he was telling the truth as he remembered it. But if he did become confused shortly after leaving the house, he still could have come back and shoved his wife to her death, and then left again without remembering doing so.

They needed to dig deeper with Dan Thurmond and Edward Gregory. And they needed to do more research on the whole family to see if there was anything in any of their backgrounds that might help put pieces of the puzzle together.

29

The Investigation

First thing Thursday, detectives Allen and Gonzales made the long drive to Aberdeen, Washington. Dan met them at the sheriff's office there at 11:00 am. They questioned him for half an hour or so, then requested that he take them to the exact location near Rainbow Falls where he told the Grays Harbor County Sheriff's deputies he spent the weekend camping. He led the way with his vehicle, and they followed in their unmarked Snohomish County Sheriff car. Grays Harbor's Sergeant Lang and Deputy Millard followed right behind Deputies Allen and Gonzales, in their rig.

When they got to the place in the woods several miles south of Rainbow Falls where Dan had stopped on his return from the Muldanos' place on Sunday evening, he parked his rig, got out and told the deputies, who had gotten out of their rigs, "This is where I was." It had rained steady for several days, so all tire tracks on the roads were washed away.

"Where were you parked, and where was your campfire?" said Sergeant Allen.

"I was parked right there." He pointed to a spot ten feet from where he was standing. "I didn't have a campfire."

"You camped for two days and you didn't have a campfire?" said Allen. "That seems odd to me, especially this time of year."

"There are many times when I don't have a fire. When I sleep in my vehicle, I bundle up in my sleeping bags and do a lot of reading or listen to the radio. Sometimes I do have a fire. Sometimes I bring a lawn chair and my camp stove, maybe even an overhead tarp in case it rains. Last weekend, I just wanted to get away and do some reading."

The officers looked around the immediate area a little and came to the conclusion they weren't going to find any evidence that could confirm or refute his claim to have camped there over the weekend. Finally Allen told him he could go home. They would be in touch. Allen said they still weren't convinced he wasn't involved in Maureen's death, and it would be a good idea to get himself a lawyer. Dan thought the only way I'm doing that is if I'm arrested.

The next morning, Friday, one week after the crime, Brenda's nephew, Edward Gregory got the same treatment Dan Thurmond had received. Only this time it was just Sergeant Allen and Deputy Gonzales who followed him to his parking spot at Troublesome Creek, and then hiked the one mile up hill in the woods to his camping spot. They were pleased to find he had actually had a fire. The problem for Edward was that no one had camped with him, and his camp was not nearly as far away from Monroe as Dan's had been. His vehicle was parked about forty minutes away from the Muldanos' place. It would have been no problem for him to commit the crime and still get his camp set up well before midnight on Friday night.

Sergeant Allen and Deputy Gonzales knew that figuring out this case would take plenty more work and probably some luck. They had three suspects with motive, opportunity, and no alibis. Yet, it wasn't coming together. On Tuesday morning the CSI team had returned to the Muldano house looking for anything they might have missed, but found nothing helpful. There was no evidence at the scene that could convict any of the three. All fingerprints and DNA found there from family members proved nothing other than that the relatives had been in the house at some time. That wasn't a crime. The only evidence found on the victim was the bruising on the chest with distinct finger tip imprints. Unfortunately, the bruising was diffused so the size of the perpetrators fingers could not be determined from the bruises. Judging by the amount of blood on the carpet at the scene and the size of the bruised areas on her chest, Mrs. Muldano must have lived at least ten minutes after the fall.

After spending all-day Thursday questioning Dan and checking out his camping spot, then on Friday interviewing Edward Gregory and checking out his camping site, deputies Allen and Gonzales spent Friday afternoon doing background checks on all of the Muldanos' relatives who could possibly have been close enough geographically to commit the crime and, at the same time, strong enough to drag Maureen four feet side-ways across the floor.

They listened to the 911 call repeatedly, and they had a voice analyst, using computer technology, filter the 911 message in order to determine what the man's actual voice sounded like. They had recorded all of their in-station interviews with all three suspects. Unfortunately, none of their voices matched the 911 recording. Either the person making the call did an excellent job of disguising his voice, if it was one of the three, or he was not one of the three, but someone else altogether. That would mean either someone else committed the crime, or perhaps, the person who committed the crime got another man to make the call. That didn't seem likely. What were they missing?

During the background checks, Conner, Brenda and Maureen were the only local family members found to have criminal records. The assault charge against Maureen didn't surprise them in light of what they had gleaned about her controlling, powerful personality. They did, however, find her driving record interesting, particularly the number of times she had rear-ended other drivers. They were each glad they didn't have to pay her auto insurance premiums. Unfortunately, her assault charge and poor driving record did nothing toward solving her death, but they did reinforce the deputies' suspicions that she may have pushed the perpetrator before being pushed herself.

Brenda's one charge was for petty theft. When in her early twenties, and working part time as her church's secretary, she embezzled money from the church over a nine-month period. Some churches would have followed Biblical principles and handled the crime in house. Not the Assembly of Christ Church she attended. The good, self-righteous, legalists weren't letting her off that easy. Originally, she was charged with embezzlement, a felony, but the church leadership finally relented after considering her circumstances of being a poor single mother of two boys. The leadership agreed to a plea bargain of petty theft instead, saying they weren't sure exactly how much money was taken. Informally Brenda admitted taking $4,000, and as part of the plea agreement was allowed to pay back the money over twelve months. She also spent forty hours shampooing the churches' carpets as her community service time. When the carpets were clean, she switched her membership to a different church. Brenda had never told Dan about any of it, not surprising considering how deceitful she was about a lot of things.

Conner's criminal record immediately intrigued the deputies. The felony conviction for his involvement in the gang rape when he was twenty had cost him four years of his life; he did hard time in the Washington State Felons Center. In the years since then, he had three misdemeanor convictions for assault and battery—two while he was under the influence of alcohol. He also had a misdemeanor conviction for harassment. He was probably guilty of plenty of other conflicts where the victims didn't report him. Violent people usually only get reported for a minority of the cases in which they are guilty. Obviously, Conner had some issues.

Sergeant Allen decided they needed to probe deep into Conner's life and do some intense interviews with his card-playing buddies, some of the people at the gym, fellow employees, and anyone else they could think of who might be able to give them a true picture of the person Conner's criminal record indicated him to be. What they didn't consider was that Conner intimidated these people so much, that most would never say a thing about him that would make him look guilty of any kind of physical violence.

30

The Memorial Weekend

Throughout Friday afternoon, and well into the evening, out-of-town relatives arrived in the Everett-Monroe area, by automobile or airplane, to join the local area Muldano-Gregorys at Grandpa and Grandma Muldanos' place. It was one week after Maureen had died. The memorial service was scheduled for two o'clock the next day, Saturday afternoon. More relatives would be arriving in the morning.

The Muldano-Gregory clan was huge, at least eighty-five people in all. Many friends would come to the service as well. When the three younger Gregory kids were in high school—Doug and Brenda never attended Monroe High—they were excellent athletes and known and watched by many people in the Monroe Community. The memorial service would be at the Monroe Assembly of Christ, a church that would hold several hundred. Maureen and Horay had first been members there right after they got married. Since then, they had bounced around between over a dozen churches in the Monroe-Everett area, including coming back to the Monroe

Assembly of Christ for two other stints. They were not members there now.

This family gathering, like most, had plenty of good food, and non-alcoholic drinks. Alcohol was looked down on within the Muldano-Gregory families, though there were a few alcoholics among their numbers. The drinkers had to bring their own booze, and do all their drinking and smoking outside where it wouldn't offend the righteous. Plenty of the Gregorys were practicing Christians, a number of whom tended to be legalistic, thanks to their heavy Assembly of Christ backgrounds.

It was an especially sad time for the family, not only because of Maureen's death, but because of the circumstances of her demise. Making it sadder yet was that Horay, Edward, and Dan were all being investigated as suspects. As of Friday afternoon, Conner was also being considered a possible suspect, though neither he nor anyone in the family was aware of that yet. Most of the Muldano-Gregory clan had always liked Dan. His only real enemies had been Maureen, Horay, Jan, two of Brenda's sons (Conner and Leroy), and her daughter, Jackie. Of course, Brenda finally crossed the line when she left him.

No one wanted to believe Maureen was pushed to her death by someone in the family, including Dan, the soon-to-be divorced-out-of-the-family member. No one, that is, except the surviving wolves, who, he guessed, all hoped he would be found guilty and sentenced to die. That would mean all of the real family members were off the hook.

One thing that surprised Dan was that Brenda hadn't put the divorce proceedings on hold so that if he was found guilty in Maureen's death, she would probably get all of the property instead of just the half she was hoping to get. Of course, she probably hadn't had time to think that through or to talk to her attorney.

Dan was sure the small coven of his enemies would huddle to gossip at some time over the weekend. He wondered who the ramrod would be now that the bitch was dead.

Late Saturday morning in the Muldanos' living room—

"We all know who pushed Grandma," said Conner, "that worth less bastard Dan. First he comes in and tears the family apart. Now he has killed Grandma. I hope he gets the death penalty."

"We really don't know yet that he was the one who did it," said Brandon, the Texas lawyer, Conner's next younger brother. "They haven't even arrested him, or charged him."

"You damn right he did it," insisted Conner, who never did see eye to eye with brother Brandon.

"We don't have to resort to cussing," said Brandon, the one genuine Christian among Brenda and her children.

"I'll cuss any damn time I want to."

"Well I don't feel like being a part of this discussion if you're going to get elevated."

"Suit yourself. We don't need your legal input anyway—"

"Conner!" snapped Brenda. "Can you lay off him for once?"

"He deserted our family years ago when he moved away to Texas," said Conner. "He's a damn Longhorn fan now."

"You drove him away," interjected Leroy, surprisingly, since he's never been one to rock the boat.

"No one drove me away. I moved to Texas because Daleen (his wife) has family there. We love it in Texas, and it's been a good place for me to practice law."

"You always were pussy whipped by her," said Conner.

"I'm done here," said Brandon, who got up from his chair to leave the huddle. "Trying to hold a civil conversation with Conner in the mix is even too tall an order for a Texan."

"Now he's a big, bad Texan," mocked Conner. "Damn traitor." Brandon went into the family room to join the friendlier family members.

"Why couldn't you just be nice to him for a change?" said a tearful eyed Brenda.

"I'm sorry Mom, but he's always been a damn pip squeak. I

don't care whether he makes hundreds of thousands of dollars a year or not. He'll never be a real man." As if Conner, in his mid-thirties and still pumping septic tanks, is anyone to judge that, especially after helping his friends rape that woman when he was twenty.

"Here we are in your grandma's house, a week after she's been killed, and you don't have the decency to be cordial to your rarely seen brother," said Brenda. "It breaks my heart all over again. I don't care what he said about Daleen's family, we all know that if you hadn't alienated him by always being so hostile to him, it's doubtful he ever would have moved that far away from home."

"Sis, Conner," said Horay. "Can we just stop and pray?"

"Why should we do that?" said Conner. "It's not going to bring Grandma back."

"No, but maybe it can help us to get along better."

"That's a good idea, Poppa," said Brenda, this from the woman who has rejected God's plan for her marriage and family, and has an unbiblical restraining order and divorce proceedings against her husband. But she's always played the spiritual game well. No reason to change now.

Horay prayed. But *no mountains* would be *moved* by this coven. God only answers the prayers of the righteous. The only truly spiritual one among them already got up and left.

The memorial service later in the afternoon went off without a hitch. Several family members and friends of the family got up and lied about what an encouragement Maureen had been to them over the years, or what a good parent she had been.

Even the devil would have lots of good words said in his memory if he were to die, that is, if such a thing were possible. It's amazing how wonderful people get after they die, no matter how unfriendly, immoral, unlawful, self-righteous, contemptible, or sinful they had been when they lived. The best thing that can happen to some people is to die. They go from being hellions to being "the lights of the world" in a few days time.

Maureen's body was still in cold storage in the Snohomish County Coroner's Office, so the internment had to wait. After the memorial service, most of the family members and a number of friends gathered at the Muldanos' place again for a couple more days of untimely reunion. Some families only get together for marrying and burying, but the Muldano-Gregorys aren't one of them. They at least tried to maintain close family ties. Well, at least most of them did. Unfortunately, those that didn't—like Conner, who was selective about which family members he wanted anything to do with—were actually destructive to the family ties. Maybe with Maureen gone, some members will pull together like they haven't done in years. Even if they do, it's too late for Dan. He's out, and there's no stopping that now. He wouldn't go back if he could.

31

Conner Interrogated

When Conner Willingham came in for questioning on Tuesday morning following the memorial weekend, the detectives put him in a room by himself. They let him sit alone for about fifteen minutes getting good and nervous. Then Detectives Allen and Gonzales entered the room, took seats across the table from him, spread out the papers containing his criminal records on the table, and proceeded to use the team approach, alternating questions between them. Conner was wound tight, but they couldn't read too much into that. Anyone with his record would be very uncomfortable being interviewed about his past and his possible involvement in a current homicide, whether he was guilty or not.

The detectives informed Conner that he did not have to answer any questions that he didn't want to and that he could have an attorney present if he desired one. They told him that if he chose *not* to answer their questions, they would have him subpoenaed for questioning. They also informed him that anything he said could be used in a court of law. Conner said his criminal record was a matter of public record; he had paid for his past crimes, and had nothing to hide.

The interview was recorded. Conner hadn't said a single word while present during the interviews with Horay Muldano. Therefore, they had no previous recording to compare to the 911 recording the night of the death. They would now. Maybe Conner hadn't said a word because he didn't want his voice to be heard.

After well over an hour of interrogation, the deputies let Conner leave. He was a nervous wreck by then. His short, curly, black hair was soaked, as were the front and back of his gray shirt. The table had puddles of sweat from his head and arms, and his seat was soaked from sweat, as well. He had drunk five cans of pop, which the deputies had provided, and made two trips to the restroom. The deputies had drilled him relentlessly about his criminal record, his problems within the family, with Edward and Dan, and his activities the night of the crime. They suspected there was plenty more about the dark side of Conner that they didn't know. And they hadn't even learned anything from him or other family members about his having swindled his own uncles out of thousands of dollars in the years immediately following his release from prison.

When the deputies were finished, they still had nothing that would implicate him in his grandmother's death. His alibi seemed rock solid. But something just didn't add up. They would hammer his card-playing buddies next, separately, to see if they could find some inconsistency in their accounts on the night Maureen Muldano died.

A couple points in Conner's favor that were gleaned earlier from family members were that he had a wife and two young sons that dearly loved him, and, by all accounts, he was a good father and husband.

Unfortunately, late Tuesday, after doing a comparison analysis, the voice analyst informed the deputies that Conner's voice did not match the voice on the 911 tape. The call was not made by Conner. A big setback?

Detectives Allen and Gonzales believed the crime was almost certainly done by a family member, but they were going to have a tough time proving who did it, unless they could find someone who saw the person make the 911 phone call Friday night. Or, if the caller was not the killer but a second person—who was recruited, by force or for cash, by the killer into making the call— they would need him to come forward with his knowledge. Otherwise they would just about have to get a confession from the perpetrator. The other possibility was that the crime was, in fact, committed by someone other than their four suspects.

Of the four family suspects, Horay looked like far and away the best candidate for the crime. He admitted having an argument— though he said it was not an argument, but rather, Maureen chewing him out relentlessly; it was all one way by his wife. He also put himself at the crime scene within an hour or so of when she died. But he said he left to avoid saying or doing something regrettable.

If Horay told the truth about when he left and he did not come back and commit the crime in a confused demented state in which he couldn't remember pushing her, then someone else did it. That other person would have had to come to the house shortly after Horay left, probably argued with Maureen, and then pushed her. The person may have moved her away from the table with the idea of trying to help her, saw the seriousness of the bleeding and maybe saw the flexibility in her neck. She would have been either unconscious, or conscious and moaning as she was dying. The person, probably a family member, panicked and left. The person was probably heart-broken, wanted to help her, but knew he would be guilty of at least manslaughter, if not murder, if he called for help from the scene and then stayed there until the law arrived.

Detectives Allen and Gonzales decided to place a short appeal in the Everett Daily News asking for anyone who made a call around 9 pm from the pay phone near the Monroe branch Liberty Realty Office on Brigham Street on Friday evening on March 10th, *or* anyone who observed someone else making a call, to please contact the Snohomish County Sheriff's office. They both knew they were grasping at straws.

Chances were that the person who made the call, or any persons who observed the call, wouldn't even see their notice, and if they did, they probably wouldn't contact the Sheriff. If it was a person with any kind of substance abuse issues or criminal history, they most certainly would not want contact with the police. Furthermore, if the person was paid off for making the call, or made the call under duress, he would probably be afraid to admit he made the call, otherwise he would have already come forward.

Their best chance was if someone had observed the 911 caller, from across the street or anywhere nearby, and he or she could pinpoint the time and give a description of the person or persons near the phone booth. The witness may have been walking by and, therefore, wouldn't have been there when the Monroe Police tried to locate anyone in that area later Friday night. It was early enough in the evening that surely someone was nearby. But then again, the caller may have waited a minute or two to make the call when no one seemed to be in the area. There were a lot of possibilities, and none of them gave the detectives much hope. But they had to give the appeal a try.

They knew if they could mention the connection—but of course they couldn't— between the caller and the Monroe woman's death in their public notice, plenty of people would be curious about it. They would probably receive lots of calls, but none with any helpful information. Most people, who might have seen the caller, wouldn't want to get involved at all if they knew the caller had killed someone. They might be afraid that *he saw them*, too. If he killed one person, they could be a target for his brutality as well.

32

Poker Players

Detectives Allen and Gonzales interviewed Conner Willingham's four card playing buddies individually at their homes on Wednesday and Thursday evenings. The first interview was with Frank Wilkens. His wife and two kids stayed occupied in the living room, though she kept one ear trained toward the dining table where the detectives sat talking with her husband.

"Did your card game occur on Friday evening, March 10th, 2006, at 34862 Woods Creek Road at the residence of James Pallen?" asked Allen.

"Yes, that is correct," said Frank Wilkens.

"Was James Pallen home that night?"

"No, he drove down to Kelso to his brother's place. He and his wife are divorced. She lives in Longview with their two grade-school-age kids. He sees the kids two weekends out of the month. One time his ex brings the kids up to his house on Woods Creek Road, the other weekend he takes his kids to his brother's place for his visit. It works out pretty good for him."

"Do you always play your game at his house?" said Allen.

"Yes."

"I take it he's not a poker player."

"He used to be, before he ended up with a gambling problem," said Wilkens. "That's what ruined his marriage. But now he's staying away from cards, casinos and any other potential pitfalls that could lead him back into gambling; he's hoping to eventually get back together with his ex-wife.

"What's your connection with Pallen?"

"I met him playing softball ten years ago. Before his marriage broke up, we used to bounce around between each other's places for our card games. After his divorce, when his visitation schedule was established and he started going to Kelso, he offered his place for our monthly game. We've been playing there for over a year now. Works out great. We always clean everything up so the place looks good when he gets back on Sunday nights.

"You mentioned softball, is that where you all know each other from?"

"All of us except Warner, he works at the mill with Lonner. The rest of us all went to high school together, too."

"So, who was at the house that Friday night?"

"The usual five, Jay Maul, Tim Warner, Mike Lonner, Conner Willingham and myself."

"What time did the game begin?"

"Just after nine," said Wilkins. "We ate some pizza, drank a beer and shot the bull a bit before playing. Pretty much the usual routine. You know how it goes."

"Yes, I do," said Allen. "When did Conner Willingham get to the house?"

"He got there at just before 8:30."

"You're certain of that?"

"Yes. He gets there at that same time for our game every month. Comes right over after he leaves the gym where he works out," said Wilkens.

"Had he been drinking?"

"No."

"Did he receive any phone calls from his wife or other relatives while he was there?"

"No," answered Wilkins. "He had his phone turned off, just like the rest of us. We all figure it's our one night a month when we can get together with the guys, play cards, eat some good food, drink some brews and not be bothered by our wives or anyone else. I'm sure you can appreciate that."

Sergeant Allen overlooked that last comment, and said, "It seems awfully convenient for Willingham to have his phone off and several buddies who will alibi for his activities that evening."

"It may be convenient, but it's the truth," said Wilkins getting defensive. "Think what you want."

Sergeant Allen considered probing deeper into the card players' reasons for their secrecy, but thought better of it.

"Would you lie for Willingham to provide him with an alibi?"

"Absolutely not; not for him or anyone else."

"I think you have answered all our questions for now, but we'd like to talk to your wife for a minute, if you don't mind," said Allen.

"What do you need to talk to her for, she wasn't at the game?"

"We just want to confirm a couple points."

"Well, I do mind. And as far as I'm concerned, this meeting is over. I'll escort you both to the door."

After the deputies got to their unmarked squad car, Allen said to Gonzales, "I think I definitely touched a nerve, don't you."

"No doubt about that, Sarge. But what does it mean?"

"I don't know if it means anything in connection with this investigation, but it could mean a lot in terms of what actually goes on at card night."

"I'm with you there," answered Gonzales. "His account of the evening and the owner of the house lined up perfectly with Conner's. Do you think they're telling the truth, or do you sense, like I do, that they're covering something up?"

"I can't say for sure. I think we may get a better feel for what's going on after interviewing the other three."

Both detectives interviewed Warner, Maul and Lonner, but got nearly identical responses. All five of the card players were either telling the truth, or hiding something. Only time would tell.

33

FM: The Revelation

Windy drove up and spent the Muldanos' memorial weekend with Dan. Her girls stayed home. On Saturday afternoon, Dan and Windy drove out to Copalis Beach. What a romantic setting, with the turquoise blue sky partially covered by stratus clouds stretched over the ocean, showing their various shades of orange and red as the sun shone through them. As the sun set slowly down behind the horizon, they listened to the waves beating against the rocks and the seagulls squawking on the beach and in the sky above them.

Dan had been wrestling with telling Father Michael about Maureen's death and his being considered a suspect, but hadn't. The Aberdeen News, as well as the local radio and television stations, briefly reported the story of Maureen's death, and of Horay's missing and then being found. But there was no way Father Michael would have made any connection between Dan and those reports. Dan had never told him his in-laws' names. Windy thought it would be good for Dan to talk to him about the whole thing; she had no idea what "the whole thing" really was.

In mid-afternoon the following Wednesday, Dan met with Father Michael in his office at the church. He visited briefly with Julie while waiting to be called back to the father's office. Dan hadn't told Julie about Windy yet, but was sure she sensed something was different. Since he had never asked Julie out, neither of them was invested emotionally in the other. Dan was sure Julie would meet a good man at some point in the not-too-distant future, *maybe even a Catholic*. If it hadn't been for Windy being available, Dan knew he definitely would have pursued Julie.

After working through the preliminary greetings with Father Michael, Dan said, "Father, "I've told you a lot about me before now, but what I tell you today will surprise even you. I hope you'll still be my friend afterwards."

"You don't have to worry about that, Dan," he said. "I've learned enough about you to know what kind of a heart you have, and to know who you really are."

"I don't think you have any idea who I really am, Father. I don't mean to argue with you on that. I just mean that I'm a whole lot more sinful than you realize."

"Well, no matter how sinful you are, or think you are, just remember that I don't think you could tell me anything that I haven't heard before from someone. I've been at this a long time, between being a psychologist and a priest. I've listened to the confessions of thousands of people, including serial rapists, murderers and even pedophiles. Mankind is sinful, and I'm just a servant of God, not a judge. So, Dan, you can tell me whatever you need to. It will stay between you, me and God."

"Thanks for saying that, Father. I've really sensed God's love through you. Have you read or heard any of the news reports about the old couple in Monroe?" asked Dan. "The woman was found dead at home, and the husband was missing for several days, then turned up."

"Yes, I read about that in the Aberdeen News."

"That couple is my mother and father-in-law."

His eyes got big, "You're kidding me. What do you know about that situation?"

"I've heard that she was pushed by someone, fell backwards and hit her head on a coffee table, which broke her neck and split her head wide open," said Dan. "Whoever pushed her left the scene; the police received a 911 call reporting that she was in serious condition in her home. I also know that I'm one of their prime suspects." He still hadn't decided how much he wanted to tell Father Michael. But it was killing him to keep all of his clandestine activities of the last seven months to himself.

"You didn't push her did you?" he asked, pointedly, but speaking in a non-judgmental tone.

"No, I didn't do it. But *I was there*."

"So you saw who did it?"

"No. I mean I was at the house when the police showed up after the caller had reported it."

"I'm sorry, I'm not following you."

"I know it's confusing," said Dan. "I went into the house after she was already injured, or dead, actually."

"You saw her?"

"No. I was in one of their bedrooms when the cops came in the house. I was there getting my watch."

"Now, you really have me confused," he said, wrinkling his eyebrows.

"I went there to kill her and her husband. *But not that time*. I had gone up to Monroe three weeks earlier and snuck into their house with my pistol after dark. I waited in the little bedroom near the garage until after midnight. I wanted to make sure they were asleep." Dan paused for effect. "Now you know why I said you really don't know me."

"I wouldn't say that yet. You obviously didn't kill them then. Tell me more."

"When I went there to kill them, I actually stood at the foot of their bed with my loaded pistol, though I wasn't going to use it. My intention was to use *one of his pistols* to make it look like a murder-suicide."

"Why didn't you go through with it?"

"As I stood there running through the scenario in my mind, staring at them snuggled up like a couple of love-birds, even though they fought like cats and dogs during their waking hours, I started having second thoughts. My conscience started bothering me. *You might even say* the spirit of God was speaking to me, though I probably wouldn't give my thoughts that kind of credibility. At any rate, I finally decided I couldn't go through with it, no matter how much I hated my mother-in-law and everything she did to tear our marriage and family apart."

"I think you're wrong about me not knowing you," said Father Michael. "You're not a killer, even though you took some serious steps in that direction. I believe your extreme feelings and reactions have a great deal to do with how much pain and rejection you have been dealt throughout your entire life, not just during this marriage."

"Father, I haven't told you everything yet."

"Somehow, I don't think anything else you will say will end any differently than what you just told me," he said. "I've always sensed that in your heart you really do want to do what God wants. You really do want to do the right thing. You have just been over-whelmed by your circumstances."

"It's very kind of you to say it that way, Father; but I came close to committing murder three times in the past seven months. And every time it would have been multiple people that I killed."

"But you didn't do it, did you?" he said rhetorically. "You are not a killer, so you couldn't go through with it."

"Is that what you told all those other people who confessed their heinous crimes to you, that they were not rapists, murderers, pedo-philes and all the rest?" said Dan, regretting those words as soon as they left his mouth. He knew it was no way to speak to a man that loved him the way he knew Father Michael did.

"No, that's not what I told them," he said calmly, with no defen-siveness. Undoubtedly, his compassionate words had been tested plenty of times before. "Remember, they actually *did* commit the crimes. But even at that, I tried to speak God's love and forgiveness to them. I told them that if they were truly sorry for those sins, that God would forgive them, if they would only ask him to. Some of those people were already in prison when they told me about their crimes. Others were in the middle of the legal proceedings against them. Still others would need to take responsibility for their crimes and go to the authorities themselves, in their own time, to accept whatever penalties the legal system meted out to them."

"So you think everyone who ever committed any of the crimes you spoke of earlier should admit them to the authorities and serve time?" said Dan.

"Not necessarily," said Father Michael. "In some cases, nothing would be gained by that. If the person was truly sorry for his crime and repentant, such as when a parent has molested their child, then their going to prison would only compound a very sad situation. I believe that God, ultimately, wants to help people and families to be successful, to forgive and to overcome their failings of the past. I know that viewpoint wouldn't be popular with many people. But it's based on my own convictions, and what I understand God to say in His Word. God is about forgiveness and restoration."

"You need to go preach to my old pastor at the *Church of the Uncompassionate*."

"Well, I don't know about that. But I do know that you have to move on with your life now, forgetting what lies behind, and press on to the high-calling of Christ. If you dwell anymore on your wife, your in-laws, your ex-pastor, or your wife's lady friend in that church, and all the ways they have hurt you, you will only do yourself more harm. Let it go. You *must* let it all go.

"At some point soon," he went on, "I hope you will forgive all those who have wronged you. I know it's very tough. But recall the words that Jesus spoke in reference to the soldiers and religious people who had put him on the cross. He hung there dehydrated, bleeding, beaten and bruised, bearing the sins of all mankind, a righteous, sinless man, God himself. Yet he could say those words and mean them, 'Father, forgive them, for they know not what they do.' You already know all this. It's time you get back to the faith you once had in God and go forward."

"I know you're right, Father. You are so right. And you are so much a man of God, a messenger of God, even if you are a Catholic Priest." They both laughed. Dan knew he wasn't ready to forgive those people yet, but maybe someday he could. But not right now.

"Dan, if you were in the house when the police arrived, how did you avoid getting caught? And what about DNA evidence and fingerprints you would have left behind?"

"When I heard the police outside, I quickly crawled down under the house through the access hatch that, fortunately, I had earlier observed in the closet of the little bedroom. As far as the DNA and fingerprints, I didn't go into the main part of the house the night I recovered my watch. Oh, I forgot to tell you. I had worn a diver's suit and a full head mask when I went there to kill my in-laws, and somehow I had dropped my watch in the small closet. I went back there the night my mother-in-law died to try to find it. Talk about poor timing. Although, I guess, it was actually probably great timing. If I hadn't found my watch and the cops had found it, I would have been up a creek."

"It seems to me you got up the creek already by going there the first time."

"You're right on that, Father," Dan conceded. He didn't feel the need to tell Father that the night he lost the watch was actually his second time in the house intending to commit murder. Dan knew now that it had to have been God that kept him from disaster on Thanksgiving, as well. At least he wanted to believe it was Him.

"You said earlier that you are considered a prime suspect in the death of your mother-in-law," said Father Michael. "Why is that?"

"I didn't tell you that while I was there hiding under the house, I managed to hear some of what was being said above me by the cops, as well as by my wife. She actually implicated me by telling them how much her mother and I hated each other, how we had had words, and that I had actually threatened her. Then, when the Grays Harbor County Sheriff's deputies came to my house that night and I wasn't there, and I didn't show up until very late Sunday night, it only added to their suspicion."

"Obviously, you couldn't have told them where you were the night of the death. What *did you* tell them?"

"I lied to them. I told them I'd been camping in the woods several miles south of Rainbow Falls off Highway 6, which I knew wouldn't serve as much of an alibi, but neither could they prove I wasn't there that weekend, either. I did come back through there on my way back from my mother-in-law's house."

"I assume that, by now, they questioned you and even checked out your story on your camping trip."

"Yeah, they have."

"Since they haven't arrested you, they must not have any good evidence against you."

"That's my hope," said Dan. "My father-in-law looks guilty, from everything I've heard—though they are also looking hard at one of my wife's nephews. And I just heard yesterday, they are also quite interested in my wife's hog of a son, the oldest one, the 400 pounder, who I told you about earlier. The nephew is a great kid, about twenty. Personally I hope it turns out to be the oldest son."

"Is there anything I can do to help you in the case?"

"No, Father," answered Dan. "Well, you can pray, of course. Yeah, I definitely could use your prayers. Pray that they figure out who is guilty."

34

The Fire

By the end of March, the Snohomish County Sheriff's Department
had pretty well ruled out Edward Gregory as a suspect in his
grandmother's death, despite his not having an alibi for the night
she died. The deputies had come away from their conversations with
Edward with a good impression of him. That was only reinforced by
what everyone else—including many family members, several of
his college and high school friends and team mates—had said about
him. The only person in the family who spoke ill of him was his
cousin Conner. Deputies Allen and Gonzales concluded that nothing
about Edward indicated he would lose control and physically assault
his grandma.

A number of family members said they greatly respected him for
speaking out the way he did on Thanksgiving, and also because no
matter how many times his grandma had verbally assaulted him, he
had never been disrespectful to her in return, at least not that they
had ever seen or heard about. No one ever remembered him getting
mad enough at anyone to get physical with them, or threaten them.

They said his nickname, "Gentle Eddie," reflected that. Those that played sports with him, or watched him compete, said he always gave a hundred percent, but at the same time he was always a good sportsman and was admired for his Christian testimony.

No detectives had talked to Dan in over a week, so he was hoping that meant they were losing interest in him as a suspect. From what he had learned, the Snohomish County Sheriff detectives on the case were focusing primarily on Horay believing that he, in fact, returned to the house shortly after initially leaving it that night, and, in his confused state, argued with and pushed Maureen. Dan felt bad for Horay, in spite of Horay's hatred for him.

Conner was prominent on the detectives' radar because of his criminal record. His personality had not made points for him either. Unfortunately, his poker playing buddies were all sticking to their stories confirming Conner's presence at the house on Woods Creek Road almost a half hour before the 911 call was made from Monroe. If they were telling the truth, Conner could not have committed the crime.

On Friday night, April 7th, 2006, at 7:50, Conner Willingham parked his 1994 Chevy pickup across the street from the Seven-Eleven store at 951 Middle Street in Everett. He stopped to pick up a gallon of milk and a dozen donuts, his usual post-workout fare, while on his way home from lifting weights at Gold's Gym. Both windows of his truck were rolled down because he was still hot from his strenuous workout.

He started to open the driver's door when he noticed a couple of attractive girls about seventeen walk up to the front of the store, giggling in that playful way that attracts the attention of so many men. One of them was smoking a cigarette, while the other one sipped on a can of Mountain Dew. Conner, despite being married to a trim, beautiful woman, hesitated on opening his door. He wanted to enjoy watching the teen girls for a minute. When they walked into the Seven-Eleven, he immediately got out of his truck, crossed the street, went into the store, and struck up a conversation with them. He wasn't about to attempt to pick up on them, but he enjoyed flirting with them, all the same. They teased him for a minute or so, then picked up some malt balls and sodas, paid for them, then exited the store.

After Conner paid for his milk and doughnuts, he walked out, told the same teen girls that were standing there, to "Stay hot," (little did he know) and walked back across the street to his Chevy pickup. No sooner had he gotten in his truck, twisted the lid off the milk and taken a long swig, when, suddenly, a man on the sidewalk just outside his passenger window yelled,

"Hey Hog, you're never gonna threaten me or anyone else ever again." Instinctively, he turned his head toward the voice, just in time to see a large flash of light. Then he was on fire. A burning gallon can of gas had landed on the seat right next to him, splashing burning gasoline onto his right side. His clothes caught fire instantly. He lunged out the driver's door and sprawled onto the pavement next to his truck, crying out in pain and surprise.

The teen girls across the street screamed and ran inside the store. A small man, about forty, dressed in shabby clothes like many of the homeless people in that part of town, ran up to Conner who was rolling and writhing on the pavement, obviously in significant pain. The bum took off his long trench coat and thrashed it at the flames on Conner's clothes. Within seconds, the flames were out. But the fire inside Conner's truck was growing larger.

The bum pulled on one of Conner's arms to try to drag him away from the truck, but he couldn't budge him. He yelled at Conner, "You've got to get away from your truck before it blows!"

"What happened?" said Conner, dazed.

"A man threw a can of burning gas into your truck window," said the bum. "I saw him do it. Then he ran off. Come on, you've got to get away from the truck, now!"

Conner managed to get to his feet, and with the bum's help, limped forty yards down the street, just before the gas can exploded.

The windshield and back window were blown out. Flames poured out on all sides.

Several people, including the teenage girls who had ducked into the store when Conner dove out of his truck, burst out of the store and ran down the street to get farther away from the burning truck. Almost at once, sirens could be heard in the distance; someone had called 911. Within a minute, two fire trucks pulled up and the firefighters immediately sprayed foam and water into the burning cab. The fire was put out within seconds, but the fighters kept the water going to cool things down and to prevent a re-flash. Fortunately the pickup's fuel lines and tank did not ignite.

Conner stood next to the bum, shivering in pain. He was still somewhat dazed.

The bum asked, "Who would have done that to you?"

"I *know* who it was," said Conner. "It was my mom's soon-to-be ex-husband. I didn't see him, but I recognized his voice. He yelled at me just before the fire hit me. I'd know his voice anywhere."

"What's he look like?" said the street bum, looking up at Conner's face above his massive belly and shoulders.

"He's fifty, a little over six feet and probably weighs around 200 pounds. He has dark hair."

"I think you're right. That's what the guy looked like," said the bum. "Yeah, that's definitely right. He ran past me. There's no doubt about it, it had to be him."

A Snohomish County Sheriff car and two Everett Police cars had pulled up about the same time as the fire trucks, and more pulled up momentarily, as did an ambulance. As soon as the fire was out, the policemen began asking the many onlookers who had gathered if they had seen anything. Two officers came over to the bum and Conner and, even in the dim light of the street lamp, noticed at once that Conner's clothes were burned.

"Is that your pickup?" one of them asked Conner.

"Yes."

"You need medical assistance. Medic, over here!" he yelled.

Two medics rushed up to Conner, carrying their boxes.

As the medics cut Conner's blackened clothes away and spread coolant over the burns on his right arm, right side, hip and right thigh, one of the deputies said to Conner, "Do you have any idea who might have done this to you."

"I know exactly who it was," he said. "It was Dan Thurmond, my mom's husband. She's divorcing him. She has a restraining order on him."

"How do you know it was him? Did you see him?" said the deputy.

"Ooh, that stuff's cold," said Conner. "I didn't see him, but just before the burning can of gas landed beside me, I heard him yell at me."

"What did he yell?"

"Something about threatening him or anybody else," said Conner.

"Does that make any sense to you?" said the deputy.

"The man is a jackass. We had a couple of run-ins in the past. Everyone in the family hates him. He treated my mom like crap."

"Did you ever threaten him?"

"I don't know," said Conner. "I might have, in the heat of an argument or something. You say things sometimes. You know how it goes."

"What makes you so sure it was him that yelled at you?" he said.

"It was him alright. I wouldn't mistake his voice in a crowd of a hundred people."

The deputy then asked the bum, "Did you see any of it?"

"Saw the whole thing," said the bum. "It was just like he said. The man yelled at him, then tossed the burning can in the truck."

"Where were you when it happened?"

"I was standing just down the sidewalk from the front of the truck. Right over there." He pointed. "The man tossed the can and ran right past me."

"Did you hear what he said?"

"Sure did. He yelled, 'Hey Hog, you're never gonna threaten me or anyone else ever again.' Then he tossed in the can. Looked like it had a paper torch or something that was on fire."

"What did he look like?"

"He was about fifty, dark hair, six foot or so and I'd say at least 200 pounds."

"We'll need to get an official statement from both of you. Do you know if anyone else saw him?"

"I couldn't say," said the bum. "Other than there were a couple of teenage girls hangin' in front of the Seven-Eleven."

Another cop was already in the process of getting their testimony. They said they saw the initial fire and the burning man dive out of the truck, but panicked and ran into the store. From there they had seen a man run up and put out the fire on the man and help him get away from the truck just before the explosion inside the truck. They did not see anyone run off.

Conner was transported by ambulance to Everett General Hospital, where he was examined and treated by Doctor Howard Folker in the Emergency Room.

As Dan completed his morning walk through the woods on his property in Aberdeen on Saturday, April 8th, three Grays Harbor County Sheriff's rigs pulled up his driveway. His chest tightened; something was terribly wrong. With difficulty, he stepped out of the trees into the driveway to face whatever the bad news was.

Three deputies jumped out of the three vehicles with their hands on their holstered pistols. One yelled, "Get on the ground *now*, Thurmond!"

He dropped to his belly on the wet ground, terrified.

The deputies surrounded him, but didn't draw their guns. Two of them stooped down and grabbed his arms, twisted them behind his back and cuffed him. "You're under arrest for the murder of Maureen Muldano on March 10th, and for attempting to murder Conner Willingham last night," said the deputy who cuffed him. He realized it was Sergeant Lang.

"What is this all about?" he asked.

Sergeant Lang pushed his face down onto the wet gravel and said, "We have an eye-witness who saw you throw a burning can of gas into Willingham's pickup in Everett last night. And we have evidence from the Muldanos' home indicating you were there when she was killed."

"I was here last night. And I definitely wasn't at the Muldanos' when she was killed. I already showed you where I was that night."

"Before you say anymore, I want you to know, 'You have the right to remain silent, if you give up that right, anything you say, can and will be used against you in a court of law, you have the right to an attorney, if you cannot afford one, one will be appointed on your behalf.' Do you understand?"

"Yes," Dan answered, "I'm not guilty of either of those crimes. I was here at home last night."

"Do you have anyone that can verify that?" said Lang, as the deputies glanced at each other.

"No, I don't. Both of my kids spent the night at their friends' houses."

"You sure have a way of never having an alibi when you need one, don't you Thurmond?" said Lang, as he and the other deputy pulled him up to his knees, then to his feet. The other officer then quickly frisked him. The only things Dan had on him were his lucky pocket watch, a comb and handkerchief. His wallet and keys were sitting on the dining table.

"When you live out here in the country, you're alone a lot of the time," said Dan. "At least I am. If I didn't commit a crime, why would I think that I needed an alibi? You have the wrong man. I don't care how it looks, or what the so-called eye-witness said. What kind of evidence do you think you have against me at the Muldano house?" He was afraid they had gotten under the house and found his DNA and fingerprints all over the place.

"The Snohomish County sheriffs found one of your hairs in the

Muldanos' bedroom."

He felt relieved that they hadn't been under the house, but at the same time he feared it was only be a matter of time now before they got under there.

"You've got a single hair in a house that I had been in many times and that makes me guilty of murder? You've got to be kidding me?"

"There's plenty more than that."

"Yeah, what then?"

"The circumstantial evidence, your threats, no alibi. Then your being identified by a witness last night, along with Willingham's own testimony that it was definitely you who yelled at him just before the gas can landed on the seat next to him. Your vendetta against that whole family is no secret."

"That's all bull crap. That family has wanted my hide for years. Willingham hated me. This is the perfect setup for them to nail me. In fact, how do you know that the whole attack on Willingham last night wasn't staged for this very purpose?" He was desperate.

"You're smart enough to know that no one is going to stage a situation in which they get torched, to make someone else look guilty," said Lang.

"What happened to Willingham anyway?"

"He managed to quickly jump from the vehicle," said Lang. "But he received second-degree burns on his right arm, right side, and right thigh. His vehicle was totaled in the fire, but fortunately fire crews arrived on the scene within a couple of minutes and put the fire in the cab out before the truck's gas tank could ignite. I guess you didn't stick around long enough to see that though, did you?"

"I wasn't there," Dan insisted. "I didn't see any of it."

Well, we have to take you down to the jail and book you. You need to get a hold of your lawyer. If, in fact, you are telling the truth, you have nothing to worry about." Yeah right.

He was loaded into one of the squad cars, taken to Aberdeen, and booked into the Grays Harbor County Jail. With his phone call, he contacted Father Michael, filled him in on the situation, and asked if he could recommend a good attorney.

After hanging up with Dan, Father Michael called his good friend in Everett, Brent Slusherman, one of the top criminal defense attorneys in Washington. His name fit beautifully because he had the reputation of turning a jury into slush in his hands. Prosecutors hated him.

35

Dan's Lawyer

On Sunday morning Dan was extradited a few hours away to the Snohomish County Jail in Everett. First thing Monday morning, he was taken from his solitary cell to another room where his new attorney, Brent Slusherman, a striking looking man in his sixties, with a bad case of male-pattern baldness, was sitting at a wooden table. What hair he did have, on the sides and back of his head, was solid gray, as were his mustache and goatee. Wire-rimmed glasses rested on the bridge of his nose. When he stood, Dan could see Slusherman was about three inches shorter than him. Slusherman shook his hand, and introduced himself with his deep voice. The jailer locked the door on his way out.

"Dan Thurmond, I'm Brent Slusherman. Your priest, Father Michael, called me yesterday and explained your situation. He asked if I could help. We go way back to our Vietnam days. I was a pilot operating off the same aircraft carrier. He told me you are a cold-war submarine veteran who is innocent of the crimes you're accused of."

"It's nice to meet you sir," said Dan. "Father Michael is not actually my priest—at least I don't go to his church. But he has become a wonderful friend and spiritual mentor to me over the last year. I don't know that I can afford your services."

"We'll worry about that later. Somehow we'll make it work."

"Why are you so willing to represent me?"

"Two reasons, actually," he said. "Father Michael spoke of you as if you were his own son. That means everything to me. I met Father Michael, who was Lieutenant Phil Michael back then, in the officer's chow hall one day in 1968. We've been like brothers ever since. One of those things you can't explain. It just happened."

"The second reason is that I know what it's like to be wrongly imprisoned. I spent over three years in the Hanoi Hilton in North Vietnam after being shot down over the Ho Chi Min Trail at the South Vietnam-Laos border in November 1969."

"Thank you for your military service, Mr. Slusherman," said Dan, "and for your willingness to represent me."

"And I thank you for your military service, as well," he said. "I was never on a submarine, but we did some exercises with them."

"What all did Father Michael tell you about my situation?" said Dan, anxious to get down to the legal case against him. He needed to know how long he would be in jail and what his chances were of being acquitted.

Slusherman understood Dan's anxiety, and said, "He just told me that you had been arrested, what you were being charged with, mentioned your submarine background, and said how much he liked you and believed in you. One thing about Phil is he really believes in and holds to client or parishioner confidentiality. I'm the same way. Whatever you and I discuss will never go any further unless we both agree that some of it is necessary to properly defend you."

"I appreciate that, Mr. Slusherman."

"By the way," said Slusherman, "you can call me Brent when we're in private and Mr. Slusherman would be fine in public."

"Thanks, Brent. I understand."

"When you were arrested, what did the cops say you were being charged with?"

"Supposedly I murdered my soon-to-be ex-wife's mother, my mother-in-law, Maureen Muldano, four weeks ago, and attempted to murder my wife's oldest son, Conner Willingham, this past Friday."

"Are you guilty?"

"Absolutely not."

"I'll assume you have no alibi for the time that either crime was committed, and that you did have motive, at least from the law's point of view. Did they tell you what evidence they have against you?"

"Yeah. On the mother, they say I had motive, that I made threats against her, they said they found one of my hairs in the mother's bedroom, and I had no good alibi."

"When did you threaten her?"

"I never actually threatened her. I just told some people what I would like to do to her for how she destroyed my marriage and family. I later heard that someone had told her and others in the family what I had said. Who knows what she was actually told."

"Can you tell me about the hair?"

"I had been in the mother-in-law's house many times in the first two years my wife and I were married, before the extended family relationship went to hell, thanks to the mother. I don't know how the hair got in the bedroom, though?"

"You were never in the bedroom?"

"No." At least not without the diver's suit on, he thought, and he knew he couldn't have lost a hair in there then. At this point Dan wasn't going to tell Brent about his actually being in the house the night of the crime, or his previous visits. He hoped he would never have to tell him.

"Where in the house was the mother killed? And what were the circumstances?"

"She was found lying in the entryway between the family room and the dining room, with a pool of blood around her head. The police determined that she was pushed backward, fell and hit her head on an end table, gashed her head and broke her neck. Then, whoever pushed her dragged her four feet to the side, before leaving the house. The person had to be quite strong; she weighed over 300 pounds. A 911 call was made at 8:58 from a phone booth on Brigham Street in Monroe, reporting the mother as being seriously injured at the Muldanos' residence east of Monroe. That's it."

"I read about that in the newspaper and heard it on the news. That was your mother-in-law, huh?"

"Yeah, unfortunately."

"I'll tell you right now, they can't begin to make a case out of the one hair, even if it was found in the bedroom. A single hair can be carried into another room on someone's socks or shoes. Since you were admittedly in the house as a family member on numerous occasions in the past, the hair means nothing."

"That's what I thought, but I couldn't help but worry."

"I understand," he said. "What about the son-in-law?"

"I was at my home in Aberdeen that evening. I don't know what happened, other than what the cops told me."

"What was that?"

"Just that I was supposedly seen by a witness, who gave a description of the perpetrator that matched me. They said I had tossed a burning can of gasoline into the cab of my wife's son's pickup while he was sitting in it parked on the opposite side of the street from a Seven-Eleven store. And the son, who escaped with some second-degree burns on part of the right side of his body, said that it was definitely my voice he heard yell at him just before the burning gas can was tossed in beside him."

"Was it you?" he asked. "I'm only asking this directly, to hear it from you."

"No. Like I said, I was at home, over two and a half hours away, at the time it happened."

"That's all I wanted to know. And I think that for now, I have all the information I need. That is, unless there is anything else you can tell me that might be helpful."

"No, that's it, I think. Well, you should know that my wife has a restraining order against me."

"That's helpful to know. Your arraignment will be first thing Thursday morning. That will give me time to gather up all the legal information and the evidence on file in each of these cases. I will meet with you again late tomorrow afternoon to go over my findings and to get a little more background on you, such as any school, community or church service you have been involved in, where you have worked, that kind of thing—anything to show positive character."

"Is there any chance of getting me out of jail right away?"

"Absolutely," he said. "I expect to get you released immediately following the arraignment. We will plead innocent and ask that the case against you be dismissed due to lack of evidence. If they don't dismiss the case outright, which I don't expect they will, I will request that you be released on your own recognizance. The prosecutor will object on the grounds that you are guilty of violent crimes to two different people weeks apart and are not only a risk to others in that family, but a flight risk as well. He will also bring up the restraining orders to try to strengthen his argument. I will object, pointing out that you have no prior criminal record and *have only been accused* of these crimes and certainly have not been found guilty."

"Since you have no history of violent crime and no felonies, and there's no good evidence against you, I have very little doubt that the judge will release you. But I do expect him to set bail at around $100,000, just to cover his butt and to appease the prosecution. Do you have any way to pay the ten percent required?"

"I have a $50,000 home-equity line-of-credit."

"That's good. Is there someone who you can get to take care of getting the money for you?"

"Yes, believe it or not, Father Michael already offered his services and will be here late Monday morning with the necessary documents."

"He's something else, isn't he?" said Slusherman, "Willing to run around to do some errands, then drive up here?"

"You're telling me. I don't know what I would do without him, right now. Or you."

"Well, we veterans have to pull together to win this battle. Try to get some rest, and try not to worry. You're in good hands with Phil and me."

"I know I am. Thanks again."

Dan was removed to his cell. Three hots and a cot; I guess I can stand it for a few more days, he thought.

36

Arraignment

At 8:45 Thursday morning, April 13th, Dan followed his attorney, Brent Slusherman, into the courtroom, wearing the street clothes that Father Michael had brought to the jail the day before. Dan saw him sitting toward the back on the left side. Slusherman led the way to the defendant's table and chairs at the front on the left. Father Michael immediately moved up to the first row directly behind them on that side.

Brenda, Conner, Horay, Jan and a couple others of their family were seated mid-way back on the right; from there they could easily root for the prosecutor to keep Dan in jail until the trial. It really hurt Dan to know he hadn't committed either of the crimes, yet his once beloved wife and the very family members that had attended his wedding, hugged and congratulated him afterwards, and ate the dinner and some of the wedding cake, were there to intimidate him and cheer for his conviction. He thought it was bad enough, eleven months earlier, when Brenda brought some of those very people, along with her satanic mom, into his own church two weeks after having him served with a restraining order. How did he not see what Brenda was really all about before he married her? She was ruthless. Did she even have a conscience? Dan didn't think so.

"*Please rise* for the Honorable Judge Leroy Laney," said the bailiff.

Judge Laney, a distinguished-looking, strong-featured, gray-haired man in his fifties, explained the preliminaries and then asked the prosecution for a motion. The prosecutor, Julian Haadapa, handling only his second murder case as the new Snohomish County District Attorney, briefly described the crimes that Dan had allegedly committed, listed the evidence against him, and asked that he be remanded to the continued custody of the State until such time as the trial.

When Haadapa was done, Mr. Slusherman, entered not-guilty pleas to both charges on Dan's behalf, then proceeded to show his eloquence in presenting the reasons why the cases should be dismissed. Dan could see why he had a reputation.

Dan held his breath as Judge Laney then said, "I am not the least bit impressed with the evidence against Mr. Thurmond on the murder charge." Dan took another big breath and held it, as he glanced over in the direction of the Muldano clan. He could see by the looks of disbelief on the wolves' faces that they were very disappointed. "However," the judge paused. "I do believe that the prosecution has better evidence on the charge of attempted murder." The Muldano faces lit up, no one's more than Conner's, who was sporting ace bandages on his right arm. "Therefore, at this time, I am not going to dismiss either charge. I expect the prosecution will have much better evidence before bringing the murder charge back to my courtroom. I'm going to release Mr. Thurmond on $200,000 bail."

"But Your, Honor—"

"No *but* anything!" Laney said to the new DA. "This is my courtroom, and I will have the last say. Is that clear?"

"Yes your, Honor," said the DA.

At the conclusion of the arraignment, Mr. Slusherman assisted Dan in getting the bail posted, and he was released on his own recognizance. Slusherman then joined Father Michael in signing Dan out of the Snohomish County Jail.

From there they went, fittingly, to the Pho Ha Vietnamese Restaurant for lunch. Brent commented that the food there was much better than the daily bowl of fish-eye rice-soup that Ho Chi Min's boys served him; they had done a nice job of carrying on the recently deceased North Vietnamese leader's legacy (Ho Chi Min died September 2, 1969). Brent said Nutri-System had nothing over those boys; he lost sixty pounds on their diet plan. The regular prison-camp body massages (torture) were an added bonus. They all roared as they shot military stories and quips back and forth. Dan got to see the pre-priest side of Father Michael. He felt so lucky to have both of these fellow ex-sailors as his friends and allies in this latest attack on his life, or rather, on his freedom.

They spent two and a half hours at the restaurant, said their temporary farewells to Brent, then Father Michael drove himself and Dan back down to Aberdeen. There wasn't much Dan could do to prove his innocence, but Brent would be working hard to prove there was insufficient evidence to convict him. They would all hope that the Snohomish County Sheriff's detectives would find, and put together, the missing pieces to the puzzle—now puzzles—on Maureen's death, and now the attempt on Conner's life.

37

Mystery Man

At two o'clock, Friday afternoon, the day after Dan's arraignment, the Snohomish County Sheriff's Office got a call from an old lady who complained about an old, dirty pickup sitting on the street at the end of her driveway in her Everett neighborhood. She said it had been there for about a week. Some guy in old clothes had come to the pickup a few days earlier and tried to start it, but was unable to. She said she didn't go out to talk to him, but through her open window it sounded like he ran his battery dead turning over the motor. She wanted to know if there was anything the Sheriff could do to get the guy to move his truck. It was blocking her view of the neighbor's house across the street which she was supposed to be keeping an eye on.

She wasn't entirely candid. The truth was, the thirty-some-year-old guy in the house across the street liked to bring a different gal home every few days, and she didn't want to miss any of the action that took place between the car and his front door. Neither did her lady friend that was usually on the other end of the phone when the old lady described what the guy was doing with his hands with each of the young women. Neither of the old women was related to Maureen, *but they could have been.*

The deputy asked for her address, and upon determining that it was in the same area as the Seven-Eleven store where Willingham's pickup was torched, he told the woman he would send an officer over to check it out. He relayed her message to a deputy in the field, and mentioned that the address was three blocks away from the Seven-Eleven where the attempted murder had taken place the previous Friday evening.

In the days immediately following the fire, detectives had questioned all of the neighbors they could find at home within a two-block radius of the Seven-Eleven. No one had seen the man who supposedly set the fire.

When the patrol deputy arrived at the old woman's house, he parked in front of the house next to hers. He got out of his car and walked over to the rusted, faded-blue, 1971 GMC pickup, and looked into the cab. Immediately, he spotted what looked like a small piece of burned cloth lying on the floor near the stick shift. His curiosity was instantly aroused. He went to the back of the pickup to look at the license plate, then radioed in the license number to dispatch, and mentioned the burned cloth.

As he waited for the dispatcher to get back to him, he tried to open the driver's side door, but found it locked. The passenger's door was locked as well.

Dispatch came back over the radio a minute later, "That truck is registered to James David Pungent, 1139 Charles Street, in Monroe. He did two years in Ralston for felony drug-dealing in 1991. There are no other crimes on his record."

The deputy then went to the door of the residence and, as he reached out to knock, an old lady opened the door. She had been watching him through her front window.

"Are you Mrs. Dorothy Mauney?"

"Yes, I am. Did you guys figure out who the owner of that truck is?"

"We know who it is registered to—some guy in Monroe. I'm Deputy Wilson. What did the guy look like that tried to start it?"

"He was a medium-size guy with a medium build. His hair was short. I'd guess he was about forty. Are you guys going to get him to move the truck?"

"We're definitely going to talk to him," said Deputy Wilson. "When exactly did you first notice the truck here?"

"I went out to dinner with my friend Ethel last Friday night about seven. We ate at Marie Callender's, then went over to her house and watched an evening soap opera. When I got back a little after ten, the truck was there. I figured it belonged to someone visiting one of my neighbors."

"When did the guy come to get it?"

"It was Sunday afternoon, about three."

"Well, I can't do anything about it until we make contact with the owner, but we will do our best to get it moved for you," said the deputy.

"I'd appreciate that."

"You have a nice day Ma'am." The deputy returned to his squad car and conversed by radio with Detective Allen.

"We're sending a couple deputies over to Pungent's residence in Monroe right now," said Allen. "Were you able to nail down a time on when that truck was left there?"

"The old lady said it wasn't there when she left her house a little before seven, last Friday night, but was there when she returned at ten."

"You're sure there is some burned cloth on the floor?"

"Yes, but I can't get in. The truck's locked."

"I'll be there in a few minutes."

Sergeant Allen arrived ten minutes later. The two deputies looked the truck over in the same manner as Deputy Wilson had done thirty minutes earlier.

"That's definitely burned cloth. It looks like it could be part of a shirt, like the end of a sleeve," said Allen. "I think this truck could be our perpetrator's in that torching incident in front of the Seven-Eleven."

"Sergeant Allen?" a voice came over the radio.

"Yes, this is Sergeant Allen, go ahead."

"I'm at the Pungent residence in Monroe. No one's home, and there are no vehicles here. The house is pretty run down, but I think someone is living here. The backyard is loaded with garbage, and some of it is fresh. Do you want me to hang around for a bit?"

"No. We'll get the Monroe Police to check back periodically there to try to catch Pungent at home. We're going to stake-out this truck with an unmarked car. I think the guy who drove this truck here was definitely involved in the attempted murder at the Seven-Eleven last Friday night. Sooner or later he has to come back."

On Monday afternoon, a medium-built man about forty, carrying what looked like a jumper battery and a small tool kit, was spotted walking up to the GMC and opening its hood. The stake-out cop immediately radioed the dispatcher, who sent three other deputies to the scene. The three additional deputies parked down the street from the old truck and coordinated their approach to it with the stake-out deputy. The jumper battery was sitting on the ground in front of the truck, while the guy was leaning in over the radiator working on the engine with a couple of wrenches when the four deputies eased up within thirty feet of the truck, with their guns drawn and pointed at the ground near the man's feet.

"James Pungent," said deputy Murray.

The man startled, then turned to face the voice. Surprised to see two sheriff's deputies, the man responded, "Yes. I'm James Pungent."

"Step away from the vehicle, please."

"What's going on?"

"Please, just step over onto the grass and lay down on your belly."

Pungent noticed the other two officers, and walked the ten feet to the grass and lay down.

"Is the truck unlocked?" asked Murray.

"No. What do you want?"

"You're under suspicion for the attempted murder of Conner Willingham Friday night, April 7th, in front of the Seven-Eleven store up the street?"

"You've got the wrong man. I don't know any Conner Will..., whatever his name was," he said, raising his head up as he protested.

"Keep your head on the ground, and carefully hand me your keys" said Deputy Brock. "We have a warrant to search your vehicle."

Pungent put his head on the ground and reached back with his right arm for his keys.

"Look at that," said Brock. "He has a burn on his hand."

Brock quickly holstered his gun, put a knee in Pungent's lower back, grabbed his right arm, cuffed his wrist, and quickly jerked his left arm around to his back and cuffed it.

"You're under arrest for attempted murder. You have the right to remain silent..."

After quoting Pungent his rights, Brock rolled him partially to his left and grabbed the keys from his right, front jean-pocket, and tossed them to Deputy Murray.

Murray unlocked the passenger side door of the truck and tossed the keys to one of the other deputies to unlock the driver's side. Murray then bent into the truck and upon closer examination of the burned cloth, said, "That's definitely burned clothing material. Get a camera, get some shots, then bag up the cloth. Get some photos of Pungent's burns too."

"Yes sir, Sergeant," said the fourth deputy.

Brock frisked Pungent and then ensured that he remained belly-down on the grass, while Murray and the other deputy searched the truck. They found no other evidence.

"Where did you get burned?" asked Murray.

"I burned myself cooking French fries last week."

"You can do better than that."

"It's the truth."

"Yeah, what is the truth about the burned cloth in your truck?"

"I took my garbage to the dump last week."

"You must have had a ton of garbage, because two of our deputies were by your house a couple days ago and said the back patio was loaded with garbage."

Pungent didn't say anymore. He had been taken by surprise and knew there was no point in getting in any deeper. Deputy Brock then pulled him to his feet, led him to his squad car and took him to the Snohomish County Jail, where he was booked for attempted murder.

Pungent was arraigned the following Wednesday, charged with attempted murder. Brent Slusherman, Father Michael, Windy, and Dan, along with the Muldano-Gregory clan, including Conner, were all in the courtroom for the arraignment. The District Attorney moved for a quick trial, because he was convinced they had enough evidence to convict Pungent already, and knew they would have an airtight case within a few months. Judge Laney set the trial for September next, and ordered Pungent to remain confined, without bail, to the Snohomish County Jail until the trial. He then announced he was dropping the charge of attempted murder against Dan Thurmond.

Mr. Slusherman then addressed Judge Laney, "Your Honor, I would ask the court to also dismiss the charge of first-degree murder against my client at this time, as well, due to insufficient evidence. I would remind the Court that much of the circumstantial evidence against my client was connected to the alleged attempted murder of Mr. Willingham and the sour history he, and others of the Maureen Muldano family, had with my client. Since Mr. Pungent has now been charged with the attempted murder of Mr. Willingham, there is no longer a circumstantial connection between my client and Mrs.

Muldano's death. The only supposed evidence the State has against my client is a single hair found in the victim's home, a home my client had, admittedly, been in numerous times prior to the night of Mrs. Muldano's death.

"Your point is well taken, Mr. Slusherman. The Court *will*, in fact, drop the charge of first-degree murder against your client, Daniel Thurmond.

Pungent's court-appointed attorney, Brian Green, consulted briefly with Pungent, before he was led out of the courtroom by two deputies and taken back to his maximum security cell at the Snohomish County Jail. As Pungent was taken away, Dan looked at the Muldano-Gregory clan and got a few dirty looks in return. At least he didn't get Maureen's satanic glare.

Part Two
Pungent Trial

38

State's Case

Dan and Brendas' divorce was final July 13th, 2006. She had renewed her restraining order in April 2006, by telling the judge that Dan was a continued threat to her. (Of course, she had no idea that for months he actually was a much greater threat than she could have imagined.)

Dan was amazed that the same person who initially wanted to reconcile with him after she left him, three months later got a restraining order against him and then kept it in force until the divorce, that she filed, was final fifteen months later. In all that time, she never spoke to him except for saying his name in The Wong Place the previous June. If that wasn't a chicken-crap way of handling things, he didn't know what was. But looking back, it didn't surprise him. Brenda's way of dealing with everything related to her family's interference and influence in his home and marriage was to stick her head in the sand and pretend it wasn't happening. She should write a book on, "How to behave like a child when dealing with your marital problems or breaking up."

Dan was awarded the house and property in Aberdeen, but he was ordered to pay Brenda fifty thousand dollars, less than a fourth of the equity, as an equalizing judgment. On one hand, she was unhappy with the settlement, because she wanted half the equity, plus half his inheritance from his parents, and alimony to boot. On the other hand, even she had to admit she took him to the cleaners, considering she brought nothing but thousands of dollars of hidden credit-card debt into the marriage and no assets, other than an old run-down Volkswagen bug. No one would consider *her family* an asset.

Now she was free to pursue a fifth future ex-husband, who she could subject to her family's constant critiquing and criticism. Of course, with Maureen out of the picture now, at least Brenda wouldn't be married to two people at the same time when she did remarry. Maybe she would quit trying to *play Christian* and go back to shacking up with her lovers again instead of marrying them— although now that she had figured out how lucrative it could be to marry and divorce someone that had even a small amount of money, she probably wouldn't settle for shacking up again.

Dan and Windy were getting married in January 2007. Finally, he would have the woman of his dreams for his wife. Since Dan's release from jail in April 2006, they had spent almost every weekend together. After their wedding, she would be moving in with him in his house in Aberdeen. He had a bright future.

As of September first, Dan had not been recharged in Maureen Muldano's death, and his attorney, Brent Slusherman, assured him that he would not be charged at any point in the future. He told Dan that when his new client, of four months, James David Pungent's attempted murder trial went to court at the end of the month, Dan would be very pleased with the facts revealed at that time. Obviously, due to attorney-client privilege, Slusherman did not disclose any of his findings to Dan.

Horay Muldano had suffered only one brief period of dementia in the last several months. The medication he had been taking for

Alzheimer's Disease, since the week following Maureen's memorial service, was working well. Unfortunately, he hadn't been able to recall any more details of his activities for the night Maureen died than he did in his initial lucid interview several days after her death. Detectives Allen and Gonzales, as well as the District Attorney's Office had determined that he would likely never be able to recall anything from that time period. Therefore, even if Horay was guilty of pushing Maureen down to her death it was unlikely he would ever be charged. From what the detectives learned about Maureen, neither could blame Horay if he had pushed her. Of course, as law-enforcement officers, those feelings didn't have any bearing on their efforts to solve the case.

At 8:30 a.m., Tuesday, September 26th, 2006 the case of *The State of Washington Versus James David Pungen*t convened in the Snohomish County Courthouse, Court Room 3—the Honorable Judge Leroy Laney presided.

The courtroom was packed as expected. At least twenty of the spectators were Conner Willingham's relatives, there to see justice brought to the man who tried to kill him. They were sitting together toward the back on the right side of the room, the same side as the twelve-person jury. Conner and the other prospective witnesses were not in the courtroom, as both sides had moved to exclude witnesses. Father Michael and Windy were seated beside Dan toward the front of the courtroom on the left side, a few rows behind the defendant, James Pungent, and his attorney, Brent Slusherman. Numerous news reporters were present, as were various law officers.

Mr. Slusherman was leaning back in his chair behind the defense table, relaxed and confident, as if he were contemplating whether to go and get a big bucket of buttered popcorn to munch on while waiting for a movie to begin on a big screen in front of him.

By contrast, the new District Attorney of six months, Julian Haadapa—a slightly built, black headed, physically unattractive, fifty-three year-old, with a pock-marked face hidden only slightly with a thin black mustache—was fidgeting noticeably in his chair ten feet away, as he flipped continuously through the pages of the thick, black notebook in front of him with his right hand, while alternately groping at his black tie, and constantly sipping from his large glass of water with his left hand. He had won all three of the murder, and the one attempted-murder, trials that he had prosecuted to date. But as simple as the Pungent case originally looked to be, he knew he was up against the best in the business and could be in for the fight of his life.

After Judge Laney explained the charges, trial agenda and various other legal preliminaries he said, "Mr. Hadaapa, you may proceed with your opening statement."

The District Attorney walked over to the jury box, slowly scanned each juror's face and said, "The State will prove that the defendant, James David Pungent, did, on the night of April 7th, 2006, deliberately attempt to kill Conner Willingham by tossing a burning can of gasoline into his truck while he was seated in it, parked across the street from the Seven-Eleven Store at 951 Middle Street in Everett, Washington."

The District Attorney went on to give a brief description of what a low-life human-being James Pungent was—that he had spent years plotting how he would one day get revenge against Conner Willingham for supposedly telling Pungent, while both were briefly together in prison, that when Willingham got out of prison he would someday rape Pungent's younger sister. The DA said he would show Pungent to be a liar and the murderer that he tried to be.

When it was his turn to give an opening statement, Brent Slusherman, representing the defendant, stood in front of the jurors, in like manner as the DA had done, and said, "The Defense will prove that the defendant, James David Pungent, is not guilty of attempted murder at all—but, in fact, acted in self-defense after a long history of physical abuse, threats and intimidation by Conner Willingham. That when he attacked Willingham that night in April, he believed it was the only way to escape Willingham's years of control and domination over him and, in fact, the only way to save his own life."

Murmuring began in earnest among a number of spectators who were shocked at the audacity of the arrogant defense attorney. The audience could see that with Brent Slusherman representing the defendant, the case was not going to be the slam-dunk most of them had anticipated. In fact, they were in for a much better show than they realized. A few of the Muldano clan began bickering. A spectator in the back left said, under his breath, "Conner deserved to be attacked, the way he pushes everyone around."

Fortunately, none of the Muldano-clan heard him. They were too busy bickering among themselves. "Don't you dare start in on Conner," said Brenda to someone in her family. "He needs all of our support right now."

"Order!" Judge Laney demanded, slamming his gavel down several times.

After order was restored, Mr. Slusherman completed his opening statement.

Judge Laney then told DA Haadapa to proceed with the prosecution.

"Thank you, Your Honor," said Mr. Haadapa. "The State will call Conner Willingham as its first witness."

Conner entered the courtroom from the back and waddled down the center aisle, dressed in his usual casual attire, a light-red, short-sleeved sports-shirt, black jeans, and white, low-top Nike tennis-shoes. He was sworn in, then took a seat in the witness stand. The chair creaked under the strain of his 400 pounds.

"Mr. Willingham, would you please describe what happened to you on the night of April 7th, 2006."

Conner related the details of his going to Gold's Gym in Everett for his usual Friday-night workout, leaving there at 7:45, stopping by the Seven-Eleven for a snack, getting back in his truck, hearing a man yell at him, seeing a flash, his clothes catching on fire, diving out the door, and finally being helped down the street by the bum, though Conner didn't refer to him that way.

"Did you see who yelled at you and threw the burning gas can?"

"No."

"Do you recognize the defendant, James Pungent?"

"Yes."

"Where have you seen him before?"

"I did some time in the State Felons Center back in 1991. He was an inmate there then."

"How well did you know him?" said Haadapa.

"We spent a few weeks in the same cell. Other than that I had very little contact with him," said Willingham.

"That's BS!" blurted out Pungent.

"Order!" said Judge Laney. "Mr. Slusherman, I'm not going to put up with any comments from your client. If he cannot control himself, I will charge him with contempt of court."

"Yes sir," said Slusherman, who immediately had a quick huddle with Pungent.

"Can we resume?" asked Laney, fifteen seconds later.

"Yes, Your Honor," answered Slusherman.

"Have you had any contact with James Pungent since you were released from prison?" Haadapa asked Willingham.

"No, I haven't."

"Can you think of any reason why he would have thrown a can of burning gas into your truck?"

"No. I didn't even know he was in this area. Like I said, I haven't seen him since I got out of prison."

"Did you have any problems with each other in prison?" asked Haadapa.

"No, other than I told him he had a nice sister, and I might look her up some day."

"How did he react to that?"

"He got angry and cussed at me, and said something about

staying away from her. But I figured it was just a passing threat. I mean it was years ago."

"Would you please describe the injuries that you sustained in the truck fire?"

"I was very lucky Mr. Haadapa. I had second-degree burns from just above my right knee, clear up to my chest, and around to my back on my right side. My right forearm also had extensive second-degree burns. If the guy hadn't put out the flames on my clothing, I would have been in critical condition with third-degree burns over that same area and probably burned a lot more of my body."

"Thank you, Mr. Willingham. That will be all from me for now."

"Mr. Slusherman, your cross-examination," said Judge Laney.

Mr. Slusherman walked deliberately up to Conner in the witness stand, looked sternly into his eyes, pointed his right index finger at his face like a father scolding his young son, and said, "You're Lying!"

"Objection! Mr. Slusherman is trying to intimidate the witness."

"Objection sustained," said Laney. "Mr. Slusherman, I'm not putting up with your intimidating tactics in my courtroom, so you can stop that approach right now."

"Yes, sir," said Slusherman, as he continued to glare at Conner. "Mr. Willingham would you please tell the court why you were in prison and for how long—"

"Objection. That's not relevant," said Haadapa

"Objection overruled. The relevance better become clear, Mr. Slusherman," said Laney. Please answer the question, Mr. Willingham."

"I was in prison from 1991 to 1995," answered Willingham, avoiding saying why he was there.

"And why were you there?" pressed Slusherman.

"For assisting in a rape." Slusherman let that sink in for perhaps ten seconds.

"You said that you knew the defendant from prison," said

Slusherman. "But what you failed to be candid about was how long you were in the same cell with him, and what kind of a relationship you had with him. Wasn't it true that you were cell mates for well over a year?"

"No."

"And wasn't it true that you made him *your boy*."

"No!" shouted Willingham.

"Objection, Your Honor," said Haadapa. "Not only is Mr. Slusherman planting a garden in the jurors' minds, he's continuing to call the witness a liar."

"Your Honor," said Slusherman, "Mr. Haadapa is correct in saying that I am trying to show that the witness has lied, because he has. He knows that he spent considerable time in the same cell with the defendant and that he not only physically abused him, but he constantly intimidated him into doing favors for him while in prison. Basically, he owned the man."

"Mr. Slusherman, you will have the chance to call your client to the witness stand and let him tell the court himself about his relationship to Mr. Willingham."

"But, Your Honor, I'm trying to establish a history between Willingham and my client that would show my client was acting in self-defense when he attacked Willingham." Slusherman was, in fact, intending to plant some serious doubts in the jurors' minds about Conner's overall character and his honesty. But he was also doing his best to shake him up.

"Then do it when your client is on the stand," said Laney.

"Yes, sir."

Mr. Slusherman then walked over to the jury box, containing five men and seven women, and carefully studied each juror in the eyes as if trying to discern whether they were man or woman enough to handle his next revelation. Then he turned toward the witness stand and said, "Isn't it true, Mr. Willingham, that you were at your Grandmother Maureen Muldano's house the night she died, and that you—"

"Objection!" yelled the District Attorney, at the same time slamming his hand down on the table as if to cover up anymore of Slusherman's words. Slusherman had no intentions of saying one word more, but the DA timed his response perfectly for the drama Slusherman was building.

"Objection sustained," said Judge Laney. Before he could say anymore, chaos erupted among the courtroom audience. One person in the Muldano-clan section shouted obscenities at Mr. Slusherman.

"Order! Order in this courtroom!" yelled Laney, pounding his gavel repeatedly.

Within a minute the roar from the audience had been reduced to a low rumble; many observers continued to quietly speculate among themselves about the meaning of Mr. Slusherman's last question.

"Jurors, you are to disregard Mr. Slusherman's last question," said Laney. Of course, none of the jurors could forget Slusherman's words, or avoid pondering their significance.

"I've had enough, Mr. Slusherman. I'm well aware of your tactics, and your ability to re-direct the attention of jurors away from the potential guilt of your defendants. I won't allow you to side-track this case with speculation and conjecture. Is that clear?"

"Yes, Your Honor."

"Mr. Willingham you may step down, unless the district attorney has some more questions for you," said Laney. Slusherman had accomplished precisely what he had intended.

"I have no questions, Your Honor," said Haadapa, knowing the last thing he or Conner needed, was for him to remain on the stand any longer.

Sweat poured off Conner's brow, his red shirt was soaked across the back and down the middle in front, he breathed hard, and his hands trembled noticeably, as he waddled out of the courtroom. He needed to go get a gallon of milk and a dozen donuts after the workout he had just been through. It was ten minutes after noon.

"The court will recess for lunch and re-convene at 1:30," said Laney. "I want both counselors in my chambers."

Father Michael, Windy and Dan walked out into the hallway. While Windy went to use the lady's room, the two men visited.

"You weren't kidding when you said Brent is an excellent defense attorney, were you Father?" said Dan, smiling. "I guess you've seen him in action."

"You bet I have. I don't know anyone better when your back's against the wall. And if you think this is good, you should've seen him with a Navy F-4 Phantom fighter-bomber. Talk about an acrobat."

"He told me that I would be pleased with what he brings out in this case," said Dan. "He wasn't fooling."

"He has obviously learned more about both cases than any of the detectives," said Father Michael.

"I'm not too impressed with Pungent's character," said Dan. "Don't you think Brent's putting a lot of trust in him?"

"Brent's like me in that respect. He has a great feel for who is telling the truth and what is really inside a person. You can be sure that he has plenty of support for his position. I wouldn't worry about him getting in over his head. He knows exactly what he's doing."

"Well, let's just hope he doesn't catch a SAM (surface-to-air missile) like he did with the F-4."

"Just sit back and enjoy him, Dan. The show has only begun."

When court resumed after lunch, District Attorney Haadapa spent half the afternoon attempting to somehow establish Conner Willingham's credibility with the jurors. He called to the stand Conner's boss at Pump It Baby Septic Service, his wife, two people from Gold's Gym, and two of his poker-playing buddies, Mike Lonner and Jay Maul.

Mr. Slusherman opted not to cross-examine any of these witnesses. He would call Lonner and Maul later when the Defense presented its case. He also reserved the right to call Conner's wife later, but knew if he did he would have to be careful not to alienate the jury by putting her on the defensive. He knew he had the evidence to shatter any straw-man credibility in Willingham that Mr. Haadapa managed to create.

At 4 PM, immediately following a fifteen minute recess, Mr. Haadapa called Wayne Weller, the bum, to the stand.

"Mr. Weller, would you please tell the court what you witnessed on Friday night, April 7th of this year."

"I was walking on the sidewalk toward Mr. Willingham's pickup on the same side of the street, when I saw a flash of fire, a man yelled, then a larger flash of fire flew into Willingham's pickup through the open passenger's side window. A man then ran past me. It looked like one of his sleeves was on fire. He ran down an alley not far from where I was."

"Where were you standing, when this took place?"

"Actually I wasn't standing; I was walking up the side-walk toward Willingham's truck. I was about fifty feet away when the flames went into his truck." At that point, Haadapa set up a very large schematic of the crime scene and had Weller stand by it and point out the details of his position, the perpetrator's position and actions, as well as the truck's position and where Willingham ended up next to the truck, etc.

"After the man ran by, what happened next?" said Haadapa.

"Right then, I saw Willingham's driver's door come open. Next thing I knew, he landed on the street beside his truck. I saw immediately that he was on fire, so I ran up to him, took off my trench coat and waved the fire out. I tried to drag Willingham away from the truck, but couldn't move him. He's a huge man. I yelled at him that he had to get away from his truck before it blew up. Finally, he got to his feet, and I helped him to walk away from the truck. A few minutes later, the police and medics came up to us and did their thing."

"Did you get a good look at the guy that ran past you?" said Haadapa.

"I looked right at him. I got a good look."

"Is he in this courtroom?"

"Yeah, he's right over there." Weller pointed at Pungent.

Haadapa walked back toward his bench, looked at Slusherman and said, "Your witness."

"Thank you, Counselor" said Slusherman, as he got up and walked up to the witness stand, smiled at Weller and said, "It was a great thing what you did in risking your own life to help Mr. Willingham get away from his burning truck that night. I'm sure I speak for all of Mr. Willingham's family when I say, thank you."

Weller wasn't sure whether he should say: your welcome, thank you, or say nothing in response to Mr. Slusherman, since he was defending the person who set the fire in the first place. He remained silent.

"Mr. Weller, in your testimony a few minutes ago, you said that you heard the defendant yell something just before he tossed the burning can into the truck. Is that correct?"

"Yes, it is."

"I thought it was interesting that Mr. Haadapa did not ask you to tell the court what it was the man yelled. Would you mind telling the court now, what you heard the man yell?"

Weller squirmed in his seat, looked at the DA for guidance, but received a frown in return, then said, "He yelled, 'Hey Hog, you're never going to threaten me or anyone else ever again.'"

Immediately, Slusherman walked over to the jurors, looked at the oldest juror, a man of sixty-five sitting in the center of the section, and said, "I want to get this straight, just before you saw the flaming can thrown into Conner Willingham's truck, you are sure you heard a man yell, 'Hey Hog, you're never going to threaten me or anyone else ever again.'?"

"Yes, that's what I heard."

Still looking at the oldest juror, Slusherman said, "Didn't that strike you funny? I mean didn't you consider why anyone would say such a thing unless he had, at some point, been seriously threatened or hurt by that individual?"

"Objection. It doesn't matter what Mr. Weller might have thought about what he heard Mr. Pungent yell. He reacted like the good citizen he is, and saved Mr. Willingham's life."

"Objection sustained."

Mr. Slusherman thought about questioning the witness about the big discrepancy between the description he gave the police at the scene of the crime and Slusherman's client's actual physical size and appearance, but he thought better of it. He needed the jury to trust this witness's testimony, particularly the part about what he heard David Pungent yell that night. He also wanted them to wonder about the reason he would have yelled those words.

"No more questions, Your Honor."

"Any follow up questions, Mr. Haadapa?"

"No," he said.

Weller stepped down and walked out of the courtroom. Judge Laney then called a recess for the evening.

At 9:00 the next morning, Wednesday, the 27th, court reconvened.

The Muldano clan had grown by five or six people. Many in that section seemed apprehensive. Undoubtedly phones had rung off the hook at theirs and other relatives' homes after court yesterday as they gossiped and speculated back and forth, and bad-mouthed the arrogant defense attorney and his tactics.

"The State calls Snohomish County Sheriff's detective Sergeant Jay Allen," said DA Haadapa.

The stout and rugged-looking Sergeant Allen walked in and took the witness seat after being sworn in.

"Sergeant Allen, how did you determine that David Pungent attempted to murder Conner Willingham on Friday night, April 7th of this year, in front of the Seven-Eleven store at 951 Middle Street in Everett?"

Sergeant Allen told the DA about Dorothy Mauney's phone call and her observations of when the pickup was first left in front of her house, and when the man came back to try to start it. Allen then told of he and Deputy Wilson's seeing the burned cloth, the stake-out, the subsequent return to the truck by Pungent, and the ensuing arrest in which they confirmed the burned cloth and discovered the burn on Pungent's right hand and forearm. Allen also said that he determined that Pungent had no alibi for the night of the crime, and that he and Conner had shared a cell at the Washington State Felons Center in Ralston in 1991.

While Allen was on stand, the State also presented various physical evidence including the burned cloth recovered from Pungent's truck, all of Willingham's burned clothes and various photographs showing Willingham's burned truck, his burns, the burned cloth inside Pungent's truck, Pungent's burn at the time of his arrest, and Pungent's truck parked in front of Dorothy Mauney's home three blocks from the scene.

The State next called Doctor Howard Folker, who treated Willingham in the Everett General Hospital Emergency Room. Folker testified about the extent of Willingham's burns and showed the court photographs taken in the ER. In the photos, Willingham's burned clothes were dangling down from where they had been cut away at the scene.

After lunch, the State called Doctor Dean Randolph, General Practioner for the Snohomish County Jail. Doctor Randolph testified that when he examined David Pungent within hours of his being booked at the Snohomish County jail, he observed and photographed what he determined were week-old, second-degree burns on Pungent's right hand and forearm. The burns were consistent with burns caused by burning gasoline and clothing material. Mr. Haadapa showed the court the photos of Pungent's burns taken at the jail.

The state then called Dorothy Mauney, who verified the pickup's status in front of her home, and positively identified Pungent as the man that she saw try to start the pickup during the week following the crime.

The state called the two teenage girls as its final witnesses. They didn't see the defendant run off, but they did see the fire in the truck, and Weller putting out the fire on Willingham and helping him to get away from the truck.

Attorney Slusherman cross-examined only one of the State's witnesses for the day: Sergeant Allen.

The State then rested its case.

At 5:23 pm, Judge Laney dismissed the court and said the Defense was to begin presenting its case at 8:30 the next morning.

39

Defense Case A
Franklin, Pungent

Mr. Slusherman opened the Defense's case, on Thursday morning, the 28th, by calling retired Washington State Felons Center Corrections Officer Jeremiah E. Franklin Jr.

"Mr. Franklin, you were a corrections officer at the Washington State Felons Center in Ralston during the years 1991-1995, is that correct?"

"Yes."

"Do you recall inmates Conner Willingham and David Pungent during those years?"

"Definitely, though Pungent was only there from 1991 through early 1993."

"Did they ever share a cell together?"

"Yes, for a little over a month in late 1991, they shared a two-man cell during lockup hours. But from late 1991 through 1992 they also shared a large group-cell for several hours a day."

"Did you ever hear the phrases, "boy," "my boy," or "his boy," used in the prison?" said Slusherman.

"Often," answered Franklin.

"What did those terms or phrases refer to, and in what context were they used?"

"Men confined in prison often dominate and intimidate fellow prisoners. They form a definite hierarchy among themselves. I'm sure most people on the outside are aware of that, if they've seen any movies involving prison life. When a prisoner dominates another prisoner, he often refers to him as 'boy,' or 'my boy.' It can be very humiliating for the 'boy.'"

Even under oath, Franklin had no intentions of revealing anymore details about what the narrower meaning of '*boy*' was, because to do so would incriminate himself and all the other prison officials for knowing certain activities went on and not putting a complete stop to them. The *ACLU* would be at the Washington State Felons Center in a heartbeat to stick up for the *boys*' rights if they heard the truth from an inside official. Never mind that the prisoner might have done some horrible and sordid things to be put in prison in the first place. The good ole' ACLU.

"Did you ever hear Willingham use the term "boy," or "my boy," in reference to David Pungent?" asked Slusherman.

"Objection!"

"Your honor, I am trying to establish the history of intimidation and abuse to my client by Willingham that drove my client to take the only action that he believed would end the domination that began in prison in 1991 and continued for all the years since Willingham's release from prison in 1995, and up through March of this year. These facts are important to this case; and, if you will allow me some liberty, I will pull it all together at the appropriate time."

"I'm going to allow it," said Laney; "We need to see the whole picture."

"But, Your Honor—" said Haadapa.

"I said I would allow it, and I meant it."

"Yes, Your Honor."

"Again, Mr. Franklin, did you ever hear Willingham use those terms in reference to Pungent?" said Slusherman.

"Yes, I did." The crowd began mumbling.

"Order!"

"Did you ever see Willingham physically abusing Pungent?"

"Yes, I did. He was slamming him around inside their cell one evening when I made the bed check. Pungent had a bloody mouth and nose."

"So what did you do?"

"We removed Willingham from the cell and put him in twenty-four hour isolation."

"And when his isolation time was up, what did you do with him?"

"We put him back in his cell."

"With Pungent?"

"Yes."

"Did Willingham's time in isolation put an end to his roughing Pungent up?"

"We thought it did. But, unfortunately, almost two weeks later, about the time Pungent's mouth and nose were healed up, Willingham rammed him into the bars and, this time, broke his nose and knocked out a tooth," said Franklin. "We put Willingham in isolation for the next week. Pungent spent the night in the infirmary. The avulsed front tooth was broken, and so it couldn't be saved. The dentist had to make him a flipper. The day Willingham was to come back, we moved Pungent to a different cell."

"Would you say that Willingham thoroughly humiliated Pungent?"

"Objection, Mr. Franklin is not a psychologist," said DA Haadapa.

"Objection sustained. Your witness's testimony speaks for itself, Mr. Slusherman. You don't need to belabor the point."

"Yes, Your Honor," said Slusherman. "Mr. Franklin, earlier you testified that Willingham and Pungent shared a group cell for several hours a day throughout the remainder of 1991 and all of 1992, is that correct?"

"Yes."

"Were there anymore problems between them?"

"I couldn't say for sure. I can tell you that there were several more incidents where Pungent had to be taken to the infirmary, but we could never put a finger on which prisoner, or prisoners, had beat him up. And he wasn't about to tell us himself. Not unless he wanted even worse treatment."

"What do you mean by worse treatment, Mr. Franklin?"

Franklin's brow furrowed, as he looked nervously around at the faces in the audience. He knew some of them had to be related to Willingham. Then he looked at Pungent sitting hopefully at the defense table.

"Worse beatings—you know—that sort of thing." Franklin again avoided revealing the extent of the "beatings," or exactly what "worse beatings" might include, but most everyone in the courtroom came to their own conclusions.

"Did you observe any of the interaction between Willingham and Pungent in all the time they shared a group cell?"

"Oh yeah," said Franklin. "Willingham ordered him around, and called him 'boy'... or 'my boy.' Pungent cowed down to him. It was actually pathetic. But with the size difference between the two of them, and the beatings that Pungent had sustained from Willingham previously, and those he probably got from him in the group cell, but didn't divulge, I could partially understand it. Who wouldn't do what they could to avoid another *beating*?"

"Were there other prisoners that cowed down to Willingham?" asked Slusherman.

"Objection!"

"Overruled. Answer the question please."

"Yes, there were," said Franklin. "I mean the guy weighed about 250 pounds, he was about six-two and solid as a rock. Then throw in his having a very aggressive personality. He scared many of the inmates."

"Thank you, Mr. Franklin," said Slusherman. "Your Honor, I'm done with this witness."

The Clan was furious with Slusherman. He had brought out Conner's seedy past, a huge black-eye on the history of his pseudo-spiritual family. But none of them even had a clue of just how low Conner had stooped while in prison or since then.

"Mr. Haadapa," said Judge Laney, "your witness."

DA Haadapa slowly got up and walked to within six feet of the witness stand.

"Mr. Franklin, if, in fact, Willingham abused Pungent in the way you described, why would you have ever put them in the same group-cell together after you moved Pungent out of the shared two-man cell?"

"First of all, I wasn't the one who made those decisions. Second, in prison, it is impossible to separate all of the individual inmates from each and every person with whom they have a conflict. There is not the room or the staffing. The best thing a prisoner can do to avoid prison conflicts, is to get his act together when he gets out so he doesn't end up back in prison." Slusherman cringed at that last statement. He didn't need Franklin to say anything that would lessen the severity of what Willingham had done to his client in prison.

Haadapa asked a number of other questions attempting to undermine Franklin's credibility as an eyewitness, but finally gave up.

"No further questions for this witness," said Mr. Haadapa.

"Nothing further, Your Honor," said Slusherman.

After lunch, sitting tall and confident in his chair at the defense table, Mr. Slusherman announced, "The defense calls David Pungent as its next witness."

Pungent got up from the defense table, was sworn in, then took the witness seat.

"Mr. Pungent, you have heard all of the testimony up until now. It is clear that the State has sufficient evidence to find you guilty of throwing the burning can of gas into Mr. Willingham's truck on Friday, April 7th, of this year. Do you deny doing that?"

"No," said Pungent. "I did it."

"Why did you do it?"

"I hated Willingham for what he did to me in prison years ago, and for the many times he came to my house in Monroe over the years after he got out of prison and threatened to abuse me if I didn't transport dope for him. Then, in March of this year, he came to my house on two different occasions and threatened to kill me if I ever turned him in."

"That's bull crap!" said someone in the Muldano-clan section.

"Order! Bailiff, would you keep an eye on that section, so we can throw the next person that speaks up out of the courtroom," said Laney.

"So, Mr. Pungent, you genuinely feared for your life?"

"I was scared to death. When you've been assaulted, and abused, and dominated, the way Willingham did to me, you believe him when he threatens your life. I couldn't go on living like that, with the fear of him. I was never able to have a successful long-term relationship with a woman after what he did to me in prison. And I was never able to hold down a decent job in the years since I got out of prison, because I always had problems with nervousness, caused by my fear of his ongoing intimidation."

"Mr. Pungent, would you show us the flipper you wear in your mouth because of the tooth Willingham knocked out that day in your prison cell fifteen years ago." Pungent pulled the device with the artificial tooth out of his mouth and held it out so everyone could see it.

"Why didn't you go to the law and report Willingham's activities and threats against you?" said Slusherman.

"Do you think any cops would put any stock in what I had to

say? I'm an ex-con. I did time for dealing drugs to kids. I live in a run-down house. I mow lawns and pull weeds for a job. I drink heavy, and I still transport dope, because if I don't Willingham will make me his boy. Throw in the fact that I would be a dead man as soon as Willingham found out that I spoke to the police. Does it sound to you like I would have been smart to go to the cops? What if they didn't believe me, but then brought my name up to Willingham? Do you see my problem?"

"Yes, I do. And I think everyone in this courtroom, who is truly honest with himself, would agree that you were caught between a rock and a hard place," said Slusherman. "Now, would you please tell us when it was that you made up your mind that you were going to kill Willingham?" A needle could have been heard dropping.

"A little over a week before I torched him, Willingham had come back to my house. He said the cops had been questioning him hard, and that if I ever said anything to them about him, he would kill me. He had already threatened to kill me a couple weeks earlier. I made up my mind that last time that the man had to die, or I was going to end up dead soon."

"Would you describe the manner in which you followed Willingham, the materials you used for your fire, and then how you completed your mission?"

"I knew that Willingham went to Gold's Gym on Friday nights, because he once told me he had just come from there. So on the first two Friday's following his last threatening visit to my house, I went to Gold's and parked in a dark area where I could watch his truck, and then followed him to the Seven-Eleven Store after his workout. I figured that since he had stopped there both weeks I followed him, it was a pretty good bet that he stopped at the Seven-Eleven after every Friday workout. So I knew that would be the time and place to burn him up."

"Go on."

"The next Friday evening, April 7th, I parked three blocks away. At 7:30, I got out of my truck, then grabbed the gas can which was in the back of my truck, grabbed the part of an old hand towel I had brought for that purpose, and hustled up the street to a thick hedge across from the Seven-Eleven. I waited there for a few minutes. Pretty soon, Willingham pulled up in his Chevy truck, parked where he had the previous two weeks, and went into the store. I quickly took the lid off the full can of gas, stuffed part of the towel into the can, shook it around to get the towel soaked, then waited a couple more minutes for that fat tyrant to come back out.

"After he got in the truck, I ran out from the hedge, used my lighter to light the cloth fuse, then yelled, 'Hey hog, you're never going to threaten me or anyone else ever again.' Then I tossed the burning can into his truck. I immediately ran past some guy on the sidewalk, and ran down an alley just down the street and circled around behind a row of houses to get back to my truck.

"But I couldn't get the truck started. So I locked it and ran away toward the Madison Street Bridge. My shirt sleeve had caught fire from the fuse and I had burned my right hand and forearm. So I went down to the Snohomish River a bunch of blocks away and cooled my arm off. I hung out there for over an hour, constantly dipping my arm in the icy river water. Then I hiked the jogging trail over to Reynolds-Baker Park, stopping periodically to dip my arm in the river. At the park, I crawled into some bushes for the night. I wasn't able to sleep much because my arm hurt so bad. In the morning, I dug a hole with a stick, and buried my burned shirt and jacket. Then I walked to Saint Vincent De Paul on Robert Kennedy Boulevard and bought a cheap jacket. From there I hitch-hiked home to Monroe. I wasn't home much from then until I was arrested at my truck."

"You said that Conner Willingham used regular threats to force you to transport drugs," said Slusherman. "How often did he make you transport the drugs?"

"About three times a year."

"What drugs did you transport? And where did you take the drugs?" said Slusherman.

"He dealt in methamphetamines, usually about ten pounds. I had—"

"He's lying," yelled someone in the Muldano-clan section.

"Order! Bailiff did you see who yelled that?"

"I'm sorry, Your Honor, I didn't see who it was," said the bailiff.

"Which one of you people said that?" demanded Laney, as the bailiff walked over to the Muldano-clan section. No one confessed, and no one squealed on the offender either.

"If I hear another outburst from your section, and I can't determine who is guilty, I will throw the whole bunch of you out. Do you understand me?"

"Yes," said several of the clan.

"Mr. Slusherman, you can continue questioning your witness."

"Thank you, Your Honor," said Slusherman. "Mr. Pungent you had started to tell us where you had to take the drugs; will you please continue."

"I had to take them down to Weed, California. Willingham would contact me by phone, a week ahead of time, using code-language that we both understood. He would then bring the drugs over, give me money to pay for my gas and a few meals, then leave. An hour after he left, I would make the trip to Weed—scared as hell. I'd exchange the drugs for cash, and head home.

"Willingham always gave me two hundred bucks for my time. I never counted the cash he received for the drugs, but it was a stack. I didn't want the two hundred bucks. I didn't want anything to do with the drugs. I never wanted to go back to the joint again. I already had one life-long monster to contend with after my first time in prison. You can't imagine what prison was like for me, or what my life has been like since I got out, thanks to Willingham."

Slusherman walked back to his table, grabbed some papers and returned to the witness stand. He then held the papers out, one set at a time, so that Pungent could read them and asked, "Mr. Pungent, would you please tell the court what these papers are."

"They are my Qwest Telephone Records of all incoming and

outgoing phone calls to and from my home phone for March 2005, August 2005, November 2005, and February 2006," said Pungent.

"Notice the lines that I have highlighted on each of these statements," said Slusherman. "They are in the incoming call port-ion. Would you please tell us the phone number and the dates of each of those calls?"

Pungent said the number, 360-288-3621, and confirmed that same number appeared at each highlighted entry, twice in each of the months previously noted. Mr. Slusherman then took all of those records and handed them to Judge Laney, then to Mr. Haadapa, and, finally, to the jury foreman, who looked at them, passed them around the jury, and then handed them back to Mr. Slusherman, who then remained standing directly in front of the jury box.

"For the record, Your Honor, Mr. Haadapa, and jury," said Slusherman, "the phone number on each of the highlighted entries is Conner Willingham's cell phone number.

"Mr. Pungent," Slusherman continued, "I don't think anyone can argue with these phone records. Would you tell us what it was that you and Conner Willingham discussed during each of those two phone calls that occurred in each of the four months already noted."

"Like I mentioned earlier, Willingham would call me up a week before bringing his drug shipment to me. That's the first call in each of these months. The second call is ten days later, the day after I made the delivery to Weed, California. He would call to make sure I had returned home with his payment from Weed; then he would come right over to pick up the money."

"I guess it is obvious," said Slusherman, "that Conner Willing-ham lied to the court about not having any contact with David Pungent since he got out of prison in 1995. In fact, based on these phone records, we now know that Conner Willingham contacted the defendant, David Pungent, on eight occasions in just one year, including two times within one month of when Maureen Muldano was killed."

"Objection!"

"Sustained."

"Thanks for your testimony, Mr. Pungent. It must have been hell for you," said Slusherman. "Your Honor, I am finished with this witness for now, but I intend to call him up again later, if that will please the court."

"As you wish, counselor," said Laney. It was 12:20. Judge Laney ordered a recess be taken for lunch and that court would resume at 2 P.M.

Haadapa began his cross examination by getting right in Mr. Pungent's face and asking, "Mr. Pungent, why should I, or anyone else in this courtroom, believe a word of what you have said regarding your relationship to Mr. Willingham?" said Haadapa.

"Objection!"

"Overruled. It sounds like Mr. Haadapa is using some of your tactics, Mr. Slusherman."

"Answer my question, please, Mr. Pungent. Why should we believe any of your testimony?"

"Because I'm telling the truth, and my phone records don't lie."

"You're still dealing in drugs, and you admitted you're an alcoholic. I bet you use drugs, too."

"Objection! Mr. Pungent already explained that he was being forced to transport drugs, and he never said he was an alcoholic. Hr. Haadapa is drawing conclusions rather than asking questions of the witness. Mr. Haadapa doesn't like the truth—"

"That's enough, Mr. Slusherman," said Judge Laney. "Your objection is sustained. District Attorney, if you want clarification on certain points of Mr. Pungent's testimony, then ask specific questions regarding those points. You're not going to accomplish anything by your generalizations."

"Yes, Your Honor, you're right," said Haadapa.

"Okay, Mr. Pungent why should we believe that Mr. Willingham dominated you in prison and, supposedly, made you his boy?"

"Objection! That's ludicrous."

"Objection sustained," said Laney. "Mr. Haadapa, the court, and you, already heard eye-witness testimony from a retired Washington State Felons Center Corrections Officer regarding Mr. Willingham's physical, emotional and mental abuse of Mr. Pungent. Please, please come up with some better questions, or I'm going to dismiss this witness."

"Yes, sir."

"Mr. Pungent, anyone could make the claims that you have regarding years of intimidation and exploitation by Mr. Willingham," said Haadapa. Heck, if I was charged for attempting to murder someone, I could drum up some similar defense, myself."

Pungent would love to blurt out the whole story right now, but he has been sternly warned by Mr. Slusherman that the time has to be right. If certain facts were revealed prematurely, his case would be hurt, rather than helped, so he bit his tongue.

"Mr. Pungent, do you think all of us in this courtroom are naïve enough to believe that your relationship with Mr. Willingham over the years since you left prison wasn't a mutually beneficial relationship, even a friendship?"

"Showing a spark of anger, Pungent answered, "What do you take me and all the rest of the people in this courtroom for, fools? Did you see any phone calls on those records made from me to Willingham? No you didn't." Pungent is acting like the lawyer now. "I've never called the man, nor would I. I just wanted him out of my life. Believe me, he was never my friend. Don't you get it? The man did unspeakable things to me in prison. He... He... *He raped me*! And now he threatened to kill me, not once, but twice, while roughing me up."

District Attorney Haadapa realized that, at this point, it wasn't going to help the State's case to keep Pungent on the stand. He knew that Willingham's credibility was already shot, but nothing he had heard justified Pungent's attempt on Willingham's life. He was also sure that the jury had to have plenty of doubts about Pungent's testimony, as well. He would still get a conviction.

"Your Honor, I'm through with this witness, at this time."

"I'll pass," said Slusherman on his rebuttal.

"Defense, you may call your next witness," said Laney.

Slusherman then called, in order, three Monroe residents, whose lawns Pungent had been mowing for between two and four years, to testify regarding Pungent's character and dependability. And then court was dismissed for the evening at 5:15.

40

Defense Case B
Old Man Goldmin

Friday morning, September 29th—

"The defense calls Myron Goldmin."

Goldmin, an old man in his early-eighties, limped down the aisle, wearing some worn gray slacks, a white dress shirt, a light, gray sweater, and some black, plastic-rimmed bi-focal glasses. He was sworn in, and took the witness stand.

"Mr. Goldmin, how long have you lived in Monroe?" said Slusherman.

"I've lived there fifty-two years. Raised my family there. The town was a lot smaller back when I moved in." The courtroom audience chuckled, as he stated the obvious. The old coot.

"I understand you served on the Monroe School Board."

"That's right. I was on the board for twenty years. Was on the booster club and even did some coaching when my kids were in school. I also served on the Monroe Chamber of Commerce for years."

Goldmin went on for several minutes about his public service.

Since it was first thing Friday morning and he was the only witness scheduled for the day, no one, including Judge Laney, was bothered by getting a bit of Monroe history. DA Haadapa figured Goldmin's dissertation would prove he was well beyond his mental prime and thereby help discredit his forthcoming testimony. Haadapa mistakenly thought Goldmin was in court solely as a character witness for his long-time neighbor, the defendant. He was in for a rude awakening.

Finally pulling things back to the present case, Slusherman said, "Thank you for your dedication and service to your community, Mr. Goldmin. Do you recognize the defendant, David Pungent?"

"Certainly; he's been my neighbor, two doors down for about ten years, or so—at least he was until this past April, I haven't seen him since then. He hauled my garbage off to the dump for me the last two years. My back got too bad. He was a good neighbor."

"So he's been a good neighbor to you for a lot of years?"

"Absolutely."

"Can you see his house from yours?"

"Oh yeah, that is, if I'm out in the front or back yards. We've got a neighbor between us."

Mr. Slusherman walked over to the defense table and grabbed a 9 by 11 manila envelope and came back over to the witness stand. He then pulled two 8 by 10 photos out of the folder, spread them out on the edge of the stand and asked, "Have you ever seen this man before?"

"Sure, I saw him six months ago, in March of this year."

"Where did you see him?"

"At David's house. I saw him speak briefly to David on his front porch, then they went inside. I had also seen him on numerous other occasions during the time David lived there."

Slusherman then handed the photos to Judge Laney, who looked at them briefly, then handed them to the bailiff to take to Mr. Haadapa. The courtroom was silent, as Haadapa glanced at the photos and handed them back to the bailiff. His expression grew even more sour than before. The bailiff then handed the 8 by 10 photos to the jury foreman, who looked quickly at them, then passed them to the juror beside him.

Slusherman waited for the jury foreman to get the photos back and hand them to the bailiff, then he said, "For the court's record, the man in both photos is Conner Willingham." A loud moan was heard in the Muldano-clan section.

"Mr. Goldmin, how do you know that you saw Willingham at David Pungent's this last March, specifically?"

"I was out front working in my flower garden when he pulled his Chevy pickup into David's driveway. When he got out, he walked very deliberately up to David's front door. I got the impression he was pretty angry, by his demeanor and the tone of his voice."

"But how do you know it was in March when you last saw him?" Some murmuring could be heard in the audience. Undoubtedly, some of them were speculating about how bad the old fart's memory probably was, and how he couldn't possibly know it was in March when he last saw Willingham.

"He had come to David's house in a helluva hurry just a week and a half earlier, on my birthday."

"And what day was that?"

"March 10th." The Clan gasped. Some, "oh no's" were heard.

"I want to make sure to get this right for the court's record," said Slusherman, basking in this latest revelation. "Mr. Goldmin, are you saying that you saw Conner Willingham come to David Pungent's house on March 10th of this year, 2006? And you have no doubt whatsoever that it was on that date, because that was your birthday?"

"That's exactly what I'm saying."

"What time of the day was Willingham there?"

"Well, he actually came, picked David up, left for ten minutes or so, then brought David back and dropped him off. He squealed his tires a bit when he left the second time."

"What time did he arrive to pick David up?" The old coot was making Slusherman work for every detail.

"It was several minutes before nine," said Goldmin.

"And how do you know that?"

"I watch Larry King every Friday night at nine. I always take my dog out front in the yard to do her job in the hedge-row before King's show starts."

"And you can see Mr. Pungent's house over your hedge?"

"The hedge isn't that high, and it's on the opposite side of my yard from David's house, anyway."

"I see," said Slusherman. "If you were in the house watching the Larry King show ten minutes later, when Willingham and Pungent returned, how did you know they came back at that time?"

"I was sitting in my rocking chair, in the corner of my living room, like I always do. I can easily look out the window."

"So you just happened to be looking out the window when they came back?"

"No. I heard an engine rev up from someone downshifting just as it got in front of my place. I turned my head to see, and I saw it was Willingham's truck. I thought it was odd that they were coming back so soon, so I watched them pull into David's driveway. Willingham barely pulled in off the street, stopped for a few seconds, and I saw David get out and go toward his house. Willingham yelled something at him, but I couldn't make out any of what he said, being I was in my house. Willingham then immediately backed out, and slammed the truck into a forward gear while the truck was still rolling backward. That's when he peeled out a little. After that I went back to watching the King Show."

"I'm just curious, Mr. Goldmin. Did you know that an old woman was killed just outside of Monroe that night, that is, on your birthday?"

"I remember reading about it in the paper and hearing it on the news, but I had forgotten that it was on my birthday," said Goldmin.

"So why should the court believe that you can remember Mr. Willingham and Mr. Pungent going for a short ride together on your birthday, if you didn't remember the old lady being killed on your birthday?" said Slusherman, addressing an issue he knew Haadapa would have brought up in his cross-examination.

"I had no connection to the old lady, so why would I remember the specific day that happened? The reason I remember Willingham picking David up on my birthday, was because I had never seen David go with him before, or after. And Willingham had never been in that kind of a hurry before. Nor had he ever come back the same day after leaving. When that kind of thing happens with your good neighbor-friend on your birthday, it is easy to remember. You have an association."

"Did you ever see Willingham at David Pungent's house at other times besides the two times last March?"

"Oh yeah. I saw him there a few times each year for almost as long as David lived there."

"Thank you for your testimony, Mr. Goldmin," said Slusherman, who then turned confidently to the district attorney. "He's all yours."

Haadapa, grabbed his notepad, and got up slowly from his chair, contemplating how he could clean up the situation he now found himself in. He walked over to Goldmin in the witness stand and said, "Mr. Goldmin, would you mind looking at the clock above the court entryway and telling me what time it says." Everyone in the courtroom turned to look at the clock.

"It is 10:17," said Goldmin.

"And what does it say right above the clock?"

"Court Room 3." Goldmin certainly had no problems seeing things at that distance with his glasses on.

Attorney Haadapa considered asking Goldmin how he could possibly know that the black man he saw at a distance in his neighborhood was the same black man in the photos he had been shown, and not some other black man, but knew such a question would be racial suicide. Instead he asked,

"Did you ever see Mr. Willingham up close? I mean you told us you saw him at Mr. Pungent's house a number of times, including the night of March 10th."

"Yes, I actually visited with him briefly a couple times over the years, when he walked by my place on his way to David's house. He struck me as being friendly, but a little hyper."

"You told us earlier that you saw Mr. Willingham drive to the defendant's house on several occasions, but now you are telling us that he walked there. Which was it?"

"Actually I only said that I had seen Willingham drive to David's house three times," said Goldmin, continuing to display his still-sharp mind. "But, in fact, I did see him drive that same Chevy pickup to David's house numerous other times over the years. And a few times I saw Mr. Willingham walk to his house. I can't say that I didn't wonder about that, but I'm not a nosey person, so I never asked. I knew David was a good neighbor to me, and figured none of the rest was my business."

"Did you know that your good neighbor was an ex-con, who did two years for pushing dope to kids, and that, by his own admission, continued to peddle dope for all the years since his release from prison?"

"Objection! Mr. Haadapa is twisting the earlier testimony of my client."

"Objection sustained," said Judge Laney. "Mr. Haadapa, re-word your question."

"That's all right, Your Honor," said Goldmin. Slusherman cringed. "I knew that David had done time for selling drugs and that some of the drugs were sold to kids. But I also knew that he regret-ted all of his past, and that he was not selling drugs anymore."

"Mr. Goldmin, your good neighbor David Pungent has already testified before this court that he was still involved in transporting drugs. What do you have to say about that?" said Haadapa.

"If that's what he said then what difference does my opinion on that make?" Goldmin was too shrewd to get sucked along on this line of questioning. "I know what kind of a man David Pungent is regardless. He is a good man."

Slusherman relaxed again, finally convinced that Goldmin was too quick to get caught by anything Haadapa could throw at him. In fact, Goldmin was beginning to remind Slusherman of his own father (a retired brain surgeon) whose mind was still sharp as a tack at the age of eighty-nine.

"Did you know he had a drinking problem?"

"Yes, I did. But there are plenty of good people who have drinking problems. That doesn't make them drug pushers, does it? How about you Mr. Haadapa, do you ever get drunk?" The court-room audience—including the jury—roared, that is, except the Muldano-clan members, who were still numb from the damaging testimony they just heard. Even Slusherman and Judge Laney had to restrain themselves.

"Mr. Goldmin," said Haadapa, wishing he could tear his head off, "are there street lights illuminating the defendant's driveway?"

"Yes, I had no problem seeing both David and Conner Willing-ham, and Willingham's Chevy pickup on Friday, March 10th, since that's where you're going, right?"

"No more questions," said Haadapa, disgustedly, seeing he was only hurting his case with this witness.

"No follow up questions, Your Honor," said Slusherman.

"The court will recess for the weekend, and reconvene at 9:00 Monday morning," said Judge Laney.

Father Michael hooked up with Brent Slusherman for dinner, while Dan took Windy out to the Olive Garden. Dan felt great knowing the heavy burden he had carried for months was gradually being peeled away from him, as Brent worked like a surgeon in the courtroom. Dan was certain now that his past was soon to be behind him for good.

By contrast, Conner's past was growing like a cancer, looming heavy in his future. Dan had already gotten his retribution with

Maureen, and now he was finally getting it with Conner, and certainly with Brenda and the other wolves. It felt good, but he knew some day he would have to let it all go. He wouldn't be much of a man if he reveled in even *their misery* for too long.

He didn't envy the Muldano-clan one bit, and he was thrilled he was no longer part of it. What started out as a family united behind Conner in this trial, as superficial as that might have been, had turned into the pack of wolves several of them really were. It was now taking all the self-control some of them could muster to keep from arguing in the courtroom. But as soon as each session of court adjourned, they broke out into open bickering.

Dan was sure Conner had violated the judge's order that no witnesses were to talk to other witnesses during the trial. No doubt he had gotten to his poker-playing buddies to make sure they all had their cards in a row. If they could all come through for Conner, it wouldn't matter what Pungent or his senile neighbor had said, because it would be the word of two people against the word of Conner and four reputable buddies. Or so Conner thought. Well, at least that's what he hoped. But he was running scared.

41

Defense Case C
The Players

On Monday morning, October 2nd, court resumed at 9:00 a.m. sharp.

"The Defense calls Mike Lonner," said Slusherman.

Lonner had done a nice job in his earlier testimony of speaking highly of his and Conner's relationship, of Conner's good character, that he was an excellent husband, father and employee, not to mention the big homerun hitter on their softball team in the summers. Of course, Conner had to smack the ball over the fence to get a homerun. No way he could haul his 400 pounds around the bases fast enough to earn an inside-the-park homer.

"Mr. Lonner, we heard your earlier testimony describing what great friends, poker-buddies and teammates you and Conner Willingham have been over the years, so we won't get into that now." Lonner was doing his best to act relaxed, but his forehead was perspiring. He had heard plenty about Mr. Slusherman, but was spared doing battle with him when he testified earlier for the State. Slusherman had passed on cross-examining him.

"What time did Willingham arrive at the card game on Friday night, March 10th of this year?"

"Objection! Why is the Defense continuing to beat a dead horse? Mr. Willingham is not on trial here. Why can't Mr. Slusherman figure that out?"

"Your Honor, Mr. Haadapa doesn't seem to want to accept that I am trying to prove that my client attempted to kill Conner Willingham for the sole purpose of keeping Willingham from killing him," said Slusherman. "I need some leeway here in order to prove that, but I can."

"Objection overruled. Proceed carefully, Mr. Slusherman," said Judge Laney.

"Yes sir. Thank you, sir."

"Mr. Lonner would you please tell the court what time Conner Willingham arrived at that card game on March 10th?"

"He got there just before 8:30."

"Mr. Lonner, before I proceed any further with my questions, I will remind you that you are under oath, and if you lie on the witness stand, you will go to jail for perjury. Do you understand that?"

"Completely."

"What time did Conner Willingham arrive at James Pallen's house on Woods Creek Road on the night of March 10th of this year?"

"Like I have said every time I have been asked before, and will say every time I am asked in the future, Willingham arrived there just before 8:30."

"One last chance…"

"Objection! Your Honor, Mr. Slusherman is badgering the witness."

"Your Honor, I'm only trying to keep the witness from perjuring himself as Conner Willingham has already done to himself earlier in the trial."

"Objection sustained," said Laney. "Mr. Slusherman, you have given the witness plenty of opportunity to answer your question to your satisfaction. Move on please."

"Mr. Lonner, I've heard a rumor that you guys did more than play cards on Friday nights. Is that true?"

"Objection! Whatever the witness and his buddies did on Friday nights has no relevance to this case. Where's the guy coming from?" asked Haadapa.

"Your Honor, I'm attempting to prove that the card players did more than play cards on their game night—that they brought special guests to the house for extra-curricular activity. And that all of the card players are lying, not only because they have all been threatened by Willingham, but they have to lie to protect themselves too, or their extra activities will become known to others outside the game, including their wives."

"I don't like it Mr. Slusherman, but I will allow your questions for now. But I better see some progress."

"Yes, Your Honor."

Slusherman continued to hammer questions away at Lonner from various angles, but Lonner remained steadfast in his testimony that Willingham had arrived at the game just before 8:30. He also repelled any of the probes Slusherman made to determine what those Friday nights were actually all about. Slusherman finally released the witness, and Mr. Haadapa passed on cross-examining him. One for Conner, zero for Slusherman.

Slusherman called Jay Maul next, but did no better with him. Conner two, Slusherman zero.

Frank Wilkens came next, and it was the same story. Conner three, Slusherman zero. Conner was almost there. These poker buddies that had gone to high school with him, and played dozens of softball games a year with him, were all right. *He knew* they would be there for him.

Slusherman determined that he wasn't getting through with the card players the way he had hoped. They had each proven willing to perjure themselves to protect Conner and ultimately themselves. But each of the card players he had questioned so far had a long history with Conner going back to their childhoods. That wasn't the case with Warner. At any rate, Slusherman didn't want to end up losing zero to four with the card players, so he decided to take a different approach. He asked Judge Laney for an early lunch recess, then planned to recall David Pungent as his witness immediately after lunch.

42

Defense Case D
Pungent Recalled

At 1:05 Mr. Slusherman called David Pungent to the stand once again. After Pungent was seated in the witness stand, Slusherman asked, "How was your lunch?"

"Objection. None of us cares how his lunch was."

"Get on with your examination please, Mr. Slusherman," said Laney. Of course every question, in fact, every word Slusherman spoke had a purpose. He had an IQ of 170, and a brain that worked like a computer.

"Mr. Pungent, we're going to get down and dirty now. We've played games on this case long enough. *It's time.*" A lot of squirming and under-the-breath conversation was going on in the Muldano clan section, which had grown to over thirty-five members. It added four more after lunch. Their cell phones were awfully hot now.

"I'm going to get right to the point?" said Slusherman.

"Did Conner Willingham come to your house on the evening of March 10th and threaten to kill you?"

"Yes." Haadapa started to object, but then decided that

Pungent's credibility was undoubtedly already questionable with the jury, and that, if necessary, he could bring it down further in his cross-examination.

"What time did Willingham get there?" said Slusherman.

"About ten minutes to nine."

"What did Willingham say?"

"He said, 'Pungent you will come with me right now, or I'm going to kill you.' I was terrified. He had never come to my house that scared and angry before. I knew something bad was up. *Then I saw it.*" The courtroom was silent, no one moved a muscle.

"Saw what?"

"I saw the blood on his right cheek. It looked like he had swiped at it, but there was still plenty there. I knew something bad had happened and if I didn't do what he said, I wasn't going to see the morning. I could hardly breathe as I hurried out to his truck behind him. When we got in the truck, he drove us over to Brigham Street and made me make a phone call to 911. He told me exactly what I was to say. He was breathing right down my neck as he half-dragged me to the phone booth."

"Did the blood on Willingham's cheek look like it was coming from a cut on him?"

"No. I couldn't see any signs of a cut on his face, or that he was bleeding himself. It just looked like he had had his face against someone else who was bleeding, got a face full, and then tried to wipe it off."

"Did you see any blood in his truck or any blood on something that he could have used to wipe his face?"

"No. He probably got rid of whatever he wiped his face with."

"What did he tell you to say on the phone?" asked Slusherman.

"That, 'someone is seriously hurt at…,' and he had me read the road address that he had scribbled on an empty donut box. It was some place on Ben-Howard Road. That's all I said. I disguised my voice, because I didn't want the people at 911 to be able to figure out that I had made the call. As soon as I hung up, Willingham drug me back to his truck. He then drove me home, all the while threatening me that if I ever said a word, I was a dead man—and it wasn't going to be a quick death. When we got to my house, I jumped out, he yelled at me some more while I was walking to my door, and then he peeled out of there."

"Did he tell you who the injured person was or how they had been injured?" said Slusherman.

"No, and I wasn't about to ask."

"Did you find out who had been hurt, or try to figure out who lived at the address you gave 911?"

"No, not until I was charged a month later with trying to kill Willingham. I don't read the paper much and to be honest with you, I went out into the woods for a few days after that night in case Willingham came back. I was scared like I hadn't been since prison."

"Weren't you curious?"

"I can't say. I was so scared, I don't think I was even thinking straight," said Pungent.

"If you made the call, and since you have a criminal record and fingerprints in the system, why didn't your fingerprints show up when the CSI team dusted the phone on Brigham Street later that night?"

"I never touched the phone myself. Willingham dialed the number and held the phone."

"Then why didn't his fingerprints come up?"

"He wore some cloth gloves."

"Your neighbor, Myron Goldmin—as you know—testified that he not only saw Conner Willingham come and pick you up on March 10th, but that he came back a week and a half later, and he seemed quite angry. Would you tell us what he came back for?" said Slusherman.

"He came into my house, shoved me up against the wall, grabbed my throat, and lifted me up in the air to his eye level. I could barely breathe. He held me there eye to eye with him, his face only a few inches away from mine, his nasty breath blowing hard into my face. He looked like a wild gorilla, and said, 'If you think I gave it bad to you in prison, you haven't seen a thing. The cops brought me in for questioning today. If I ever find out that you gave them any information about our little phone call, I will gut you out.' I promised him I would never say anything. He finally let me down and left. I knew then that I had to kill him. I had no choice, or I was a dead man. Even if I never said a thing to the cops, if he believed that I had, I was still a dead man. What choice did I have?"

"It doesn't sound to me like you had much of one," said Slusherman. "So why are you telling us this now? Even if it turns out Willingham is found guilty of a crime in relationship to his dead grandmother, your life will still eventually be in danger."

"I'm already dead," answered Pungent. "He knows that I tried to kill him. Do you think he's going to let me live. That's why I'm telling it all now. I've been safe in the jail all this time. But when I get out, I'm dead no matter what."

Slusherman walked over to the jury and scanned their faces. "Mr. Pungent, you really *didn't have a choice*. Not if you were going to keep from being killed by Willingham. You tried to kill him in self-defense. You did it to save your own life. If that isn't self-defense, then there's no such thing.

"Ladies and gentleman of the jury," Slusherman asked rhetorically, "would any of you want to have been in David Pungent's place? *What would you have done?* You know that the only thing you could have done was to try to save your own life. With a man like Conner Willingham, the size and temperament of Conner Willingham, who had already abused you unspeakably in the past, and now threatened your very life, if he found out you had spoken to the cops about him, or if he even thought you had spoken to the cops about him, he was going to, quote, 'gut you out,' and kill you, what would you have done? Exactly what David Pungent did. Oh, you might have done it by some other means, but you would have had to end his life, or get someone else to end it for you, in order to save your own life. That is why you will find my client, the defendant, David Pungent, not guilty of attempted murder. *It was self defense*."

Brenda and several other Muldano-clan women were crying. Brenda felt the same sickening feeling fifteen years earlier, when Conner was on trial for the rape. She wanted to leave the courtroom right now, to go hold her big baby Conner. But she had to sit and hear the rest. Conner wasn't guilty of anything yet, for sure. He couldn't be, she told herself. Nothing had been proven. They would get him a good lawyer. There had to be another Brent Slusherman around that could get him off. That could prove that things weren't the way they sounded right now.

"Your Honor, I have no further questions for this witness," said Slusherman.

Court recessed for twenty minutes and then the State cross-examined Pungent.

Mr. Haadapa, who had been scribbling furiously off and on throughout Pungent's latest testimony, got up deliberately, and carrying his note-filled pad, walked up to Pungent to try to salvage what he could.

"Mr. Pungent, even if by some fluke, you get off now because the jury happens to believe your sad tale, you and I both know that you are still a murderer. You tried to kill Conner Willingham and nothing changes that. You could have gone to the police at any time during all those years that Willingham supposedly abused you and forced you to sell drugs. You could have gone to the police after the night Willingham supposedly made you call 911 for him. You could have gone to the police the second time he supposedly threatened your life after supposedly forcing you to make the 911 call. But you didn't," said Haadapa. "*You didn't*. You didn't go to the police, because you decided to take the law into your own hands and kill another human being. As the District Attorney for Snohomish County, the man who the entire county holds responsible for prosecuting cases against murderers like you—"

"Objection!"

"Sustained."

"As the man responsible for prosecuting cases against attempted murderers like you," said Haadapa, "I don't swallow your sad story, and nobody else in this court room should swallow it either.

"Right now, the only substantial testimony that this court has that you had any contact with Mr. Willingham since you left prison, or in particular, on the two nights in March that have been alluded to, is your neighbor, Myron Goldmin. We already know we can't take your word on anything for obvious reasons."

"Objection."

"Overruled."

"For all we know you made up the whole fantastic story about the 911 call based on scuttle-butt you have heard from guards or other jailbirds while you have been in jail. I find it quite interesting that neither yours, nor Mr. Willingham's fingerprints were on the phone that you said you made the 911 call from. I guess he just happened to have a pair of cloth gloves in his truck for just such a time as that, right?"

"Think what you want, Mr. Haadapa. I was there," said Pungent. "I know what happened. My neighbor saw Willingham. Are you going to try to discredit him too, a man with his record of public service?"

"We have already heard from three of Willingham's poker buddies that he was with them at the time the 911 call came in," said Haadapa. "There's your evidence, Pungent! And this jury is smart enough to see that. Mr. Goldmin is an old man, who could very easily have his times and dates confused."

Brenda was suddenly feeling more hopeful. This prosecutor might just get his attempted murder conviction yet. After all, she did hear that he was four for four in getting convictions on his three murder and one attempted-murder trials in the six months he has been the district attorney. He would pull it out for her, and for

Conner. He had to. And she knew there was no way that Conner was involved in her mom's death. He was at the card game. All of his buddies said so, and they hadn't changed one word of their testimony, no matter how hard they had been pressed by that manipulative Mr. Slusherman. But there was still one card-playing buddy that hadn't been called to testify yet. He would say the same thing. It was the truth. What else could he say?

The DA asked Pungent a few more pointless questions and then concluded his cross-examination.

Mr. Slusherman got up for rebuttal just long enough to basically recap his pre-closing argument regarding why Pungent had to do what he did. That Pungent was telling the truth, and expressing his faith in the jury's ability to not have their judgment clouded by an over-zealous prosecutor.

After his rebuttal, Slusherman called Snohomish County Sheriff's contracted Voice Analyst, Judy Barrow, to the stand.

The petite, attractive blond-haired, lady in her late-thirties, Ms. Barrow played the tape of the 911 call that was made from the phone booth on Brigham Street in Monroe at 8:58 on March 10th, 2006. The call was brief.

"This is 911, what is your emergency?"
"Someone is seriously hurt at 23759 Ben Howard Road near Monroe."
"What is the nature of the injury?"

Then there was just the dial-tone. The caller hung up. It was apparent to everyone in the courtroom that the caller was a male who was clearly attempting to disguise his voice.

Ms. Barrow re-played the tape four times to give everyone in the courtroom plenty of opportunity to listen.

"Ms. Barrow," said Slusherman, I understand that through your computer technology you were able to clean the recording up so that the caller's actual voice could be heard. Would you please play the clean version for us now?"

The courtroom was silent except for the sound of the cleaned recording playing. She played it again, then one more time. Everyone in the courtroom recognized that voice. They had just heard it twenty-five minutes earlier.

Ms. Barrow, you have had plenty of opportunity to listen to recordings of Sheriff Detectives Allen and Gonzales interviewing David Pungent in the Snohomish County Jail. In comparing the cleaned up 911 call we just heard with the recordings of David Pungent's voice during those interviews would you say that the voice heard on both those recordings is the same person's?"

"Yes. There's no doubt about it."

"And whose voice is it?"

"The defendant, David Pungent's." No one was surprised.

Slusherman turned to Pungent, and just to reinforce that the recorded voice was his, asked, "How have they been treating you at the jail, Mr. Pungent?" Pungent answered that the guards have treated him fairly, that the food wasn't bad, but that the isolation was killing him. There was no doubt that the cleaned recording voice was David Pungent's. Slusherman thanked Ms. Barrow and said he had no more questions; DA Haadapa said he had no questions for her, and she was released.

At 5:35, Judge Laney ordered the court recessed for the evening and said the Defense would call its last scheduled witness first thing the next morning.

43

Defense Case E
Warner, Don't Do It

Both attorneys spent a restless Monday night. Julian Haadapa felt that he still had a great chance of getting a conviction providing the jury took seriously his argument that even if the things Pungent said about Willingham were true—though Haadapa believed they were lies—he still could have and should have gone to the police, rather than take the law into his own hands and try to kill Willingham. In his closing argument after the final witness in the morning, Haadapa would convince the jury that they *had to come back* with a guilty verdict in this case, or they would be opening up the door for anyone else who is threatened in any way to take the same action toward his oppressor that Pungent had taken.

Brent Slusherman was restless because he knew from the start the difficulty in getting a jury to see an attempted-murder as an act of self-defense, particularly when the self-defense reaction occurs after any passage of time from when the perceived or real threats or assaults were made. The present case was even more difficult because his client, who was claiming self-defense, had a documented criminal record—no matter that he had not committed another crime in the last thirteen years, since his release from prison. Slusherman knew that old man Goldmin's testimony, as well as the testimony of the Felons Center corrections officer, Jeremiah Franklin, had to carry a lot of weight. But he also knew that somehow he had to get the last card player to break, to reveal the truth about Willingham and his buddies.

Tim Warner was a stereotypical lumber-mill worker. He was about five foot ten, with a barrel chest and bulging biceps from pulling green-chain, and he had only a little over a year of college to his credit. Unlike all his card-playing and softball team buddies, Warner was not married. At twenty-seven, he was also eight years younger than the rest of them. He had only known Conner Willingham for the last six years and been playing cards and softball with him for that same length of time—points that Slusherman intended to exploit. In fact, Warner's much shorter history with Willingham, his youth, and his marital status were precisely the reason Slusherman held him back as his last card-playing witness. Slusherman believed Warner would prove to be his ace-in-the-hole. There was no doubt that Conner had to be very concerned about Warner, and probably even laid some heavy threats on him over the last few days.

Members of the Muldano-clan were more anxious than any of the previous four days of the trial. They were all talking loud and fast.

"Renee (Conner's wife) said Conner didn't come home last night!" said a concerned Brenda. "No one in the family that I've talked to knows where he is. None of his friends that I talked with knows where he is either." The rumors circulating among the Clan quickly made it around to Dan's section.

Apparently Conner never came home last night. He was last seen at lunch yesterday when the family met at *Tower of Babbling Buffet* between court sessions. There was speculation among the family that—because of the revelations that had come out in court testimony, and then relayed to Conner by the usual family channels and over lunch—he was hiding out somewhere, certain that the devil was about to jump up in Slusherman's hand. Even though his friends, family, co-workers, and card buddies had all stood strong for him (though some hadn't been so supportive of him behind his back), he told Jay Maul that things weren't looking good for him. He said, "There's no way I'm going back to prison for anything or anybody." Did he believe he committed a crime that would send him back there?

"The Defense calls Tim Warner to the stand," said Slusherman, at 9:02, Tuesday morning, October 3rd.

The Muldano clan settled in, though none of them look relaxed like most of the other spectators in the courtroom. Like Haadapa, they were pinning their hopes on Warner's testimony corroborating Willingham's and the other three card players' testimonies. If all four were telling the truth that would mean David Pungent was lying about Willingham coming to his house on March 10th. If he was lying about that, then it would call into question everything else he had said, and most certainly result in his conviction on the attempted murder charge. Also if Willingham was, in fact, at the card game when the 911 call came in and had actually arrived there by 8:30, he could not have been at his Grandma Muldano's house at all that evening, which would also rule him out of any involvement in her death.

There was no doubt now that David Pungent made the 911 call. Perhaps he went to the Muldano house intending to rob them, and got in over his head. Or maybe he knew the Muldanos were related to Conner and figured he could take out some flesh on them, for what Conner had been doing to him. If David Pungent was the one who actually pushed Maureen Muldano to her death, then he had used his neighbor Mr. Goldmin, Conner Willingham, and even Mr. Slusherman to steer the attention away from that crime as well.

During the Muldano death investigation the CSI team recovered a number of other hairs who's DNA could not be traced to the family suspects, nor to anyone whose DNA was in the police files. Every house has plenty of stray hairs lying around on carpets, no matter how meticulous the carpets are cleaned, so many, if not all, of the recovered human hairs could have belonged to other family members or friends.

After Pungent's arrest and incarceration, the police obtained DNA samples from his cell and eating utensils. None of the hairs at the Muldano house had matched his DNA. That, of course, didn't mean he wasn't there the night of March 10th. It only meant there was no evidence at the scene to prove his presence. The police had also searched his house following his arrest last April, but found nothing that placed him in the Muldano home at any time. Of course, since he was not considered a suspect in the Muldano death, the police had not specifically looked for evidence in his house that would connect him to that crime. That was an oversight, considering they were so willing to charge Dan Thurmond with both crimes, when they thought he had torched Conner.

"Mr. Warner, we have already heard testimony from Conner Willingham, Jay Maul, Mike Lonner, and Frank Wilkens regarding Friday night March 10th of this year. Each of them basically regurgitated the same stories they gave when they were interviewed back in March and April. But we have a problem. We know they are lying."

"Objection!"

"Sustained."

"I know they are lying. And I believe other people know that as well. I know you weren't in here for their testimonies, but I have no doubt that the five of you coordinated your stories to cover up not only Conner Willingham's arrival time that night, but to hide what it is you guys actually do besides play cards at that one-Friday-a-month boys-night-out.

"Mr. Warner, the court already has plenty of evidence to prove Conner Willingham was somewhere else, and not at the card game, when the other four claim he was there. And based on that evidence, the detectives in the Maureen Muldano death will be digging deep now to find the answers to that puzzle. That includes more interviews with you and your buddies, possibly making you take a lie-detector test, any number of things to try to get to the truth. They are not going to give up until they solve that death."

"Objection!" said Haadapa. "Mr. Slusherman is trying to scare the witness. He is acting like he is the investigators, the judge, jury and warden all in one. Can you please keep him on track here, Your Honor?"

"I don't need your help to keep anyone on track in my court-room, Mr. Haadapa," said Laney, "And unless you change your approach, we may be hiring a new district attorney. I will run my courtroom. You won't. As for your objection, Mr. Slusherman has brought out some interesting points throughout this trial, and at this juncture I have every intention of hearing him out. Is that clear?"

"Yes, Your Honor."

"Your objection is overruled. Please continue Mr. Slusherman."

"Mr. Warner, you being a card player, you can appreciate this one. The kicker about your present situation is that if you purge yourself today on this stand with me, you are going to jail. Add to the perjury charge, obstruction of justice, and you could be doing some hard time. Believe me I'm going to get the truth, one way or another."

Warner was sweating badly, and keeping his hands from trembling by tucking his fingers under the outside of his thighs. He looked like a kid that just got caught stealing cookies. And he hadn't even said a word yet.

"Now I know that you have only been friends with Conner Willingham and two of the other guys at the game for six years. All of them, however, have been buddies since junior high. That already puts you outside the inner circle. Then add the fact that they are married and have a lot more to lose than you do if the game-night activities become known. Surely you can see why they would lie about it." Slusherman had no evidence that anything illicit actually went on, but he knew it was not an unusual scenario for such private guys-only nights, and it was also his best bluff. "You, on the other hand, are not married, so if you screw around with women on Friday nights, you aren't cheating on anyone." Haadapa wanted desperately to object, but Laney neutered him the last time, so he wasn't willing to take another chance. "I've given you this long introduction to try to simplify things for you now and in the near future."

"You don't understand anything, do you?" Warner let slip.

"What was that?" said Slusherman. There was a loud cough from the Muldano clan.

"Nothing."

"What is it that I don't understand, Mr. Warner?" Another cough.

"Nothing."

"Your Honor, someone in that section there," he pointed to the Clan, "seems to have a tickle in his throat. Would you mind having the bailiff see if he can figure out who it is? It seems to be affecting Mr. Warner." The bailiff walked over and stood near the Clan.

"Mr. Warner, what time did Conner Willingham arrive at that card game on Friday night, March 10th of this year?"

Warner looked down at the floor between him and the Clan as he debated *whether the price* to speak freely about what he knew *would be greater* than going to jail for perjury and obstruction of justice. "You already know what time he arrived. You don't need to hear it again from me," he said, trying to find a happy medium, but certain Slusherman wouldn't let him off that easy.

"Answer my question, please, Mr. Warner," said Slusherman. "You're not leaving this courtroom without answering my questions." The courtroom was silent. No more itchy throats, not with the bailiff watching.

Warner started to speak, but couldn't. Fifteen seconds passed with nothing but silence in the courtroom. Even the judge understood this couldn't be easy for Warner and cut him some slack. "You must answer Mr. Slusherman's question, Mr. Warner," Laney finally said.

With his eyes still glued to the floor, the courtroom silent, Warner said softly, "Conner got to the game at 9:30." Warner wasn't going to jail for anyone, not even Willingham. Brenda broke into tears. Someone said, "Finally, *someone tells the truth.* I knew they were all lying."

Slusherman let Warner's words of revelation hang in the courtroom for thirty seconds without saying a word. He had just been dealt the royal flush he held out for. He relaxed for the first time in thirty hours. But he wasn't about to let up now.

"Mr. Warner, when Willingham arrived at the card game did he have blood on his face?"

Knowing there was no point in holding on to his losing hand, Warner folded. "Yes," he answered.

"What side of his face was the blood on, and how much was there?"

"It was on his right cheek, near his earlobe. There wasn't much at all. It looked like he had wiped the rest of it off."

"Did anyone ask him about it?"

"Yes, Jay Maul did."

"And what was Willingham's explanation?"

"He said there had been an accident. He practically burst into tears. But he wouldn't give us anymore details. He said none of us could ever say a word about it no matter what. We all had our secrets and we all needed to protect each other. After all, we were brothers."

"And no one asked for any more details?" said Slusherman.

"Believe me, when Conner said not to say a word about anything, we all knew him well enough to know that if we didn't want to get hurt like others we had heard about, we best not even say another word to him about it."

"Did you guys ever talk about it later, among yourselves, when

Willingham wasn't around?"

"Not as a group, but sometimes when a couple of us were together, we did."

"Did you know that Willingham's grandmother died that same night?"

"We heard about it on the news."

"Did you put two and two together?" said Slusherman. "I mean the blood and him showing up to the game an hour later than usual."

"Of course we put it together. But we also believed him when he said there *had been an accident.* We all knew he had a criminal record and that no matter that it was an accident, since he must have panicked and left his grandmother's house, he would be charged with at least manslaughter. None of us wanted Conner to go to prison." At those words, Brenda, still crying, burst from her chair and ran out of the courtroom. Her sister, Jan, ran after her.

"You said that no one said anymore to Willingham about where he had come from and why he was late. How did you all come up with the 8:30 arrival time?"

"Just after the card game started, Conner, who was very nervous, told us that if anyone ever asks us what time he got to the game that night we were to tell them his usual time of 8:30. None of us liked the situation we found ourselves in, but we all agreed on the 8:30 time. It was a simple detail that we could all keep straight. Any other explanation we would use would be the same one we had all agreed on months earlier regarding our activities on card night. After all, it was our night for fun, and no one else needed to know anything."

"So what actually went on at those card games besides playing cards?" asked Slusherman.

"Warner, you damn traitor!" yelled someone just outside the Muldano section.

"Bailiff, remove him from the courtroom!" ordered Laney.

The bailiff and another deputy from the back quickly grabbed a man wearing a blue baseball jersey and escorted him out the main courtroom entry. Then the bailiff returned to his position overlooking the Clan.

"What went on at the card games?" Slusherman asked again.

"We used to just play cards. But a year ago, Jay Maul brought a couple hot broads with him. He said he had picked them up at Jiggles. When we saw them, none of us told him they had to leave. What guy would have? We played some strip poker. You can figure out the rest."

"What you're telling us is that you and all four of the married men at your games had sex with the women?"

"Yes." Warner said softly as if that might ease the blow to the other players' wives and family members who were in the courtroom.

"So did you have women there each month from then on?"

"Yes." He didn't tell him that it was never the same women, and that they were always beautiful and big-busted. Nor did he mention that they had anywhere from two to five women there on any given game night. Things could get pretty wild with the *games* going well into Saturday morning.

"Were there women at the game the night Willingham arrived late?"

"Yes."

"And you talked about the accident in their presence?"

"No, Conner had called us all outside on the porch. The women that night never knew anything had happened. We made sure the blood was wiped off Conner's face before he came in the house."

"Thank you for your testimony, Mr. Warner."

"No thanks. I might have kept myself from doing time, but I just lost four friends and probably a lot more."

At that moment, one of the Clan, who had just received a text message on her cell phone from Brenda, blurted out to those around her, "They found Conner. He's threatening to jump off the top of the Hilton Hotel." The whole clan stampeded from the courtroom and downstairs to hustle through the security area and run to the

Hilton several blocks away.

As soon as the Clan was gone, Judge Laney quickly asked Mr. Slusherman if he had any more questions. When he said no, Laney asked the prosecutor for cross-examination, but Haadapa knew he was beat with this witness and said, "No questions." Haadapa wasn't conceding defeat on the attempted murder charge; he just knew that nothing this witness would say would help him.

Judge Laney dismissed the court for the remainder of the day, due to this latest development and said closing arguments would be heard beginning at nine the next day. He hoped that the Willingham drama would have played out, with no one hurt, by then.

As soon as Laney left the courtroom and David Pungent had been taken away by the sheriff deputy, Brent Slusherman, Father Michael, Dan and Windy, along with most of the rest of the audience, quickly made their way downstairs and through the security check, then jogged up the several blocks to the twelve-story Hilton Hotel. Everett Police and Snohomish County Sheriff deputies had the street blocked off at the front of the Hilton so no one could get to the entrance to the building. As the spectators stood across the street, they could barely see Conner's back as he stood up against the three foot wall at the northwest corner of the terrace, ten stories up. He was talking back and forth with several people on the terrace. In addition to the lawmen, several firemen were on the street along the front of the hotel, as well.

Several Everett Policeman and two sheriff's deputies were on the terrace trying to talk Conner out of jumping. Brenda and Jan were both there, and were both crying. No one dared approach for fear that would force Conner's hand and he would jump over the edge. He demanded that no one come any closer than the forty feet they were standing away from him. None of the law men had their guns drawn. They could see he was unarmed and only a danger to himself.

At one point Conner turned and put a leg over the edge.

"Don't do it, Conner!" Brenda and Jan screamed. "I love you, Son! No matter what you have done."

"You don't understand, Mom. You'll never understand," said Conner. "I didn't do the things Pungent said I did. I didn't deal drugs."

"It's okay, Conner. I don't care about any of that. I love you. I always have and I always will. Didn't I show you that for all your life? Didn't I show that by breaking up with Dan and coming back up here to Everett to be with all of you guys? You were one of the main reasons I did it. I couldn't take not having a normal relationship with you and your boys, or Grandma and Grandpa, or Jan, and Leroy. I missed all of you so much. But I missed you the most. You were my firstborn." Just then Brenda's third-oldest son, Leroy, was allowed out on the terrace next to Brenda and Jan.

"Conner, you can't do this to Mom," said Leroy. "You can't do this to any of us. How do you think it felt for all of us those four years when you were away before? We can get through anything with you, but we couldn't take it if you killed yourself."

"You guys don't understand," said Conner. "I killed Grandma. I didn't mean to. It just happened. (Like all the other assaults, right?) She fell backwards and hit her head. I've been dying inside every day since it happened. But I couldn't tell anyone, because I knew they would put me back in prison, no matter that it was an accident." The lawmen continued to let the family members talk back and forth without their involvement, knowing that the best resolution in these circumstances was usually obtained by letting loved ones talk to the distressed party.

"No one in our family would ever believe it was anything but an accident, Conner," said his Aunt Jan.

"What happened that night, Conner? You can tell us," said Brenda. "We know it was an accident. We know it had to be an accident, because you always loved Grandma so much."

"Mom, I stopped by Grandma and Grandpa's because Grandma had called me a couple days earlier and said she needed to talk to me in person. I figured I would just swing by there after working out at Gold's on my way to the monthly card game. I got there at 8:30. Grandpa was gone, and Grandma was all upset. She was even mad at me, and I hadn't even said anything. You know how she could be. Well it was worse that night for some reason. She said my wimp grandpa had left almost an hour earlier to get away from her. The way she was acting, I could understand why he left.

"I never even got a chance to sit down. We were standing by the entry between the family room and the dining room. Just out of the blue, she said I was *a nigger*, that she knew that because I helped rape that girl in Bellingham years ago. She said she always thought of me as a nigger after that, in the back of her mind. You remember how she chewed me out when she came to the jail that night way back then. What you didn't know was that she continued to get her subtle digs in about it all those years since I got out of prison. I knew she never forgave me. And I also knew I was the only black man in our family. That's one of the reasons I always took her side about everything. I always wanted to earn her favor for being black and for what I did in Bellingham."

"It's okay, Conner," said Leroy. "All of us always tried to earn her favor. But the price was too high. Your being black never mattered to any of us. We all loved you and always will."

"How did Mom fall, Conner?" asked Brenda.

"She pointed her condemning finger at me and said, 'Conner, *you'll always be a nigger*. You're the only one in the family.' I lost control, Mom. I pushed her, and she tripped when she stepped backwards to catch herself. She was knocked unconscious and her head was bleeding badly," he said, slumping down, sobbing. "I'm so sorry, Mom. I'm so sorry!"

Brenda started to move toward him, but one of the police officers held her back, and said softly, "Not yet."

Conner continued bawling. "I'm so sorry, Mom, for all the ways

I've hurt you over the years. I knew I was a bastard kid. I always knew I was just a nigger."

"That's so wrong, Son," cried Brenda. "I have always loved you more than you will ever know. We all love you." Before the deputy could stop her, Brenda ran over to Conner and knelt down beside him, clung to him as if he were her newborn again, and cried. She said over and over, "I love you, Conner. I love you, Conner."

The law men moved right in and positioned themselves within a few feet ready to tackle him if he made any move toward the edge of the roof. They allowed the family to cry together for a minute, then forced Conner down onto his belly and handcuffed him.

Brenda cried out, "My son, my son. Don't hurt him. I love you, Conner. We will be with you through all of this. We all love you." The deputies led Conner away and back into the stairwell.

Conner Willingham was taken to the Snohomish County Jail and booked awaiting formal charges.

44

The Verdict

On Wednesday morning, October 4th, District Attorney Julian Haadapa gave his closing argument imploring the jury to find David Pungent guilty of attempted murder. He said none of the testimony or arguments presented by the defense negated the fact that Pungent pre-meditated and deliberately attacked Conner Willingham on April 7th, 2006 with the intent to kill him. He could have gone to the law at any time with his claims of intimidation and alleged death threats. If the jury let Pungent off for such a crime, then in the future many other juries would be confronted with the same or similar circumstances. It was this jury's duty to not set that kind of precedent.

Defense Attorney Brent Slusherman followed up with his closer insisting that what David Pungent did was done for one reason: *to save his own life*. David Pungent did it to prevent his own certain death by this tyrant of a man who had intimidated and abused him unspeakably for years. This tyrant, Conner Willingham, busted up David Pungent and raped him numerous times in prison in 1991 through 1993. This tyrant forced David Pungent to transport drugs for him for years. This tyrant had blood on his face when he came to David Pungent's house the night of March 10th, 2006, and forced David Pungent to call 911 in order to cover up his just-committed act of violence. This tyrant then came back to David Pungent's house on March 23rd, choked him and told him he would gut him out if he ever said a word. David Pungent did the only thing he thought he could do to save his life. He did what anyone in his shoes, with a similar background, confronted by the same or very similar circumstances, would have done. He defended himself. *It was self-defense.*

After an impotent rebuttal by Haadapa, the case was then turned over to the twelve-person jury.

The jury deliberated all afternoon on Wednesday, October 4th, all day Thursday, and up until 10 Friday morning, before returning with a not guilty verdict for David Pungent on the attempted murder charge. They determined that David Pungent had, in fact, acted in self-defense. He was subsequently released a free man.

On Tuesday, October 10th, 2006, Conner Willingham was arraigned on the charge of involuntary manslaughter in the death of his grandmother, Maureen Muldano. No other charges were filed against him at that time, though harassment, perjury, obstruction of justice, assault and battery, and drug trafficking charges were being considered and might be sought in the near future. Conner was released on $300,000 bail until his trial scheduled for April 2007. Judge Laney also sternly warned him that if he ever went near David Pungent again, Laney would charge him with every crime he could and personally see to it that Conner never saw the light of day again.

Conner's three card-playing buddies who lied on the witness stand were initially charged with felony perjury and obstruction of justice, but all three of them admitted their fear of reprisal from Conner Willingham played a role in their dishonest testimonies. Additionally, they each agreed to testify against Conner in exchange for the reduced charge of misdemeanor contempt of court.

In March 2007 the three players were each sentenced to six months in jail, with 90 days of that suspended, and a year of bench probation. Jay Maul's wife was granted a divorce from her husband, on the grounds of adultery, while he was nearing the end of his jail sentence. Conner's other two married card-playing buddies' wives hadn't filed yet, but that was still a possibility.

Conner Willingham's case never went to trial because he agreed to plead guilty to involuntary manslaughter in exchange for the Snohomish County District Attorney's Office not filing the numerous other charges considered in the intervening months since his arraignment in October 2006.

At Conner's sentencing hearing on April 22, 2007, Brenda and several other family members begged Judge Leroy Laney for leniency based on the impact that Maureen Muldano's death had already had on the family, and that Conner had grade-school aged boys who needed their dad around. Conner admitted that he had made a terrible mistake in how he handled the situation that night and in the months that followed.

Judge Laney reprimanded not only Conner, but also Brenda and other family members who had excused and enabled Conner's behavior for years. (Too bad Laney hadn't had a crack at Conner's Grandma Maureen Muldano. Of course she wouldn't have listened to him anyway.) Laney said Conner was more concerned about protecting his own neck than in immediately calling for the medical help that might have saved his grandmother's life if it had arrived within minutes of her accident. Not only that, he had left her to die alone. Laney also emphasized Conner's prior ongoing criminal record, his years of intimidating not only David Pungent but numerous other people, his drug dealing, and his willingness to let other people, particularly his mom's ex-husband, be charged and go to prison for his crime.

Conner Willingham was sentenced to four years, back at the Washington State Felons Center in Ralston, Washington. You're finally going home BIG BOY—*back to where you once belonged!*

Brenda wept bitterly at the reading of Conner's four year sentence. It would be four more very sad years for her, but at least her first-born son was still alive. Maybe this time he would finally learn his lesson and get out of prison to become an honest, respectable, decent human being. That was not likely, however, considering his Grandma *Maureen Muldano's blood still runs through him.*

Ironically, Conner's wife actually forgave him for everything he had done and was going to hang in there raising their boys while he did his time.

Dan Thurmond and Windy were married by Father Michael in Aberdeen on January 6th, 2007. Their early months of marriage were like heaven on earth for both of them, because they fit like a hand in glove in every way imaginable. They are both looking forward to a long love-filled marriage. And now Dan is finally loved by all of his wife's relatives who, of course, have always been his relatives as well.

An Interview with
Author Wesley Murphey

Lost Creek Book's Jill Curtis: Wesley, you've really hit on a hot topic with **To Kill a Mother in Law**. And you have great insight into problems common in many families. How did you come up with so many interesting characters and such an amazing plot? And specifically how did you come up with this rogue mother-in-law Maureen Muldano?

Wesley Murphey: There are a lot of interesting people out there, with an amazing variety of problems in their lives and in their family relationships. I guess I just observe people a lot and have listened to many people talk about their family problems. Along the way, I've heard some very harsh things said between people—stuff that just blows you away. That stuff makes great material for a great fiction story like this one, a story with some intense dialogue and creative monologue.

Curtis: But why did you, Wesley Murphey, write about Maureen Muldano?

Murphey: I really liked how the name Maureen Muldano fit this obese, squatty-body, controlling matriarch. Of course Maureen is completely fictional. She has to be. No one could be that bad a mother or mother-in-law could they? I would hate to meet them if they could. Same thing with Conner. The guy doesn't have a clue. His life is all about running over people. Conner's brother Brandon, the lawyer, couldn't even last twenty minutes in the same room with him. And then to hear of the things Conner did to David Pungent. That's one bad dude. All of my characters are fictional.

I'm sure many people who read this book will see some—and perhaps a lot of—similarity to real situations in their own marriages or in the marriages of friends or family members. I only hope that those who are a bit like Maureen, Conner or the other wolves will see themselves that way and maybe try to change, to stay out of the business of other family members. I also hope that others, who see themselves as the characters that would never hold Maureen or Conner accountable, will get brave and stand up for their loved ones against such wolves.

Curtis: One thing I struggled with as a reader was whether I could like your protagonist, Dan Thurmond. At times I felt sorry for him, but I also saw him as somewhat of a hypocrite himself, not only because of the murderous plots he considered, but because he actually sought to kill people. How can you defend that?

Murphey: Most people who have read the Bible or sat in church very much have heard the true story of "Cain and Abel" as recorded in Genesis 4. God showed Abel favor over Cain based on certain circumstances, and Cain became very jealous. God warned Cain that sin was crouching at his door, desiring to have him, but he *must master it*. Unfortunately, sin ultimately mastered Cain: his jealousy caused him to murder his brother Abel.

In this Mother story, Dan Thurmond, like Cain, believes he has been wronged (only Dan actually was wronged) and is confronted with the same challenge that the Bible's Cain faced: take matters into his own hands, or let God's way win out. Dan chooses to take matters into his own hands, except that ultimately he doesn't complete the violence he plans. Some, like Father Michael in this story, would say that God stopped him, and maybe they are correct.

In real life, good people in desperate situations sometimes do cross the line in their thoughts and actions. I have one friend that lives near me who told me he once aimed a loaded rifle at his ex-wife from 150 yards away fully intending to shoot her. He just didn't pull the trigger. Because of his pain and anger, he came that close to spending the rest of his life behind bars. Yet no one who knows him would know that he almost committed murder. And his ex-wife doesn't know how close she came to dying. These are the sort of things from which part of my story comes. And these things make fiction come alive in a way that true life events never can.

Curtis: You're other new book **Girl Too Popular** is connected in some way to this story. Can you tell me how?

Murphey: The star-athlete and most popular girl, Carly Cantwell, in **Girl Too Popular,** is actually the same girl as little Jackie in **To Kill a Mother in Law**. She's older, and I've changed her name, circumstances and the locations, but readers will enjoy the strong correlation between the two books. One big difference is that Carly's grandma is still alive in the *Girl* book.

Curtis: Of your first four novels, which is your favorite?

Murphey: Definitely **Trouble at Puma Creek**. I love the criminal character Del Hensley's sarcastic sense of humor, and actually feel the pain he lives with because of his traumatic service in Vietnam. Also, I think the POW/MIA issue is brought out better in my book than in any other work I've read on Vietnam. I believe in time that book will earn the recognition it deserves for that and its insight into the plight of Vietnam veterans, among other things.

I will add that I also especially like **A Homeless Man's Burden** because the story was so real for me personally, and I am actually my character, Shane Coleman. Much of what is described in that story related to Shane, his father and the little girl is factual. From 1965-1972, I picked in the bean field where the murder occurred, my dad was the mail carrier who believed he knew who killed the girl, there actually was a homeless man in a sleeping bag under the I-105 bridge on my trapline, and many other details are real. But I also altered certain details. For instance, Shane mentions working for the murdered girl's father for a short haying season when he was a teenager. But, the fact is, when I was fifteen, I worked for the actual deceased girl's (Alice Lee's) father, Ernest Lee, for nearly a year riding around with him on Saturday and Sunday mornings each week punching papers on his Eugene Register-Guard route.

Curtis: That's interesting. Tell me about your four books scheduled for release in 2013.

Murphey: All four are outdoor nonfiction books. Three will include many of my deceased father's and my published articles on hunting, fishing and trapping and some unpublished articles as well. The final one is a collection of many of my published trapping articles. I also have a **novel** in my head that begs to be written; we'll see.

About the Author

Wesley Murphey was born and raised in Dexter and Pleasant Hill, Oregon and lived in Lane County, Oregon until 2003, when he moved his family to Central Oregon where he now resides. He and his beautiful wife enjoy fishing, hunting, hiking, swimming, camping, and doing numerous other outdoor activities together. He has no mother-in-law problems. With *Girl Too Popular* and *To Kill a Mother in Law* both released in 2012, Murphey now has six books in print, with four more scheduled to be released in 2013. Three of the four upcoming books will feature numerous outdoor articles written by Wesley and his now deceased father, Don Murphey. The fourth book will be a collection of many of Wesley's published articles on trapping.

See back of this page to order Wesley Murphey's books-

Lost Creek Books
PO Box 3084
La Pine, OR 97739
email: lostcreekbooks@netzero.com
website: lostcreekbooks.com

Wesley Murphey's books make great gifts!

Get more information and order more of Wesley Murphey's books at lostcreekbooks.com. Credit cards accepted. Or order through your local book store.

_____ Cut here _____

Quick order form for Wesley Murphey's books

Fiction:	Price	#books	Ext.Price
A Homeless Man's Burden	$14.95	____	_____
To Kill a Mother in Law	$14.95	____	_____
Trouble at Puma Creek	$14.95	____	_____
Girl Too Popular	$12.95	____	_____

NonFiction:			
Blacktail Deer Hunting Adventures	$12.95	____	_____
Conibear Beaver Trapping inOpen Water	$11.00	____	_____
(Plus total shipping regardless of quantity)			$3.50
Total Price			_____

Send check or money order to address at top of page. Be sure to include your name and address. A phone number should be included with large orders.